The
REINDEER
of CHINESE
GARDENS

The REINDEER of CHINESE GARDENS

BARBARA SJOHOLM

CEDAR STREET
EDITIONS

The Reindeer of Chinese Gardens
Copyright @ 2025 by Barbara Sjoholm

Cover design: Ann McMan/Treehouse Studio
Text Design: Raymond Luczak

ISBN: 979-8-9911206-0-9 (print)
ISBN: 979-8-9911206-1-6 (e-book)
LCCN: 20249114901

Cedar Street Editions
PO Box 1705
Port Townsend WA 98368

For Betsy and Ellen

Five journals remain.

Two journals bound in brown calf, rough-skinned at the spines; two more journals with linen covers, one navy blue, and one tan, the last badly stained by mud and rain. They cover the years 1897 through 1907. One journal no longer exists; it was burned by mistake. There's also a fifth journal: heavy gray cardboard with red leatherette corners, big and blocky. Inside, pale blue lines are overprinted with vertical red lines to make columns. It was purchased as a household ledger and starts out with weekly budgets but includes entries about Alaska in 1899; it bulges with handwritten manuscript pages, newspaper clippings, and letters still in their envelopes.

I'm writing in this household ledger now, in its clean back pages, writing in Norwegian, while sitting on the small balcony overhanging the rocky shore. The leaves of the birch trees we planted are just beginning to turn canary yellow and the sun is mild through a warm, pale mist, a dazzling blue cupola above. The tide is out, and the smell is muddy, almost rank. Seagulls peck for clams and shriek out in triumph from time to time.

Out in the wide fjord I glimpse a seal's head. Its wet, round eyes stare back at me, as if to ask, "What now, Dagny?" I'm sixty-seven and I've been in America thirty-five years. We bought this small cedar-shake cabin as a retreat on the Hood Canal because it reminded us both of Norway: no electricity, a wood stove, everything simple. A good place for fishing, walking, reading, and remembering.

I drove here yesterday from our house south of Tacoma, with the journals and a box of photographs that I took from my old sea chest in the attic. The journals are from my first twelve years in America and beyond, and today I mean to begin rereading them. It seems time to see who I was and consider what words I want to leave behind. I haven't gotten very far this morning, have only glanced at the first few entries in their rather awkward English.

After that false start I switched to Norwegian and continued to write in my mother tongue, even as my English improved.

Old days, old memories, beginning in the closing years of the last century. Many of the events took place not too far from here, in the small city of Port Townsend, about fifty miles north. I've not yet decided whether to try to drive there this week. We've only had our new Ford six months, and my husband has worried about me taking it out for such a long trip. Highway 101 is still new and gas stations are few and far between. I often take his advice, but this time may ignore it. I have two gasoline cannisters in the truck and I know how to change a tire.

In the past, we traveled by ship and wagon. My foster son Kjell still doesn't own a car, but he has a truck and tractor now. I'll see him and his family on the farm in Chimacum, even if I don't get all the way to Port Townsend.

For now I sit in a battered old wicker armchair with my feet up on the railing. The first journal is in my lap. The scent of old paper and ink mingles with the reek of the brackish low tide. I recognize my neat handwriting, learned first from my mother. I look out at the shining water, the refracted autumn mist. I look at the water for meaning, as I have often stared out at Arctic seas and southern oceans, fjords and bays and straits and rivers around the world. The seal's head vanishes as a fishing boat bears down on it with a rackety motor. I wave back to the man standing at the wheel, inside the cabin with its open windows. He's wearing a thick sweater and a watchman's wool cap and calls out a greeting that's lost in the sound of the motor. I was about fifteen the first and last time I pretended to steer a big sailing ship, but I've never forgotten the heft of the polished wooden wheel in my hands.

The First Journal
Port Townsend

January 1897 - January 1898

My Husband has purchased me this Journal in Calf Leather. For a Christmas Present. To practice English Writing. I had no Time to write before this. He was sailing two Days after the New Year to San Francisco and there was much to get ready. Only now begin I to write. No. *I begin,* in my poor English. Always before I write in Norwegian. *Hjemmespråket.* My Home Language, the Mother Tongue. Although I speak English often now and can read the American Newspapers, I have had not much use to write it. I write in Norwegian. Letters to my married Sisters, Solveig and Marit, on their farms on the Sognefjord, to my Cousin Katrine in Bergen, just as I always have since I married and set sail with Captain Edvard Bergland. Edvard speaks and writes good English from his early Years on British Ships.

Sometimes, besides my long Letters, I have written Sketches of Life at Sea and in faraway Ports which my Cousin Katrine places in Norwegian newspapers. As a Girl I dreamed of writing a Novel. That was when I first came to Bergen from Sognefjord to live with my Aunt and Uncle. I was fourteen. Before then, I could read, but we had only one shelf of books at home. In my Uncle and Aunt's house there was a whole bookcase of Norwegian, Danish, and French books, even Charles Dickens in translation. I thought sometimes how exciting it would be, to write Something like those Stories about People who loved and lost and hoped and died.

Then kind and quiet Captain Edvard Bergland was introduced to the Household, for a Purpose: to give me a Place in the World and a Family of my Own. He is older than me. He has always been older than me. He will always be older than me.

Tenses.

I was almost eighteen then and he was thirty-six, with red-brown Hair and a full Beard and, I found out, a Tattoo on his Arm of a half-naked Lady. I am thirty-two now and he is fifty. I have been to South America often, each Voyage lasting one or two Years, with some Weeks or Months spent in Peru and Chile each Time. I have been to Hawaii, Hong Kong, Bombay, and Cape Town. That was on a Trip that took three Years, all around the World. For fourteen Years altogether I lived mostly in two Cabins in our three-masted Barque, the *Matilde*. But now I do not sail with Edvard up and down the West Coast with Cargos from Port Townsend to San Francisco. The *Matilde* is gone, and my Husband now captains a two-masted Schooner belonging to the tight-fisted Swede Carl Olafsson, who runs Ships with Lumber from the forests here to San Francisco.

After the Loss of the *Matilde*, Edvard said he would not use the Insurance Money to build another Ship. There are more Steamships than Sailing Ships now, and he has no wish to captain a Steamship. He wishes us to have a Land Home now, a House, and this House should be in America, here in Port Townsend. So with the Insurance Money he bought the House and took an ordinary Job that anyone could do. I keep the House, as they say in English, not keep to the House, though it comes to the same Thing.

Maybe someday we go back to Bergen, but not for a long while. Even with his ordinary Job he makes good Money here, and Money is important, especially in America. Edvard has no Family in Norway now that his Parents have died. His Brothers died at Sea long ago. I am his Family, along with Kjell, our Foster Son.

There are Things that are the same about Bergen and Port Townsend. Hills. Wharves. Ships in Port, Ships from Europe, England, China. Here the Ships sail and steam up and down the Pacific Coast and into Puget Sound to Seattle and Tacoma. You can look out from the Top of the Hill where we live, which has no Trees since they were chopped down, and instead see a Forest of Masts and Sails coming and going through Admiralty Inlet or anchored in Port Townsend Bay. You can see many large Buildings as well from our Home: the Customs House, the Marine Hospital, Learned's Opera House, the red-brick City Hall with the Clock Tower, the Blocks of Wooden and Stone Offices, Shops, and Hotels on Water Street. Ten Years ago they said Port Townsend would be the biggest City on the West Coast north of San Francisco, especially after the Train would come here from the East Coast. It was to be the "Key City." Dozens of Buildings went up. Hundreds and Hundreds moved here. But then the Train did not come to Port Townsend after all. It stopped in Seattle and Seattle is now "Queen of Puget Sound." In 1893 there was a Banking Crash. A thousand People left Port Townsend almost at once. This Town is not a Ghost Town, and many Ships are in the Harbor. Still, the Streets look empty, almost surprised. The tall stone and brick Buildings are now too grand for the Town. They are like Royalty seated here and there along Water Street and on the Bluffs and Hills. They wait for the Party to begin, a Party that is put off for another Day.

There are two Towns, really. Down and Up. Water Street and Uptown. Water Street has a nice Quarter, but down by the Wharves it is all Saloons and Hotels and Boarding Houses, dirty, noisy, unsafe for Ladies and unwary or drunken young Seamen. I know about these Port Cities. I am not innocent. I have seen the worst of Human Nature in ports like Bombay and Callao. But we do not have our nice new House down by the Port. We live high on hill, in Uptown. Heaven above the Hell below. Up here on the flat Bluff are Streets and Houses, Bakers, Grocers, a Blacksmith, Stables, many Churches, a School, even a Theater. All so the nice Families never have to walk down among the Riffraff (an amusing English Word) along the Wharves. I don't care about being with the nice Families.

I miss the Sea. *Jeg længer til Sjøs.*

January 10

I continue now about our House. I said it was new. It is eight Years old, built by a Banker whose Bank failed in the Crash. It stood empty for some Time, then my Husband bought it for a good Price. It is more than we need with six Bedrooms, Servants' Rooms, a Cellar and an Attic. One Bedroom has a round Turret with Windows to the Sea on three Sides. This is my favorite Room. Here I have my Sea Chest, painted with Rosemaling, and Photographs framed on the Walls. The attic has a small Door that leads out to an iron-fenced Balcony facing the Sea. I am told this is a "Widow's Walk," where Wives, many with their Husbands still living, go out to watch for his Ship to return. Why should a Banker's Wife need to look out to Sea? Better she should have looked at the Bank Ledgers.

The leather Journal Edvard gave me has a Lock, and that is typical of my Husband. He respects my Privacy, even now when I have my own Room. There are many Things we do not talk about. The Night the *Matilde* burned and sank in San Francisco's Harbor. Edvard's scorched Arm and Hand. The two Children. One a Boy in the Atlantic Ocean now, and one an infant Girl, in the Pacific off South America. And we do not talk about the Fact we find it hard to try again. Edvard says, "When we are settled in the Town, there is Time to raise a Family, a Speaking-English Family, who will go to School and be Americans."

If we have Children here, we will not go back home to Bergen.

We do not discuss this much and also he is so often at Sea. Loads of Spruce, Cedar, and Fir go down to San Francisco. Ballast and City Goods return. When the Ship comes in, my Husband sends me a Message and I walk down to the Wharf with Kjell. He was our Steward on the *Matilde*. Kjell misses the Sea as much as I do.

I tell my Husband, *Jeg er rastløs på Landen*. I am restless on the Land.

"We try this, Dagny," he says firmly. "This House, this Town. You will make Friends." Not a Command. A Hope.

But I have never had Women Friends, though I was always very glad in my Sisters Solveig and Marit and I still miss Cousin Katrine as much as the Day I last saw her in Bergen, three Years ago. We stood on the Wharf, and I said, "We will be back from South America in two Years, maybe less." She is a Schoolteacher.

Sailing around the World is not a Tea Party; you do not make Lady Friends. On the *Matilde* I was the only Female among the Crew. There is Something odd about me, I feel now, in Port Townsend. It is not just my Accent, because the Shopkeepers understand what I say. But these Ladies in Uptown, yes, and they *are* Ladies, New England Ladies like Mrs. Jane Mills and Mrs. Helen Witherspoon, they never smile and never say hello.

We are not rich, but we have Money enough. My Husband bought us a big House and Piano. Dresses and Hats in the latest style he brings from San Francisco. All what is needed for me to look like a Lady, I have. But the Port Townsend Ladies do not see me as one of them.

You do get brown and leathery at Sea in the southern Latitudes. You cannot always carry a Parasol in the Sea Wind.

And you sometimes forget and you swear. *Fy faen!* you shout when the Horse rears. *Din jaevl!* You Devil! And worse. And the Ladies understand, even if it's Norwegian, what the Meaning is.

Mrs. Mills' Husband owns a Bank.

Mrs. Smith's Husband is the Methodist Minister.

Mrs. Witherspoon's Husband is the School Principal.

Mrs. Petersen's Husband has the Grocery Store and Ice Cream Parlor here in Uptown.

Mrs. Barker's Husband owns three Saloons and (they say) a Whorehouse, where (they say), Mrs. Barker once worked. Cecilia Barker occasionally speaks to me. It is no Comfort that she is not seen as quite "nice enough" either.

Emma Smith, the Methodist Minister's Wife, also speaks to me, because she is a Godly Woman. A Good Woman, too, I must add.

This Christmas, Uptown was decorated with Fir Boughs and red Balls and Ribbons. It snowed and Sleighs passed each other on Lawrence Street. At Night, if I took a Walk, I saw Families gathered in their brightly lit Parlors around a Christmas Tree. Sometimes there were Parties. No one invited us. Edvard's Ship was delayed, so I told myself I could not have gone to a Party alone, even if I had been invited. On Christmas Eve, after Edvard had returned, we went to Trinity Methodist Church and listened to Kjell sing Carols, and then came Home. We toasted each other with hot Chocolate (Kjell is a Temperance Follower) and tried not to think too hard about Norway.

But I had a long Letter from Katrine with a Photograph of her and my Aunt Inger, now a Widow. My Aunt sent a Package of Norwegian Sheep Wool and a Pattern, for me to knit Edvard a Sweater. Katrine sent Books in Norwegian—Novels. She told me that one of my Stories, about Lima, Peru, had appeared in a

Newspaper in Kristiania and won some Praise from the Editor. She sent me the Clipping. I have put the Photograph of my Family in a Frame and the Frame is next to my Bed. Because it was Christmas Edvard came to sleep with me. He told me he was lonely and not to turn away. Our son, Jan, had my Husband's Eyes. He was just five when he was swept from Edvard's arms into the Sea by a Wave.

April 15

I have not written in some time and now I find, if I am to continue with this *dagbok,* this daily journal, it would be better to continue in Norwegian. Only in Norwegian do I feel myself fully. In English I make too many mistakes, with the verb tenses, with the nouns that look wrong if they are not capitalized, and I feel my sentences are choppy as waves and my meaning is lost. If this journal is to be not just a copybook to practice English, but a record of my new life in America, then I must write in the language that is mine, especially when the events are hard and the soul is trampled.

I could not write because I was ill and low for weeks after my "miscarriage," as they call it in English. That sounds less harsh than our *abort.* The dictionary says that plans can also miscarry and so can justice. The doctor came to see me after it had happened. I was not far along, six weeks perhaps, but of course you still feel the shape of the being-not-to-be as it leaves your body. Cramping before and after. Kjell helped me. He has seen blood enough on a ship. Together we wrapped and buried the bundle in soggy ground under a bare shrub in a far corner of the garden. A stone for remembrance from the shore.

I didn't lie abed more than two days but for some weeks I lost my interest in life. The winter snow lasted only briefly, and afterwards came heavy, gray rain and then the wild winds of March. Late February was when the miscarriage happened. I dozed during the day and was awake at night. Edvard had to be told when he returned from San Francisco, that was the worst part of it, almost. His long, kind face grew longer still, so the furrows in his cheeks seemed like dry rivers. I have never seen him cry, not even in the San Francisco infirmary with his burns. He may have cried when our son Jan was swept away in the stormy Atlantic, when the rain itself was like crying. Or when Agnete died. This time he had allowed himself to have a little hope, as I had. Now that was gone. He was in port for a week in March, before leaving again.

"I do not like you to be so alone, dear Dagny. Kjell is not companion enough for you. You must have a housekeeper-cook or at least a maid. We can afford it. Can't you ask the other ladies in town to help you find someone?"

In the seven months we have been here, we've had two cooks. One drank and one left after quarreling with Kjell about how to marinate herring. We also had trouble with a chamber maid, who stole the silverware. Now it's just Kjell. He makes porridge and coffee for breakfast, does some shopping, and is preparing to plant some vegetables. I bake bread and prepare soups and meat for our *middag*. I dust and sweep, but the house is large.

So I've begun again to search for a servant who can cook and clean. What I've heard from the shopkeepers is that the fine ladies here in Uptown often brought their servants with them from California or the East Coast, since there are few decent single women available to work as maids. As a result some families in Port Townsend employ Chinese servants, mostly men.

In Lima, when we were in port there once for many weeks, we rented a house with Chinese servants. The Chinese were brought to Peru to work in the terrible guano mines offshore on the Chincha Islands or to labor in the fields on the haciendas. But after their contracts were over, they moved into Lima, and some of them married Indians or *chulas*, Indian-Peruvian girls. That was the case with our Chinese houseman, who had taken the last name Rodrigues, and his *chula* wife, Maria. I liked them very much for the short time I knew them.

I have seen these Chinese people—the locals call them Celestials—going quietly about their business in Uptown. They are slender and narrow-hipped, wearing cotton tunics or pajamas under their padded jackets, and they have long black pigtails. Besides the servants in Uptown, who live with families, at least several hundred Chinese are to be found in Port Townsend's Chinatown down by the wharves, several blocks of shops, noodle parlors, boarding houses, and laundries. There is one big shop, the Zee Tai Company, and many little ones that are also opium dens. So it is said.

For some time now, since the stealing maid was let go, our laundry has been washed in Chinatown. A laundryman by the name of Ah Song comes once a week. He carries two big baskets swinging from his shoulders, a contraption almost bigger than he is. It was Kjell who engaged him. It seemed like a good solution to the washing at least, just to have someone come and take away linen and clothing and bring it back clean and pressed. A slightly foreign smell, but a good one.

Today when I paid Ah Song I asked him, "Do you know someone from Chinatown who might come here to help us?"

"Gardener?" he said. The Chinese are the gardeners of Port Townsend, I understand, and not just in the front yards of Uptown. They labor on farms not far from us in a place called Chinese Gardens, and also on many acres out of town at Station Prairie. They raise fruits and vegetables in great quantities in spring and summer, and then load them on wagons and sell them in the neighborhoods.

"I was thinking, maybe, a young woman, to cook and clean. She could live in or live out. Someone perhaps who works in the laundry and would like a chance to better herself."

He did not look at me. "No girls in laundry. Nice ladies not work. Nice ladies married."

"But surely some Chinese girls are not married?"

"Some ..." he stopped, embarrassed. I suppose he meant those working in the brothels.

"Just think about it," I said. I know that lower Port Townsend is full of whores. Few are as lucky to escape as Cecilia Barker who now has a large house in Uptown. I suppose some of the whores are Chinese too. "A young man is also fine, if you know one."

May 1

Two days ago, along with Ah Song, another fellow came to collect the laundry. He looked very much the same, in cotton trousers and a padded jacket, but younger. His jaw was determined but his cheeks were soft like a child's and his lower lip full. He said nothing; I wasn't sure if he understood any English, though his eyes followed me with a curious look. Usually Kjell deals with the laundry, but he was out to buy some garden tools, since the rain has brought so many weeds.

After I paid Ah Song and saw to putting the sheets and towels away in closets, I went back to the dining room and continued writing a letter to my cousin Katrine in Bergen. The spring sun came through the lace curtains and made a filigree pattern on the dark walnut wood. Katrine has asked me for more stories. "I spoke with an editor here in Bergen," she writes, "He is interested in your impressions of America. He writes me, tell Mrs. Bergland to describe what she sees in the Wild West— especially bloodthirsty Indians, sharpshooters, card sharks, and opium eaters. He says he will print whatever you write. Dagny— such an opportunity!"

Katrine was the one who first urged me to write articles based on our life at sea and my impressions of some of the port cities. My letters, she told me, were so interesting. Surely the Norwegian newspapers would be interested in tales of a sea captain's wife? Over the years I sent her a number of sketches to place for me. While I was at sea, I only thought of Norwegian newspapers. But I've realized that here in America there are newspapers published in the Norwegian language, for all the tens of thousands of immigrants who have settled here and don't know English well. Earlier this year I sent away for copies of the *Minneapolis Tidende* and the *Decorah-Posten,* two of the largest. I also subscribed to a women's monthly journal in Cedar Rapids, Iowa. It impressed me to learn *Kvinden og Hjemmet*—*Woman and Home*—had been founded by a woman, Ida Hansen, and that it has such a large circulation: 40,000 subscribers. But after looking at the first two issues, I put *Woman and Home* to the side. It seemed to be full of recipes for American-style meals, like berry pies and meatloaf, and advertisements for farm tools, patent medicines, and beauty creams. The Norwegian immigrant reader must live on a farm, I thought. Or perhaps she was a young housewife in a Norwegian neighborhood in Minneapolis or a mother trying to raise daughters to be patriotic Americans while still teaching them how to knit and make *lefse*.

I couldn't imagine writing for the Norwegian press in America, or at least not *Woman and Home* in Cedar Rapids, Iowa. True, occasionally I read the articles in *Ladies' Home Journal* to practice my English or studied the illustrations and photographs to get a better picture of this country. I might skip over the articles on fashion and gardening, but I enjoyed the short stories and serialized novels. I couldn't help noticing that the young American heroines seemed to be rather different than those in Norway; they appeared to have more freedom, and sometimes they were "boyish" and got into "scrapes." They didn't swear but they did say inexplicable things like "By golly."

Another piece of paper lay beside my letter to Katrine; it was a list of different things I might write about for the editor she mentioned in Bergen, but I had not gotten very far. I saw obstacles as well as possibilities. Water Street and the wharves are full of life, as port cities always are, but this life is lived mainly by seamen, rough-spoken and often drunk. I'd seen plenty of sailors but no cowboys on the coast. As a lady living in Uptown, the world of card sharks and sharpshooters is unknown to me.

Wild Indians, there are none. At the edge of town, at Point Hudson and along the rocky shore, you could sometimes see people camped, digging clams and weaving baskets to sell. They're called the Klallam, as far as I understand—the "Strong People," and their village here was called something like "kuh-tai," which is now the name of a lagoon. The coastal people lived here for a long time, they say, at any rate long before the Europeans came. With their woven cedar hats and quiet ways, they are not the kind of Indians we Norwegians are familiar with from Karl May's books about the American West, those living in tipis and fighting on horseback with bows and arrows. These Pacific Northwest tribes are water beings who appear and disappear through the sea mists, now in town, now gone again.

Chinatown holds some possibilities, if what the editor in Norway wants are opium eaters. Several times Kjell and I have shopped at the Zee Tai Company for porcelain cups and plates, but further into the quarter, near the dormitories and hotels and brothels, we haven't ventured, on the orders of my husband, who fears I might be seen there and criticized. In Lima I walked with Edvard in the Barrio Chino along Calle Capón, and in San Francisco we had often done the same, on Grant Street. In Hong Kong we had wandered together through alleys reeking of opium tar and bitter herbs and sweet smoke from charcoal braziers, and whenever I was near Port Townsend's Chinatown and smelled the same scents, I felt connected to my old life—my old seafaring life.

If I were to choose a subject for my next article, I suppose it might be easiest to write about the ships anchored in the harbor. I could look for ships with Norwegian captains and crews and interview them and their passengers. Perhaps I might find men who came from Bergen or Ålesund, where Edvard's family once lived. Perhaps I would even meet someone from the Sognefjord—stranger things have happened—who could give me news of my sisters. But here again my mind came up against the warning face of my husband, and the horrified raised eyebrows of Mrs. Mills, the banker's wife, and her equally proper friends. Nice ladies do not wander around the wharves alone.

After I wrote this, I tore up my list of possible subjects, and went to my turret room, out onto the small balcony. Not to look for any particular ship off the coast, but to feel the sea breeze on my face. I married to have a larger life, and now I find myself confined to a house, and I cannot even use my pen to free myself.

May 6

Today the two Chinese fellows came again with laundry, and this time they had a proposal. Ah Song gestured to his young companion. "He is Henry Soon. He says he will work for you. Work hard. Cooking, cleaning, garden. You give him food and a room, he very happy. A little money. You decide."

"Does he speak English?"

"Not so much, he is new to the country. But he is clever."

"He looks very young. How old is he?"

The two conferred. "Twenty."

I found that hard to believe—Kjell is twenty—but in looking more closely I realized that the boy might be at least seventeen. He looked well able to perform household tasks that any woman can do. "We don't need help with everything," I said. "Kjell and I manage all right. But there is still much to do. Yes, then."

"Thank you," said Ah Song, smiling.

"Thank you," said Henry Soon. His voice was low, almost a whisper, and he did not smile. "Thank you."

Again, Kjell had been gone when I decided this. He was not satisfied. He hoped, I think, for a young local girl, so he could practice his American English. But Henry was so quiet, so swift in his movements, so quick to pick up our ways, that within two weeks it was hard to imagine how we had managed without him. The sweeping is done almost before we wake up, and no dish ever sits on the counter more than a few minutes. Henry has taken over making the breakfast and baking the bread, and then helping me with the *middag*. Himself, he eats only rice, vegetables, and a little fish. In the afternoon, he pulls weeds in the garden and piles fish bones around the small plants. He asked for permission to make a better vegetable garden for us in a sunny spot, and he and Kjell built a fence around it. Out the window I have sometimes seen Henry standing in the garden, pausing to look out to sea.

His room is up the backstairs. He goes to his room every night right after washing up the few dishes from the bread and cheese we take in the evening. We do not know what he does up there all evening—he is light of foot and there is never any sound— but of course it is not right that he sits with us in the parlor. We imagined he would seek out his own kind down in Chinatown, but he does not appear to go anywhere to meet other Celestials except sometimes to the Chinese Gardens, where he returns with the green vegetables he likes. Kjell found the New Testament for him in Chinese, and a simple grammar of English. We talk to him in English, and I see that he understands more than I thought. We all learn English through practice. The more I read and write in English, the better it goes. My dictionary is always open. Sometimes Kjell and I speak to each other in English, and sometimes, just for old times' sake, in simple Spanish. When my husband and I first met Kjell in Lima, he only spoke Spanish and just a few words of Norwegian that he remembered from his parents. I had to learn Spanish to speak to the boy in order to teach him Norwegian.

May 20

My captain is back for ten days. He brought many presents from San Francisco, two new dresses for me and underclothes (he is not shy buying such things). He had with him this time a fine velvet sofa for the parlor, with matching wing-backed armchairs, hauled up the hill by horse and wagon. Also two lamps, three little tables, some curtains, and a large turkey carpet. On his next trip he says he'll buy more beds and chests for the empty bedrooms. This house seems to need a lot of furniture to fill it. More to dust. But I was happy to see him. For most of our married life we lived practically on top of each other in the *Matilde*. It has been a strange thing to rattle around this large house without his step and his voice nearby.

Edvard is well pleased with Henry who does the work of two and is in motion all day long. Edvard does not share the strange prejudices held against the Chinese. When he was a boy, just an apprentice seaman out of Liverpool, his first passage to South America was on a guano ship, the worst kind of ship if he had known. Most of the work mining the seabird fertilizer was done by enslaved Chinese, working with picks and shovels on the cliffs of the Chincha Islands off the coast of Peru. They transported the guano to holding areas and eventually down to the shore, where barges brought the fertilizer out to the waiting ships. As a lowly sailor Edvard had to wear a mask and stand in the hold shoveling the guano in piles. It could take three months to fill a ship's hold with guano. It was poison to breathe and burned his eyes so he could hardly see. But it was better to be a lowly Norwegian seaman than a Chinese laborer. Edvard saw sights he would never forget—boys and men lashed until the blood ran, screaming in agony and throwing themselves off the cliffs into the ocean waters. They had been recruited in China with the promise they were going to the California to mine gold, then enslaved and tortured in Peru. To see such sights as a boy of fifteen burns the eyes like ammonia.

The first evening Edvard was home, when Henry was upstairs, he asked me if Henry was legal, and I had to tell him I did not know.

From our time in San Francisco I remember stories about how the Chinese first came to America to pan gold. They stayed to build the railways to connect this country east to west. They blasted and they dug and they hammered and pounded in the heavy snow and rain. They were paid very little and when the work was finished no one cared about them. Many went to work in canneries or farms or moved to cities. They had their shops and laundries. But even such useful work they could not do in peace. Edvard told me this evening that only about ten years ago there were anti-Chinese riots in Tacoma and in Seattle to expel the shopkeepers and business owners. Already, in 1882, Congress had passed the Chinese Exclusion Act. Only Chinese merchants and a few select ladies and children could come into America. The rest were excluded. It was meant to be for ten years. In 1892 the Act was renewed for another decade, and that is the situation now. The Chinese already here must obtain a certificate of residence, or they will be deported.

"Imagine," said Edvard. "To single out one kind of people and exclude them. If there was a Scandinavian Exclusion Act there would be no shipping on the West Coast."

That is because half the captains and seamen from California to Alaska are Danes, Norwegians, Finns, and Swedes.

"How to do you suppose Henry came to be here?" I asked Edvard. "If the Chinese are prevented from emigrating?"

"He must have arrived secretly. It is not yet prohibited for the Chinese to sail from Hong Kong to Canada. They must pay a head tax, but they can come. They arrive in the Port of Victoria and pay to be smuggled by boat to Port Townsend. If the sea is calm, it's a crossing of only two or three hours."

I see how civil Edvard is to Henry. My husband is a fair man. As a captain he rarely meted out the harsh punishments he received as a young seaman. He also believes in democracy and American ideals. Edvard is eager to belong to this country.

I, less so.

May 23

Last September when we arrived in Port Townsend from San Francisco, with the few items we had left from the *Matilde* (items like my sea chest that happened to be onshore with us in a hotel room when the drunken second mate knocked over a lantern), it was warm and sunny with a blue sky and so many dark green trees that I felt as if I were home in Norway. Soon after, in October, the rains began and they continued all winter, sometimes just drizzle, sometimes a raging windstorm, sometimes snow in December and January.

But this May has been fair, with hardly a cold day and very little rain, just the refreshing sea wind. The daily sunshine and growing warmth do my heart and body good, and Edvard feels it too. We would not be human if we did not grieve, nor human if we did not also see how beautiful the world is.

Edvard is often busy during the day down at the wharves, but in the long bright evenings he and I sometimes walk for many miles around town and over to the bluffs above the lighthouse. This summer the government will begin to construct a defensive fort on the bluffs, one of three at the entrance to Puget Sound, to protect Seattle and the naval station at Bremerton. The construction will help the town's faltering economy too, says Edvard. But right now, in May, they have not yet begun to cut down trees and build the gun batteries.

Last evening we walked through those big fragrant trees— cedar, fir, spruce, and the pistachio-green and orange-barked Madrona—out to the edge of the bluff. From up there you get the widest possible view. To the north, the white cone of Mount

Baker; to the south, the vaster white cone of Mount Rainier. Winter and summer they glisten with snow and ice. Their summits are so high they never melt. The tide was far out, and we descended to the lighthouse to walk around the rocky point to North Beach. It was not so light as it would be in Norway in June, but it was still light enough, and the clouds were only a little pink at the edges. Edvard, in spite of the burned arm, is a tall, strong man with long legs, and he walks quite quickly. It is a pleasure to walk with him, for I walk at a good pace too, not caring when with him that my skirt gets muddy or sandy. In town I cannot walk as I like but must take smaller steps and carry a parasol.

We did not speak much as we walked. Yet we knew the other's thoughts. We had lost another baby. Should we try again this May night and the ones to follow? Edvard sails in a week and will not return until the end of July. First, he will take the *Fidelius* to be loaded at Port Ludlow nearby and then down the coast to San Francisco. The ship will go into dry dock and Edvard will oversee some needed repairs to the ship. Then, he will start up the coast again carrying merchandise, furniture, and tools for the towns and lumberyards nearby.

In bed last night I noticed that my husband's chest hair is now entirely gray. The tattoo of the woman on his left arm is distorted from the burns; her head is still the same, but her body is twisted and erased in places by pink scar tissue. We must be careful of the arm, because some muscles were damaged. The arm has grown weak. He cannot prop himself above me as in the old way. I must astride him. This I did last night, but I rolled off before he finished. How is it that I care for my husband but yet will disappoint him? Too many memories crowd my mind on such occasions. "Patience," I ask, when what he wants is passion.

The evening light was soft, glowing as we strolled the beach. Saltwater makes the air shimmer. Perhaps I am not so romantic as a woman, but I am romantic as a writer. I wanted a pen in my hands to describe this gold light, this sea, this moment. I had only been once to North Beach with Edvard. It has no harbor and is hardly even an inlet. The Klallam people used to put in their canoes carved from cedar trunks on the shore here and then portage them over to the other side of the narrow peninsula, through a valley with several ponds to the lagoon of "kuh-tai." Last September we came here by carriage and saw the fields of greens, corn, and tomatoes: the Chinese Gardens. Barefoot Chinese men in wide cotton trousers and straw hats hoed and weeded. Edvard and I walked among the Gardens and wondered at the strange green vegetables among the familiar green beans and potato vines. We bought beans and dahlias from a small stand.

This evening, as we came walking along the shoreline, we could not see over the low dunes to the gardens. Instead what we saw in front of us, standing out on the tidal flat, was a clump of men in their loose trousers and jackets waving their hands, and making sounds of fright. It was Edvard who understood it first and immediately he began to run, holding his left arm close.

I looked out to sea. A large dinghy had overturned, and heads were visible in the waves. Some people hung on to the hull. Some were swimming toward shore. Others simply disappeared. Edvard reached the crowd. He had been a strong swimmer once, but no longer. He waved at the men on the flats with his good arm, pointing to the overturned boat with the clear message: they must swim out to the others. But I could see the reluctance in the men's bodies. Perhaps they could not swim either. One man plunged in, and then another and met with the swimmers and helped them ashore. They were also Chinese.

In the end, six men survived the wrecking of the boat. We never knew how many had died. Edvard said the boat was likely overloaded. It had perhaps been lowered from a larger ship and then foundered in the rough waves near the shore. He shook his head and cursed his useless arm, but I was glad that he had not jumped into the cold waves after the drowning men. The six soaking survivors were incapable of speech. Wrapped in blankets they were led away, to disappear among their own. Later the bodies of the unlucky would wash ashore and be buried, probably secretly.

Was this how Henry arrived in America?

This morning Kjell and I stood on Union Wharf a long time, watching the schooner *Fidelius* slip its hawsers and catch the outgoing tide. The sails were set, the wind was fresh, the sky unclouded. We both wished we were on that ship. Edvard probably wished himself ashore. His heart was not aboard a ship any longer, he had told me last night in the darkness of the bedroom. He was no longer master of his own beloved barque; now he went where the owner wished. Edvard hoped now only to set more money aside and then in another few years leave the sea. He wanted some quiet years with me, here in Port Townsend, if possible, with a family.

I sometimes wondered why Kjell did not sail with him as steward, but I suspected that Edvard had made him promise to stay with me, for safety's sake. I knew there were a few rumors in town about Kjell. He is much younger than me. Why would a young seaman be content to just live with the captain's wife and do chores around the house? Cecilia Barker, the former whore, once asked me if he was my brother, and she winked.

My own view is that Kjell would shoot away if something better came along, but for now he seems content to practice his English and learn new ways. Kjell is a devout young man. He finds his own delight in visiting the many and various houses of worship in Port Townsend. Back and forth he went between the Lutherans and the Catholics, the Presbyterians and the Episcopalians. Now he is a Methodist. At Trinity Church in Uptown he joined the choir, and his fine baritone is a good addition. He may have also had an eye for one or two of the pretty girls in the choir. He certainly never in a hundred years would cast his eye covetously on the captain's wife. I am also his foster mother. I am only a dozen years the elder, but much of my life already seems behind me.

After the *Fidelius* was no longer to be seen, Kjell and I found ourselves in a strange, restless state. If he had not been feeling the same way, I doubt I could have persuaded him to accompany me on a walk around the streets. I hid the fact that what I really wanted to see was more of Chinatown. Since the incident on

North Beach a few days ago I had been thinking more about the Chinese people. Would not Henry's story of how he arrived in America be an interesting one to write about?

Our first stop was the familiar Zee Tai Company on Water Street, a large well-appointed shop of teak cabinets and shelves holding bolts of lush silks and embroidered satins. The shop sells painted fans and ivory figurines and pale green celadon vases. But the shop is not only for trinkets and treasures. Large tea tins lined the shelves, along with boxes of spices and remedies. The shop smelled of star anise and bitterroot and sandalwood, like shops in Hong Kong and Lima. The Zee Tai Company has its own rice-packing machine, and big bags of rice were loaded from the back door onto carts, not just to feed the Chinese in town, but those all over the Northwest.

I felt in the mood to buy myself a present and some jade objects in a glass case caught my eye. The merchant came over to help me. His clothes, a tunic and trousers, were very finely tailored and his cap red satin embroidered with a dragon motif. He was a well-rounded man with a smooth face and friendly eyes who spoke English. I pointed to a cloudy, pale green jade pendant on a silver chain.

"Yes, the jade gourd," he said smiling. "It is good luck. Good luck for ladies. Good luck for travelers. Good luck for life. Much good luck."

It was smooth and plump, and the green was like ocean water after a storm. I thought of my husband and how we needed luck to go on with our wish for a family. Kjell helped me put the chain around my neck after I purchased it. The man bowed many times and we parted with kind words.

Then Kjell and I ventured out into the twisting little alleys a few blocks away from the Zee Tai Company, where much smaller shops, some hardly wide as a door, with signs only in Chinese, offered piles of roots and other unfamiliar things in baskets and boxes. In the street, the sickly-sweet tar scent of opium mixed with human sweat and urine, and soap clouds, for the laundries stand in the midst of it all, along with fragrant steam from the noodle parlors upstairs. This is the world of Ah Song and Henry Soon, a world in Port Townsend as unknown to me as if it was

Hong Kong itself. A closed door. Yet what is the task of the writer if not to try to open that door, if only a little?

June 14

I am newly curious about the Chinese in our town. Today, in order to acquire a few more facts, I went to the *Morning Leader,* the best of the town's daily papers, though only eight pages with many advertisements. I asked for the editor. Mr. Duffy invited me into a back office for five minutes that stretched to twenty after I said I was a correspondent for a Norwegian newspaper and required information about Port Townsend's Chinese population. This seemed to surprise him greatly. That Norway had newspapers? That a woman would write for a newspaper? That anyone in Norway would spare a thought for the Chinese here?

Actually I wondered about the last question myself.

"The situation has changed over the years," Mr. Duffy told me, as I took hungry glances at the room's bookshelves and framed illustrations. He had a big Underwood typewriting machine on his desk and long sheets of paper all marked up, and in the corner a young man sat reading page proofs at a desk. On the way to his office I'd glimpsed two men standing in front of cases of metal type and a third worker setting blocks of type into a square frame. The big, steam-powered press was quiet, but two platen presses clanked busily, printing stationery and business cards. Today's morning paper was already old news, and they were working to make up tomorrow's paper to be printed this evening.

Now, seated across from me in the office, he said, "Only ten or twelve years ago the Celestials were in mortal peril. Their shop windows were smashed, knife fights were the order of the day, and more than one honorable Chinaman had his pigtail cut off. But still it was far better than what happened elsewhere on the West Coast, where the Celestials were lynched and murdered, and their homes and businesses burned down. There were no anti-Chinese riots in our town, and the Chinese were never packed on ships and sent off, like they were in Seattle. Port Townsend instead attracted the Chinese who were afraid for their lives elsewhere."

Mr. Duffy rocked back in his wood chair. He was a man of less than forty, and there was something of the fox about him: a brush of light brown hair and beady brown eyes behind spectacles. His accent, I thought, was from a New England state. He was earnest too, like some of those Maine or Massachusetts whaling captains we had encountered here and there in our travels. He had no ring on his finger and no paunch pushing at his waistcoat, so I imagined he was a bachelor.

"It doesn't mean that the Chinese are always liked here. There is the opium trade. There is the smuggling. But it is recognized that they are hard workers. They are good for business." he said. "You may not know it, but the Zee Tai Company is the most successful business now in Port Townsend. The Celestials are honest too. They always pay their loans back. Which is more than you can say for many local businessmen."

He asked if I wrote in English. "Your accent is so charming," he added, with a smile.

I said, regretfully, no, I didn't write English very well, at least not yet. I added that my husband, a sea captain, was fluent. At the mention of my husband his interest in me suddenly waned. "Is there anything else I can help you with, Madam?"

I had many questions for him, all about writing for newspapers, but I rose, and he rose, and that was the end of my interview. Nevertheless, as I walked out of the office and back through the print room, my spirits lifted. This was the first time I had presented myself as a writer to someone besides my cousin in Bergen.

June 18

This morning I've been upstairs in my bedroom at the small desk by the window, writing a letter to Cousin Katrine, telling her about my meeting with Duffy, his recounting of the past violence and current prejudice against the Chinese, and my attempts to describe the Chinese in Port Townsend. I'll enclose the letter with the newspaper article I have written for Katrine to place. Henry is part of the story though I do not name or give other details. He is described as one of many who made their way to America from China, only to be treated with disdain.

As always, I look at Katrine's framed photograph on the desk from time to time. Not the one Katrine recently sent me, of herself with her mother. Both of them are stiff as boards and Aunt Inger is wearing mourning still, though my uncle died five years ago.

The framed one on the desk is from ten years ago, when we were in our early twenties. I made my cousin go with me to a photography studio and both of us had pictures taken. Katrine rarely smiles, at least not widely, but I can still see she's pleased by the experience. She is trim and tidy, a cameo at her ruffled collar, but otherwise her dress is sober, as befits a schoolmistress. Her light hair is parted in the middle and drawn back into a coil. Only the hat is fashionable. I brought it to her from London. I had a baby son by then, and had been to South America and back twice, with stops in New York, in São Paulo, and London. I remember I thought myself quite the sophisticate, far from the fourteen-year-old girl who had first appeared at the house in Bergen with Uncle Theodore, in my wooden shoes, shy and eager and homesick all at once.

Katrine was not shy at all, though she was even then, at sixteen, a serious young lady. But she rushed forward and took my hands, rubbed them to make them warm and said, "*Velkommen til oss!* Welcome to us!" That was the family phrase—everyone who came to the Vestermans' Bergen house was greeted that way—but it touched me then as it still does. You become part of a new family when you're welcomed in those words.

Aunt Inger, corseted like an hourglass, with pearls in her ears, and tightly curled hair, still blond then, said indulgently, "Katrine has talked about nothing else since your uncle sailed to fetch you, dear Dagny. She is an only child, you see. And now she will have a companion. You'll join her at school soon and she'll take care of you."

I wished now I had a photograph of Katrine and myself in

those early days. Over the four years I lived in that house, we grew close as sisters. She stood up for me at school when girls laughed at my dialect and my innocence. She encouraged me to read and admired my first efforts at writing. She thought for a long time I'd study to become a teacher, as she meant to do. I did my best to be like her, but I was dreamy, even then, and often I dreamed about foreign places, of taking passage somehow on a ship going to South America or China. Although Aunt Inger celebrated all the holidays in good Norwegian fashion, objects in the house (conches, carved statuettes, raffia baskets) hinted at the exotic, and visitors spoke of Java, Brazil, and Kenya—anywhere there was coffee.

My mother had told me only a little about Uncle Theodore's company, though I knew it was to do with coffee, since every Christmas a box with an enormous sack of roasted beans arrived at our farm by mail boat. In fact, my uncle's coffee importing and roasting firm, Bryggen Kaffe og Kakao, was the largest in Bergen, and the Vesterman family was rich because of its success. The firm had been built up by his father-in-law's father, who began by sending salt cod to Brazil. The ships returned with coffee beans. It's well known that Norwegians drink more coffee than almost anyone, so of course the business prospered. Uncle Theodore had a warehouse down by the wharves as well as a roastery in another part of the city. There was no shortage of money in the house and no shortage of coffee either. But what I liked more than anything was my new proximity to the world of wharves, warehouses, and ships that unloaded sacks of green coffee beans from Brazil.

Not framed, but in a photo album, I have a picture of myself on one of those special visits to the wharves with Uncle Theodore. Katrine rarely joined us, but I never missed an opportunity to go aboard a ship if I could, to walk around the deck of a barque or a clipper newly arrived from South America and to pretend that I was a sailor or even the first mate. Sometimes a mate or even the captain might walk the deck with me and tell me the parts of the ship and the kinds of rigging and sails on her. Thus I learned *bowsprit, foremast, main mast, mizzen, quarterdeck, forecastle, shrouds* and *stays.* I was most fascinated by the helm and the explanation that the ship's wheel was connected to pulleys and a tiller below decks to the rudder. By turning the huge wheel clockwise or counterclockwise you could turn the rudder and thus the whole ship to port or starboard.

I was told not to touch anything but on one visit I couldn't help myself. When I thought no one was looking, I went to the helm and put my hands on the handles of the polished wooden wheel. I pretended I was steering the ship through the South Pacific. A photographer for a Bergen newspaper happened to be present and took my picture. I was fifteen or sixteen, and after the photograph was published with the caption, "A Young Girl Dreams of the Sea," Aunt Inger didn't allow me to accompany my uncle again to the wharves. The photographer gave me a print, however, and from time to time I would look at it and remember how it felt to be in charge of the ship's direction in the vast blue sea, even though we were firmly anchored in Bergen's harbor.

Since Uncle Theodore died, Bryggen Kaffe og Kakao is run by other men, but Aunt Inger still lives on coffee profits and my cousin with her. Katrine still doesn't think of marrying. When we were young, we discussed marriage sometimes; she was against it, and I was also skeptical at first. Yet I knew that I didn't want to be a teacher and I didn't want to go back to Sognefjord. Education had changed me. Was I to be a farmer's wife? Katrine suggested I might be able to earn a modest living with my pen. We read the newspapers avidly, but whenever I submitted poems and little stories to the papers, they were rejected. I smile now at my hopes. Because I still seem to have them.

June 23

I've been in a continuing state of nostalgia for Norway and the past these days. The Americans don't celebrate Midsummer as we do "at home." Soon I'll go downstairs and cook a pot of *rømmegrøt* to serve with fish cakes for *middag* today. Tomorrow it will be pancakes, Kjell's favorite. I've tried to teach Henry to make my favorite sour cream porridge, eaten so often on the farm as a child, but he shies away from it. "Missus, you make." It's true, there is an art to *rømmegrøt*, and it doesn't conjure up the same warm feelings in everyone any more than *lutefisk* does.

This morning I opened my sea chest and took out the bunad that Mor, as we called our mother Signe, made for me when I was eight, a dark wool skirt with green trim and an embroidered dark bodice. With it I wore a white linen blouse. It wasn't a full dress, it lacked a belt and an apron, but I had been delighted with it as a child before I grew out of it. It was the tradition in our family that a full bunad was sewn when a daughter was sixteen or seventeen and had her woman's figure. It would be a treasure she could wear on special occasions all her life, as my mother wore hers. Solveig made one for herself and so did Marit with Mor's help. But when I was sixteen, I was living in Bergen, where the custom of the household was fashionable dresses from patterns created in Copenhagen and Paris. Aunt Inger, for all her support of Norwegian culture, would not have worn a bunad. That was for country folk at the time. But she did give me a beautiful silver brooch, a *sølje*, when I turned sixteen. I was as proud as I could be of this first real piece of jewelry, a round, silver filigree pin with six shining silver discs. She presented me with another *sølje* when I married, a much larger and more dramatic piece that was stolen from me years ago when the ship was docked in New York.

I've kept the bunad from my childhood. I thought Agnete might wear it, or another daughter.

This morning so many memories came back to me as I stroked the soft black wool of the skirt and let my fingertips roam over the embroidery. I wondered how I would describe the family farm to someone like Henry.

It was called Kvamnes, for our last name Kvam and the Norwegian name for headland: *nes*. It had been in my father's family since the 1700s, it was said. We had a modest house, of logs, and several outbuildings, added to by successive generations. The goats were pastured higher up, the cow lived off the rich grasses of our pasture. We were on the north side of the Sognefjord, a fjord that is the longest in Western Norway. We did not have a horse. We walked any distance easily or skied in winter. For longer journeys, we came and went by water, dragging our boat, the double-ended *faering*, from the boat shed on the rocky little headland into the fjord. We all rowed, we girls, and were taught how to help set the square sail when the wind was right. We steered with the oars. Our papa, Jakob was his name, though we called him Far, would go out with other men into the deeper fjord and fish, often in one of the larger *faerings*. He was a tall man, with powerful arms, and usually a good eye for the weather.

When my father was alive, we managed well enough, with the cow and goats and fishing. Trees were chopped up for the stove, my mother baked bread, oatcakes, and flatbread or *lefse*. She churned butter and pressed cheese into round molds. We girls learned all those things. We herded and milked the goats. We picked berries, and we dried fish on wooden racks in the summer and autumn. We planted potatoes and carrots and kohlrabi in the spring. All of us girls knew how to knit, to chop wood, to fish. In good or decent weather we traveled by boat to the nearest village of Kyrkebø on Sundays and for weddings, christenings, and funerals; in winter we stayed home and read the Bible aloud on the Sabbath. We had a few other books, chiefly those of the Wergeland family. The famous Nicolai Wergeland, who helped write the Norwegian Constitution, had been born on the other side of the fjord from us, and both his children had become writers. We had the collected poems of Henrik Wergeland, who died young, and a novel by Nicolai Wergeland's daughter, Camilla Collett. Her book, *The Governor's Daughters,* was too difficult for me, but I marveled, always, that a woman had written a novel.

What I mean to say is that even though we were far away from the capitol, news came to us in the form of pamphlets and shared newspapers, along with rumors of possibilities abroad. Young men left for the sea or the cities, like my mother's brother Theodore Vesterman, who went to Bergen to apprentice as a coffee roaster. He became the manager of the roastery, then a merchant when he, against all odds, married his employer's daughter. Some families packed up and went to America. The more who emigrated and wrote letters home about their successes, the more who wanted to emigrate. But my parents were perfectly content with their lives in Norway.

I was the youngest by six years and often played alone. My sisters were close in age and much alike. Solveig, the elder, and Marit. They weren't interested in books but in women's work. Solveig was good with a needle and Marit knew everything about raising healthy goats. She was the one to take them up to the higher pastures in the summer. When I was eleven, Far died suddenly. He and other men were out in the fjord fishing one autumn day when a violent storm suddenly blew in from the west. They all drowned when the boat overturned. The farm and all the animals were sold, and my sisters both married, perhaps sooner than they had wished, but happily. Solveig's husband had more land and a better farm than Marit's husband. Marit had more children. She writes to me more often than Solveig does, though still not often and her letters usually speak of difficult times.

My mother and I moved into the village of Kyrkebø to a parish cottage and Mor did what she could to keep me fed and clothed. She made cheese and churned butter, she baked biscuits and cookies, she knit and sewed. After the money from the farm sale ran out, we occasionally had to take handouts from neighbors and the church. There was a school in the village, but only up to the age of fourteen. Although I was judged to be clever, I had to accept that I too would have the same life as my sisters. I did not complain about this. Only sometimes, in the evening I would stand looking out at the fjord edged by mountains, at the sunsets in the west. The Sognefjord led to the sea. I thought that I would like at least once in my life to see open water and the horizon.

Mor said that she would write to her brother for advice, and one day Uncle Theodore appeared in Kyrkebø on a hired schooner from Bergen. He was bald and well-nourished with a decisive manner. I had never met him before. He and my mother talked a long time, and the end of it was that when he returned to Bergen, he offered to take me with him. I don't think Mor had planned for this, but she wanted more for me than she could easily give. And I was not reluctant, though I cried.

We gathered together my small bundle of clothes, including the bunad that no longer fit me, my Bible, and a large cheese as a present for Uncle's family. I was to live with them for at least four years, to finish my schooling and to train to be a teacher, like their daughter Katrine was planning to do. Or, if I found a suitable husband, I could marry.

One morning I woke up and life was the same as always. By the end of the day I was in a schooner heading out to sea and then south to Bergen. Mor went to live with Solveig and her husband after that. She died a few years after I was married.

I will make *rømmegrøt* today, just as Mor did, and fry up fishcakes. Henry can eat some too, with his vegetables. And tonight Kjell and I will light a bonfire in our garden. It seems long ago and far away that I was a child in Norway. Will I still celebrate Midsummer's Eve if I spend the rest of my life here in America? I would like to talk to Henry about what it means to be an immigrant, about all the things that you forget and that you still remember.

July 4

I asked Henry if he would like to go with me and Kjell to the Independence Day celebration at a local park, but he shook his head, surprised that we would even ask. My efforts to engage Henry further have petered out, but still from time to time I try. Kjell was enthusiastic and once we arrived at the park, he saw some of his friends from church. I wandered a little by myself listening to the music. Flags waved and local people made speeches. It was a sunny day, rather warm, and Kjell brought me some lemonade.

I recalled how last year the *Matilde* put into port in San Francisco several weeks before the 4th of July. We planned to be in the city at least two weeks while a cracked mast was repaired, but the time was extended into July. We'd been to San Francisco twice before but there had been great changes since the last time. The city was still rowdy and rough, yet it had also grown more elegant and modern, with cable cars and a grand new park, the

Golden Gate. After living onboard for some time, we eventually booked into a hotel not far from the docks, bringing Kjell with us, and the three of us disported ourselves for a few days with oyster dinners and vaudeville shows. On Independence Day we attended a public celebration with music and speeches. Americans seem to love speechifying about their country and its many virtues.

As Norwegians, of course, Edvard and I had attended the parades in Norway in honor of the 17th of May, our Constitution Day, but they were altogether smaller affairs. In San Francisco I could see that Edvard was moved by the speeches about the United States, the "most prosperous, the greatest, the most freedom-loving country in the whole world!" Edvard compared the freedoms in America to Norway's. "We are not even a proper country, Dagny!" he said. "Under the thumb of the Danes for centuries, and it's hardly better with the Swedes. The Union with Sweden is a disgrace. Not to have our own king. Not that I care about kings, but why should we have Oscar living in Stockholm as our sovereign?"

There were fireworks and a singing of the "Star-Spangled Banner." Very high notes. A few in the crowd wept and many put their hands on their hearts. This country seems so harsh to me, but people are enthused about its possibilities. In Norway we talk about our past, our Viking times, our traditions. In America it is only the future anyone cares about.

It was July 5 when the *Matilde* burned. And sometime after that, Edvard decided that we should move to Port Townsend and live as Americans.

July 20

GOLD! GOLD! GOLD! GOLD! was the headline of the *Seattle Post-Intelligencer* a few days ago. We get the Seattle morning newspapers by packet boat, but in this case the town already knew all about the big gold strike in Alaska. The Seattle newspaper reporters were in town on July 16. They had hired a tugboat to take them off to Cape Flattery to intercept the *Portland* as it began to make its way into Puget Sound from Alaska. The steamship carried a ton of gold and sixty-eight newly minted tycoons, returning to Seattle to celebrate and realize their wealth.

It was last summer that prospectors discovered gold nuggets in the sands of the Yukon River and staked their claims. The news stayed in Alaska over the winter until the ice melted. Then the prospectors sailed downriver from Dawson City, 1700 miles to the sea. There they took passage for Seattle and San Francisco.

The reporters got the story and returned to Port Townsend. They telegraphed the details to the *Post-Intelligencer* and the next day when the *Portland* arrived in Seattle, there were 5,000 people on the dock to meet the steamship. Now there will be a stampede north, everyone says, and this can only benefit Port Townsend. Merchants and hotel and restaurant owners are laying in food and dry goods as fast as they can. Advertising circulars are already in print: LAST STOP BEFORE THE YUKON! Overnight, bankers are loaning money again and storefronts that were empty for the last several years now have new proprietors, new signs, and new stock. Water Street now resounds day and night to hammering and sawing and urgent voices. The summer in Alaska is short and the race to get north is to the swift.

Because of the railway, Seattle is the main terminus for goods and people now flooding into the city from all over the country. How will Port Townsend fare in the competition with Seattle? For now, Port Townsend will prosper from the fact that many ships in port are ready to sail north at a moment's notice, having changed their schedules to accommodate the stampeders. Local men are booking passage on whatever seaworthy vessel they can find. A kind of mania has taken hold in just a few days. Young men who only last week were serving customers at the shops or shoeing a horse at the blacksmith or singing in the choir on Sunday and about to propose marriage to the minister's daughter are now down at Union Wharf with a trunkful of flour, molasses, cornmeal, and sardines, with long underwear and socks, with picks and shovels.

July 30

The *Fidelius* came into port several days ago, Edvard safely at the helm. But the ship wasn't filled with the usual furniture and dry goods, but with passengers, would-be prospectors from California. Carl Olafsson, my husband's employer, can make more money from hopeful gold miners than from lumber. A group of twenty San Francisco men have chartered the *Fidelius* for a trip up to Alaska, with Edvard as captain. They will not go to Skagway where most of the ships land, but to St. Michael on Norton Sound, much farther north. Then they will hire a boat, a sternwheeler it is called, to take them up the Yukon River to Dawson City.

The schooner makes a stop in Port Townsend to take on more supplies and even a few more eager passengers, those who will pay top dollar, before setting off for Alaska in two days. It takes two or three weeks to get to St. Michael and the same to return if the weather holds. The *Fidelius* is not equipped for icy seas and snowstorms, so Edvard must bring the ship back by the end of September. He receives a bonus from Carl Olafsson for going north and another when he returns. I worry about the ship. It was built for hauling lumber. How shall it sail in such northerly seas?

All has been activity in the ship and in our house to get things ready and Edvard has hardly been home, only to sleep briefly. He telegraphed last week to me and Kjell a list of all he needed. I retrieved his bearskin coat and hat from the attic, along with a quantity of knitted underclothes and thick sweaters. Kjell repaired and polished Edvard's fur-lined boots and sewed up his skin gloves. Kjell and I also bought up all the food we could, and I taught Henry how to bake ship's biscuits. I taught Henry how to can fresh food as well; for two days we put up fruit and vegetables in glass jars, then wrapped them in hay and set them in heavy crates.

Down at the wharf Edvard has been supervising the loading of the *Fidelius*. The passengers bought more supplies at high prices from the outfitters who suddenly appeared in town. I feared that too many of the men from San Francisco had no understanding of where Alaska was or what the conditions might be as winter set in. They seemed to imagine that they would strike gold in a few weeks and return before autumn, and many of them have been passing their time drinking in the saloons and frequenting the ladies. My husband could have taken on more passengers, but he set a limit and kept to it. The *Fidelius* is not our sturdy *Matilde* with a crew of twenty to thirty depending on the route. The usual crew for the schooner to San Francisco is only eight to ten men. Now, instead of lumber piled on deck and in the hold, there are to be twenty-four passengers to Alaska and only a few extra stewards hired to serve them.

It would not have surprised me had Edvard asked Kjell to join the crew as a steward—and Kjell earnestly wished to go. More than wished, I knew he was wild to go.

But Edvard told him, in my hearing, that he was worried to leave me alone, with just Henry for protection. The town has swelled with ruffians, smugglers, and chancers. Uptown seems to be a world apart but it is still only uphill from the flats where the worst sorts of vices and robberies flourish.

"There are many women in Port Townsend who live alone with their servants," I told my husband when we were alone. "It is you I worry about, sailing in unknown northern waters. If Kjell were with you, you would at least have someone to take care of your linen and feed you properly."

"I fear that Kjell would jump ship in Alaska to become a gold miner and I'd never see him again."

The night before Edvard left, he wanted to lie with me and be inside me and I said yes. I wore the jade pendant for fertility and good luck. For him and for me.

He woke a few hours later and we had coffee together while everyone else slept.

I saw him to the door. And then he was gone. To Alaska.
Oh, Edvard.

August 3

Kjell has been in low spirits since the *Fidelius* left port. More than that, I have observed a contrary streak not in evidence before now. He would stand up for his opinion, like any good stubborn Norwegian, but he respected authority. How could he not? He was our foster son, who had come to us from a Lima orphanage at age eleven to be a cabin boy on the *Matilde* and had been with us ever since, eventually becoming my husband's steward and clerk. But although there was much affection on both sides, on a ship there can only be one captain. My husband never whipped his men, never imprisoned them below decks unless they had murdered anyone (which happened once or twice), and only rarely put them off the ship in foreign ports (though that had happened too). But the crew knew the captain could do all those things and had a right to do them. He could place them on meager rations, demote them, change their watches, set them to any tedious task he liked. A captain is the small god of a ship at sea, the judge and jury, the jailor and the merciful liberator, the minister who reads aloud the Bible on Sundays and who consigns the dead to the waves. And that is as it should be, probably, for someone must be in charge at sea.

But happy enough as Kjell had been on the *Matilde* and accepting enough of his mandate to take care of me and the house in Port Townsend for the last months while Edvard skippered the *Fidelius,* Kjell was a young man of twenty used to the sea and foreign lands. It tormented him to see Port Townsend's wharves and streets aswarm with landlubbers newly arrived from all around Puget Sound and ports along the West Coast in their just-bought mining outfits (sombreros, canvas trousers, and Mackinaw jackets), with trunks of food and shiny copper pots and pans. Many of these men were young, and they had never been aboard a ship in northern waters, had no idea of snow and ice, of winter's darkness—all things Kjell was well-acquainted with.

The best chance of getting up to the Yukon goldfields would go to those who embarked as soon as possible for Skagway, in Kjell's opinion. "From there," Kjell told me today over morning coffee, "it's just a climb over Chilkoot Pass and two weeks trek to Dawson. I could be there in September and have time to stake my claim and then spend the winter, so I was ready to pan as soon as the snow melts in spring. If I went, I wouldn't be like these fools with their trunks of clothing and sacks of flour and cornmeal, all those iron kettles and ropes and shovels. How will they climb the pass with all that on their backs? No, if I went, I'd travel light, with just my rucksack, bedroll, some dried foods for the voyage and a rifle. There will surely be wild game in Alaska."

He had clearly thought about this all night, and "If I went" notwithstanding, there was something in his whole manner that told me it was not a matter of "if." He was going to be leaving— maybe as soon as tomorrow or next week. I had the choice to tell him no, on behalf of the captain who had ordered him to stay behind. Or I could help him prepare, as well as possible, and see him off at the dock, knowing he might not come back.

I chose the latter.

Today we put together his kit and while I sewed a patch or two on his trousers, Kjell went down to the harbor to see about working his way up to Skagway on whatever vessel he could find. He was in luck. The steamship *Castlekeep* was in port and had need of a steward to serve meals on the journey. The ship was crowded with men who had come from Olympia by way of the Hood Canal. Tickets were going for hundreds of dollars. But although Kjell would have to share a berth, he'd pay nothing. He would be working fourteen hours a day to get the prospectors their meals. The ship is due to leave tomorrow, which gave Kjell time to buy a new pair of boots and a hat from Waterman & Katz's mercantile at inflated prices. He could not find a rifle for sale, so I gave him permission to take Edvard's old handgun.

I did not telegraph my husband for permission—where would I send a telegram? He would be making his way much more slowly up the Inside Passage. Unlike a steamship, a schooner had no need of coal to fuel its engines. The *Fidelius* would arrive in Norton Sound by sail. God willing.

August 6

Today I waved good-bye to Kjell on the *Castlekeep*, as I had waved farewell to Edvard just four days ago. In both cases the mood was frenzied. There was greed, of course, propelling men (and women too, as it turned out—I saw a sprinkling of them on the deck of the *Castlekeep*) up to Alaska. But there was something else, a final grasp at adventure. With most of America now explored and settled and the twentieth century soon upon us, this seemed to many their last chance to be pioneers in the wilderness, to experience what the 49ers had felt in California, and twenty years ago in Leadville and other silver towns in the Rocky Mountains.

If these sentences sound like a newspaper article, it's because they are—attempts at least. A telegram arrived for me a few days ago, the day Edvard left on the *Fidelius*. It was from Katrine, urging me to write about the Klondike, news of which had now reached Norway. She believed that she could place anything I wrote about the gold strike in the Yukon.

This is perhaps why I was less reluctant to let Kjell go. He could be my eyes and ears on the Chilkoot Trail and in Dawson City this winter.

August 10

I seem to have made a new friend since I last wrote, as well as increased my acquaintance with two other ladies. The friend is Adele Pennybaker, a name that amuses me. She is a dressmaker. I first required her services last November, when Edvard suggested I have a gown made for Christmas parties. She fitted me with care and produced a beautiful blue satin gown (which, however, was never worn). Her shop is on Polk Street, just off Lawrence, and a very pleasant little shop it is, painted pale green with white curtains. The front of the shop contains a table and two chairs and on the table are illustrated fashion books, very up to date. On the walls are shelves with bolts of cloth and some wholesaler's books of sample fabrics. Through a door are found dressing rooms and a workspace. Miss Pennybaker keeps two apprentices steadily at work on seams, ruffles, buttonholes, and lace trim, while she does the fittings and final adjustments.

I went to see her again the day Kjell left, to order two

new dresses for the autumn. I went back again three days ago for a fitting and then again yesterday for the sheer pleasure of talking with her again. Adele is a small woman, precise in her movements. Not surprisingly, her clothes fit her beautifully and emphasize her narrow waist and pretty hands. Her complexion is lovely; only fine wrinkles at her eyes show she is past thirty. It is her low-pitched voice I find most appealing, as well as her curiosity about life. As a dressmaker it's necessary for her to show a gracious attentiveness to her customers, befitting her position as a woman who must work for a living and yet whose opinion is earnestly valued. She never gossips about her clients, but her blue eyes record every tiny detail. As a "recorder" myself I notice where her eyes go: To the weathered look of my face that contrasts with the white, lightly freckled skin of my shoulders; to the scar on my wrist, where a kitchen knife slashed me when the ship heeled unexpectedly; to the missing side tooth whose absence I mask when I smile with closed lips. If I had not been wearing my corset, I assume she could have read from my soft, sagging belly that I had been a mother.

I asked her a little about herself and she told me willingly that her father had come west, on the Oregon Trail, as a young child in a covered wagon, as had her maternal grandparents. Her mother and one aunt were dressmakers in Portland. Another aunt was a midwife. Her aunts were unmarried, and rather happy about it, Adele's father having proved to all, through his business schemes, that having a husband could be less advantageous than assumed.

"But my father is a wonderful storyteller," said Adele, "and he raised me and my younger brother Knox on tales of wagon trains and Indian scouts and herds of buffalo. Knox and I wanted to be pioneers as well!"

The two had tried Astoria first, and then came to Port Townsend. Knox Pennybaker began as a carpenter, and then bought a shop at the edge of town. He lost title to it in the financial crash and was now the assistant manager of a general store. He was considering moving to Seattle, now he was married and had two young sons. Adele had opened her own shop several years ago and lived above it in rented rooms.

What joy, I told her, to be able to support yourself and even to hire apprentices. To my surprise she envied me as well.

"They say you have been all around the world by ship, Mrs. Bergland. To China and India and South America. And how brave you must be, to live on a ship, the only woman among so many men."

I looked at her quickly to make sure she wasn't insinuating anything, but I could see that she was genuinely curious and admiring. That is not a look I've been accustomed to see in the eyes of the ladies of Uptown. It would not do to tell Miss Pennybaker that much of daily life at sea is rather ordinary. I never found it tedious, but it can feel circumscribed. You have the enormous dome of sky above, unbroken by buildings, shining at night with a million stars. You have the smell of salt water and the surge of waves. Anything can happen, from lack of wind to a hurricane, from a whale sighting to a broken mast. Yet you also eat and sleep and raise your children in small spaces, and your walks are confined to certain areas of the deck, only at certain times of the day.

Instead I began to tell her about Lima: often blanketed in fog in the mornings, but with brilliant red and orange sunsets. Plaza Major on Sunday, religious processions and bands. Colonial mansions with balconies like those in Sevilla or Cadiz. Such a mix of people: Indians, Mestizos, Germans, French, Italians, and Chinese. While the *Matilde* anchored in the harbor of Callao, I would stay in rooms off a quiet plaza in Lima. Once, some years ago, I spent three months there, in a grand casa, with servants.

"Oh, how I would love to sail the Pacific Ocean," said Adele. "I have only traveled by sea from Astoria to Port Townsend, and it was a calm two days at that. I should love to be at sea in a storm!"

"Never wish for that," I said.

"Don't you wish your husband would take you with him on his voyages now? I should not like to stay always at home, not once I had lived aboard a ship."

"I miss the sea," I said slowly. Yes, I told her, I miss the sea. And that is why, perhaps, I think Adele is becoming a friend. She allowed me to say that aloud: I miss the sea.

*

I have also taken tea with Cecilia Barker and Emma Smith, the Methodist minister's wife. I would not have gone if Cecilia had not assured me Mrs. Smith would also be there. Cecilia's house on the corner of Clay and Adams is the same size as my own, but much more splendid, with an imposing oak staircase rising from the entryway, and two parlors, one for everyday and one for more formal occasions. We sat in the latter, on velvet settees and surrounded by a remarkable collection of furniture and ornate paintings, most of which had been purchased in Boston, where Mr. Barker hails from, and shipped overland. Added to this were many rare and beautiful objects from the Orient: celadon vases holding peacock feathers; silk screens painted with mountains and birds; of mahogany chairs and busily carved footstools; and cunning, red-painted cabinets with many drawers. All these came directly from China to Port Townsend, to the Zee Tai Company.

Cecilia wore a silk tea gown with wide sleeves and looked very charming. She is young, perhaps not even twenty-two, so could not have been in a brothel very long. She is very pretty, white-skinned with naturally curly black hair, and a bow mouth; she seems quick-witted and gay, though slightly uneasy in her new circumstances, eager to do the right thing.

Mrs. Smith is a comfortable sort of woman in her upper forties, well-corseted, well-dressed, and refined in her manner of accepting a china cup and a small biscuit from the tray offered by a maid servant dressed in a white apron and cap. As a minister's wife, Mrs. Smith easily took the lead in chatting about the weather and some recent developments in town and church circles ("We have lost a good quarter of our male congregation to the Klondike! And Mrs. Bergland, I understand we now can count our young baritone Mr. Fossen among those who have succumbed to gold fever.") before steering the conversation firmly and gently in the direction of charitable endeavors. Namely, Mrs. Smith wished our help in caring for indigent members of the town, particularly women who had fallen into difficult circumstances.

"Widows and abandoned or persecuted wives, formerly genteel ladies," she said briskly, lest we suspect her of any reference to Cecilia's former profession. "Widows with children, in particular, but also women whose husbands have fallen into arrears with their mortgages or have lost their businesses. Very frequently the men, often once upstanding citizens, have either descended into drink or have left town, perhaps with intentions to make a fresh start in Seattle or Tacoma and to send money home, money that is not always forthcoming."

"Of course I can contribute," I said. "Those of us who are fortunate enough to have husbands and property must help other women. Please put me down for two dollars."

If Mrs. Smith expected more, she was polite enough not to show it. In fact, Edvard and I are not so wealthy that I can afford to simply give money away. He bought our house here in Uptown on the proceeds of the insurance for the *Matilde,* and with savings we had built up. But I would be reluctant to touch the remainder of our savings in any way. Every seaman's wife knows she could become a widow overnight.

Cecilia smiled, but nervously. "I'm afraid my husband, so generous in many ways, does not believe in charity. Nevertheless," she added, speaking in a more refined tone than I was used to from her, "I believe I could persuade him to contribute something. I don't have money of my own, you see. He prefers to do our finances, and I just order what I need from the shops and have the bills sent to him."

"Yes, that is common," said Mrs. Smith equably. "But please do speak to him about it. I fear that as this Klondike fever spreads, we will see more destitution for women here in town. The men are rushing off with no thought to what awaits them in Alaska if they don't find gold. I predict many will return penniless. In the panic of 1893 you found women digging clams on the beaches for food for their children. I would not wish a return to that."

"Not everyone is going to Alaska," Cecilia said. "My husband says the real money is to be made from the prospectors. He has been doing a roaring trade since this all began last month."

"Then perhaps he will feel generous," Mrs. Smith said with a smile, and stood up to make her departure.

I accompanied her outside and we walked together along the street in the direction of her church.

"Mrs. Barker has a lovely house," she said. "Six servants too, I'm told, though we just saw the maid and housekeeper. Personally, I don't know what one would do with all those people underfoot. I grew up on a farm in western Massachusetts. We were a large family, and we had no servants at all. Now I must keep a maid and cook and a gardener, all so we look respectable. But I sometimes think I could do a far better job myself with cleaning and cooking."

"Yes," I said. "I grew up on a farm as well." I did not mention that I'd lived a life of some luxury in Bergen and rarely cooked or cleaned on the *Matilde*. "Of course, one must have servants, for appearance's sake, but I do not like too many about. We have our houseboy, Henry. He is a hard worker and very quiet and neat."

"Then you are most fortunate to have found him," said Mrs. Smith, bidding me good-bye at the corner of Taylor. "You must join me sometime for tea, Mrs. Bergland. I am at home most afternoons. Please call."

"Thank you. I ... I am not a member of the congregation."

"Yes, I imagine you are Lutheran, being Norwegian," she said, with a slight twinkle, as if she suspected I didn't go to church much at all. "You are still very welcome in our parlor."

August 14

When Kjell was here and when Edvard was at home, I admit there were times when I hardly noticed Henry, who moved so silently and lived so anonymously in the small bedroom upstairs. We spoke every day to discuss the meals and tasks to be undertaken. My attempts to learn more about him had never gone far. Yet, he often appeared, unbidden, when I was writing at the dining room table on one of my stories, or attempts at stories, with a pot of coffee. His eyes rested on the papers, and I know he was curious. I heard him sometimes practicing English in his room. Words floated out from under the door: *kettle, fish, ice box*. But we had little conversation ourselves, by his choice.

This evening, I was so restless I could have screamed. The western sun shone over the strait filled with all manner of craft, from fishing boats and tugs to lumber schooners and clipper ships from China. Men were still leaving daily, almost hourly for the Yukon, but the tumult of the docks wasn't visible from here. Only the coal smoke from the steamship engines could be seen, along with the wind filling the top sails of the three and four-masted windjammers. Even though many ships were loaded with lumber they appeared to float lightly on the waves because of the billowing sails. The largest of them were under tow; tugs would take them out through the Strait of Juan de Fuca to Cape Flattery and release them upon the open sea like butterflies.

Before I married Edvard, I had no experience of the open sea. I came to Bergen by schooner through the Sognefjord to the Norwegian Sea, and then we sailed south through islands, keeping near the coastline. But I would often look down from the hill where my aunt and uncle lived and watch the ships navigate their way in and out Bergen's harbor. Even after Aunt Inger put an end to going aboard the ships with their coffee cargos, my favorite Sunday walks with Katrine were along the wharves built for the Hansa traders centuries ago. It was this fascination with ships that made my uncle believe a sea captain would be a suitable match for me. I longed for foreign places and adventure, an audacious life I was unlikely to have if I prepared myself for teaching as Katrine did or married a man in trade. Without me at first understanding why, various ship's captains and merchants began to visit my aunt and uncle's house for dinner. Edvard was the only one, ever, who appealed to me. Perhaps it was because of his kind blue eyes or the shiny buttons on his blue jacket, more likely it was because of the way he spoke of his new three-masted barque. The other men spoke of money, to impress me. Edvard spoke of freedom.

The first time I set foot on the *Matilde,* hoisted aboard from the tender, and saw the white canvas of the folded sails, the coils of hemp rope, and smelled the seasoned timber of the decks and spars, I was caught by the throat with love. Not for Edvard, no, that came later, but for his newly built ship. Four hundred tons of wood and iron and shiny brass, built to his specifications in

Glasgow, with a broad beam and deep hull for cargo. Edvard showed me all over the ship and smiled when I put my hands on the handles of the big ship's wheel. He left the captain's quarters for last. A spacious cabin, wood-paneled, spanned the width of the stern, with a skylight and polished windows offering a view of the harbor. No expense had been spared with the fittings: brass trim glossy as sunshine around the portholes; brass kerosene lanterns; a massive captain's table fixed to the floor; cabinets for charts and logs; and instruments secured to the sides of the ship. There was even a small upright piano, and a lady-like chair in one corner. A room off the great cabin held a bed, with cabinets built underneath. I knew only a little about what went on in marriage beds at that time and shied away from even looking too closely. Still, I remember thinking how pleasant it would be to sleep in this cozy little bedroom, rocking on the high seas.

I was still standing at the window when Henry slipped into the parlor and asked, as he usually did before going up to his room, if there was anything else.

"Yes, there is, Henry. Please talk to me. If you would not mind."

His smooth face froze. As usual he wore a silk cap with his plait down his back. The laundryman's rough blue tunic and trousers had given way to a set of finer cotton pajamas, with a high collar, and embroidered slippers for the house. "What have I done wrong?" he asked.

"You've done nothing wrong, Henry. I never have a complaint about you. It's only that—I suppose it's just that— with Captain Bergland and Mr. Fossen gone...."

He continued to look alarmed. "Mrs. Bergland. I go up now." He bowed quickly and fled.

The poor boy. Could he really imagine I had any thought of seducing him?

I write here in my journal for lack of anything better to do. I write about the *Matilde* and her pretty brass fittings and skillfully made cabinets. And I cry a little to think of her in flames, even though at times I have also hated her and the trouble she brought us, the losses.

August 15

Today, after lunch, I tried again to engage Henry. As he cleared away my simple dishes, I said, "You and I, Henry, we have something in common. Please, don't look so frightened. I mean, we are both strangers in America. I come from Norway."

At his half smile, I added, "Of course you know that. But do you know where Norway is?"

"No, Missus." He stood there with the tray in his hands, but I was determined not to let him go.

"It is very far away, farther off than China by sea, because if you were to sail there you would have to sail down the coast to Cape Horn, up the coast of eastern South America and then across the Atlantic. I could show you on a map. Put down the tray."

For the first time he looked slightly interested, but he did not put down the tray. "I know you all speak your own language with you each, among you." He gave a perfect imitation of "*God dag!*"

I laughed. And after a moment he did as well.

"But now we are Americans," I said. "Now we must speak English."

"*You* are American," he said. "You are *lo fan,* white person."

"In Norway we are white, mostly," I admitted. "But in America people are from many places."

"No one thinks I am American."

I persevered, going to fetch a book of maps from the parlor's bookcase. I opened it on the table. "I am from a small farm in Norway. See here."

He finally placed the tray back on the table and bent to look. There, on the Sognefjord, was the village of Kyrkebø. I pointed to a spot on the map, about two miles from the village, to an invisible cluster of farm outbuildings, wooden logs and heavy painted doors, grass growing on the roof of the *stabbur.* Apple trees that bloomed white in spring. A view of the fjord. "My family were farmers. We grew hay for the animals and planted potatoes, and we had a small herd of goats and one cow. After my father died in a boating accident, the farm was sold. My sisters married and my mother and I lived in Kyrkebø. Later I was sent to a city." I pointed out Bergen, on the coast. "There I lived with my uncle and aunt. My uncle was the brother of my mother, and they sent me to school. Then I married the captain, and we sailed away in our ship, the *Matilde*." My finger traced loops around the world's oceans and ports.

Henry said, "I too. Farm family in a village. No school, just work. Near Canton. Where?"

I pointed out Canton on the map. "I have been to China, not Canton, but Hong Kong. With my husband on our ship. We delivered a cargo of lamp oil there some years ago."

He said nothing but looked fixedly at China.

"You must have left China's coast to sail to Victoria ... Is that where your ship came in, to Victoria?"

He closed up like a clam. "I must go now and wash windows."

A beginning?

August 20

I pride myself a little that Henry now speaks to me much more. I have told him that it is no use practicing English by himself; he must begin to speak to people—people like me—if he is to learn to make his way in the world. I am impressed by how many English words he already knows. His accent is difficult at times—the "r" especially. I dropped my dialect when I came to Bergen and adopted the city's special "r" with gusto. The Bergensers sound like the French, they say, with our "r" deep in the throat. Henry's 'r' is like an 'l.' I have heard people in town make fun of that sound—"the Celestials like their lice," and so on. They also make fun of Norwegians and Swedes, of course—"Ya, ya, you betcha,"—and of the Irish, Italians, and the local Indians. And Negroes. If you would go to Learned's Opera House and see one of the traveling shows, you would hear plenty of jokes in Negro dialect on stage by people with their faces painted black with shoe polish.

As if there was only one way to speak English. As if only one kind of American could live in America. A white person from England.

However, it doesn't matter what I say to Henry. He knows what he knows, and things have happened to him that I do not have a clue about. If I could, I would write a real story about his experience and send it to the Norwegian paper. But whenever I ask about his voyage to America he looks away and does not answer. Instead we talk a little about his family. He says he had a brother and a sister. The brother also came to America. There was an uncle who helped them. His family had a pig once, and a goat. They farmed land they did not own. They often had nothing to eat. I asked what happened to the brother who came to America with him. Henry says he went to Butte, Montana, to join their uncle. I don't believe that is the real story. He does not know anything about Butte except its name. And yet he says he is saving to go there and join them.

Each time we talk, Henry tells me a little more. Then he stops. Whenever he speaks of his sister, who he calls Lian, his eyes grow wet. There is a story there, but a sad one. I believe he misses her greatly. I do not know why he calls himself Henry. He has never told me his real name.

What I write now, about the Klondike, is scraped together from what I can learn from the *Morning Leader* and the other papers, especially those from Seattle. Two days ago I received a letter from Kjell, written in Skagway when he first arrived. He has a clear hand, but the letter was short and seemed composed in haste. He wrote in fragments about chaos on the docks, a friendship struck up quickly, a horse purchased. He and his new friend were setting off immediately for the Yukon. The horse would take them and their goods over White Pass. With luck they would reach Lake Bennett and sail up the Yukon River to Dawson City before winter came. I should not expect to hear from him until the following spring. I put some of his words in my article and sent it off to Katrine.

Nothing has come from Edvard. Still, I think that he must have reached St. Michael by now and deposited his passengers. There is little information in the papers about that route to Alaska. Newspapers have sent their reporters up the Yukon, but no one has sent reports back from Dawson City. Instead the papers have news about Skagway and Dyea. Chaos, as Kjell says, is the order of the day.

September 7

Out of boredom I have begun attending services at Trinity Methodist and have now visited Mrs. Smith twice during her afternoons "at home." Today she came here, and we sat in the parlor while Henry served us China tea in fine porcelain cups, with an apple cake I had made myself.

I had asked him to wear his finest. Last week I gave him money above his wages for an embroidered tunic; he wore that today, over silk trousers. He has begun to fill out a little since he came to work for us. I saw Mrs. Smith glance at him with approval. He was so graceful and polite, an attractive young man, and I knew now, a clever one. Over the last two weeks I had begun to give Henry back copies of *Century Magazine* and *Ladies' Home Journal.* He is not able to read the stories very well but is fascinated by the illustrations, fashionable ladies and gentlemen, and scenes of city life. He asked me what the stories were about, and I gave him the shortened versions. I told him I had found the magazines a way to learn about America.

Henry prefers these conversations to anything of a personal nature. I suppose it's because he does not really trust me, and I cannot blame him. For he most certainly arrived in Port Townsend without the proper papers. He had given me to understand that he would save up money to travel to Butte where his uncle had a shop. But I never saw him write to this uncle or receive a letter. Henry seemed, as far as I could tell, to avoid the other Chinese servants in Uptown and he only rarely went to Chinatown. But sometimes, when Ah Song came to deliver and pick up the laundry, the two of them had a cup of tea together. It is important to speak your own language, so you do not lose it. At first, I thought they were talking "Chinese," but Henry corrected me. It was "Cantonese" they spoke, one of many Chinese languages.

Mrs. Smith wanted to discuss, once again, the plight of women who had been left without funds by husbands, sons, and brothers who had gone to the Yukon. "Many scraped together money to outfit their men, on the understanding that it was crucial to be in on the first claims. Now it is becoming apparent that it takes longer and is more arduous to reach the Yukon than previously thought. It may be a hard winter for the men, but it will also be hard for the women left behind."

She wanted my help organizing a bazaar to raise money. It would have a harvest theme. Could I be on the food committee? Nothing could appeal to me less, but I wanted to please, so I said yes. "I think you'll enjoy the others," Mrs. Smith said, naming a few women from Uptown, one of whom was Adele Pennybaker. "And it will get you out of the house and a little more into society. The first meeting is tomorrow morning at ten, at the church. I hope you can join us! And by the way, shall we call each other by our first names? I am Emma."

"Dagny." I smiled and said I would come tomorrow morning. I had, of course, never mentioned to her that I wrote articles and stories for Norwegian newspapers. Since Kjell has been gone, I've fallen into a routine of writing every single morning, and I dislike the idea that instead of writing I'll have to make chit-chat over coffee and plan a harvest festival. Still, perhaps I can write a story for the Norwegian newspapers about the women left behind in the rush to get to the Yukon.

September 16

Preparations for the bazaar go on. I am not only head of the food committee but, with Adele, have taken on the task of sewing small items for sale at a table of our own: aprons, children's clothes, capes. Adele was pleased to see that I could sew quite well and though I do not enjoy sewing half as much as she does, I am quick and neat with seams and can cut a pattern out. Onboard ship I often made clothes for myself, Edvard, and Kjell. I made clothes for my children.

Of late I have had less time to speak with Henry, who has withdrawn into himself again. Perhaps that is as it should be. When Edvard returns, which may be any time now, it would not do to be too intimate with our Chinese houseboy. Of course, it will be obvious I have been making do without Kjell and have not hired any other servants, but I will explain everything to Edvard. If only he is safe and on his return voyage!

I wrote to his employer in San Francisco, Carl Olafsson, who assured me by return post that other ships had returned from St. Michael to San Francisco, and they reported seeing the *Fidelius* in Norton Sound in late August unloading passengers and taking on supplies for the return voyage. Mr. Olafsson said he hoped that *Fidelius* would be back in Port Townsend in early October at the latest.

Adele and I spend evenings now in the parlor sewing together.

This evening she said to me, "Your houseboy—how much do you know about him?"

"Henry?" I felt protective. "Very little, really. Only that he is an excellent fellow to have about the house. Why do you ask?"

"I was only a bit curious. I have never been around a Chinese person, so close. I have seen them, of course, in Uptown." She paused and, embarrassed, added, "One of my lady clients said she would not have a Celestial around her two boys—she has heard they steal small children and sell them. I wish I had spoken up, surely that is not true."

I flushed. "It is not true, it is malicious gossip. In Lima we had a Chinese servant and his wife, a Peruvian of mixed heritage. They were quite honest, quite ordinary. They had a beautiful daughter. Why would they want the bother of stealing a white child?"

"*I* don't think that, of course."

"Henry comes from a small farming village, just like I did. He came to America to better himself. He has an uncle with a shop in Butte, and when he saves up enough money, he will take the train to Montana. He deserves a chance, just like all immigrants."

"Well, then," said Adele, but I had the impression she was thinking something rather different. She looked down at her sewing, as if she were wondering about something she didn't dare to ask.

What do I know of Henry really? What is the key to his heart? I know he had a sister, and the thought of his sister made his eyes damp. Girls could not come to America. Girls in China lived behind closed doors, with bound feet; they traveled in enclosed sedan chairs. I had seen this in Hong Kong. But the daughter of a farmer would not have bound feet. Perhaps she had allowed herself to dream of a different life, like girls around the world. I thought about this girl Lian and decided that I would write a fictionalized story about her and Henry and send it to the newspaper in Norway. Perhaps Norwegians would see that our Scandinavian ways are not so different than those of the Chinese, that women everywhere struggle to unbind their feet and walk freely.

September 22

I have heard nothing from my husband, nothing more from Kjell. I find that I am not sleeping well, and last night was particularly bad. Yesterday I told Mrs. Smith I could not attend yet another meeting about the bazaar, I had something else to do. I spent all morning writing my article about Henry and Lian to send to Katrine. I called Henry in once to ask him more about life in China, but he was close-mouthed and alarmed to see my hand hovering over the papers on the table.

"My story?"

"A letter to Mr. Kjell," I lied. "I thought only to tell him a little about you, since he always was your friend."

Henry said nothing. He only took away my cold coffee and brought another steaming pot.

At first, I felt jubilant, the way I often do when finishing a piece of writing, and I hastened to make a fair copy and put it in an envelope for the afternoon post. But last night, as I tossed and turned, I wished I could recall my letter and the story. What I had written about Henry and his sister seemed so thin and ignorant. I had no real idea of how they lived and who they were, and because I did not know, I made a moral at the end for Norwegian readers. I wrote neither fact nor fiction. For if I had wished to make things up, I could have invented a tale of Henry's passage across the Pacific, a tale I could have embellished with my own memories of the sea.

Surely all those memories of the oceans of the world could be used for something?

Last night I dreamed of my little boy, Jan, of those last few minutes before the wave took him. In reality I still don't know how it happened. It was raining, a warm, heavy rain, but not storming. The sea rocked with swells as we approached the coast of Brazil. The sails were set and reset to catch the contrary winds, yet our progress was impeded by waves that came from several directions. Still, there was nothing unusual about that, it was only sometimes jarring when the ship heeled, or we slid into a trough.

Jan was, I thought, with the cook in the galley. He had been taught, he had been warned from the time he could crawl, never to go on deck without me or his father, but still somehow, that day he climbed up the ladder. Perhaps he was curious about the thumping around, perhaps he only meant to stick his head up, and then saw something that demanded a closer look. That day might have ended in no more than a whipping if it had not been for the wave. He was only up on deck a few minutes, I would guess. By the time I came dashing up the ladder, not having found him in the galley, Jan had been scooped up by Edvard, wearing his rain slicker and hat. How angry I was, and yet relieved, so relieved I burst out laughing.

Their faces had turned toward me. Jan couldn't help laughing too, to see just my head popping up. He was a handsome child already at five, growing into a boy, but still with the dimples of a baby when he laughed. He had Edvard's reddish-brown hair. Then the deck tilted down behind them as we slipped into another trough, and at the same time a vast wave roared up. Edvard, trying to steady his feet and move to the center of the ship, away from the rail, saw my expression change from laughter to horror. He turned his head.

Did he let go of Jan in that instant? No, he swore later. He said the wall of water slammed him down on deck and tore the boy from his arms. I had fallen back down the ladder and hurt my arm, but I clawed my way back up again as the *Matilde* righted herself.

Edvard was on his knees, soaked, hands scrabbling at the deck, and the boy was gone, along with one of the crew.

We ran to the side; the sailor could swim. A rope was thrown to him, a boat lowered, "faster, faster," no sign of the giant wave or of our little boy, only that strange churning of the sea, trough and swell.

Those in the boat lurched here and there, and they shouted and shouted. But the sea was louder, the sea was larger. And Jan was already deep away.

Years later that wave comes back to me in dreams. I hear Jan's laugh, and my laugh, like a mockery, a mother laughing just before her son is drowned.

After those dreams, I wake convinced that Edvard is drowned, and that Kjell will die as well. The wave seems an omen, telling me that everyone I know will die violently at sea. I find I miss Kjell desperately these days. "He was your charge," Edvard will say when he returns, if he returns from Alaska. "How could you simply let him go?" Our second son, our replacement.

Kjell came into our lives three months after Jan was swept away.

The *Matilde* had continued down the coast of Brazil and Argentina around the Cape to deliver our goods to the port of Callao, six miles from Lima. The rounding of the Horn with its screaming gales had caused the foremast to crack. There were other repairs in order for the damaged *Matilde*. And new sails must be rigged to replace those ripped to shreds. We planned a stay in Lima of two or three months. We found rooms in a colonial mansion belonging to a hacienda owner who came rarely to the city. The casa had many unusual details, a Moorish wooden balcony and ornate doors and windows; it was surrounded by gardens and several fountains. Along with the rooms, we were offered the services of two servants, a married couple: Chan Rodrigues, formerly a Chinese laborer on the owner's estate south of the city, and his wife Maria, of mixed background. She cooked and he tended the garden and saw to the affairs of the house.

The Andes form a mountain wall behind Lima and the marine air cannot push over it. The skies are often gray, like Bergen's, but no rain falls. It is rarely hot. It is never very cold. The stillness in the air is like time has stopped. After the restless movement of the sea, the reckless winds and thieving waves, Lima was both haven and prison. Unlike my husband, busy with the multitude of repairs to the *Matilde,* I had too much time to think.

My left arm had been broken in the fall down the deck ladder off the coast of Brazil. The surgeon in Rio had reset the arm and pinned it in a sling, but it was slow to mend and still caused me pain, so I could not do as much as I wished. I went out in a carriage to visit the sights and I sewed a little. The hacienda owner had a small library, but the books were in Spanish, of course. Instead, I reread some of my Norwegian novels, Camilla Collett, Bjørnsterne Bjørnson, and Amalie Skram. I did not write to Katrine. I could not bear to see my pen forming the truth-telling words on the page.

Edvard and I never spoke of Jan's death. We did not blame each other—if anything was to blame it was the sea itself or the ship for not protecting us better. But the sea was also our great love and the *Matilde* our familiar home.

Although Edvard came when he could to Lima, the problems with the ship were such that often he had to spend morning to evening onboard and some nights as well. The Rodrigues family members were my only companions for days on end. Maria, rather plump, with silver earrings and silent bare feet, brought me dishes to tempt my poor appetite. Chan, not old but thin and stooped, with a cough to announce himself when he entered a room, gave me fresh flowers from the garden. The Rodrigues had a daughter of about eight, Rosalia, brown-skinned like her mother, with her father's eyes. A livelier little girl I've rarely met. She danced and sang all day long and made me laugh even when I fell into bitterness because I had no child of my own. She always spoke Spanish to me, of course, and in this easy fashion I began to learn the language, through games and songs. Sometimes we walked in the garden together and she and her father recited to me all the names of the plants that grew there in tropical splendor. Neither Chan nor Maria told me much about themselves; it was through Rosalia I learned that her papá had been born in China and had worked hard for many years as an indentured servant, before attaining the paid job of houseman and gardener.

One day a letter, written in Spanish, was delivered to the house, addressed to *los Noruegos*—the Norwegians. I was astonished, for I knew no one in Lima. Neither Maria nor Chan could read; I had to puzzle it out myself with the help of a German merchant who could read Spanish. It came from a nun at one of Lima's orphanages. A boy of five had been left in their care six years ago. His parents were Norwegian missionaries who had died of a fever on their ship, en route to San Francisco. There had been an attempt to contact relations in Stavanger, but no one ever came for the little boy, nor were funds sent. He was now eleven and near the age when many children left the orphanage as indentured servants.

The question was put to me and Edvard: Could we think of taking the child on as a cabin boy and somehow, eventually, let him work his passage back to Norway? I showed this letter to my husband. He was as eager as I to meet the boy.

The same nun who had written the letter brought him to us. I did not understand the name she gave us. But the boy said, "Kjell Fossen," and it was recognizable enough even with the odd Spanish twist he gave it. Both Edvard and I spoke to him in Norwegian, but his name and just a few words—*mor* (mother), *far* (father), *kirke* (church), *skip* (ship)—were all he seemed to know. How strange it was to see a boy, in appearance like any other farm lad from Norway, straw-haired and blue-eyed, rough in dress and barefoot, speaking only Spanish and clinging timidly to the hand of a nun in voluminous robes.

It grew easier when Edvard spoke to him in Spanish. Then we learned Kjell had some education, could read and count anyway, and Edvard told me he was intelligent enough in his answers. But did he want to come with us? Did Kjell even understand what was being asked of him? I heard the words *barque* several times as Edvard tried to make the boy comprehend that he would have to live and work on a ship at sea, but that we would take him back to Norway.

Kjell balled his fists, he said he would not leave Lima. He did not want to leave the nuns, nor the orphanage and his friends there. The nun heard him out and then was firm; all he did was cry and cling to her even more. Edvard and I looked at each other. Could we take him against his will? Then Rosalia came running into the room with her usual abandon, singing some song from the street about a girl with a parrot. She stared at Kjell and then held out her hands to him. "*Tan guapo!*" So handsome, she said, delighted. "*Ojos de cielo.*" Eyes of sky.

I said in Norwegian to Edvard that we should not rush things and frighten the boy. There was no hurry after all. Perhaps he would like to make a visit to this house and play with Rosalia? This I ventured in Spanish, with a smile, and Kjell agreed.

Of course, I knew from the first moment he came into the room that we would take him with us.

The next several weeks proved to us all that it was possible to trust in life again. It was a happy time, almost to my surprise. My health improved rapidly and so did my Spanish, which I spoke much of the day now. He went back and forth to the orphanage the first week, but then came to stay for good. I had new clothes made for him, and boots. I trimmed his hair and clipped his nails. And I taught him the language of his parents. Kjell's education gave me something to do. Every morning we had Norwegian lessons: grammar, reading, and sums. The afternoons were for playing after the siesta. Often in the evenings Edvard managed to return, and we all had dinner together. After a month of such regularity and reassurance, I took Kjell in the carriage with me to Callao to see the *Matilde*. What boy doesn't love to see a ship with all its movement and noise? He remembered nothing of the voyage from Norway many years before. His parents' names were Karoline and Hans Fossen, of the Evangelical Lutheran Mission in Stavanger—that was on a paper that came with him to the orphanage and all he knew of his heritage.

We did take him back with us to Norway and by the time we arrived, he was twelve and spoke and read Norwegian very well, with not even the hint of an accent. We had done our best, Edvard and I, to make him a countryman and to prepare him for Stavanger and the missionaries there. We read the Bible to him and Luther's *Small Catechism* and discouraged the use of the rosary. We explained temperance, which struck Kjell as a good idea, and Lutheran ideas about sin and salvation, which he thought peculiar and severe.

By the time we sailed into Stavanger on the *Matilde,* I felt confident that the straw-haired boy was sufficiently ready to meet his relatives. But willing relatives there were none. His mother's parents had died, and his father's mother was in failing health and had no use for a strapping grandson. The pastor of the mission church and his wife said they would take him in. It was their duty. They were sour-faced and stern with Edvard and me, grilling us in Kjell's presence about his exposure to sinful native ways (they had obviously never heard of the grand churches of Lima, but imagined Aztec sacrifices and other heathen goings-on). The wife said, "We will not tolerate laziness or speaking back." This was all in their parlor in Stavanger, a room made strange by mementos of their years in Africa—elephant tusks on the walls next to paintings of Jesus on the Cross. They had been in Africa when the young Fossens set off for their mission in America, so could not even claim to be taking in Kjell for his parents' sake.

If the sour-looking couple had had any real claim on him, we would have had to leave the boy. As it was, Kjell firmly refused to stay behind in Stavanger, and so we simply sailed away, up to Bergen, without a backward look. In just six months he had become like a member of our family. Moreover, Kjell was proving to be quite helpful in any number of ways. His temperament was agreeable and his Spanish far better than Edvard's. Even in Callao he had proved adept at bargaining with the workmen on the ship, having overheard and understood their slangy comments about cheating *el capitán noruego.*

In Bergen we outfitted him with clothes and showed him the sights. Edvard sorted out his papers and had him properly bound as a seaman's apprentice, but Kjell would never really develop an interest in climbing rigging or learning celestial navigation. And Norway would always remain something of a mystery to him. He found the people pale and stony-faced, he confided to me, grim unless they were drunk, and far from easy-going. He remained a bit of a South American, and he always looked forward to getting back to Lima again. He and Rosalia's friendship was not to last, however. The last time we were there, two years ago, we arrived to find her married. She was just sixteen, but very pretty, and her new husband was rich. Her parents were pleased for her, a girl of Indian, Chinese, and Peruvian birth, to marry well. Kjell of course was devastated. She was his first love, and first loves are hard to forget.

I know that Kjell is a grown man now and that he himself has made the choice to go to Alaska and seek his fortune. Still, I fear for him. The conditions, from all I read, are harsh now that the weather is cooling. No word comes from him, which either means he has managed to get to the Yukon River and to Dawson City. Or that something has happened to him.

And if that is true, Edvard may well believe that it is my fault for letting Kjell go.

September 24

This morning when I came down to breakfast, there was no sign of Henry. I first assumed he'd gone out early to the garden to continue some of his tasks or perhaps to do errands, though it was early. But as the morning wore on and he didn't return, I left the parlor where I had expected to have a much-needed few hours to write or to read the new issue of *Century Magazine*, and made my way along Lawrence Street, asking at different shops if they had seen Henry. No one had, but Mrs. Cozzen, the butcher's wife, did feel moved to tell me, "You can't trust those Celestials, they're low and underhanded." Had I checked my silverware and valuables?

Offended, I told her that Henry must have been delayed with errands on Water Street. Nevertheless I did return home quite soon after that. Nothing was missing from the parlor or kitchen or storage. Hesitantly I climbed the backstairs to the small room above and knocked on the door. No answer, and I opened it. I had allowed Kjell to deal with Henry regarding the room, and the meagerness of the furnishings now embarrassed me. Just a cot, not even a bed, and a single chair with a table next to it. A wash basin on a stand. No wardrobe or dresser, just some pegs on the wall. It was empty now, the sheets and blanket carefully folded. A magazine Henry had borrowed was placed on the cot. Other than that, there was no indication he had ever been here.

September 26

I waited for two days. I told myself Henry had decided to set off for Seattle's larger Chinatown or even for Butte. Of course he would not say anything to me for fear I might betray him. I knew he was afraid of being sent back to China. Perhaps he had overheard Adele asking about him. Perhaps I had asked too many questions about his life in China. I recalled his alarm as I sat cheerfully at my table writing a story about him and his sister. Foolish of me, however well meant, to lie to him.

And yet it didn't seem like Henry just to sneak away without saying good-bye. He was protective of me, somehow, and took pride in his work. Would he really depart and leave me alone with no servant at all? The frightening possibility crossed my mind that he had been set upon by men looking to bait a "Celestial" and to cut off his queue. What if Henry had fought back and had been arrested? Or what if he'd been crimped, pressed into service on a ship and was even now down in the hold in shackles?

And yet—he had folded up his bedding and taken all his things.

Today I could wait no longer. I set off for Chinatown and Ah Song's laundry and see what I could discover. I had, of course, never been inside Ah Song's laundry before, though I had passed it on the corner of Madison and Washington Streets, giving off gusts of steam and soap. The door was open, and I saw only more clouds inside. Then ghostly figures scurrying, some away from me, a few toward. One, fortunately, was the familiar figure of Ah Song, who pulled me back outside. "I come tomorrow like always. You want clothes now, they not ready."

"I want to know what happened to Henry. He has disappeared."

At first Ah Song would tell me nothing. He had not seen Henry. He had not heard from Henry. Maybe Henry had gone away. I didn't believe him, of course. Ah Song knew something—

he had been the one who introduced Henry into my house. They were friends.

Finally I was reduced to a threat, I'm sorry to admit. I stood like a fishwife on the street outside the laundry, in view of all passers-by, and thundered, "I will take my business to another laundry if you don't tell me where Henry is. I don't believe that he has left Port Townsend."

Ah Song flinched. "Okay I tell you truth. Henry tired of working for you. He comes here, tells me he needs a new job. So now he is a houseboy down here in town."

"Down here, what do you mean? There are no respectable houses down here."

"Female Boarding House always needs servants."

"Female Boarding House! But why would Henry work in a ... in a boarding house?" These Female Boarding Houses were the brothels of the town.

"I tell you only he no more wants to work for you."

"At least tell me which boarding house."

Ah Song shook his head. "No. Nice ladies do not go there. Forget him."

I flushed hotly. Could Ah Song possibly think ... could Henry have said anything that indicated I felt some interest in him? Tired of working for me? It was true, I *had* pried into his life. I had written about him. But I had not treated him badly, I had paid him the going rate. I thought of the cot and the wash basin on a stand. Not even a dresser.

In confusion I left the laundry and walked quickly away, down Water Street. I passed Waterman & Katz and came to the Central Hotel and continued walking past all the sandstone-faced buildings thrown up in that short dizzy span of a few years. The street seethed with prospectors, horses, mules, and wagons. Even now, late September, with all the rumors that snow was already falling in Skagway, people were still embarking for Alaska.

October 14

I received a brief letter from Edvard, from Juneau. It came

by steamship to Port Townsend and was delivered by hand to the house by a crew member, who could not tell me any further details and left immediately to board his ship again, its destination Seattle. Edvard, sailing south from Alaska more slowly on the *Fidelius,* writes that he had to put into Juneau for more supplies and to attend to some business. He doesn't explain further. He merely apologizes that his return to Port Townsend is delayed, and assures me that all is well, he is healthy, and he looks forward to seeing me later in October.

It has now been over two months since my husband left for Alaska, and all that I've had from him is a letter from Dutch Harbor on his way north. He likely did not write from St. Michael because he imagined no letter could reach Port Townsend before him. There are, as yet, no telegraph wires or underwater cables in Alaska, and an organized postal service up north is almost non-existent. Captain's wives should not complain, not as long as their husbands return, but I do not like the notion of Carl Olafsson's old lumber schooner sailing along the northwest coast in these stormy autumn months. Nor have I heard anything more from Kjell since he let me know he had arrived in Skagway. If he is on his way to Dawson City, of course, there is no letter box on the trail.

To keep me company and help around the house I have hired a girl, a fifteen-year-old girl named Sarah, with pimples, a runny nose, and bad breath. I put her in an upstairs bedroom, just in case Henry were to return. I've left his simple room the same. I find I miss him more than I would have expected. I cannot have much conversation with Sarah, and so, sadly, we each eat our meals separately, she in the kitchen and me in the dining room. Sometimes I read novels in Norwegian, old-fashioned tales that take place in another world, another time, and yet still speak to everything we struggle with today: women's emancipation. The author Camilla Collett died just two years ago, in straitened circumstances. After she became a widow, she lost her house and had to send her children away to be raised by relatives.

The harvest bazaar finally took place; it was a great success and raised a good deal of money. I managed the displays and sales of all the cookies and cakes very well, Emma Smith thought. Adele and I sold almost all our needlework (it helped of course that she is Port Townsend's best-known dressmaker), and now I seem to be accepted by Uptown Society, taken under Emma's wing as I have been. I've been going to Trinity Methodist every Sunday for some weeks. The Uptown ladies like to see a woman who comes to church regularly in a nice dress and who spends her free time organizing charity bazaars to help widows and destitute women.

I can't help but wonder, if Edvard comes to grief on his homeward voyage, if I might find myself a widow as well. In that case I will have to turn our home into a boarding house, I told Adele. Not a Female Boarding House. A Ladies' Boarding House. There is a difference.

"It's wise to be prepared," Adele said. "But don't do anything too rashly. At least he managed to get to Juneau and must be on his way to Ketchikan. Once a ship is safe within the Inside Passage there is protection." She thought she knew all about the Alaska trade from her brother, Knox, whose mercantile supplies the prospectors. But Adele is no seafarer and has never relied on charts to steer a passage. How could she know that sailing close to land can be far more treacherous than crossing open water?

Adele was not surprised that Henry had left suddenly. "There was something secretive about him," she said. "But no matter. And although it's not the best work in a Female Boarding House, it is work. And he is closer to his people, in Chinatown."

"Yes," I said. I thought of Henry more than I cared to admit. Now that the bazaar was over, I was free to return to my reading and writing every morning. But it was not the same with my snot-nosed little maid clanking around breaking teacups and singing off-key as she washed up. I missed Henry's intelligent eyes and the way he had listened. More than anything I wondered *why* he had gone. I must have thoroughly frightened or angered him with my curiosity. And for that I wished I could apologize.

October 20

I thought about it for several days and then I finally got up my courage and went to call on Cecilia Barker.

I found her alone in her overstuffed drawing room, playing cards with her maid. She looked as pretty as always, though beginning to put on weight. She asked Bertha to bring tea and added, "Ask Cook for some of those plum tarts, with vanilla cream." She seemed very happy to see me, but less happy when she heard what I hoped she might be able to do for me.

"Quite impossible! I haven't been down to the flats for three years. I have put that all behind me, and if I'm lucky, eventually fewer and fewer people Uptown will know about the life I led before. It's not the sort of place that any lady should be seen."

"But if we went disguised ... in the twilight ... no one would recognize us."

She shuddered. "But Mrs. Bergland, I don't understand. Why would you even want to go looking for your former servant, especially one who has *chosen* to work in a brothel?"

I invented. "Because he has something that belongs to my husband."

"Well, go to the police then."

"It's more complicated than that. It's something that Edvard gave him, as a present. But now that it appears Edvard might have encountered some problems at sea, and perhaps will not be coming home at all, I have been thinking of this small box—it is ivory scrimshaw—and wishing I had it back—as a memento. I wish to buy it from Henry."

"Why would your husband give a Celestial anything of value?" Cecilia asked, but she was wavering, the kind-hearted girl.

"Henry did Edvard a service," I said mysteriously. "I'm not at liberty to say what. But it was information that helped Edvard quite a bit."

"Oh, all right then, but let me think about the best way to manage it. There are over a dozen houses. *I* never worked in a house, as you know, only sang for a few months in my husband's saloon. But I knew the world, of course, and who was who. I can make a list for you. That's all I'll promise."

I thanked her profusely and then, as Bertha had returned with the tea and plum tarts, we devoted ourselves to gossip of a more pleasant kind, about how all the ladies of Uptown had comported themselves during the harvest bazaar and what they had bought and how much money had been made.

A day or two later Cecilia came by to give me an envelope, which contained the information I wanted. "Please do not mention my name," she said. "But if you meet Mrs. Purfoy and she is still healthy, that I would like to know."

I gave Sarah two days off to visit her widowed mother across the water on Whidbey Island. In the evening, after she was gone, I slipped through Uptown to the flats, at twilight, wearing a pair of Kjell's old trousers and the patched boots he had discarded for a new pair to take him to Alaska. I wore his pea coat, too big for my shoulders, but with a collar I could turn up, and a derby hat, under which I could stuff my hair.

I'd had occasion some dozen years ago, always with Edward by my side, to dress in male clothing, when we found ourselves in some rough port city, and likely to be set upon and robbed if we promenaded openly, he in his blue coat and brass buttons and captain's hat, me in a hobbling skirt and trimmed bonnet. I was young then, scarcely twenty the first time we tried the ruse, and I was delighted that I was mistaken for a sailor out with one of my mates, an older fellow in a patched pea coat. My build has always been angular, my chest rather flat, and my face, hair hidden under a cap, oddly masculine in the mirror. Edvard was amused to dress me in a jacket and trousers—and, later, undress me—and to teach me the finer points of acting like a man. Swearing like a sailor he did not allow, or at least only some of the minor oaths. I wasn't permitted to carry a weapon of any kind lest it be turned on me. Edvard had his knife and revolver—he would defend me. We were never in peril, both of us tall and strong-looking, striding along confidently, and no one came forth to challenge us—but I liked to pretend we were in danger, just to imagine how I would run and dart and vault over a fence or wall.

Now I was older, softened by motherhood, weakened by dusting and sweeping, with only stairs to climb. But I found my sailor's swagger and manly stride came back to me. I was helped in my disguise by the fact it was raining hard—and a dark evening to boot, without a moon. A few lamps were lit in the saloons and shop windows; they cast a blurred light out onto the boardwalks and muddy streets. The wind was in the creaking of the masts and hulls offshore and in the water slapping under the docks. Because of the downpour and the early evening hour, few were out on the streets. I sloshed through mud puddles to get to the first Female Boarding House. I screwed up my courage, pulled my cap down and my collar up and knocked.

From brothel to brothel I trod the streets, until I had exhausted Cecilia's list of six of the better-known places. Sometimes the madame herself came to the door, resplendent in feathers or modest as a shopkeeper's wife. Other times it was a maid who let me in to stand dripping in the foyer, to catch glimpses of women in the parlor room playing cards or talking, their breasts bulging out above half-laced corsets, all visible through lace-draped robes.

The answer everywhere was the same: no Chinese were employed here. Finally, at the last place on Cecilia's list, a maid brought Mrs. Purfoy to speak with me, a lavishly dressed lady, stout and flushed. Her red hair flamed in a pompadour. This was the woman who had perhaps been Cecilia's employer. She certainly looked healthy enough and had as kind a face as you could expect given her line of work.

"I am seeking a Chinese servant," I mumbled, husking up my voice as best I could manage and finding it easier now that I was so soaked and chilled.

"I do not have Chinese girls in my employ ... sir." She hesitated. "If that is what you seek, you will find an establishment near here, close behind the Yee Hay Sook shop, with the red lantern. And I advise you not to ask for servants, here or anyplace. My girls may not be entirely respectable, but they have their pride too. None of us are any man's servants."

To explain I was looking for a male servant named Henry Soon would only complicate things, so I simply nodded my thanks. She sent me off again into the rain with one piece of advice, and a wink: "You would do well to tuck up a strand of hair or two back into your derby."

I fled in the embarrassing knowledge that a long, wet lock was trailing down my neck.

The Yee Hay Sook Company was one of several very small Chinese stores that had been created in the wake of the Chinese Exclusion Act. Instead of one owner, there were ten or even twenty, only a few of whom actually were employed there. They were owners on paper only; this allowed them more freedom of movement. As "merchants" they were allowed to travel back to China and re-enter the United States legally, something denied to mere "laborers." These shops were in many cases more known for their fan-tan games and sleeping rooms for opium addicts than for their merchandise, and this was true of this seedy shop, with only a small window and a door that stuck as I pushed at it. Two kerosene lamps on the counter were all that lit the room, perhaps ten by fifteen feet, and the shelves were almost bare, just a few bags of rice and tins of tea. Zee Tai Company's shop tickled the nose with scents of ginger, clove, and tea buds. Here I could smell only urine, tobacco, and opium smoke issuing from the rear rooms where muffled voices signaled a card game. The man at the counter, indeterminate in age, with one blind eye and stained teeth, was courteous enough, but seemed to expect some direction from me. Obviously, I had not ventured out on this wet evening to purchase tea. Only need could have driven me, for opium or women.

"Girls?" I choked out. "Red lantern?"

"Backside door, you go," and when I hesitated, he repeated, "Red lantern. Girls."

The rain was as black as the sky and as I stood on Adams Street wondering whether the man meant I should squeeze through the alley by the side of the shop, I questioned whether I should not run as fast as I could in the other direction, up to my warm kitchen.

I knew this part of town not at all and it no longer seemed like an adventure to be wearing a pea coat and boots, but a tempting of fate. What if the man was steering me wrong and it was a trap? What if in going through the alley I found myself coshed, bound, and shackled by crimps, only to awaken in the hold of some ship heading out to sea? Once they discovered I was a woman, I would be done for.

Nevertheless, having come this far, I told myself I had to at least try to find Henry. Fists balled and head down, I charged through the alley to find only a set of rickety stairs leading up to a second story porch, with a red lantern hanging under the eaves.

There was no madame here, only a few girls sitting in the shabby front room, who looked at me in astonishment as I came in without knocking. I was streaming with water and probably wild-eyed with fear.

"English?" I said. "Do you speak English?"

Very little apparently. I realized their trade must be with the Chinese. Although their faces were painted, red on the cheeks and lips, eyes outlined with black, they wore only tunics and trousers, not corsets and lace.

"You wait," said one of them quietly. Another came to relieve me of my pea coat, hat, and boots, but I gestured her away. Henry could not be here—maybe one of them was going to get someone to drug and shanghai me. I turned to fumble my way back out the door, when I heard a familiar voice, English.

"Please sir, do not go. May we help you?"

It was Henry's voice, but it was not Henry.

A young woman stood in the room, wearing a worn calico dress with an apron. I recognized the dress as a cast-off of mine that I had put in the rag-bin. The apron, also one of mine, was not large enough to disguise the bulge of pregnancy pushing at the woman's waist.

"Mrs. Bergland!'

I do not know which of us was most astonished.

That evening I did not get the truth out of her, but she did finally agree to pack her few things and come back with me to the house. We were lucky in that Sarah was away that night and I meant to keep her away. When she arrived back home the next day, I met her at the kitchen door and gave her a month's wages and a referral in lieu of notice.

Only then did Lian, for that was her name, not Henry, feel safe enough and sure enough of me to tell me the story of how she came from China to Victoria, lost her brother to illness on the ship, and managed to be smuggled from Vancouver Island to North Beach.

She said she had left my service because she feared I would
throw her out anyway once I learned she was a girl and pregnant.
I convinced her that I would not turn her in to the immigration
authorities. That I would take care of her. But I asked her if there
was any possibility that she could marry the father of her child.
I assumed that was Ah Song.

"Ah Song is married. In China. Ah Song is faithful husband."

"Is it someone else in town then? One of the merchants or
other workers? Someone who might be persuaded to marry you?
I could help, Lian."

"No one will marry me, not now," she said. Her lips pressed
together. She would not allow me to see her cry. "You will see,
when I have my baby."

I feel relieved to have her back with me, and so foolish for
ever having thought she was a boy. Lian was the sister I imagined
had been left behind in China. Instead it was a brother who
stayed at home and another brother who died on the ship from
Hong Kong to Victoria. Only after a few days did she tell me the
story of the "white devil" who is the father of her child. It is a
strange tale and a sad one that I write here.

Smuggled to America: The Story of a Chinese Girl
by D.B. Bergland

L. woke face down in a pool of brackish saltwater that
smelled like vomit, and at first she could not remember
anything. Her cheeks rubbed against rough wood; she
was no longer in the dark hold of the ship, but on the
tilting deck. The back of her padded jacket and trousers
were soaked from rain. Light, gray as it was, hurt her
eyes when she turned her head to see boots next to her.
A man was bending over her, asking something. It was
all gibberish, the white man's language. She stiffened
for a beating. But his face, when she raised her head a
little, was not the indifferently cruel visage of one of
the seamen, who twice a day came down to the hold
and gave them some kind of rice or porridge. The man
was dressed better. He wore glasses, and his face was
concerned.

He seemed to be asking a question. It could have been, how did you get here? Or, is something wrong with you? Or, what is your name?

She didn't remember the answers to any of them. He picked her up then, as if she were a small pile of rags, and she did not know whether he was going to take her back to the hold or throw her overboard. The deck rolled and her stomach rolled with it; she coughed and retched, though there was nothing left in her stomach. She almost didn't care if she ended up among the fishes. Let me drown.

The man did neither. He took her in his arms, gently, and brought her to his surgery. He was the ship's surgeon.

As the day passed, the waves calmed. She was able to take some broth and some tea. A translator was brought up, a man named Ah Song, who knew a little English. He spoke something close to her dialect of Cantonese, and he told her she was "dried out" from vomiting and lack of water and food. He said she must have "lost her mind" and crawled up to the deck. They had been on the ship for two weeks and due to the storms, they were only halfway across the Pacific.

"My brother?" thinking she had only dreamed his death. "May I see my brother?"

Ah Song shook his head. Many passengers in the hold were in the same state she was, and some had died. He spoke softly, as if to a child, and did not finish his sentence.

The pieces began to come together, as if in some nightmarish puzzle.

An older cousin of her father's—they called him Uncle—came one day to the village, bragging about his wealth and success in Butte, Montana. He offered to take the two eldest boys to America and set them up as merchants. She remembered her father's gratitude, her mother kissing Uncle's hands. Muffled crying from Soon Gee, the second brother. He did not want to leave home. And murmuring voices late at night as she slept;

she thought she heard her name. Courageous, the next morning, she begged to go in Soon Gee's place. They only laughed. "Girls cannot go to America." But that they had spoken of her, she was sure.

She was a thin, strong girl, as tall as Soon Gee, but not as big as her eldest brother, Soon Hay. Her feet had never been bound, and she had been raised to work. Not only to help her mother around the house, but in the fields, sowing and harvesting, and leading the animals to water and home. Her oldest brother was her companion, and together they protected tender-hearted Soon Gee, who was always singing and who often smiled when he dreamed.

L. drank her broth and watched the surgeon come in and out. He had ginger-blond hair, wire-rim spectacles, and neat, strong hands. His teeth were poor, even though he was not old. He had moved her to his cabin. His name was Arthur Dennison. He was Scottish, he told Ah Song. A decent man. "A decent man," Ah Song translated, but his eyes looked sad. "He says he is not like the other white men on the ship. He is working his passage back to Edinburgh where he has family. He will travel by train across Canada to New York."

Arthur Dennison told her she could stay in his cabin for the rest of the trip. Now that he knew her secret— for he had undressed her and put her in a rough cotton shirt—he told Ah Song to tell her she would not be safe back in the hold. He would protect her.

She lay there, in the narrow berth, hardly daring to breathe, as afraid of staying as of going back to the dank and frightening hold, keeping quiet as Arthur Dennison had instructed her. More memories returned. How Uncle told her parents he already had the tickets for the passage across to Canada. The boys were to travel immediately to Canton; he would travel with them. From there they would take a small ship to Hong Kong, and then board the big ship with many sails.

Oh, L. was so envious! Uncle seemed to see that on her face, and his face softened. "Little girl," he said, "Perhaps you would like to come as far as Canton with your brothers? I will undertake that you are returned safely to her parents."

She was sixteen. What did she know of Canton, or of travel? Because her parents said yes, L. imagined that the city was just a few hours away, and that she would be back the next day. Afterwards she understood with bitterness that her parents knew about Uncle's plans for her, and were willing to accept money from him.

Soon Gee cried to leave home, but Soon Hay was impatient to be gone. The trip to Canton was much longer than L. imagined; it was mostly by sampan along the river delta. How large the river was and how great the city, unlike anything they had ever seen before, a thousand buildings, and so many people her eyes grew tired looking at them. They went to a noodle shop and ate as much as they wanted, and Uncle bought new clothes for the boys. Then they came to the hotel where they would stay overnight. Now Uncle began to drink rice wine, and not long after that he sent L. and Soon Gee into another small room to sleep. They heard him talking drunkenly to Elder Brother Hay for a while, and then there was silence.

L. could not sleep, partly from excitement and partly from worry. She did not want to lose her brothers. She did not want to be sent home. She wanted to go to Hong Kong and America too. How could this Uncle, who seemed to have money and to be kindly disposed toward her, be persuaded to buy her a ticket, too? She was still awake when Soon Hay crept in and knelt by her pallet. He whispered what Uncle had told him. That tomorrow, after the boys had sailed to Hong Kong, he would deliver L. to another merchant from Butte. They had traveled back to China together, and this merchant had even more wealth than Uncle. The merchant had one wife, but he wanted another, a younger one for his old bones. This was to be L. He was going to pay handsomely for her.

"That is why our parents agreed to send you to Canton," whispered Soon Hay. "They knew you would not come back, but that Uncle would send them money.

They were persuaded it would be a better life for you."

"I will not stay in Canton," said Lian. "I will not stay to be sold like a goat or a pig."

Soon Hay thought for a while. "We have our tickets, but Soon Gee does not want to go to America, and you do. If you dress in his clothes and we leave right now on an earlier boat to Hong Kong, Uncle may not follow us. Are you willing? I cannot think of another plan. To argue with Uncle is futile, and if we wake Soon Gee, he will also argue and cry. Uncle will wake to see what is wrong, and you will be married within the week."

L. only nodded. She had always trusted her older brother to help and protect her, and all the way to Hong Kong they discussed in low voices how they would manage. They would either stay in Victoria and find work or be smuggled to America. "We will not go to Butte, in case Uncle comes after us."

They were both very brave and very ignorant of the world outside their village. And yet, as far as they could tell, in her brother's clothes, L. was just like any of the other Chinese passengers, all of whom had their own fears and hopes to preoccupy them when they boarded the ship and didn't spare a glance at the two village peasants who quietly found berths in a dark corner of the hold.

The ship flew a British flag, and had a British captain and mates, but many of the crew were from other races. It was a clipper ship, said Ah Song, who came up another day to translate for a sick passenger who later died, and stayed to talk to Lian. The ship traded in Oriental wares and opium but made its money carrying Chinese immigrants to Canada in crowded conditions. Invariably many passengers died. Not the twenty who were traveling first class, whites and wealthy Chinese alike, but the hundred or so other passengers jammed into the hold among the rats and lice, with no privacy, little water to wash with, and only rice and sometimes bits of fish to eat. The Scottish doctor was kept busy tending to the Chinese.

Arthur Dennison had told Ah Song that it was not his first experience on a ship like this, but it was the worst. The captain was not so much cruel as callous. The Chinese were merely cargo to be delivered. They had already paid for their passage, so if "one or two" died en route, it mattered little. The burials at sea took place at night, so as not to disturb the other passengers, and without benefit of prayer. "For the captain believes the Chinese to be heathens," said Ah Song.

Lian's brother was one of the many who died on that voyage. Something got hold of Soon Hay and almost overnight he turned a gray color and could not stop vomiting.

It was when they came to take him up to the deck to throw him overboard that L. had crawled up the ladder behind them, crept into a corner, and ended up lying there as the waves beat the sides of the ship. She was sick too, but the reason she came on deck was to see where they were taking Soon Hay. They merely threw him overboard. That was when everything went black.

The surgeon knew her secret, but he did not immediately take advantage of it. It was only after a few days that, with gestures, he put it to Lian: she could either return to the hold and possible death. Or she could stay in his cabin. She knew, without him telling her directly, that there would be a price for his protection.

L. paid that price without much shame. She realized she would rather be alive than dead.

She never knew if the captain was aware about her continued presence in the surgeon's cabin, or if he simply assumed the Chinese boy had been returned to the hold with the rest of the cargo. Arthur Dennison had her remain in his narrow berth and keep quiet all day. She often heard people come into the surgery; she heard groaning and even screaming as well as the gibberish that was English. Everything that happened at night between them was quiet. He rolled on and off her and did not hurt her. He was gentle. Still, he never asked her if she wanted this. She was given better food and kept everything down. She forced herself to eat. She forced herself not to think of her parents who had agreed to sell her to Uncle's rich friend, of the sight of Soon Hay's body being flung over the rail.

Once a day Ah Song appeared, usually with a sick person. He did not look down on her. He pitied her, but he was not the sentimental type. He had a sister, and a wife. He was not as young as he looked, and this was his second voyage to Gold Mountain. He had been there for three years, in Victoria first, and then in Puget Sound. There was much work there for those willing to work. In the canneries, laundries, and hop fields. This time he planned to get to Port Townsend as soon as he could. That would involve running the sea in a small boat, from Canada across to America. But he had done it before; he knew how.

Their conversations were not long, but they strengthened Lian's nerve. She did not ask him, "Can I come with you?" She thought he would say no. But she made a plan that she would stick by him when they left the ship. She would follow him.

That did not happen.

She was in the surgeon's cabin when the ship docked and at first, she feared that Arthur Dennison simply planned to leave her there, a prisoner. Instead, he eventually came with finer clothes for her, though of man's cut. He asked for her papers and made some changes. He pointed at her: "Henry," he said. Without Ah Song to translate she could not make out at first what his plan was. Only that she was to do as he said, and that she was now called Henry. It was only later that L. realized Arthur Dennison had done her a kindness. He bribed the customs official who came onboard, passed him something in a parcel—she suspected it was opium. The official then quickly escorted L. past the other passengers, explaining something in gibberish as he went. Ah Song was in the long line of passengers, and she couldn't help sending him an appealing look. She was certain she was being marched to prison or something worse. Instead, the official walked her through a side exit in the large building near the wharves, and simply let her go. He turned his back and let her go.

She was free, and in Gold Mountain. Her name here was to be Henry. Yet her troubles were not over.

L. had a few bills and some coins in her pocket from the surgeon, but she did not know their worth and was reluctant to spend them, or even show them at first. More valuable perhaps was the paper-wrapped parcel he had given her, somewhat like the one he'd given the official, but smaller, and which she had secreted away in the inner pocket of her jacket. Arthur Dennison had not kissed or embraced her when they parted; he had said something with a sheepish smile and pointed to the parcel. She guessed this was a kind of apology.

But she did not feel he needed to apologize. He had given her her life. That was the only way she could think about what had happened between them. Anything else was too painful.

At first, L. waited around the building where she had last seen Ah Song, but he did not come and did not come. And eventually evening fell. All she could do that first night was sleep under a wagon she found; in the morning she made her way to the nearby Chinese quarter. It was like Canton and like Hong Kong, but very much smaller. She walked the tight alleyways, smelling the stream of noodles, and eventually mustered up the courage to ask the cost of a bowl. The money she offered turned out to be sufficient and she was given more coins back. She did not find the people unfriendly, and most of them spoke some dialect of Cantonese. The clothes she wore showed that she was a boy of standing. They asked her family name and she said, "Soon." There was a merchant by the name of Soon in Victoria; they assumed she was a family member newly arrived.

L. thought it would not be long that she could maintain this story, but perhaps by then she might run into Ah Song or someone else from the British ship. Nights she slept in hidden places away from Chinatown, where she feared being robbed. Days she wandered around. On the hillside on the other side of the harbor from the Chinese quarter were streets lined with trees, large houses of wood with porches, and grand buildings. Men in beaver hats rode on horses, and carriages rumbled by her. A few Chinese people were here, but they seemed to be servants. She dared not speak to them; she spoke little to anyone for fear of them guessing her secret. Yet eventually she managed to find out, through overhearing others speak, that some Chinese worked here in Victoria as servants; some were merchants or had noodle houses; and others left as soon as they could, to earn money elsewhere. Many still spoke of going to America to see relatives or work on farms or in the canneries. L. determined that she would try that too. If she could get to Port Townsend and find Ah Song, she was sure he would help her.

She learned that if you wanted to be smuggled to this place in America called Port Townsend, then you must go to a beach some distance from Victoria at night and there wait for a fishing boat to anchor offshore. It cost money to cross the water to America, and she doubted she would have enough from the small store of coins, but the bills might be enough. She found the beach only because she was picked up by a cart on the way there by a driver who was carrying several Chinese men hidden under bales of hay, along with goods that were to be taken across to America. He picked her up for a few coins and she was grateful, because the way was much longer than she had imagined, and she never would have found the embarkation spot in the dark.

Later, when she thought about it, safe in a room in Port Townsend, L. would wonder what drove her forward that night. Everything seemed frightening and many times she wanted to simply turn back to Victoria. The sky was clouded over, and the water was black except for the line of white that rolled onshore. They could not see the rowboat until it was almost on the beach, and they heard its hull scraping on the pebbles. Two men stepped out of the boat, white devils in slick rubber coats, like eels. They had beards but she could see nothing else about them, not even their eyes, until they lit a lantern and began to count the Chinese. Fifteen is all they would take, and fifteen was five too many for the fishing boat. Everyone knew that and yet everyone pushed forward to pay and to be first on the rowboat. The rowboat took seven men and came back for more.

Now was Lian's moment of truth. She held out her bill and coins. The answer was a laugh and the word "Too little," one of the few phrases she had learned in the last week. Someone behind her tried to push her out of the way, but L. stood firm. "Opium," she said, and withdrew her parcel from her coat. The man seized it and opened it and smelled it. And then he laughed again, but this time a happy laugh. It was probably worth a good deal, but she didn't care. All she wanted was to be on that fishing boat.

The smell of salt water brought back memories of the British clipper and the rocking made Lian's gorge rise in memory. She clamped her jaw and held onto the side of the boat. The hours passed in darkness, but with the dawn came the sight of land, low hills, almost all forest, with huge mountains behind, mountains covered in snow, just turning pink, and little sight of human habitation on land, just a cabin or two with a curl of smoke.

The sails went down, and oars came out, propelling them closer to land. Now they began to see a few people on the slope of the bluff, coming down to the shore. To Lian's great relief they seemed to be Chinese. Not a single Chinese person onboard the fishing boat spoke English, so there was no understanding the words that came from the mouths of the white devils, who had begun shouting and pointing, as if at another boat behind the point. L. later wondered if there had really been another boat piloted by customs officials. She heard it was often the case that the smugglers didn't come ashore at North Beach, to save time and escape more quickly should there be trouble. They were so close to the beach that she could make out faces—and to her surprise and great joy she saw Ah Song. She was so relieved that she stood up and waved to him and shouted "It's me! Ah Song."

A moment later she had been shoved off in the rough sea, swimming for her life, and surrounded by other flailing bodies, as the fishing boat put up its sail again and headed back across the strait.

November 10

Some time has passed since I put pen to paper to describe the events of my life. I have discovered how difficult it can be to keep up to date with a journal, when events rush onward. That is not to say I did nothing in October—I was occupied writing down the story Lian told me here in the journal. I could polish it and copy it out to send to Katrine, but I hesitate. The part about the Chinese uncle and Mr. Dennison would not surprise her; she thinks rather poorly of men and how they treat the female sex. She might well wonder how I know Lian and ask tiresome questions. "Is it fiction or journalism?" "Is it the truth or have you made this up?" I hardly know what to answer. It is a story about the truth, a story I have written, without permission, about another person's life. Lian's story has been important to me, but I question whether I have the right to share it with others. So in my journal it will stay, one scrap of the quilt that makes up America: How we all found ourselves in this country.

Instead, I sent Katrine two short articles about the Klondike, one newsy and optimistic, and the other more somber and sardonic.

"See what you think, Katrine," I wrote her. "It is surprisingly complicated to learn the truth of what is happening in the Klondike Gold Rush. One continues to hear rumors of gold strikes, but while hundreds still pack the ships up to Alaska, few are returning with gold nuggets or dust as they did in the summer. Winter settles in with snow and ice. Disturbing tales come back of disenchanted prospectors who in a few short weeks seem to have lost everything. Suicides grow more frequent, and murders are common. I fear that Kjell is lost to me forever. If he has written, no letter has reached me for weeks."

I did not hire a new servant after I dismissed Sarah. I did not want word to get out that I had a pregnant Chinese girl living in one of the guest rooms. Instead of sending Lian out to shop, I had groceries, milk, and coal delivered. Ah Song continued to pick up and return the laundry. He often hid sweets and packages of herbs among the linens for Lian, but he would not stay to tea. He always had a great deal to do; like all the Chinese he works morning till night. He did tell me though, that he was glad to know Lian was back at my house, and he trusted me to keep her and her baby safe.

I must admit I missed "Henry" and his company, but in many ways, I was glad Lian turned out to be a girl. Now, at least at home, I did not need to observe proprieties quite as I had; I could come downstairs in my wrapper in the morning or sit in bed and drink my tea. Besides, Lian is an excellent housekeeper and an improving cook. I would not hear of her going back to her old room, but insisted she move into the guest room with the comfortable bed, carpet, armchair, and table. It shamed me that I had offered her so little before, that I had never invited her to sit with me in the parlor or read to her.

These evenings I read aloud the serials in the American women's magazines, and we often discuss them. We are both fond of romances and plucky heroines named Susan and Louise who stand up for themselves. We practice our English together from these stories and amuse ourselves by reciting lines. Now that I had her confidence, she would sometimes tell me more about growing up in her village, how the freedom she'd had as a girl had marked her. And I thought of myself, running up the steep mountain behind our farm to get a view of the fjord below.

As October turned to November and the gray skies darkened even further and heavy rains and winds whipped our exposed peninsula from all directions, I continued to fear that Edvard might not return to me. In due course the wreck of the *Fidelius* might be sighted, smashed on rocks or a lee shore somewhere along the long northwestern coastline, or simply declared lost at sea with all hands. Other ships had met that fate in the frenzied rush to Alaska. Greed for gold had sent thousands up to a wilderness where only the native inhabitants and a few mad trappers and prospectors had earlier braved the harsh conditions.

The San Franciscans who had chartered the *Fidelius* might strike it rich next summer. More likely, if they survived the winter, they would come limping back, frostbitten and much poorer.

When the telegram arrived, one pearly gray morning a few days ago, Lian brought it into the dining room where I sat writing. I waited three hours to learn the news, putting the envelope into my apron pocket and throwing myself into washing windows that had grown dirt-speckled with the recent storms. Lian helped me without saying a word, even insisting on climbing the ladder part-way. She had never gotten very big (as I had with my two). Ah Song had bought her a roomier, padded silk jacket. This she usually wore over her trousers and loose shirt. Her hair, she continues to wear in a braid, under a cap. Yet her face has softened and grown fuller. It's the bee-stung lower lip and calm, intelligent eyes that make her attractive, as a boy or girl, but I now see that behind the gentleness is strength of mind and spirit.

Finally she asked me why I did not open the telegram.

"If I open it, I will know my husband is dead. If I don't open it, I can pretend, for just a little while longer, that he is alive and will one day walk in the door again."

"Pretending does no good," she said. "I will read the news and tell you."

I took it from my pocket and handed it to her.

"Nanaimo, Vancouver Island," she read. "Ship broke up off Campbell River. All saved. Home this week, God willing."

I was so happy that I hugged Lian and cried. Only later in the day did I wonder how Edvard would take the news that Kjell had left in August and had not written for over two months, and that our Chinese houseboy Henry had turned out to be a young woman, and a pregnant one at that.

I had not seen Adele for a few weeks. In truth I had avoided her and told Lian not to answer the door if she saw her coming. But I needed to share the good news about Edvard, and so I made my way that same afternoon down Lawrence Street to Polk Street and her shop. She had a customer in the fitting room, but gestured to me—rather coolly, which did not surprise me—to wait in the front of the shop. A bouquet of autumn leaves had replaced the fresh flowers of the summer, but otherwise it was as tidy and fashionable as always, with its pale green wallpaper and lace curtains shielding the bow window from the street. After ten minutes she returned. I didn't stand on ceremony but rejoiced, "Adele, Edvard is alive and well. His ship wrecked up north off Vancouver Island, but he managed to get to Nanaimo and send a telegram. He will be home very soon."

"Oh, Dagny!" she said—not Mrs. Bergland as she usually calls me in the shop. Her quizzical face broke into a great smile. She took my hands. "I share your relief."

She asked then why I had not been "at home" of late. I could not tell her the truth then but asked her to dine with me that evening.

When she arrived, I had Lian open the door. I stood close behind her to judge Adele's reaction. I need not have worried after all.

"Ah," said Adele, taking off her blue wool cape and fashionable hat. "You're back—Henry, is it?"

"Lian, please, Madam."

"Well, in any case, Lian, it is good to see you again. I know that Mrs. Bergland was worried about you."

Adele and I sat and chatted at the dinner table just as in old times. Quite often these days I have no formal dinner. Lian and I simply eat in the kitchen together with a pot of tea for her and a cup of coffee for me. Tonight Lian insisted on serving the two of us a new recipe: Meatloaf and gravy. Adele and I drank some claret and grew positively merry. After Lian went upstairs, I looked at Adele. There was no need to explain the exact circumstances of Lian's transformation.

"The question is," she said. "Will you keep her on after the baby is born? People are bound to find it out eventually. I wouldn't want you to find yourself or Lian in trouble with the law. Or with society in Uptown."

I knew immediately what she meant on both accounts. The Chinese boys and men smuggled into Port Townsend all looked the same to the authorities and, as Henry, Lian had been indistinguishable from any other boy. As a woman, a mother, it would be more obvious she had come illegally. Every Chinese woman in Port Townsend was known, for there were less than ten. The baby would be of mixed race. Society was likely to think Edvard was the father. I was grateful to Adele for not pointing that out.

"Lian has relations in Butte, Montana," I said. A partial truth. "But she cannot travel with an infant. So we must keep her with us for at least a time."

Adele sighed, but with a smile. "So there will be a baby in the house? You must have more help then, someone who will not talk."

"I don't see why Lian and I can't share the baby's care. In this great house there is plenty of room. I have given birth to two babies. I can certainly help with Lian's infant."

As usual, when I spoke aloud about my children, I felt a wrench of shock that they were no longer with us. I realized I had never spoken of them before with Adele.

"What were their names?" she asked quietly.

"Jan was the little boy, five years old when he died. A wave swept him into the sea. Agnete was the girl. She was just three months old when she sickened of typhus. We buried her at sea, off the coast of Chile."

"I would find it hard to speak of them, too, if I were you." Adele put her hand on mine. "My grandmother lost two children on the westward trail. From smallpox. They would have been our uncles, my mother's older brothers. My grandmother didn't mention their names, but started a new family of three girls when they finally arrived in Oregon."

"I had a miscarriage this past winter," I confessed. "Edvard wants children very badly."

"Then you will have children," Adele assured me. "You are young still."

A silence.

"We must find a doctor for the birth, or if you don't wish one for fear of scandal, then I can attend her. I have midwife experience helping my aunt. But dear Dagny, you must see that Lian cannot stay here hidden with a child. What if her relatives refuse to take her in? I think we must equip her with skills to allow her to make her way on her own."

"She is only seventeen, but she's very clever," I said. "And she learns more every day. Could she teach school, teach Chinese people to speak English and so on?"

"There was once such a school here, run by the Baptists, but it's gone now. People seem to prefer that the Chinese keep to themselves. They respect the merchants' success but look down on the servants, cannery workers, hop pickers, a low class without rights, subject to deportation." She thought a moment. "I will undertake to teach her to sew and train her to be a dressmaker— if she agrees. Then she will at least have a profession."

November 16

Edvard has returned after fifteen weeks, mostly at sea. He is shockingly thin, and his hair has a streak of white at the temple. His beard too is rippled with white. Otherwise he seems his old self, kind and forceful by turns. He took me in his arms right away and kept me there for some time.

November 18

Edvard of course was surprised to find Lian where Henry had been, but a man who had survived three months in the Gulf of Alaska and the Bering Sea in a lumber schooner, who had been farther north in Alaska than he ever imagined venturing, with passengers who caused no end of trouble, and who had seen his ship wrecked on Ripple Rock in the Seymour Narrows of the Inside Passage, was unlikely to think a pregnant Chinese girl in the house was any great matter. He was less pleased, quite furious in fact, to find Kjell gone, gone since August, gone to the Yukon, if he'd made it that far, where he would surely starve with the rest of them, and it served Kjell right if he *did* starve. But, of course, Edvard was broken-hearted about that prospect, and worse ones. So many men have perished on Chilkoot Pass or the long route up to Dawson City through the interior.

Edvard's story is almost too long to recount here, but I will make an attempt, writing down as much as he told me. Some things he keeps to himself or considers bad luck to dwell on. For now, he is resting and building up his strength.

He has sent a letter to Carl Olafsson, the owner of the *Fidelius,* and will need to provide documents of the shipwreck for insurance purposes, but for now he wishes only to sit in the parlor and read the newspapers. To eat Norwegian food and drink hot coffee with cream. Within a week, he says, he'll seek employment with Puget Mill Company, which owns the great sawmills in Port Gamble and Port Ludlow and has a fleet of lumber schooners. He has not yet been paid the second half of his wages by Mr. Olafsson. Instead, Edvard deposited a good deal of cash into the bank, payment from two of his passengers who made the return journey. That is a story in itself.

Since I have never been up to Alaska, nor even British Columbia, I must imagine, Edvard tells me, a wilder, more forested Norwegian coastline, at least to begin with: steep mountains dark with firs and cedars that come down to the edge of narrow fjords that open up into bays and sounds; waterfalls crashing down through ferns and salmonberry. Edvard described seeing grizzly bears, taller than a man and three times as thick, fishing in a river where salmon threw themselves upstream through the rapids to spawn. All along the route, between Vancouver Island and the mainland, were the spread-out villages of the Indians. Some of the villages still thrived and others were abandoned, smallpox and other diseases of the white man having killed many.

The *Fidelius* first made port at the coal-mining town of Nanaimo. Edvard hoped to pick up a pilot to guide him through the Inside Passage up to Southeast Alaska. The schooner could have set out from Port Townsend to Cape Flattery and then northwest, but he had some worries about how the vessel with its broad beam and relatively shallow draft would handle in the open sea with such a load of people and gear. But there was no pilot available in Nanaimo, so Edvard was forced to rely completely on his charts. The greatest danger was not the rocks and islands, Edvard thought last August; it was the steamships, fishing boats, and lumber schooners, all pressed into service to ferry the prospectors up to Alaska.

North of Vancouver Island, Edvard set a course west across the Gulf of Alaska for the Aleutian Islands, through which the *Fidelius* would need to pass before heading north and east for Norton Sound and St. Michael. Conditions at first were reasonably fine; a light fog in the mornings gave way to sunshine and often stiff breezes. While the *Fidelius* could not make headway as strongly as the barque *Matilde,* with all its sails set, they looked to arrive in the Aleutians in less than a week. The mood on deck up the Inside Passage was jovial, just the way it had been on the week's voyage from San Francisco, where good humor and excitement prevailed. These men were not roughnecks, not by any means, but young and middle-aged fellows from a variety of professions, some of whom had been born in the East, but most of whom were Californians looking for the kind of wealth that had transformed San Francisco in 1849. Some of their grandfathers or fathers came west then and the new crop of adventurers had been raised on tales of luck—hard conditions to be sure, but with a payoff that made it all worthwhile. Not all were prospectors. Some had seized the opportunity to come north in the expectation that they would find ways to serve the miners and take their money, without staking claims or panning for gold.

Such a man was Clarence Harrison, the owner of a small bank south of San Francisco, a portly fellow of about thirty-five who was traveling with his two younger brothers, Jeffrey and Thomas. "Initially Mr. Harrison and I got on quite well, and I was relieved to have someone of his apparently good judgment, and calm demeanor aboard." Harrison's intention, as Edvard understood it, was to set up a branch of his bank in Dawson. He was traveling with an iron safe wrapped in chains and padlocked. Only he and his younger brothers had keys, worn around their necks. They all carried revolvers. With the cash inside the safe, they planned to buy passage on a sternwheeler up the Yukon River and to construct a bank for the gold diggers.

"Poor wretch," Edvard shook his head. "He imagined that by avoiding the rabble sailing to Skagway and the passes, he could make it to Dawson City by river, with his iron safe intact. Why shouldn't he believe there was a sternwheeler just waiting for us at the mouth of the Yukon? That's what he'd been told. Four days on the river to Dawson, they said. Easy as pie."

The fine weather did not last, of course, and midway across the Gulf of Alaska, the morning fog grew thicker, often turning to heavy rain, and the progress of the *Fidelius* was slowed by contrary winds. As the schooner tossed on the waves, many of the passengers grew ill and were forced to keep to their bunks. These rough bunks with straw mattresses had been hastily constructed in the hold and were entirely uncomfortable, especially for men accustomed to soft feather beds and carpets underfoot.

Not surprisingly perhaps, the men turned to drinking and to gambling. There was one young man who played cards very well—Lloyd Quayle, a handsome fellow with an embroidered vest and a diamond stickpin who called himself a bookkeeper, most recently in Nevada. He stuck close to the Harrison brothers, and made it clear he hoped to have a job in the bank in Dawson. No ordinary bookkeeper wears a diamond stickpin, but it was not Edvard's place to say so. He had his mind on the weather and not on the gambling below decks that grew increasingly fierce along with the weather. Violence erupted one night when Jeff Harrison, the youngest brother, lost big in a game of poker to Quayle. There were calls of cheating, but nothing could be proved. Clarence Harrison pulled Jeff out of the game, disappeared below decks, and returned with a wad of cash to pay off Quayle. He issued a stern warning to Quayle about cheating, but Quayle only shrugged. "A fool and his money are soon parted, my friend. Not that I'm saying Jeff is a fool—in fact, I think he has the makings of a cardsharp. Just needs practice."

Edvard began to keep an eye on Quayle. When he found Quayle prowling around the cargo, specifically the iron safe, without a good explanation, Edvard was forced to throw him in the brig overnight. This shocked the men badly. It is one thing to call a man Captain Bergland and another to accept his full and complete authority aboard a ship, backed up by crewmen who support him unswervingly. Quayle behaved himself after that but held a grudge against Edvard and Clarence Harrison.

It was ten days across the Gulf of Alaska, the last two days a maelstrom of wind from all directions. But Edvard had been through the Straits of Magellan; he had seen worse. The *Fidelius* managed to work her way through the passage between two of the western isles of the Aleutians and head into the Bering Sea. Here the schooner encountered icebergs. It was only the third week of August, but it seemed this ice from the past winter was only waiting to lock up its pieces again and form a solid sheet. Finally, on August 27, the coast of northwest Alaska came into view. It was a barren landscape. In Norway, the Gulf Stream warms the land north of the Arctic Circle and the sea never freezes, but in Alaska the seas are frigid and the tundra melts only a foot or so in summer. Still, there was some green along the rivers and welcome sunshine. The *Fidelius* passed the delta of the Yukon River and anchored some sixty miles north, at the port of St. Michael, with a few other vessels. The schooner had sailed over 2,000 miles from Port Townsend to arrive August 31. Edvard was eager to unload his increasingly fractious passengers and all their supplies, to swab out the ship, take on fresh water and perhaps some whale or walrus meat, and to begin the southbound voyage as expeditiously as possible. The icebergs in the Bering Sea worried him, as did the return passage across the Gulf of Alaska.

His passengers were eager to disembark as well, and to begin the last stage of their journey up the long river. They had heard the Yukon River froze over by the end of September but figured they would have plenty of time to get there before that. They disembarked with their trunks and piles of gear, only to find there were no sternwheelers, nor any other motorized vessel capable of carrying twenty-four men and their supplies 1700 miles up the river. There *had* been two sternwheelers; they were somewhere on the river to or from Dawson. The river was unusually low this summer and the steamboats were having trouble navigating through the shallow channels.

Some of the ships in harbor had brought up sections of extra sternwheelers to be constructed at St. Michael. The former mayor of Seattle (he had resigned his office to become a stampeder) had chartered a ship up to St. Michael and brought lumber and iron for such a craft. He and his fellow passengers were busy hammering and welding and hoped to head upriver very soon.

St. Michael had been founded by the Russians, and still had an onion-shaped dome on its small Orthodox church, but the town was now fully in the hands of the Americans. St. Michael was not much to speak of—wooden shacks abounded as well as makeshift summer tents inhabited by prospectors. The largest buildings were the warehouses of two trading companies. This past summer the U.S. army had built a large fort to impose some order, explained Edvard. Apparently—and with reason—the government was worried about the influx of stampeders at the beginning of the Arctic winter. For late September can be the beginning of winter, one that lasts until mid-June. Those who had lived through the last winter could attest to that.

Clarence Harrison bargained and pleaded for a boat to go upriver with his safe. He demanded to see the commander at Fort St. Michael. Lieutenant Colonel Briggs could only tell him that he and the other prospectors from the *Fidelius* would likely have to stay the winter in town. If it was any consolation, they would have a head start next spring, ahead of the prospectors who would be just arriving in June or July. Meanwhile, they could spend the next ten months cutting firewood and helping construct several more sternwheelers. Or they could turn around and take passage back to Port Towsend and then San Francisco and spend their winter in comfort. Many of Edvard's passengers elected to stay in St. Michael, and some were quite cheerful about it. Never having been through an Arctic winter, they had no notion of its hardships, and the thought of being first to get up the Yukon next summer was incentive enough. Not a few perhaps, having spent a month at sea, were reluctant to board the schooner again. Edvard announced he would take anyone who wished to return to Port Townsend, but they would be charged for the voyage, the full amount to be determined by the ship's owner in San Francisco.

Lloyd Quayle opted to stay in St. Michael, along with the youngest Harrison brother, Jeff. Clarence Harrison and his other brother Thomas, along with about ten others, prepared to leave. Only Edvard and one other man—Clarence Harrison— knew that they would not be returning directly to Port Townsend. After retracing their passage back through the Aleutians the ship would cross the Gulf of Alaska directly west to Juneau and deposit the Harrison brothers in town with their iron safe. Clarence Harrison would open his bank there, instead, for he judged Skagway too lawless. For this service, which would take the *Fidelius* at least a week longer, Harrison agreed to pay Edvard $2,000 cash for himself and his brother, with $1,000 upfront and the rest in Juneau. This full amount would not be reported to the shipping company. Instead, Edvard would explain that he chose to cut over to Juneau and then sail south through the Inside Passage because of the stormy autumn weather.

Or so Edvard worked it out at the time. In St. Michael he and Clarence made their agreement and Clarence gave my husband $1,000, which Edvard wrapped tightly in oilskin and placed in the inner pocket of his trousers. Edvard says that he didn't intend to defraud the ship owner, Mr. Olafsson, only to make sure that he had sufficient funds should there be delays. Repairs on the ship might be needed and supplies were hard to come by and expensive. By taking payment from two passengers and rerouting through Juneau he felt he was only showing prudence in the face of the unknown.

Perhaps, he admits now, he was also angry with Carl Olafsson for being so tight-fisted and with himself for having accepted a strenuous job transporting stampeders back and forth for so little money.

It took three storm-battered weeks for the *Fidelius* to work its way back through the Aleutian Islands and across the Gulf to the town of Juneau. The passengers were often seasick and complained about the food, of which there was not enough. Edvard, fearing for the men staying the winter in St. Michael, had left some of his stores there for them. By the time they sighted the shore of Southeastern Alaska and Juneau they were all weak with hunger and illness. That was when Clarence Harrison managed to get down from his berth at long last to check on his iron safe and to take out the rest of the payment to Edvard.

The safe was chained and padlocked as before, but the stacks of bills—some $100,000—were gone.

Clarence was sure that one of the men onboard had taken his money. A great commotion ensued, and the ship was thoroughly searched. Every crewman's berth and kit, every passenger's trunk. Mattresses were ripped open, along with the remaining flour sacks, boxes of tools dismantled, sails unfolded, and piles of rope uncoiled and recoiled. Most of the men were flat broke. The only significant money on the *Fidelius* seemed to be Edvard's thousand dollars. This Clarence wanted returned to him, but Edvard refused. He himself suspected that Jeff Harrison had been forced by gambling debt to fall in with Quayle, and that the two of them, with Jeff's key, had managed in the chaos of unloading and reloading over the two days spent in St. Michael, to empty the safe. A sorry trick to play on your own brother.

There was, of course, no way to return to St. Michael. The town was now locked in ice until the next spring. But Edvard submitted to a second search of the *Fidelius* in Juneau by a customs agent. Nothing was found and the *Fidelius* weighed anchor again, after taking on water and supplies that Edvard paid for. He offered to carry the Harrisons free of charge south to Port Townsend, but they declined. What the Harrisons planned to do in Juneau over the winter was unclear; Clarence probably did not know himself. All he wanted was to get off *this damned lumber schooner*. Edvard promised him he would take the matter to the authorities in Port Townsend. The safe was left onboard as evidence.

By this time it was October. Although the Inside Passage is protected from the swells of the sea and the worst of the storms, after leaving Juneau Edvard encountered days of fog in channels he was unfamiliar with. The bears were mostly gone now, and the Indian villages looked ghostly in the mists. Along with the crewmen, eight passengers were onboard, worn out with all the excitement but relieved to be homeward bound. They reached Ketchikan, took on more supplies, and Edvard pulled out the charts from the voyage north in August to guide the *Fidelius* down the coast to Vancouver Island.

In his stories about the trip, Edvard talked far more about the behavior of his passengers and the mystery of the iron safe than about the fog-bound morning when they encountered Ripple Rock. He was not on watch but wakened when they struck. He knew immediately they were going down. He remembered Ripple Rock from the passage north, but on that trip, they had steered well clear of it, and the current was in their favor. This time it wasn't. A steamboat, with an engine and propeller, could have pulled away in time; the sailing schooner *Fidelius* had no chance.

But Edvard, in all the years I have known him, has never dwelt upon disasters and wrecks. He considers it bad luck. Even now he merely explained, "So we lowered two lifeboats with as much as we could save and rowed with all our might toward shore. We sat there on a patch of gravel, silently watching the schooner smash again and again against the massive rock in the center of the narrows, until the hull submerged, and spars and timbers were born away with the current.

"And then a small band of Indians found us and showed us the way to Campbell River. There are fishing lodges there, as well as a trading post and some trappers. We dried out as best we could and then I paid two fishing boats to carry us all down to Nanaimo." There he left the passengers bound for San Francisco to deal with the situation as best they could but paid for his crewmen to get to Port Townsend.

When he first arrived home, Edvard had planned to go to the police department to report Clarence Harrison's loss, as the man had asked. He hesitated, however. First, he had become more and more certain that it could only have been Jeff who had the means to unlock the safe in St. Michael. Edvard was also certain that when Clarence had the time to think it through, he would come to the same conclusion. Would he want to see his brother arrested and possibly sent to prison? Much better would be to wait until spring when ships began to call again at St. Michael. Then Clarence would probably decide to return there himself, force Quayle to return the money, and carry out his original plan to go to Dawson. The population would be captive until June when the Yukon River unfroze, and there was the commander at Fort St. Michael to punish Quayle. So Edvard reasoned, to himself and to me, as to why he should delay reporting the theft in Port Townsend.

But my husband had another reason for not wishing to draw too much attention to his arrangements with Clarence Harrison. He was afraid that if Carl Olafsson somehow heard that Edvard had been paid $1,000 in cash by two passengers not on the manifest, that Olafsson would demand the money, without, of course, compensating him for everything Edvard had had to spend on supplies in Juneau and on transporting the passengers to Nanaimo and the crew to Port Townsend. Olafsson, that miserly Swede, would demand the whole fare that the Harrisons had paid.

Edvard is a fair and honest man, but a hard-headed one as well, who worked his way up from apprentice on a Liverpool guano ship to becoming captain of his own merchant ship. He had bargained with companies all over the world and ruled his crews for over twenty years. It galled him that Olafsson, after sending him up to Alaska in a lumber schooner only in order to extract money from innocent prospectors, now blamed him for the breakup of the *Fidelius* and was withholding his pay for the voyage until the insurance paid out. One of the reasons he has talked of taking employment with the Puget Mill Company is so he can confront Olafsson himself in his San Francisco office.

December 1

Edvard left yesterday on the *Lester*, a well-built lumber schooner about ten years old: three-masted and somewhat broader in the beam than *Fidelius*. He is now working for the Puget Mill Company owned by Mr. Talbot. The past week he's been much occupied with getting his kit together and fitting out the ship to his satisfaction, hiring crew, and of course seeing to the loading of the schooner. He hopes to sort everything out with Olafsson while he is in San Francisco, and to be back after the New Year.

Finally I have a moment to write and can say something about Lian. Her condition was of course apparent immediately to Edvard, but to my surprise he seemed almost to take it with a sense of humor.

"Well, young Henry," he said to her. "You managed to bamboozle us very well. Of course, as I look more closely at you, it seems obvious that you could be a girl just as well as a boy in those pajamas. You must stay on until you have your child, and then, afterwards, we shall see what we shall see." He glanced at me and then said more heartily to her, "*Velkommen til oss!*" It was a phrase we never used on the *Matilde,* but now that we had our own house, I'd taken the Bergen family's expression up again and encouraged Edvard to do the same. Now Lian repeated it back, with a relieved smile: "*Velkommen til oss.*" She knew it meant something friendly and kind in Norwegian. Welcome to our house, welcome to our family, welcome to us.

Edvard told me privately it would be a nice thing to have a baby in the house, even though we must have a plan for Lian after the infant was old enough to travel. There was the uncle in Butte, wasn't there? I told him that we could discuss all this in the new year, when he was home again, not wishing to go into the whole story.

Before Edvard left, we tried again to make our own baby. I was glad to have my grizzled old man in my arms and to feel his strength returning.

December 5

Lian cried out in the night, and I rose immediately. I made sure she was not suffering anything but ordinary labor pains and then set out for Adele's rooms above her shop. It was a terrible wet night, the rain slashing down like small knives. But at least no one was about at two a.m. to ask what I was doing with a coat over my flannel nightgown and a stout umbrella nearly jerked out of my hands by wind. Half an hour later there were two stout umbrellas traversing the return path up Morgan Hill.

When Jan was born, in Bremen, as we took on a cargo, I had the benefit of a spotless ward in a small German hospital and the luxury of two crisply aproned nurses and a practiced doctor whose small goatee between my knees I still recall with a smile. Edvard hovered anxiously outside the door and rushed in as soon as he heard the cry that announced his first-born. Agnete's birth was far less comfortable. She came quickly, three weeks early, in the roiling Atlantic Ocean, assisted into the world by Edvard and Kjell and the cook, who brought hot water. We had set off from Norway in the *Matilde* with the expectation of being in Lima by the time Agnete was born. Instead the seas off Chile became her grave, three months later. One of the seamen had contracted typhus in Valparaíso when we docked to take on supplies. He and two others died as well.

Today a cry pierced my house, a home that had seen no children since it was built. It was the same cry with which each of us entered the world. Adele, worn and bloody with her midwifery, wiped the screaming red baby girl with a damp towel, wrapped her in a clean cloth, and held her to Lian's breast. The former Henry broke into tears of happiness, and Adele and I began to cry as well, with exhaustion yes, but also joy.

She is a fine baby, with eyes like her mother's, and no trace of the Scottish doctor.

Susan is her name. I recognized the choice immediately from one of the frontier romances Lian and I had both read. Susan was a heroine we both admired, quick-witted and spunky, able to shoot a deer or a man, and to knock back a glass of whiskey with the best of them. It was when Lian said firmly, "I will call her Susan," that I realized Lian had no intention of seeking a place in our Chinatown. She knew she would be ostracized by her own people. The name was as clear an indication as any that she was throwing in her lot with me and Adele and with the white devils of Port Townsend.

Adele said, "Susan is a beautiful name," and I knew she was thinking the same thing.

"Susan it is," I said. We could not register the baby's birth at the courthouse, but somehow we would need to have her christened.

December 16

Today I visited Emma Smith, not during the usual afternoon calling hours, but in the morning. I found her with her cook, in the parsonage's large, light kitchen, in a frenzy of baking. The scent of butter, eggs, sugar, and cinnamon put me in mind of my aunt and uncle's in Bergen, for Aunt Inger always entertained magnificently over the holidays. I set to helping Emma and her cook for an hour, until the last batch of cookies had come out of the oven. I'd forgotten there was to be a small Christmas gathering at the church later today—for the widows and single women of the congregation. I was glad, I told her, that Edvard's safe return kept me from the unfortunate ranks of widows but said I would be glad to serve refreshments if needed. I then asked if I might speak to her alone a few moments.

Emma, daughter of one Methodist minister and wife of another, had seen something of the world and even more of human nature. She had traveled around the Horn to California with three boys and then eventually up to Port Townsend. Two of the boys had gone to seminaries in the East (the third son had initially run off with a circus, but then had returned to Seattle to study natural sciences at the new University of Washington). She is worldly and sympathetic, yet when I told her that my Chinese houseboy Henry had turned out to be a young girl, a pregnant girl who had just given birth a few days ago in my house to a baby of mixed race, Emma Smith could not help but show her dismay, and then a moral sternness I had suspected but not yet seen in her.

"Mrs. Bergland—Dagny. Pardon me if I offend you, but please be honest. Is Mr. Fossen the father? Is that why he left home so abruptly?"

Blood rushed to my face, but I controlled my voice. "Kjell was as ignorant as I that our Henry was a girl. He was simply struck by gold fever, like the rest of them, and when Edvard refused to take him to Alaska, he asked and received my permission to go to Skagway. And before you ask, my husband is not the father either. Lian was violated on the ship traveling from Hong Kong to Canada. Passing as a boy was safest for her, and doubtless she would have continued that charade had she not had the baby to worry about."

"I apologize, Dagny," Emma said after a moment, but she still looked unhappy. "Are you proposing to keep her on as your servant? With the child?"

"Yes," I said, though it was the first time I had decided that firmly. "At least until she has a profession. Adele Pennybaker is

teaching Lian fine sewing and says she can become a dressmaker."
I paused. "I come to you asking just one question: will you talk
to your husband and see if the baby can be christened? And
quietly?"

Emma didn't look completely shocked at this request, but
squared her shoulders and said, "Leave it to me. And, Dagny,
not a word of this to anyone today. I'll see you at three o'clock
here—to help with the refreshments."

So Lian's daughter was christened Susan in Trinity Methodist
early one morning in a private ceremony, with only me and
Adele to witness it, along with Ah Song, who came bearing a red
envelope of money. When Reverend Smith asked if there was a
middle or last name, I had to explain that to Lian. I suggested she
give Susan a Chinese name to reflect her dual heritage. Maybe
her mother's name? She shook her head. Her mother had, after
all, agreed to sell her to one of Uncle's acquaintances.

"What is your middle name?" she asked me.

"Berit," I said.

"Then I choose Berit. To honor you."

Susan Berit. Thus it was written in the church register. But
not recorded in any other public record.

The four of us—Lian, Ah Song, Adele, and me, with little
Susan Berit hidden under Adele's wide cloak—went back to the
house in the gray dawn. A few people saw us, I suppose, and
wondered, but the fine ladies of the town were all still abed,
and that was what mattered. We had an excellent breakfast of
pancakes and eggs, and then Lian cleaned the kitchen, and Ah
Song and Adele went off to work, and I sat at the big walnut
table in the dining room with Susan Berit in my left arm, writing
here in my journal.

December 23

Lian has remained of somewhat ambiguous sex. She emerged a
few days ago as Henry in Uptown and made some purchases at
the grocery store. She looked the same as before in her padded
coat and trousers, queue and cap. Whoever looked at her saw only

one thing: Chinese. But at home now she is a nursing mother. In the evenings, she sits in the parlor warmed by the coal-burning stove with me and Adele. Adele has taken to bringing work over and Lian sews seams and hems and adds lace to wrists and collars. I mend my clothes or read aloud to practice my English. Sitting around the parlor in the lamplight, with candles at the windows, the three of us with our needles flashing, little Susan in a makeshift cradle (we didn't dare purchase one for fear of rumor but have put her in a drawer) when she isn't being held or nursed, make a cozy scene. I must reflect on how different it is from last Christmas, my first in Port Townsend, when Edvard was still at sea and I sat here alone or with Kjell, who read his Bible or accompanied me on the piano with his fiddle.

For all that Edvard spoke optimistically of Christmas parties and made sure I had a party dress, there were no invitations last year and only one this year, to Cecilia Barker's house for a lavish buffet and dance. I had to send regrets. I supposed that once again Edvard would be delayed returning from San Francisco. He'd wired two weeks ago when he first arrived, and then a week later, but with little detail. "Complications with Olafsson keep me here longer. Will return as soon as I can."

I wondered if the Puget Mill Company here in Port Gamble would be as understanding as I was that their lumber schooner's return was delayed. In the meanwhile I found myself content in the company of two women and a baby. If Edvard did not come home, we would have ourselves a perfectly fine Christmas dinner here. Adele's brother Knox had moved to Seattle with his family recently, and Adele had not the leisure to go over to join them for the holiday.

It was close to nine o'clock last night, and Adele was preparing to go, lingering just a moment in her coat and hat in the hallway to tell me an amusing story she'd just remembered about one of the local ladies, and confirming she would return tomorrow evening for dinner. We both heard a heavy step on the porch, and the thump of a bag being set down.

"Edvard!" I said and opened the door, but it was a stranger who stood dripping with rain on the mat, in a bearskin coat and fur hat, and a thick blond moustache and beard. He was clumsily trying to remove his boots with his gloves still on.

"Mor Dagny, don't you know me?" Mother Dagny, the old name I had bid him call me in Lima as a boy.

It was our Kjell, returned to us, and the reason he still had on his gloves was because they were harder to remove than they used to be. He had lost most of his little finger to frostbite. Fortunately, as he said, it was his bowing hand, and he had never wanted to play the piano.

December 26

Yesterday was Susan Berit's first Christmas and although she will not remember it, I hope she remembers how much she is loved. Kjell took to her immediately, just the way he had my own baby girl Agnete once. As an orphan, he has a special fondness for little children and unlimited patience. Of course he was astonished that first evening and the next day (laying to rest any suspicions Emma Smith had roused in me about Susan's parentage) to find Henry changed into Lian, and Lian a mother.

"*Jaaaaaa ... Du verden*," was all he said in Norwegian. Occasionally he added "Gee Willikers," which is English for the same feeling of surprise.

Details of Kjell's grand adventure came out only gradually over the next days, and it was clear some parts of it caused him embarrassment and sorrow. But it was also clear that he was changed in ways that made him more of a man. His speech was larded with new English words for which he had no Norwegian equivalent: *bunko men, hurdy-gurdy girls, tenderfoots,* and *sourdoughs.* He had in fact been speaking English non-stop for four months and outshone us all when it came to all the latest phrases, snapped out with quite a convincing American accent. He shaved the beard off but left the moustache and kept his hair longer than before. His gait was heavier, as he had put on some weight, but he was just as graceful, as befitting a man who'd grown up serving meals on ships and more recently been a waiter in saloons packed with gamblers and hell-raisers. In that he was much like Lian, who moved economically and swiftly wherever she found herself.

Again, I write Kjell's story as I wrote Edvard's, never having seen the places they mention or having, indeed, a good idea of the geography or, in some cases, the spelling.

Back in August Kjell had shipped as a dining room steward on the battered old *Castlekeep,* a coal steamer built in Glasgow that had only been given a lick, not a polish. Coal dust drifted around the passengers as they attempted to sleep in rough racks of berths, hastily hammered together from pine and fir. The carpenters had been instructed to use as few nails as possible, so that the berths could be dismantled in Skagway and sold as building lumber. Like all the vessels sailing to the goldfields, the *Castlekeep* was overcrowded, and the two cooks had a hard time feeding the passengers on any sort of regular timetable. The dining room had only ten tables, so the service went on from six a.m. to eleven p.m., with breakfast turning into lunch turning into dinner. Plates barely had time to be rinsed before new "glop," as Kjell says, was spooned over potatoes or bread. He was on his feet at least fourteen hours a day and the promised hour off in the afternoon never materialized. He had barely enough time to eat a meal himself.

Still, he wasn't unhappy—he was off to the goldfields! All day long he listened to men (and a few women) talking about what they knew, what they'd need, and the best ways of getting to Dawson as fast as possible. The passengers were divided in that some planned to climb up the Chilkoot Trail, even though it was almost perpendicular. The rest planned to buy or rent pack horses or mules and take the longer but less steep route over White Pass. The men were from all walks of life— architects, lawyers, bank clerks, loggers, longshoremen, railway workers. Some were well-off, some athletic looking, some were half-derelict and counting on a fairytale. He listened and paid attention all the way from Port Townsend up to the Linn Canal, a fjord that ended at Skagway.

"It reminded me of Norway, narrow and clear blue and steep mountains on either side. But already, just a few weeks after the first ships had landed, the forests above the tidal flats were half stripped of their trees to build a town. The sawing and hammering echoed everywhere, along with the men shouting and swearing, and the mules and horses and dogs all making a racket on shore. Is it any reason we were all half crazy and confused even before we got off the *Castlekeep*? We were dumped into the shallow water—there was no real dock—and our possessions thrown down into scows. Crates smashed, chickens drowned, glass shattered, small chests and trunks burst open, and clothes floated off in the water. What remained of our belongings was tossed from the scows onto the beach, where it was either stolen or submerged by the tide.

"I managed only because I had made a friend onboard, a fellow named Johnny Stevens, also from Port Townsend. We stuck together like glue and one of us always had our eye on our wooden chests and knapsacks. We had both decided to go the White Pass route and before anything else we needed a horse. I knew very little about horses and he claimed to know a lot, so I gave him some money and he came back with a horse that we decided to call Maggie, after a horse Johnny had once owned."

Later, Kjell was sorry they had named the horse. It made what Maggie had to go through and what they had to see that much more painful.

Johnny had brought more or less the same things that Kjell did: dried pemmican, tins of sardines, and biscuits for the week it would take to get up the divide to Lake Bennett, a fishing rod to catch dinner in the rivers and lakes, and a rifle to kill game. They had bedrolls and one change of clothes and some extra socks, a shaving razor and soap, a canteen, and between them a collapsible shovel, a pickaxe and two gold pans. They congratulated themselves when they saw all the mess of stuff other people had, that they were traveling light. They exchanged their wooden chests for saddlebags, and without hanging around Skagway more than a few hours, set off. They planned to walk all day and most of the first night at least—the sky was so light. No matter that it was drizzling. The important thing, they knew, was to get to the goldfields and stake their claims as soon as possible so they could work them during the fall and winter and make their fortune.

Yes, it was drizzling when they set out and raining or drizzling the whole week that Kjell and Johnny were on that muddy trail. They went maybe eight miles during that time. The trail was forty-five miles long. Deceptively easy to begin with, it narrowed to the width of only two men and crawled up steep slopes and plunged down again through rocks to canyons. The steady stream of people and horses, often hauling loads far too heavy for their broken-down backs, made progress slow through the churning mud. Often, when a horse fell over a cliff or broke its leg and had to be shot, the whole vast train came juddering to a halt. Kjell and Johnny didn't sleep much—not because it was the midnight sun—but because there were few places to stop and build a fire or lay down. If you stepped off the trail for a moment, someone would take your place in line, it was that tightly packed.

Maggie gave out after five days, frothed at the mouth, and sank to her knees. Even though Johnny whipped her and got down on his knees and begged her, she wouldn't get up. The people behind them didn't care—they began stepping right over Maggie and even on top of Maggie, until finally Maggie just closed her eyes and died there. After that, the men coming behind kicked her off the trail, to join the other dead animals all along the mountain sides and valleys.

Kjell said he threw up everything in his stomach and was so dizzy he almost fell off a cliff himself under the weight of the knapsacks and saddlebags. There was no longer any reason to partner up, without the horse, so Johnny went on and Kjell made his way back to Skagway. He sold the saddlebags and everything in them. There were others who did the same, in fact, most of them had to abandon the quest to get to the top of White Pass with their pack animals, so many horses died. Kjell never saw Johnny again, never knew if he'd fallen or died on the trail or if he'd come back eventually to Skagway himself and left on one of the ships.

Kjell could have found a ship going south; he thought about it. Why didn't he? He was down but not out, he said. That was why he didn't write me in Port Townsend; he didn't want to return without his claim, without his gold. Klondike fever hadn't left him yet. It was stoked by the resolve of the five thousand people who now packed Skagway and planned to wait— or were forced for lack of money to wait—until the rain turned to heavy snow and the mud froze too, so that you could walk on top of it or run a wagon over it. It wouldn't be long, people said. November or December at the latest, the trail up and over White Pass would be fine, and some fellows were working on widening it, so teams of oxen and horses could pull wagons to the top.

Kjell found a job as a waiter in a restaurant run by a widow, Mrs. Asa Gurdy, who had arrived in the summer with two young children and a hundred dollars and several cases of beans, dried hams, and onions, along with tin cups, plates, and forks. She set up in a tent with two tables and six chairs. By September she had multiplied those hundred dollars into a thousand and had paid for the building of a ramshackle restaurant. The "grub," as Kjell called it, wasn't anything special, but she had surprising means of obtaining all kinds of meat (it was wise not to ask; fresh-killed horsemeat tasted much like beef when it was in a heavy gravy) and had cornered the market on biscuits and beans.

Just like on the ship, Kjell worked long hours, but he was satisfied to do it. Mrs. Gurdy treated him "fair and square." He set up a tent next to her small family's tent behind the restaurant. His many years at sea made him naturally tidy, and she was impressed he was a churchgoer even in these rough surroundings. Although Mrs. Gurdy wasn't a teetotaler herself, she didn't serve liquor. She employed a man named Bert to do nothing but keep an eye on the customers. They had to throw out some fellows who were too "lickered up." Or quarrelsome. Bert carried double pistols on a holster belt, even though he never had occasion to use them. That people *did* use their guns was not in dispute; every night you could hear shooting in the streets. Outright premeditated murder was unusual; fights that led to shooting and counter-shooting usually had something to do with the "hurdy-gurdy girls" or "cardsharps."

"People say Port Townsend is the worst Sodom of all the ports in America." Kjell shook his head. "But there is nothing like Skagway. I never saw a policeman, though I did see men hung for theft. Someone hung them."

But Kjell kept his head down and saved his money, including pinches of gold dust that some customers offered as tips just as freely as if it was snuff. Yes, there were still some in Skagway who had money from prospecting, and they helped keep alive the dream that, soon, a new group of lucky miners would cart out bags of nuggets and "pokes" of gold dust from behind the steep rampart of mountains that sealed off the Yukon from the coast.

In late November, with snow freezing over the mud on the ground, Kjell bade good-bye to Mrs. Gurdy, and a new understanding of what would be required. He bought food at cost from Mrs. Gurdy and re-outfitted himself with a bearskin coat and fur hat and thick gloves and thicker socks. He didn't buy a horse but scouted out a packer who would transport his gear by ox wagon. The trail was wider now, hard-packed, and thronged with similarly outfitted men. Kjell walked behind the wagon, carrying only enough food and water for the day.

It was encouragingly clear the day he set out, and he slept inside the wagon with the driver under a mound of blankets and looked at the stars. The next day was harder and steeper, but still he walked on with a good heart, buoyed by the thought of the goldfields. Later that afternoon a blizzard blew up, and he fell behind and lost sight of the wagon. He found himself sitting down with some thought of trying to build a fire and for that reason taking off his glove. That's all he remembers. A wagon heading back down the trail almost ran over him, but stopped in time and took him to town, back to Mrs. Gurdy. He lay in the camp bed with bronchitis for two weeks while she fed him soup. A doctor amputated most of his little finger. "My gear is still probably up at the top where the wagon left it," Kjell said. "Buried under snow until spring."

After that, Kjell's gold lust was over. He found a berth as a steward again on a steamship returning to Seattle. From there he came straight to Port Townsend, leaving, as he said, his dreams and his finger behind in Alaska.

December 31

And so the year 1897 comes to an end. I arrive at the end of this journal and find that I wish to keep writing. Edvard told me he would bring a new leather *dagbok* from San Francisco. Meanwhile I can report that, between Edvard's tales of sailing up to the Arctic and back again, and the difficulties the stampeders faced in getting themselves and their outfits up the Yukon before "freeze-up," and Kjell's hair-raising stories of conditions at Skagway and White Pass, we are far more knowledgeable than the majority of dreamers who continue to sail and steam their way up north from Tacoma, Seattle, and Port Townsend, ever hopeful with their exorbitant "outfits" of shovels, picks, pans, and tins of food. The Mounties have now issued stern instructions and a long list of supplies required, a year's supplies they reckon, for everyone who crosses into Canadian territory—as all must who travel to the Yukon. While the newspapers now carry a few warning reports from journalists who escaped from Dawson on a boat before the rivers froze or who mushed back to safety on dog sleds, most of the advertisements continue to entice. For every headline, "Men Who Rush to Goldmines Find There Are No Mines for Them," or "Suffering in Yukon County: Starvation in Dawson," there are ten times as many articles about hordes of people getting off trains in Seattle from all across the country and all around the world, making the merchants wealthy with their immediate need for these Klondike Kits. And the advertisements paint an even rosier picture, showing men in hunting clothing and furs striding cheerfully through the snow.

A story is circulating—Kjell heard it first in Skagway and now people speak of it here—that a man named Sheldon Jackson has convinced the War Department of a scheme to transport five hundred reindeer and their Lappish herders from the north of Norway to Alaska. The reindeer are meant to pull sleds full of supplies to the people of Dawson, after which the animals will be slaughtered for food.

Kjell tried to imagine how the government planned to transport the reindeer all that distance. Surely the beasts could not get there in time to help Dawson?

Edvard had told me that he'd seen a few reindeer up in Norton Sound. There are two or three reindeer stations in Alaska. Apparently, some Laplanders came over a few years ago, in order to teach the native people how to herd. The reindeer were imported from Siberia, which lies not far from Alaska. I told Kjell that when I was a girl in Norway, I had seen illustrations of Laplanders in Finnmark, wearing fur coats and hats, snug in sleighs being drawn by one or two reindeer or tied together in caravans, traveling over the snow.

Kjell shook his head, "Yes, but how will the Laplanders in Finnmark get to the Yukon in time to help the miners? It's impossible."

Our former cabin boy and steward has become a man of twenty-one who speaks with the authority of someone who knows what he has seen. Although much of what Kjell went through was painful, he is realizing that even though he led an adventurous life by most standards before he went to Alaska, his experiences in Skagway are now what will mark him all his days in the eyes of others. When we went to Trinity Methodist on Sunday, Kjell was mobbed by the young men. He was no longer a Norwegian with a nice baritone and "singsong" accent. He was a stampeder.

Yes, he was a stampeder and has lived to tell the tale. He has no gold nuggets and no little finger, but he has his life. He says he thinks of buying a farm this spring out in Chimacum. For when he took the "poke" of gold dust he'd collected as a waiter to the bank, it turned out to be worth quite a lot.

January 14, 1898

A few last pages left, and I must write here because Edvard forgot to buy me a new journal in his rush to leave San Francisco on the tide and return post-haste to Port Townsend to face questions about Clarence Harrison and his iron safe.

Edvard was right: Clarence Harrison did have a change of heart. He realized if he put out the story of his brother Jeff being in league with Lloyd Quayle that Jeff would surely go to jail. Apparently, Mr. Harrison, when he did not hear from Edvard, wrote to Carl Olafsson to ask for the information about the captain of the *Fidelius*. Thus he heard that the ship had gone down at Ripple Rock. Clarence Harrison must have seen an opportunity to concoct a story that might save his brother and perhaps convince the investors in his bank that the money had been stolen by the ship's captain and could be refunded.

It was all because Edvard didn't go to the police right away when he returned from Alaska in November, and because he didn't make a clean breast of things to Carl Olafsson about taking payment directly from Harrison. With the safe at the bottom of Seymour Narrows there is no proof it was empty. Harrison contacted the Port Townsend police and now an investigation will begin. Edvard has been suspended from his job with the Puget Mill Company and will not be captaining the *Lester* later this month.

I ask myself, how did we land in this dire situation: our bank account frozen, the accusation publicly aired in the newspaper, Edvard possibly going to jail or having to pay Harrison for this supposed loss? The word "deportation" has come up, along with "foreigners."

Before now I never cared about becoming an American citizen, never saw the value of it. I always thought that I would persuade Edvard to return to Norway, that we would live in Bergen near Katrine, perhaps raise more children, in a country that was our home, in a language that was our own. Now I understand that we are foreigners here and it does not help our legal cause to remain so. Yet are we to become Americans merely to defend ourselves from false accusations?

We have hired a lawyer, and Edvard has not been arrested. He is not in jail. That is all that matters now.

The Second Journal
Port Townsend

March 1898 - June 1898

Another unusual occurrence in a town where unusual events seem to be a way of life. I suppose that is because we are a port town, half lawless, full of arrivals and departures, not all of them entirely voluntary, a town almost entirely run by men on the make and people pretending to be other than they are, having conveniently left their histories behind them.

Still, this event strikes me as particularly extraordinary and more welcome than the ordinary comings and goings, involving as it does the arrival of a number of my countrymen and women at Fort Townsend, three miles out of town. True, some in my country would not think of them as true Norwegians, given their exotic dress, their nomadic way of life, and their attachment to their own language and customs. But *I* find myself quite curious, even thrilled to know that a group of Laplanders from Norway landed today at the barracks of the decommissioned fort, even if they are only to stay for a month or so before heading north to Alaska.

Most of them are women and children of the reindeer-herding families brought over from Finnmark to America a few weeks ago, along with their pack animals, to help the people of Dawson City. Now it turns out that the rescue attempt has been more or less abandoned given the march of time and circumstance in the Yukon. Over the winter many stampeders left Dawson City in a panic and others have not yet arrived there, stalled as they are by snow on the shores of Lake Bennett at the mouth of the Yukon River. Skagway is well supplied with food now, though the cost is exorbitant. In short, no pack trains of reindeer are needed in Alaska in the same way they were thought to be in December. The reindeer, over five hundred in number, and their colorful herders have been waiting in Seattle for instructions as to where they should go and what they should do next. According to the Seattle newspapers, the Laplanders have been a complete sensation in the city. Last Sunday thousands of people arrived by streetcar, bicycle, and foot to see them at Woodland Park.

Surely this is a story that newspapers in Norway would pay well to receive. I must get to Fort Townsend as soon as possible.

In beginning this new journal I realize that I leave a gap from where the last one ended, in mid-January. I simply had no time to continue. To summarize briefly, we hired a big, boisterous lawyer, Mr. Arnold Baxter, one of those Americans whose confidence shines in his face so aggressively. Mr. Baxter met with the judge and told him that there was no evidence of theft other than Clarence Harrison's feeble accusation. Let Harrison bring his ridiculous claim to the court in Port Townsend. Let witnesses be called. Let Lloyd Quayle and Jeff Harrison be called. Let the trial proceed! Mr. Arnold Baxter wagered that Clarence Harrison was a coward who would buckle immediately, and Mr. Baxter relished the thought of demolishing him.

The charges were dropped—for now anyway—yet all this took time. Edvard was temporarily dismissed from his position as captain on the Port Ludlow–San Francisco lumber ship run, but once Edvard was free from taint, Mr. Talbot of the Puget Mill Company had no qualms about hiring him back. Talbot had lost a large number of workers to the gold rush. Millhands, bookkeepers, and sailing crew had all walked off the job, often overnight. In February Edvard was offered a job sailing to Hawaii with a load of lumber. Again it was a schooner, which meant it would take three months to complete the round trip. There was a great deal to make ready for such a voyage across the Pacific and Edvard was down at the docks every day.

One thing has changed since last year. Kjell no longer resents the fact that he has become a landlubber. After his adventures in the fall and winter in Alaska, he's had no desire to travel anywhere. His small stash of gold dust was enough to purchase ten acres from a farmer on Chimacum Creek, about eight or nine miles from town. He does not wish to leave Port Townsend and our home yet, for there is no house on his parcel of land, but he intends to purchase a horse and wagon and to plant crops this spring. It is a fine piece of property. Lian thinks so as well, for she is a farmer's daughter, and though their crop in China is mainly rice, her family also grew many vegetables and raised some chickens and a pig in good years. For the moment Kjell still helps around the house, but he is also working four days a week—the evening hours—at one of the saloons belonging to Mr. Barker. There he continues to make a good deal in tips, for the mood is optimistic. There are still people taking passage for the Yukon. They continue to come from as far away as England and Russia.

Edvard left for the Hawaiian Islands the last week of February. Now we are back to rather quiet evenings. Lian is becoming an excellent seamstress, and Adele often comes by to give her fine work and teach her more. It has become known that we have a baby in the house, but Mrs. Smith has said Edvard and I took in the infant temporarily from a destitute widow as an act of Christian charity. Although it pains me to hear little Susan Berit referred to in this fashion, I have acquiesced to the false story for fear of any harm coming to Lian. Her status as Henry was illegal but tolerated. As a single woman she could be deported back to China quite easily.

I, of course, have no more friends than I used to because of what is seen as the irregular household I keep. Emma Smith is friendly (I now attend Trinity Methodist, out of gratitude for her help), but Cecilia Barker has been scarce of late. Kjell has heard that his employer Mr. Barker is under investigation for smuggling opium and liquor from Canada, so as not to pay duty.

Adele is a true friend and Lian is a great comfort. Still, I long for more varied conversation. Conversation in my own tongue, with people who know my country. I hope to visit the Laplanders' camp as soon as possible.

March 19

Today I hired a buggy to drive to Fort Townsend. The distance of three miles is one I could have easily traversed by foot, but the day was damp and the road muddy after continual rain and mist. All around me, as I drove, the thick fir and cedar forests dripped with rain. Fort Townsend was built some decades ago before the town began to grow. Although the buildings remain, the fort was decommissioned due to the lack of sufficient water (though that seems hard to believe on a day such as this). The Laplanders are lodged in the old barracks. Descending from the buggy, I could see any number of folk on the long, covered porch and steps of this dormitory building. Others walked about. There were no men, but a few older boys wore extraordinarily large hats, square in shape with four high points, stuffed with something like eiderdown. Some of the points drooped a little with wear. I recalled I'd seen these hats in the newspapers from Seattle and thought that they reminded me of jesters' caps. They did not wear furs but seemed warmly dressed in wool and tanned leather.

A one-armed man with a soldier's bearing came out to greet me and ask my business. This was Mr. Dahl, who had been hired to supervise the Laplanders. He was originally from Norway, where he had learned the Lappish language. He immediately began to converse in Norwegian and, once he knew my purpose, said he would introduce me to some of the women. He mentioned that one of them, Elle-Ristine Persdatter, spoke good Norwegian, and he went off to find her.

I confess, I was eager to meet a real Lappish lady and talk to her. While I waited by the stairs of the porch, I ventured a few words with the children, who only stared shyly at me, and with their young mothers. No one seemed to understand much of what I said, which surprised me. I confess I thought that, being from Norway, they would all be conversant in the language. Unlike Edvard, I had never seen a Laplander before. Most of them were short-statured, and many had high cheekbones and dark straight hair. Like the Chinese, some had a pronounced fold above their eyes, but the color of their irises ranged from blue to brown.

The young women wore dresses of thick, woven material, which came to below their knees and revealed calves covered in wool leggings and feet shod in tanned leather shoes without heels, something like the moccasins worn by the Indians, but more substantial. The toes of the moccasins curled up and around the ankles were wrapped brightly woven bands, connecting the shoes and the leggings. Colorful too were the women's plaid shawls: reds, blues, yellows, and greens. Their simple cloth bonnets were red; they fit tightly on their heads and covered the hair, except for a braid that hung down the back. The dresses were belted below the waist and from these belts dangled an array of objects: a knife sheathed in reindeer horn, inscribed with patterns or figures of people or reindeer; scissors and bone needle cases; a soft pouch or two. The women struck me as serious but not sober. Alert, curious, and no one's fool. They also seemed friendly, and several offered me a smile. The smallest children were like children everywhere, bashful behind their mothers' skirts, a reasonable caution considering all they'd experienced in the last two months. The older boys were curious but did not speak to me. They too wore dresses of a sort, but shorter, with a belt and leggings.

By the time everyone in the dormitory had come out to look me over, the porch had grown rather crowded, so I stepped back off the stairs to the walkway, and it was here I encountered Elle-Ristine. Accompanied by Mr. Dahl, she came walking around the side of the building, leading a most peculiar beast, white of fur and knobby of knee, with a straight-up tail and a long bony head, rather like a camel's, with small ears, a muzzle, and large, dark eyes. It appeared to be something between a large, long-legged, cloven-hoofed dog and a miniature cow. After a few seconds I realized it was a reindeer, minus the branching antlers one always sees in photographs and drawings. The animal wore a harness of plaited wood in festive colors and seemed perfectly docile.

"May I present Mrs. Elle-Ristine Persdatter Aikio," said Mr. Dahl, and the young woman and I shook hands. Her fingers were strong. She wore a simple wedding band, like mine. She was in her early twenties, I guessed. Her face already had faint lines from her outdoor life; it was a round face with a slightly upturned nose and dark blue eyes. She had on the same tightly fitting cap as many of the others; it was faded red, patterned in white flowers, with a thin line of lace around the face. She appeared to be a sturdy girl, steady on her feet, a bit thick about the middle from the heavy wool dress. Almost immediately I felt a strong liking for her, as well as a sense that she would be a good "source," as they say in newspaper writing. This sense increased once we fell into conversation. Elle-Ristine expresses herself clearly and confidently, without the apologies and discursiveness of many young women. Her Norwegian is excellent, though her dialect is that of Northern Norway. At times you hear a different rhythm, soft under the Norwegian tones.

I expressed surprise to see a reindeer here in Fort Townsend—I thought they had all gone north by ship to Alaska. Elle-Ristine explained about milking and said that Leksu, for the reindeer had a name, was very dear to her. Hesitantly I stroked the reindeer's back. Leksu had short fur, rough but pleasing to the touch. Elle-Ristine explained that each of the reindeer's hairs are hollow—the better to insulate from the cold. The all-white color of the animal is something special among the Laplanders. Elle-Ristine had been given Leksu as a wedding present three years ago, and the reindeer had always brought her luck. I thought the animal had remarkable eyes, dark brown and rounded or convex. They gave the impression of being able to see forward and behind and to the side, even as she bent her head and investigated my shoes as possible food. A necessary trait, those all-seeing eyes, I suppose, if a reindeer does not wish to be the dinner of a wolf or wolverine.

I explained that I hoped to write something about the Relief Expedition for a Norwegian newspaper, and Elle-Ristine expressed a willingness to speak to me. She seemed eager as well to find out as much as possible about this strange new world in which she found herself. Mr. Dahl offered us a room in a separate building where he lives and sat down with us.

The interview began rather awkwardly, given that Mr. Dahl was listening in. I soon learned, however, that the Laplanders had not been informed that after leaving Woodland Park that they would be split into two groups, with all the women and children and some of the older boys men to be left here at Fort Townsend, away from the herd and their husbands and brothers and sons, who would accompany the reindeer to Alaska. Here at the fort the women and children had only a short time to bid farewell to their men, with the awful realization that it would be a long time before they would see them again.

"When we signed our contracts two months ago in Norway,"

Elle-Ristine said, "we thought we were going to Alaska and would be there in a few weeks. We were told there was plenty of reindeer lichen in Alaska. I had no idea then how far away Alaska was. In Seattle they put all the reindeer in a sailing ship, the *Seminole.* Now the ship must be towed to Alaska by a tugboat. A good deal of lichen was lost in New Jersey and more in Seattle. If the journey takes too long, the reindeer will starve to death."

At this point, Mr. Dahl asserted firmly, "I understand that the tugboat is the best way to get the reindeer to Dyea as soon as possible. Everyone has the interests of the herd at heart. That is why no expense has been spared in transportation, even at such a difficult time, when the government is in need of ships for the war with Spain."

I heard the lecturing tone in Mr. Dahl's voice and Elle-Ristine heard it too. She said firmly, "Our contracts said one thing. The reality is now different."

"You need not worry, Mrs. Aikio. We all have the best interests of your group at heart."

A skeptical look passed fleetingly over Elle-Ristine's face, but she said nothing more.

If we were to continue the interview, I must change the subject. I asked where she came from in Finnmark and about her upbringing. She willingly told me that she had been born twenty-three years ago in Karasjok to a Laplander mother and a Norwegian trader from Alta. She told me that among themselves a Laplander is called a *Sáme* and in the plural *Sámit.* She was the only child, after her younger brother's death from measles when he was three. She had spent some years in Alta and had been able to study there, which is why she knew Norwegian as well as the *Sáme* language used in Finnmark. After her father's death her mother returned with Elle-Ristine to Karasjok. Her mother had then died a few years ago, after which Elle-Ristine married. Her husband Mikkel, also from Karasjok, had gone up to Alaska with the other men and reindeer.

Soon Mr. Dahl was called to other matters and Elle-Ristine and I were able to speak at greater length. I wrote down a good deal, but still had more questions. She had questions for me as well. Where did I come from in Norway? How did I come to be in America and did I plan to stay? She knew I was a married woman. Was my husband Norwegian as well? Ah, a sea captain, from Ålesund. She had never been south of Alta on the coast but would like to see those cities someday. Did I have children? When I told her no, she impulsively took my hand. She was with child herself, she said. It would be her first. "Born in America," Elle-Ristine added with a shy smile. "I have brought a cradle, the one my family used for my brother and me. I will show you sometime."

I asked if she had seen Port Townsend yet, and she shook her head. But she had seen New Jersey and Chicago from the train, small towns in the Midwest and sod houses and log cabins in the Dakotas and Montana. She had seen Seattle, though only briefly. Most of the time the group had been at Woodland Park and Seattle's population came to them.

When Mr. Dahl returned, I asked if I might be able to invite Elle-Ristine to my home for the night. Elle-Ristine was eager to visit the town, and I promised to return her the next day. However Mr. Dahl refused, for now. He wanted the Laplanders to settle in a bit first and then he would decide how many at a time could visit the town under his supervision. Elle-Ristine shook her head slightly but did not dispute with him. She asked me to come back to Fort Townsend when I could, and I agreed I would.

I liked her very much. She has awakened a spirit of adventure in me, this young woman in a foreign country, bound for Alaska.

March 30

I've made two more visits to Fort Townsend to see Elle-Ristine and meet more of her companions, very pleasant visits I must say. Most of the time the women are active, weaving on a hand loom or sewing. They drink coffee all day long and speak their own language, which is softer than Norwegian. They laugh often. Few know Norwegian, but they are trying to learn English and use my visits as a chance to practice, pointing out things and asking their names: *boot, horse, reindeer, bucket, cup.* Two women are friends of Elle-Ristine's: Margrete Utsi and Ravna Pulk. They come from a village south of Karasjok: Kautokeino. Margrete has two young children and is a bit bossy, but has a broad smiling face, with a prominent scar on her forehead. She dresses more finely than the rest; her collar, more like a sort of breast cloth, has a geometric design in "tin thread," they tell me. Ravna is quiet and shy and wears a cross around her neck. She is only twenty and married just before they left home, so as to accompany her sweetheart. His mother Inga is traveling with them.

The people are no longer restricted in their movements ("They are guests of the United States government," Mr. Dahl has told me several times. "My one concern is to make sure they come to no harm."), but Mr. Dahl does keep a rather close eye on them when they go to town and limits the parties to four or five people at most. The women do not drink or carouse, but Mr. Dahl still fears the women and children falling into the hands of sailors and white-slave traders. He is attempting to run a sort of school for the children and every Sunday a church service is held. Nothing much has been heard from the men, except for the fact that the *Seminole* did arrive in Dyea. From there the reindeer and herders were moved to Haines Mission.

This was the situation until yesterday, when I received a message at home from Mr. Dahl. He said that Elle-Ristine had taken ill and although he had alerted the doctor assigned to the Laplanders, he feared for her and her baby. From this I deduced that Elle-Ristine was in danger of a miscarriage, and I made haste to go to her. By chance Kjell had his wagon and horse in town. He had now begun to gather materials to build his house in the country, and he offered to drive me to Fort Townsend and, if necessary, transport Elle-Ristine back to the house.

In this manner, Elle-Ristine has come to stay with me for some while. I had the doctor at Fort Townsend, Dr. Gambell, on my side. He wants Elle-Ristine in a proper bed in town; she must keep horizontal and not walk about or attempt to do much. Her feet are swollen and that is not a good sign. Mr. Dahl could not say a word against this idea, because it is his job to deliver all the Laplanders safely to Alaska eventually. It is almost too much for the man. Several children have the croup; the women are restive and keep wishing to go to town; the few men are drinking too much (they say Mr. Dahl drinks as well); and everyone is worried about the reindeer herd and herders up in Alaska.

Elle-Ristine was lifted into the wagon carefully, on a makeshift straw mattress, and I sat in back with her to hold her hand. How well I knew the sensation of feeling a baby loosen its grip on life while still in the womb. She had told me she thought she was two months along. She had thought she was only seasick on the ship from Norway, but she knew for certain on the train to Seattle. The cart was bumpy, but she did not complain. She lifted her head from time to time to look out the back of the cart at Leksu. For Leksu was harnessed to the back of the wagon and trotted behind us. Elle-Ristine refused to leave the fort without her. Inside the wagon, serving as pillows for Elle-Ristine's head, were three burlap bags of reindeer lichen, a most precious cargo. Leksu was beginning to eat the spring grass, but it was important she not eat too much, and the grass around the fort was, at any rate, rather sparse because of all the tree saplings and buildings.

If my neighbors of Uptown needed any further reason to gossip about me, which they don't, they had it yesterday, when our strange parade arrived on Morgan Hill, and Kjell and I carried Elle-Ristine inside and up the stairs. Afterwards, Lian was introduced as Henry. She brewed a pot of herbs and encouraged Elle-Ristine drink it, while Kjell attended to the reindeer. For now Leksu will live in our carriage house, though this is probably not the best solution.

April 7

Sadly, in spite of a week of bed rest and herbal tea and loving care, Elle-Ristine lost her child one bloody morning. She makes a brave face of it, but I know this pain intimately. You do not only lose a half-formed baby, you lose a child's hand in yours and the future they might have had. One of her aches is that Mikkel was not nearby when this happened and will not know for weeks that he is no longer to be a father. In her unhappy eyes I see how she wishes she had never left her home in Finnmark.

Lian, still in her role of Henry, takes care of her most devotedly, but we keep Susan Berit out of sight, so as not to pain Elle-Ristine further. The reindeer seems content enough, though the issue of what to feed her if the lichen runs out will be a concern all too soon. I continue to work on my story about Elle-Ristine and the origins of the Yukon Relief Expedition. I have taken the facts from accounts in the Seattle newspapers, from a short interview with Mr. Dahl, and from Elle-Ristine's personal story of the strenuous voyage. I think to publish this article in a Norwegian newspaper, this time directly, without Katrine's help. I don't want too many questions from her about how I came to know so much about Elle-Ristine.

Meanwhile, I've changed the names of Elle-Ristine and Mikkel in the article but left Leksu as I know no other names for reindeer. As to what to call the reindeer herders, I've debated with myself about using Sáme and Sámit, but finally decided on Lappish and Laplander, so that the average Norwegian reader will understand.

In my journal, however, I am switching to Sáme. It seems the right thing.

**From Karasjok to Seattle on the Yukon Relief
Expedition: A Lappish Girl and her Reindeer
Make the Journey to America**
by D.B. Bergland

In December of 1897, stories about Alaska and the Yukon Gold Rush flew like ravens around the snowfields of Finnmark in Norway, from tent to tent in the lands where the nomadic Lapps have long lived with their herds of reindeer. A report even appeared in the *Finnmark Post:* The "gold diggers" in the Yukon were starving and needed help, and the United States was turning to Northern Norway for draft reindeer and herders. Dr. Sheldon Jackson, on behalf of the United States War Department, was to organize this relief expedition to bring food and supplies to the underprepared miners in the Alaskan wilderness. Dr. Jackson enlisted an

American born in Finnmark named William Kjellman, who spoke Norwegian and Lappish. Mr. Kjellman's job was to travel around Northern Norway, to buy as many as five or six hundred draft reindeer, and to recruit herders to drive the beasts westward over the Finnmark Plateau and through the river canyon to Bossekop on the coast of Norway, where a ship would be waiting.

The audacious plan was to load the reindeer onto this ship and to sail across the Atlantic to New York. From there they would be loaded onto trains heading across the vast landscape of America. On the other side, in a place called Seattle, the reindeer would be loaded onto another ship sailing north to Alaska. To accompany the herds, Mr. Kjellman planned to hire at least a hundred Lappish men, accompanied in some cases by their wives and children, to care for the animals. Men of Finnish and Norwegian background were also recruited for the task. They would play an important role once the reindeer got to Alaska and the overland journey began. For this they would receive free passage to Alaska, all their food and drink, and clothing too. They would be employees of the American government and be paid some $25 a month for a one-year contract to deliver the reindeer to the Yukon, after which they would receive free passage home or could stay, as they wished.

Most of the herding families on the Finnmark Plateau had heard of New York, and many had heard of Alaska. Four years ago this same William Kjellman had recruited thirteen Laplanders from Norway to come over to Alaska and teach the Eskimos how to herd the reindeer that had been brought over from Siberia. But this time, the aim was to help the starving miners, and thus draft reindeer were needed in large numbers, along with Lappish herders experienced at handling sledges piled with goods and reindeer to pull them.

Siri Andersdatter, a young Lappish wife, knew as soon as she heard about this scheme, with its promise of adventure and ready money, that her husband Lasse Gaup would want to go. Not just because of the promised monthly payment, but because of the adventure. Like many young men, he had heard of Alaska. Once the reindeer were delivered, he told Siri, they would be in the Yukon. Why shouldn't they find a claim of their own and become wealthy? Siri and Lasse had been married only a few years and had no children. She was twenty-three and he was twenty-five. They lived in a tent near the village of Karasjok. Although Siri came from a family with many reindeer, Lasse was from a poorer family. Siri's parents were both dead, or else they might have persuaded her to stay home.

In the end Siri and Lasse were two of the almost thirty men, women, and children who left Karasjok around the last week of January 1898. They took down their tents and bundled up their sleeping sacks, clothes, iron kettles and knives, wooden bowls and boxes, skis and ski poles, boots and dried hay for stuffing into the boots for warmth, and small mementos and jewelry. They dressed warmly, packed up their sleds and finally, harnessed their reindeer. Siri drove her own sled, pulled by her favorite reindeer, the all-white Leksu, which she had received on her wedding day three years before. She had debated with herself whether it might not be better to leave Leksu behind in view of the possible dangers to come. But she worried that no one in the *siida* would take care of Leksu properly.

Because Siri's father had been a Norwegian and she had been to a Norwegian school in Alta for a few years, she was the one who had to translate the contract that William Kjellman gave to Lasse to sign. Most women went as wives and mothers, but Siri told Kjellman that she wanted to sign a contract of her own, as she would also be working with the reindeer. Kjellman agreed, though her monthly salary was to be only $4.00 a month, while Lasse's, like those of the other men, would be $22.00 a month. There was nothing she could do about it.

Ten days it took them to cross the snowy plateau in their reindeer sleds—strung together in caravans to make it harder to lose sight of each other—driving the reindeer before them. They carried dried lichen with them to feed the reindeer until they arrived in Bossekop, the traditional Lappish marketplace and port outside Alta. Kjellman told them that the ship was being loaded with sixty tons of reindeer lichen, brought north on a ship from Trondheim, for the sea journey. The winds whipped the snowfields with blizzard force, making progress slow. At some points they had to stop driving, set up their tents, and sleep. The sky and moon were invisible on that trip; Siri huddled together with Lasse and tried not to think about what she was leaving behind.

In Bossekop they were joined by about sixty other Laplanders from Kautokeino and other villages in Finnmark, with another twenty-five Norwegians and Finns, mostly young bachelors, who either knew something about reindeer or just wanted the adventure. Altogether there were one hundred and thirteen passengers, including twenty women and twenty-five children. The reindeer numbered over 530, mainly geldings. The storm still raged in Bossekop, making the loading of the lichen very challenging, for it had not been bundled and tied up properly. That the lichen would be sufficient to get the reindeer to Alaska, where lichen grew abundantly, was the most necessary thing in the world. Siri had brought her own large store of lichen for Leksu but had determined not to use it unless there was an emergency. She saw the terror in Leksu's mirror-like convex dark eyes and tried to soothe the animal as best she could. Siri, while she had seen the fjord when she lived in Alta, had never seen such gray waves close up, nor ventured out upon its surface.

Their ship, the *Manitoban,* had come from Scotland. It loomed just offshore like some strange dark animal, swallowing their boxes and bags and sleds in its hold. The reindeer were ferried in rowboats out to a floating platform secured next to the ship. What a strange sight in the blowing snow: hundreds of reindeer, gray and brown and white stepping one after the next up the gang plank into the ship. All of the reindeer had had their antlers sawed off to prevent accidents on board. Siri heard Leksu's bell as the reindeer disappeared.

Loading of people went in more or less the same way later in the day, except for the fact that some of the men were quarrelsome. They had tried to bring four barrels of whiskey aboard for the voyage, but these had been confiscated. Still some men had bottles in their belongings, and these were clearly employed to ease the terror of leaving land.

The man who was organizing the whole expedition for the U.S. government, Dr. Sheldon Jackson, came aboard at the end. A short man with a sharp pointed beard, he seemed as shocked as the Laplanders at the quarters provided for the passengers, who, after all, were now temporary employees of the War Department. While the reindeer were taken to stalls on the middle deck, eight to a stall, the herders and their families were to sleep and eat down in the hull, in open steerage, with no privacy and little comfort. When some of the Laplanders saw the lack of accommodation, they panicked and wanted to go home. But it was too late for that—the ship had orders to get underway as soon as possible. Apparently, Dr. Jackson had been instructed to leave Norway no later than January 15. It was now February 3.

Siri would remember the nightmare of that long voyage across the Atlantic all her life: the dry retching that continued long after the stomach was emptied, the stink of vomit and feces, impossible to clean off clothing and boots, the children's sobs and parents' helplessness, the stark fear in so many eyes, human and animal, when the ship rocked in the heavy waves and boxes slid from one side of the open steerage to the next. Some of the stalls smashed at one point, and the reindeer began to thrash and move and only the barking of the dogs kept them together. It was dark almost twenty hours a day; the sky was dark, the ocean was dark, and the hail and the snow often looked dark too. Off Iceland, the *Manitoban* was struck by a storm that threatened to drive them onto a rocky island, at another point two weeks into the voyage, the captain ordered the engine turned off for some repairs. The sudden halt to the sounds of the boiler and the giant screw that drove the ship forward was one of the most fearsome silences Siri had ever known. In spite of her seasickness, Siri went to the stalls often to feed and comfort Leksu. In the reindeer's dark eyes she remembered home and who she was.

They arrived in New York on February 28, after almost four weeks at sea. Although the travelers stood on deck to see the Statue of Liberty, their ship did not go to Ellis Island. They tied up at the dock at Jersey City; the reindeer were led from the ship to a cattle barge and then to the cattle yards nearby, followed by the Laplanders in their furs, carrying all their possessions. A thousand curious people had come to catch a glimpse of reindeer and the Laplanders, and they cheered to see them. No one told the travelers why the Americans showed such an interest in them and their animals. In their own country they were often scorned. Rail lines ran through the cattle yards and the reindeer were loaded into cars, eighty cars it took to hold them all, along with the unbundled lichen. There were two separate trains for all the Laplanders.

Siri and Lasse were young people, and like all young people, once off the ship and in Pullman cars, with comfortable seats and windows, they recovered their interest in life and were curious and astonished at all they saw. Like almost everyone else from Northern Norway, they had never been on a train before; there were no trains above the Arctic Circle. It took them many days to cross America; they lost track, but it was at least a week. The trains steamed across rivers as broad as any they'd seen at home, but these rivers were packed with steamboats and on their banks rose whole cities of wood, red brick, and yellow sandstone. Philadelphia, Pittsburg, Cleveland, and dozens of smaller towns where they didn't halt but went right through with whistles and flagmen waving. They arrived in Chicago very early in the morning but were not allowed to leave the trains during a stop of three hours. In Milwaukee hundreds of townspeople lined the tracks to see them. Photographers took their pictures and newspapers recorded their journey. Small children shouted, "Klondike!" In several short stops they met copper-skinned Indians, who stood by the train wearing red blankets to meet the people that they had been told were of the same heritage but came from the frozen north. The Indians inspected the caps and moccasins of the travelers, and seemed to see something familiar in the Laplanders, while the Laplanders themselves were curious but a little frightened at the Indians' bare shoulders and painted faces. Here in the American West, the landscape grew lonelier and more desolate. The small towns were built of logs or rough planks with dusty streets, and people drove great wagons with teams of horses. There was no snow, not until they came to the mountains. Up and up and up the long trains chugged, along such precipices that the Laplanders had to hide their eyes lest they imagine their own death. After the last set of mountains, everything grew as green and familiar as Western Norway, but with the difference that the trees were huge and oversize ferns and plants grew under these forest canopies.

The trains halted seven miles from Seattle's center, on a trestle bridge, and they had to spend yet another night sleeping on the train, which by now, did not feel as comfortable as before, especially suspended over the bridge at Everett. A mood of trepidation began to spread. In Seattle they were to board another ship, with the reindeer, which would take them up the Pacific coast to Alaska. They now knew the vastness of the globe—a month to cross the Atlantic, many days to cross America. How long would they be on this next ship? But in the end the train never steamed into Seattle, and they did not board a ship immediately. They were taken to a small town called Fremont, and everything was unloaded there. Little explanation was offered at first; they were merely to drive the reindeer up a hill from the railway yard to Woodland Park. There the reindeer would be able to graze, and the Laplanders could put up their tents and rest from their journey. In vain some of the herders tried to explain that the reindeer would have trouble digesting the grass after their long journey; they must have their dried lichen, of which a good quantity remained. Yes,

yes, they were told: sufficient lichen would be delivered by wagon to the park, along with their belongings.

In the park the reindeer were allowed to roam free, and the large park building was opened to the Laplanders to sleep in. The cooks from the train were given a vacation, and the travelers suddenly had to prepare their own food. No one explained much of what was going on, because few in authority seemed to know. One journalist had discovered that the ship that should have been waiting in Seattle to take them to Alaska had been requisitioned by the Navy. The Spanish-American War had broken out and every available vessel was steaming over to the Philippines. In addition to that, the journalist had heard that so many miners had left Dawson City that it was no longer a question of starvation. Were the reindeer still needed in Alaska and if not, what should be done with them—and with the herders from Norway? Telegrams flew back and forth between Mr. Kjellman and Dr. Jackson, who was by now in Washington D.C., defending himself at the War Department: Why was the ship so late? Why had the herders brought so many children? What ideas, if any, did Dr. Jackson have *now*?

Meanwhile it seemed that half of Seattle flocked to Woodland Park. Some were Norwegians, Swedes, and Danes, who were able to speak with the newcomers and relay information they read in the newspapers. Some of the Laplanders went into Seattle on the trolley and came back with liquor. That evening things got loud and the whole next day all the herders and children, not just the rowdy men, were confined to the park. But the day after, everyone who wanted to was allowed to take the trolley car from Fremont to Seattle for just five cents. Lasse and Siri went along. The trolley rolled its way along Lake Union into the city, as big as any they had passed on their trip across America, but rough and new. Many shop windows displayed supplies for the Klondike, pans and shovels and pickaxes, and more merchandise spilled out onto to the sidewalks. Lasse had received their first month's wages and bought a number of things, at what seemed very high prices. Siri bought nothing with her four dollars even though she was tempted.

On Sunday it was visitors' day at the park and perhaps three thousand people came and went all day, ladies in large hats and men in plus fours and caps, little girls in lace and high boots, boys with small dogs on leashes. But it was not such a happy day for many of the Laplanders. The promised lichen from the railway cars had not appeared and Mr. Kjellman found out that some of it—probably a good deal of it—had never been off-loaded from the *Manitoban* back in Jersey City. Apparently, it had been thought of as some kind of packing material. The reindeer had arrived in Seattle in good health but were refusing to eat the park's grass, which was old and trampled. Twelve had died. It was hard for Siri to keep Leksu apart and feed her lichen separately, but she managed. One of the little children was also sick, and in the midst of the huge crowds at Woodland Park and a festivity more like a circus than anything Siri had known, the three-year-old boy, Mattis Sara, lay in bed and died.

By March 14, a week after they had arrived in Fremont, Mr. Kjellman had received his instructions. They were finally to proceed to Seattle and board a ship to Alaska. In the early morning the next day the reindeer were loaded onto railway cars in Fremont and the Laplanders with all their supplies, also boarded trains for the city docks. The night of March 17, after midnight, a tugboat began to pull the *Seminole,* a three-masted barque, from Seattle out to the Strait of Juan de Fuca. In the morning, something happened that had not been explained to most of them beforehand. Mr. Kjellman announced that the Lappish women and children would be left at a decommissioned fort near a city at the entrance to Puget Sound, Port Townsend, with a translator, Regnor Dahl, and a surgeon, Dr. Gambell.

The women and children would live there for around two months, after which they would be transported up to Norton Sound in Alaska by ship. The reindeer and men (fifty-seven of them) would meanwhile continue with the *Seminole* to Haines, Alaska, there to drive the animals overland up north. This was the plan that Dr. Jackson had negotiated with the War Department. It was a late decision from someone in the government that the women should be left behind.

No reindeer were to be taken off the ship with the women and children, they said, and the dogs would all go north as well. Siri put her foot down. She told Mr. Kjellman in no uncertain terms that Leksu was staying with her. The reindeer provided milk for the children, the only sort that young children could digest. Mr. Kjellman had no time to argue and only said that her reindeer was sure to die without lichen, just like the others if they didn't get to Alaska soon for a fresh supply. Siri had not mentioned to anyone that among her possessions she had three full bags of reindeer lichen left, for just such an emergency, and she didn't mention it to Kjellman now lest he take them from her.

Lasse and Siri said farewell on the deck of the *Seminole* in Port Townsend Bay, Siri subdued and Lasse, in spite of his worry at leaving her behind, excited. For after all he was going to the Yukon, to the land of gold.

April 20

If I ever grow to love the Pacific Northwest, it might be because of the long springs here in Port Townsend. They begin in February with a speckling of purple and white, the first crocuses. Then comes the forsythia and red currants, in waves of canary yellow and bright pink. Along with them appear the frilly jonquils and early tulips. The apples and plums planted by the settlers turn Uptown's streets and gardens all white and blushing rose. Wild rhododendrons, in tropical purples and reds, bloom at the same time as the planted lilac bushes, which make one think of England. A spring that in Bergen is a mere two months and often rainy, with occasionally sleet and hailstorms, here in the Pacific Northwest stretches to five months.

When I write such flowery sentences, I seem to be reaching

for a newspaper audience in my homeland, penning a slew of comparisons in terms that the average Norwegian will appreciate. Of course it is true that Port Townsend has jonquils—Kjell planted several dozens of them around our house last autumn— but the beauty of the Pacific Northwest is more raw and less civilized and has very little to do with fruit trees and lilacs.

Uptown is built on what was evergreen forest, and stumps still dot the yards, while new saplings—apples, plums, maples, beeches, and those peculiar monkey-puzzle trees—hardly reach the second stories. Everywhere on empty lots you see remaining stands of spruce or fir with salal and ferns growing beneath the branches. To walk in the woods here is to find tiny spring plants, twinflower and shooting star, and to hear a dozen different bird calls, half of them unknown to me. In spring comes the return of the Klallam canoes. The Chinese farmers plant their vegetable seeds at Chinese Gardens and farther out of town at Station Prairie.

Elle-Ristine has now been with us for three weeks. Her fever has passed, but it has taken her some time to regain her strength. It was eventually necessary, of course, to explain something of Lian-Henry's situation, and for Elle-Ristine to understand that there was a baby in the house, and it was Lian's. Our Sáme friend was quite surprised at first, but sympathetic. She understands that during the day, when friends and tradesmen come to the door, that it is Henry who shows them silently in. Only in the evenings does Lian the young woman emerge.

I see similarities between the two. Both are young but experienced beyond their years with loss and hardship. They have something of the same quickness of mind, the same capacity for understanding. They even look a bit alike, in the evening lamplight especially, with their dark hair and high cheekbones. Lian has returned to her slender figure while Elle-Ristine is stockier. One grew up in the fertile Pearl River Valley, walking barefoot and wearing a bamboo hat, planting and harvesting rice and vegetables under the humid sky. The other, from lands where snow and ice reign eight months a year, grew up herding reindeer and fending off wolves with a ski pole, sleeping in a reindeer sack in a smoky tent, with only the northern lights for company. Neither knows the other's world and neither can speak the other's language.

Yet both know what it means to take courage in your hands and leave your country; they know the roll of the waves and the fetid stink of life in a ship's filthy wet hold; they know the fear of not being able to determine your own fate. And friendly smiles can say what words cannot. Elle-Ristine had seen Chinese people in Seattle and in her few forays into Port Townsend. She knows the Chinese are not considered equal to white Americans from Boston and New York. It makes her thoughtful, as it makes Edvard thoughtful and sad. If America is the land of freedom for all, how can there be such differences? Lian does not ask such questions, and neither do I. But we are not idealists. We live with what life gives us.

During Elle-Ristine's illness, Kjell built a fence around our yard of split rails, so that Leksu would not roam, and soon this "reindeer corral" became a great draw. All of Uptown came by to see the reindeer and ask questions about her, and sailors and merchants from Water Street came as well. One Water Street merchant offered $500 for the reindeer in order to display the animal and charge admission; this doubtless gave Kjell the notion of passing himself off as a reindeer herder in order to collect coins from visitors to come inside the corral and pet Leksu, placidly eating her grass or lichen. He had a tailor whip up a Sáme-style hat and tunic based on a drawing published in a Seattle newspaper. Ever since Skagway Kjell has manifested a new entrepreneurial spirit.

Having purchased land in Chimacum, he's now built a one-room shack of simple boards and a tar-paper roof. His seaman's chest serves as a table. He has scavenged a chair or two and built a small bed. Every coin is precious to him, for he won't move there until he is able to plow the land and buy chickens to raise.

I would rather pay Kjell a better salary than have him dress up as a "Laplander from the Far North" and take coins from children and sailors to see Leksu. But since the captain's arrest I've felt a great unease about our financial situation. I look around at all the furniture and pretty things Edvard brought from San Francisco and try to imagine what I would sell first if Mr. Harrison renewed the charges and Edvard had to go to prison or if Edvard never came back from one of his voyages. Even savings in the bank could vanish. In America banks fail regularly.

We had a visit a few days ago from Mr. Dahl. He brought one of the Sáme women to see Elle-Ristine, who was up from bed yet still not venturing far from her room or the kitchen. This was Margrete Utsi. I could see that Margrete was not amused by Kjell in his "Four Winds" cap, so-called for the peaks that point in four directions. But even though she is a rather forceful personality, Margrete has a natural dignity that keeps her from expressing her feelings in hasty words. Margrete did say something in the Sáme language that disturbed Elle-Ristine, and Mr. Dahl explained it further, in Norwegian, so I could understand it too. Apparently, the War Department has now completely dropped the idea of the Yukon Relief Expedition. Dr. Jackson has proposed a new plan, that the Sámit and reindeer should be transported far north in Alaska. There, around field stations, the reindeer herds would be allowed to increase, and the herders would take on the task of teaching the native peoples to raise reindeer.

The herders, Mr. Dahl said, would receive the same monthly wages as promised and free housing and food for the length of their contract. At the end they could choose to stay in Alaska or have their return passage paid back to Norway. But they must accept that they were still under contract to the United States and must meet the changed needs of the government.

Elle-Ristine looked at Mr. Dahl coolly and steadily. How were the reindeer to be transported north? What was to become of the men who were herding the reindeer, including all the husbands of the women? How were the women and children to go north—how far north?—and when were they expected to go?

To all this Mr. Dahl had few answers. He had only had a letter from Dr. Jackson. There had been no communication with the Sáme men and their leaders at Haines Mission. Impossible to know what has happened to them and the five hundred reindeer.

April 30

Elle-Ristine has begun to move around freely, up and down the stairs without assistance, and outside as well. As soon as she saw Kjell in his big hat and the reindeer corral, she put an end to the sideshow. Kjell did not mind at all; his impersonation of a Sáme had grown tiresome to him, and he had gained his objective: enough money to buy a cast iron stove for his shack. Elle-Ristine's delight in being reunited with Leksu was evident, but she was taken aback at how far the store of lichen had diminished.

Kjell volunteered to take the animal to Chimacum Creek, where lush grass grew in abundance, but the farm was too far for Elle-Ristine to visit. Lian made the suggestion that perhaps Leksu might forage at Chinese Gardens, around the edges of the farms, where grass grew well, and where there might also be other food a reindeer could like in the forest nearby. That afternoon, Kjell and Lian, dressed as Henry, led Leksu over the hill to Chinese Gardens. I had to stay home with Susan Berit or else I would have gone with them, just to see the surprise on the gardeners' faces as they looked up to see a white reindeer, looking like a bony-faced goat, coming over the hill in a bright harness. Her antlers had been cut off before boarding the ship in Norway and now the stubs were gone too. She would begin to grow new antlers this summer.

Apparently, the grass and bushes in the forest nearby were very much to Leksu's liking. From then on Lian and often Kjell took the reindeer there every day.

May 5

I want to write down some of what Elle-Ristine said to me this morning. We were alone in the house, Lian having gone out, as Henry, to do some shopping here in Uptown. Kjell was in Chimacum working on his farm. I came into the parlor to fetch a book and found Elle-Ristine there reading the Bible. It was her own edition in Norwegian, well-worn, and must have come with her from Fort Townsend.

Elle-Ristine looked up at me from the wingback chair where she was curled up and said, "Are you a believer, Mrs. Bergland?"

I said only that I attended the Methodist church here in town. I've found it's best not to discuss religion with most people. I believe in God, of course, but he never feels very close to me, never has. Perhaps I stopped believing he would watch out for me and my family when my father drowned. Certainly later when I lost Jan and then Agnete I had no sense of his love, only of his vast indifference, rather like that of the sea itself.

"Most of my family in Karasjok are devoted to the teachings of Pastor Læstadius," said Elle-Ristine. "Have you heard of him?"

I said no and sat down on the sofa with my knitting. I am making socks these days for a new charity project of Emma Smith's, strong Norwegian socks of gray wool for penniless prospectors who have returned from Alaska and haunt the streets of our town, unable to find work or return to the far places they came from.

"Pastor Læstadius was partly Sáme himself, from Sweden, and he came among us to teach a living faith and tell us about a God who cared about the Sámit. He stood up for us against the state church and its priests who looked down on us. He encouraged us to read and pray, to give up false gods and confess our sins. Praying for forgiveness, singing psalms, standing in a circle, all this came to Finnmark from Sweden. The lay preachers traveled around the north and in the meetings, people fell to the ground trembling and crying out. When people were converted, they stopped drinking and stopped stealing reindeer."

She added matter-of-factly that she had seen the light as a young girl and had fallen to the ground sobbing with the spirit of the Lord in her.

I didn't know what to make of this. Was she trying to convert me, or just tell me more about herself and her people? I asked if this religion was based on Luther's teachings or another's. She responded that it was Lutheranism and Christian but existed alongside old beliefs. Many of the Sámit, except for the very strict Læstadians, had not given them up even now. She said, "Do you think that is very strange, Mrs. Bergland?"

Her round face was solemn but the expression in her eyes,

questioning and a little defiant, made me think she was one of those who still held to older beliefs.

I told her that while families in my childhood home in Sognefjord went to church or at least read the Bible together on Sundays when the weather was too bad to travel, that we had also kept old superstitions and beliefs alive. My grandmother was a storyteller and from her my sisters and I heard about witches, talking animals, wizards, and *huldras,* those tempting women with cow tails. The mountains around us were the home of giants and trolls, you could sometimes see their faces in the crags and crevices of the steep hillsides. Elle-Ristine told me that in her childhood she had been taught that everything in nature was alive—trees, stones, and water—and until recently they could speak. Now they were mute, but they could still understand human speech. She had grown up talking to the spruce and to the creeks and rivers as they tumbled through the hillsides. I told her that my grandmother had done the same, giving streams names of her own and greeting a large old tree familiarly each day. Grandmother had also believed that stone markers along mountain paths were formerly alive; they were trolls that had been frozen in time.

Lian came in with a question about dinner before we could continue our conversation. Otherwise, I could have told Elle-Ristine that Edvard half-believed in the *draug,* the seaweed-covered monster that lived in the sea and was only seen at twilight or during storms, often rowing or sailing a smashed-up ship. The *draug* was the spirit of drowned sailors. If living sailors encountered this ghost, it would drag them down to the depths.

But it's unlucky for a sea captain's wife to speak of the *draug,* so I merely got up and went with Lian into the kitchen to see what could be done with the meager cut of mutton Lian had managed to obtain. These days we all compete for provisions with the saloons and ships in harbor.

May 7

We've taken up the subject of beliefs again, Elle-Ristine and I, sitting in the parlor with a cup of coffee and some sewing and knitting this afternoon. I've known little about the northern people in my own country, and very little indeed about the Sámit. I had supposed, from stories I'd been told, that some of them practiced black magic. They were known as sorcerers who told fortunes and predicted the future. Seafarers feared their powers over wind and waves.

For both of us, the old stories lived alongside the Lutheran teachings, and we found in surprise that some of the superstitions and folktales were just the same. Both of us knew about being *bergtatt*, taken into the mountains by the *huldras*. Both our traditions had evil eyes, and herbal healing, and souls that loosed themselves to travel by magic flight. We both had ghosts and underground beings, who lived beneath us and sometimes exchanged our children for their own. These underground beings, called *uldas* in the Sáme language, lived just like us, with their own cows and goats and reindeer, but slept during the day and were awake all night. Sometimes the changelings grew up among us and we loved them just as we had loved the natural child who was stolen.

After she told me about the *uldas*, Elle-Ristine fished two small silver balls on a chain from a calfskin bag. They were heavy and unpolished and attached to them were two crude rings from which dangled silver leaves. These were protective amulets, *šiellat* in the Sáme language; *komsekuler* in Norwegian. They were to be hung in the cradle as a means of protecting the baby. I had seen Elle-Ristine's baby cradle at Fort Townsend, made of wood and soft leather, a kind of northern papoose that could be carried on the mother's back or slung over a reindeer's saddle during a migration. The silver balls were usually suspended at the head of this cradle. If the *uldas* came to exchange the baby, they would never get past the power of the silver balls.

Other Sáme folktales were different, of course; there was a demon giant called Stállu, who would suck out your brains with an iron pipe and who cannibalized small children on Christmas if they made too much noise. There were also many tales about the *noaidis*, the spiritual men and women who beat drums and fell into a trance to heal and predict the future, and tales too about the otherworld and of people who returned from the dead. Perhaps we had had such stories of drums and trances in Norway long ago but if so, I never heard them. I told her that instead we had heard stories about northern wizards who could unleash storms at sea and send arrows at great speeds to harm their enemies.

"Yes," she said, but not smiling. "I have heard these stories too, but they are not true, and they are often used against my people. We become the enemy and our magic is evil. When it is the Norwegians who have so often been to blame for our suffering."

"I'm sorry if I've offended you, Elle-Ristine," I said. "It is my ignorance." I'd seen how she suddenly prickled and drew back. "I don't think of you or your friends and compatriots as the enemy. In the south of Norway we have no Sámit, as far as I know. I met none in Bergen or my travels either."

Elle-Ristine's face changed. "You've not insulted me, Mrs. Bergland. It is a contradiction I carry in myself. I say 'the Norwegians,' knowing that my father was Norwegian."

"Can you tell me about him? You've spoken about your mother's family in Karasjok, but what about your father's in Alta?"

"My father had no family in Alta. He was born farther south, in Mo i Rana. He came to work as a clerk for a merchant in Bossekop, an old Sáme marketplace outside Alta. His employer bought and sold furs, so he dealt often with the Sámit. Twice a year the reindeer herders from the plateau would load up their sleds and come to the market at Bossekop to sell and trade furs, meat, berries, ptarmigans. It was there he met my mother and decided to move to Karasjok and marry her. My father learned the North Sáme language, *davvisámegiella*, and that was what we usually spoke at our home. He went back and forth to Bossekop, but when the merchant moved south, my father needed a different job, so we moved to Alta where he oversaw a shipping office. My father thought it might be good for me to have better schooling too, in Norwegian."

She looked down at her sewing thoughtfully and then up at me gain with a calm determination.

"We were not the only mixed family. Many different people lived in Bossekop and Alta—Finns, Russians, Sámit, Norwegians, and even English and Welsh people, because of the Alten mines nearby. But the Sámit were not treated in the same way as the Norwegians. Sámit were looked down upon. I saw my mother shrink and change. She knew Norwegian but was shy about speaking it in public. It was only after my father died and my mother and I went back to Karasjok that I became a reindeer herder. Before that, I expected that I might become a teacher at the school where I studied.

"I must tell you this," she said quietly. "My father was sincerely interested in the Sámit. He would not accept what people said about us. He told me that the Sámit were in the north before everyone else came, and there was proof of it in ancient rock paintings. Once I remember he took me to a place outside Bossekop to see the paintings. He said they were a secret that only some people knew and would not share."

I was curious, but she suddenly felt she had said enough.

I have noticed this before, how she is both trusting and not trusting. Elle-Ristine is a teacher at heart, she likes to share what she knows. But she is protective, too. What belongs to her people, belongs to her people.

May 16

After our last conversation I've longed to speak with Elle-Ristine again, alone, but the opportunity has not come. We have had more visitors from the fort, as several of the Sáme women have taken to walking daily to Port Townsend to see Elle-Ristine. We entertain them in the kitchen and parlor with cakes or pancakes with jam and plenty of coffee. Some bring handiwork, including a palm-size heddle of antler or wood used to weave the colorful shoe bands. They are curious about Lian, and I have wondered if any of them guess her secret. She usually leaves us when they are here, going up to her room with Susan Berit.

In addition to Margrete and Ravna, and Ravna's mother-in-law Inga, a teenage girl named Sunna often comes. She made the sea and train journey with her parents. She has a bewildered look most of the time but loves pancakes and jam. She told me that she'd never seen a house like mine, had never seen a bed like the one where Elle-Ristine sleeps. Imagine, she said, a bed of your very own. All four of them are shorter than Elle-Ristine, and a bit bulky in their dresses of tanned leather or wool. Their skin is brown, and Inga's is quite wrinkled. They have the same narrow eyes and high cheekbones. Inga has a few missing teeth and smokes a small clay pipe.

I come in and out of the rooms when they are here, for the conversation is mostly in Sáme. It is a soft and flowing language, with no resemblance to Norwegian or English. Elle-Ristine glides into it easily and then back out again to translate for me. Quite often they laugh. Today I heard raised voices for a time in the kitchen, but when I came in everyone was silent.

Afterwards I asked Elle-Ristine if there had been problems at the fort.

"They want me to come back," she said. "They need me, they say, to talk with Mr. Dahl. They wonder how long they will be living there, where the men are, and what we do next. They are afraid we will never go to Alaska, never see the reindeer again, and that we will become beggars here. That we will never see Finnmark again."

"If you would like to return to the fort, I can arrange it," I said. "If you feel well enough."

"Margrete told me I looked well enough to return. She wondered if I was finding life here too comfortable." Elle-Ristine smiled. "I do find it pleasant and cozy," she admitted. "But when they called me 'too Norwegian,' I felt ashamed. My mother raised me to be proud of being Sáme and to live in the Sáme way. But I admit I have enjoyed your company and the meals you and Lian make. And the house with the books and newspapers. We don't have anything at Fort Townsend like this to occupy us, just our own handiwork. We cook a little, because the food Mr. Dahl gives us is not always to our liking. Canned beans with pork." She made a face. "And the days are long."

"You still need to rest," I said, for unsurprisingly I didn't want her to leave. I too had enjoyed her company. It was balm to my soul to speak Norwegian with her, that was part of it. But she had become a friend as well, along with Adele and Lian and Emma Smith. I wished that she didn't have to go to Alaska.

"I have rested," she said, putting her hand on her stomach. "I am getting fat from pancakes and cream porridge. I will go back to the fort soon. But we can still visit each other, I hope."

"I had a miscarriage not too long ago," I said after a pause. "I did not feel myself for quite some time. The loss makes itself known in the body. One may feel rested, but not in spirit."

"I had wanted a child, but this was the wrong time," said Elle-Ristine. "If I get to Alaska, that will be a better time." Now she was the one to pause. She asked carefully, "Have you lost other babies that way?"

"Lost, yes, but not through miscarriage," I said. "Only this last one. My other children, my two children, Jan and Agnete, died in other ways. Jan in a storm at sea and Agnete from a disease called typhus. They were very young."

"Oh, Mrs. Bergland!" She wept for me. "I didn't know."

"I hope you will call me Dagny," I said. "And think of me as your friend."

May 20

Some thirty men, mostly Sámit, but also a few of the Finnish-Norwegian herders, returned two days ago from Alaska, among them Elle-Ristine's husband Mikkel. They arrived in Port Townsend by steamship and from there were ferried across the bay to Fort Townsend in a small steamboat. Here at the house we only heard about their arrival the next morning in the newspaper. Elle-Ristine set off immediately with Kjell in his wagon. After some inner struggle she left Leksu here, in Lian's care. The animal had grown visibly healthier on the verdant grass of Chinese Gardens.

When Kjell returned home, he had the story of what had happened in Alaska from one of the men, a Finnish-Norwegian herder, Carl Johan Sakariassen, who has kept a journal of the whole tragic expedition. The *Seminole* set off March 17 under tow. With the heavy winds and storms it took ten days for the tug to get the ship from Port Townsend to Dyea. Finally, the *Seminole* anchored off Haines Mission, a few miles from Dyea, where a small band of soldiers, their tents along the shore, waited to escort them up the river to Chilkoot Pass and over to the gold fields. There were Indians on the shore, who fished from their dugout cedar canoes and lived in cedar houses. The herders had only a large drafty barn for lodging.

Although there were several feet of snow when they arrived, it soon began to rain "as if a spigot had been turned on" and this weather hardly changed for the next several weeks. The expedition was supposed to be led by Army officers, but they were unfamiliar with the terrain and knew nothing whatsoever about reindeer. It was William Kjellman, the Sáme-speaking American who had recruited the herders in Norway, who realized that the supply of lichen was almost at an end and that food for the reindeer must be found if the expedition was even to have a chance of succeeding.

He organized a scouting party to the nearby mountains, but when no lichen could be discovered anywhere and the reindeer went hungry, Kjellman ordered that the herd be moved to a snow-free headland where the animals might forage on swamp weeds and chew on spruce bark. While the reindeer attempted to graze on the headland, the herders and soldiers were organized into groups to haul supplies and their snow sledges up the river to an Indian village. They had to hack their way through the dense brush growing along the river in terrain that grew steeper and steeper. And still it rained.

At the village, they rested, and some of the men were instructed to continue into the mountains with Indians as bearers, while the rest of the herders, including Sakariassen, returned to Haines to collect the reindeer, now scattered around the headland's forest and shores. The reindeer were so exhausted and starving they were hardly able to move and when the herders tried to drive them across the river, many reindeer simply drowned, even though usually they are strong swimmers.

As the scope of the disaster grew, the herders frantically offered the poor creatures any kind of vegetation they could find on the headland that the reindeer could eat, and came bearing mushrooms, grasses, and mosses, all to no avail. Finally, one of the men discovered a large quantity of reindeer lichen in the mountains nearby and the herders worked in relays, using their sleds, to bring down as much as possible. For most of the reindeer it was too late. They could not even raise their heads or chew. Over and over, with a sudden spasm at the end, they meekly died.

In the end, out of the 521 reindeer that had made it to Haines (two dozen had already died en route from Norway), only 185 survived. More were expected to die on the trip to the Yukon.

With so few reindeer left and the whole expedition in confusion, with most of the supplies now upriver, Kjellman made a drastic change of plan. Some fifteen men were to herd the remaining reindeer up the river to Chilkoot Pass and then to Circle City. The rest of the group would return to Fort Townsend to await instructions.

It was impossible hearing this story not to think of Leksu. How Elle-Ristine must be relieved she had not sent her beloved reindeer up to almost certain death in Alaska.

May 22

Elle-Ristine came walking into town today with Mikkel and they made a visit to our household for lunch. Mikkel is about twenty-five, muscular and middling tall, with a great shock of brown hair and white teeth. His face is broad with high cheekbones, scarred from chicken pox, and his eyes lively and dark as Leksu's. He speaks some Norwegian and attempts English with me ("How are you!! Thank you!") He gives the impression of great energy that has not yet found its focus. Elle-Ristine looks at him with fondness, but he seems not quite to return the feeling. Has she told him about the loss of their baby? Is he sad about it? Does he blame her?

With Elle-Ristine as translator, I inquired more about what happened in Alaska over our meal of smoked fish, cheese, and flatbread. A shadow darkened his face as he recounted the same story Kjell had told us, with new details, the most painful being the behavior of Dr. Sheldon Jackson, who, after sending the herders and reindeer to Alaska in a sailing vessel so slow it hindered their arrival, steamed past them in the Inside Passage on a faster ship. "He came to visit us in Haines one day," said Mikkel, and Elle-Ristine translated, "And there, as the reindeer lay starving, he preached a long sermon to us in English about courage in the face of difficulties and about trusting in God's will. Mr. Jackson stood there as his sermon was translated and seemed surprised at our sour faces. Then he left again. On another fast steamship. The very fastest."

Often, Elle-Ristine told me, the Sámit make a joke about the people with power, how stupid they are. But Dr. Jackson's behavior seemed to me beyond stupid. It was criminal. And the fact he was a well-intentioned Christian made it worse.

After our meal, we went over the hill to Chinese Gardens with Leksu on a leather rein. Lian came along as Henry. It pains me that when she and I leave the house at the same time, it is I who must carry Susan Berit in my arms. At home Lian sometimes straps the baby in a sling around her back as she washes and dusts. But I hold Susan in my arms, near my heart. I love to feel the baby's warmth close to me, but I am conscious of the injustice. What will we do when the girl grows older, and she begins to call Lian "mama" in public?

The four of us adults took the less-traveled path through the woods, but still we met a few people who gaped at us: the two Sámit in their wool tunics, leggings, and turned up moccasins, with Mikkel wearing his fantastical "Four Winds" hat; all-white Leksu, gay in her bright harness and lead; me, in my cumbersome calico dress, shawl, and a hat tied firmly under my chin, a swaddled baby in my arms; and finally a young Chinese man with queue, tight cap, and blue cotton trousers and jacket.

It was a beautiful May afternoon, the sea blue-green and sweet-smelling, the air so clear you could see Vancouver Island across the water. With the warm weather of late, the gardens were green and growing: peas in abundance on trellises and fencing, rows of lettuces, Chinese cabbages, green onions, and celery, rhubarb leaves massive as serving platters, strawberries in blossom. The vegetables and fruits were in beautiful, neat rows and among them walked the gardeners in their loose shirts and trousers, barefoot, with conical straw hats, making the fertile land thrive, and they looked up to see us in some amazement. But Leksu they were used to, the little northern deer-goat, they thought of her. A symbol of good luck, shining white, with her rounded dark eyes that seem to see a good deal in all directions.

I was sorry that Leksu would return to Fort Townsend with Elle-Ristine, but of course it was best for the animal to be with her friend and owner. Having heard the story of so many reindeer deaths in Haines, I fear for Leksu's fate up in Alaska should Elle-Ristine and Mikkel end up traveling there. I fear for Elle-Ristine and Mikkel's fate as well.

May 26

A party of Sáme men came to town the other night and created a disturbance with drinking, singing deep in their throats, and falling senseless on the street. So said the *Leader* this morning with distaste, though what is so remarkable about men—any men—getting drunk on Water Street is beyond me. Mr. Barker's saloons have made him wealthy from such behavior, and we have at least a dozen more saloons downtown, all filled day and night with sailors, prospectors, and the fair youth of the town. Half the time they shoot or knife each other as well. The Sámit at least are peaceful men.

As I was going downtown anyway to make a purchase, I stopped in at the *Leader*'s office and gave Mr. Duffy a piece of my mind, not only for the article about the herders' drunkenness, but for another column in yesterday's newspapers. The article was about the investigation regarding John Barker for working with opium smugglers, but it touched, in incendiary language, on the threat of Chinese opium dens to the reputation of the town.

I proposed that I write an article for the newspaper, one about the whole botched Yukon Relief Expedition and the death

of two-thirds of the reindeer, but Mr. Duffy would have none
of it. He explained that readers were no longer sympathetic to
the Laplanders in town. Word was out they were living high at
government expense, drinking up their monthly stipend in Port
Townsend saloons. As to the cruel language used against our
Chinese inhabitants, Mr. Duffy simply shrugged his shoulders
and asked in a bored voice if I thought that a newspaper should
print only stories of tea parties in Uptown and theatricals at the
Learned Opera House. Opium dens existed in Port Townsend;
if I didn't believe that the so-called Chinese merchants hadn't
brought a serious problem to our town, then I should feel free
to walk through the doors of one of the Chinese shops near the
Leader's offices. Most of them had opium dens in their back
quarters. Courteously but firmly I was shown out of Mr. Duffy's
office.

My short newspaper career was ended before it began in Port
Townsend. And not for lack of English, but for an abundance
of opinions.

After making a purchase of stockings at Waterman & Katz's
mercantile, I went to the Zee Tai Company. It had been on my
mind for some time to buy shoes and a few things for Lian. In
her current status, half Henry, half Lian, she could not move
freely where she used to, especially around Water Street and
Chinatown. The rumor, among some, was that I'd had a baby
with my houseboy Henry. Ah Song had told me this.

But I have a long history of holding up my head, and so I
bought slippers for Lian and a length of silvery blue satin for a
new jacket for her. Let the merchants think what they wished,
that I planned to dress up as a Chinese woman. I thought that
Lian might like something new to wear, from her own culture.
I had seen that, like most young women, she enjoyed looking
attractive, and I was uncertain how to meet that need, since our
only safety was in continuing to pretend that she was Henry
Soon.

Two weeks ago, while Elle-Ristine was still living with me,
Adele had come over for dinner, and the four of us had become
very lively afterwards when Lian joined us in the parlor. Adele
had brought several day dresses for Lian to trim with lace,

embroidery, and buttons. They were very pretty muslins, and Adele was seized with the notion that Lian and Elle-Ristine should try them on. Elle-Ristine demurred—she said she surely would never fit into one of those tight-waisted gowns that required a corset, for a corset is something she refuses to wear. But Lian touched the fabric of one of the muslin dresses and suddenly whisked off into another room with it. When she returned, she looked quite different. She was so slender that she was able to wear the pastel-pink muslin dress without a corset, and though it was long on her, and the sleeves were somewhat wide for her thin arms, she looked beautiful. She had wrapped up her long braid on her head and slipped a shawl around her shoulders.

We were not the only ones to think her lovely. Kjell had come in from choir practice through the kitchen entrance and stood in the doorway between the kitchen and dining room, quite transfixed. Unfortunately, he had also brought home a friend of his, Jeremiah Comstock, who also sings in choir. Although Jeremiah remained in the kitchen, and Kjell tried immediately to block the view, I'm sure his friend saw Lian in her dress. Kjell told me he spoke to Jeremiah and that he made a promise not to gossip. Kjell told him that, being slender, our houseboy is occasionally called on to model for Adele. I'm sure Jeremiah thought that possibility far-fetched.

But I decided that never again must Lian wear a dress—it was too dangerous for us and for her. Instead, I'll offer her new Chinese slippers and cloth for a jacket, even as I see her every day becoming less and less what she was, a girl who passed as a boy. Now she is a young mother of seventeen, who will not be able to pretend forever.

May 30

Our carelessness has had results. Jeremiah Comstock must not have been able to resist telling someone what he saw from the kitchen that evening. Today I had a visit from an immigration deputy from Port Townsend's Customs House, who wished to question my houseboy Henry Soon. He said nothing of rumors that this houseboy had been glimpsed in a dress, which made me wonder if I should panic just yet. I said calmly and brazenly that Henry was no longer in my employ, but had left two days ago, saying he was going to Butte, or perhaps it was Boise, to join some relatives and work in the mines there.

The deputy, a Mr. Cantwell, reminded me that all Chinese must have papers. Harboring smuggled-in Chinese from Canada was against the law.

"If that is so," I said with a smile, "then you must arrest half the ladies in Uptown along with their gardeners and houseboys. I am a foreigner here myself, from Norway, and I did not speak the language well or understand your rules when I arrived with my husband, Captain Bergland. We tried several girls out and they lied, stole, and did many other dreadful things. Then someone suggested taking on a Chinese youth. I was most satisfied, and I am sorry he has gone."

"I understand, Mrs. Bergland," he said. "But in future, think of the consequences and see if you can put up with a maidservant." He paused. "I understand you have taken a Chinese baby to raise."

"That is so," I said. "Through Mrs. Smith, of Trinity Methodist Church. The Methodists have missions and orphanages in China, as you probably know, and this little baby, through no fault of its own, was born into unfortunate circumstances. It is my Christian duty to help where I can. It began as a temporary measure, but now Mr. Bergland and I think of adopting her. Our Christian duty," I repeated.

I assumed a pious expression and the official, no doubt fearful he might receive a sermon, bowed and left. I was not sure I had convinced him.

Lian was with Leksu at Chinese Gardens, and I quickly called to Kjell, who was hoeing in our garden and asked his advice. Lian must be hidden as quickly as possible, he agreed. His shack by Chimacum Creek would be best. And Susan Berit? Susan would need to stay with me for the time being. Later we would try to devise something else. What, I have no idea.

June 3

Edvard has returned from Hawaii after three months at sea. Mr. Talbot is pleased with him and wants to send him off again soon with another lumber shipment, this time to Hong Kong. It crossed my mind that this might be a way to return Lian to her people, but I'm not sure she thinks of China as her home any longer. Besides, what would she do, where would she go in Hong Kong? She has family in the Pearl River Delta, if they are all still alive. If she went back to the village she might marry or more likely become a servant. And what would happen to Susan Berit? Can I send either of them to their fates in China? Yet, America is no easy place for them either.

I told Edvard, "The more I read about the treatment of the Chinese in America, the more worried I become about Lian. As Henry she had some small chance of survival, but here in Port Townsend as elsewhere there are almost no Chinese women— only a few merchants' wives, and the ladies of the brothels. Lian is clever. Her English improves constantly—there is so much she could do if it weren't for these terrible Exclusion Laws."

Edvard and I were driving the road to Chimacum during this discussion. I had little Susan Berit with me. It pained me greatly to keep the baby from her mother, even as I myself grew more tightly attached to the child. Her dark eyes fixed on me with a single-minded look of adoration and need. I never thought of her as Chinese or Scottish, only as a small being that I loved helplessly. I had brought Susan twice before to Kjell's shack. Each time I was saddened by the anguish on Lian's face as she gave the baby back to me for the drive home. I knew that physical anguish: how the arms yearned to tightly clasp a small warm living body, even when it was no longer possible.

Edvard said, "Now that you have put it about that we are adopting the baby, don't you think we must do it?"

"I suppose we must. After all, the child cannot remain invisible much longer. She will have a hard enough time of it in the world without having a Chinese mother in hiding who cannot provide for her. We could give her advantages and send her to school."

"Dagny," said Edvard, slowing the horse and looking at me full on. "We can not adopt her legally unless we are American citizens."

I had known this was coming. It was two years ago this June that we had arrived in San Francisco and that made us eligible for citizenship. I had thought to postpone the decision—to talk seriously with Edvard about returning to Bergen. What, after all, bound us to Port Townsend in the long run? Kjell had his farm. Edvard his work as a captain—but he could do that in Norway as well, couldn't he? Wasn't it time for us to go back home, where we belonged?

"I will think on it," I said unhappily and held Susan Berit closely for as long as I could.

Kjell was at the farm when we drove down the dirt road to Chimacum Creek. He was strengthening the fence around the potato patch and, to my surprise, a woman in a dress and bonnet that shaded her face was helping him, pounding away with a hammer. They looked like any young married couple, doing a job together. I now remembered the look in Kjell's eyes on that unfortunate evening when he and Jeremiah appeared in the kitchen and glimpsed Lian dressed up in pastel-pink muslin. This sprigged cotton dress was mail-order, but it fit Lian and the big sunbonnet hid her black hair and most of her face.

Foolish Kjell, buying her that dress from a catalog! The farm was out of the way, but did he think that sooner or later people in the area would not realize there was a woman living with him? The agreement had been for Lian to dress as Henry and to stay inside the shack as much as possible.

I meant to scold them, but when Lian came running over to our carriage, holding out her arms, I had not the heart. They showed us all around the place with pride. Kjell has built a rough outhouse and a chicken coop, and purchased chickens and a goat, which is tethered near the creek. Lian had put flowers in a jar on a table under the shack's one window. I admired the cleanliness of the room and averted my eyes from the single mattress on its iron bedstead.

On the way home Edvard said to me, "Our Kjell is in love with her."

"Yes," I said. "We must find a way to help them."

June 7

Kjell is formally gone from our employ, the explanation being that Edvard is back and the young fellow has to make progress on the farm. Judging from the single mattress and the happiness on his face yesterday when he came to pack up all his things and bid good-bye, he and Lian are now living as husband and wife. I have often thought him an innocent in the world, because of his religious beliefs and refusal to take a drink, but in truth he is well-traveled and unprejudiced. He grew up surrounded in Lima by Spaniards, Indians, Europeans, and Chinese merchants and laborers. He was always very fond of Rosalia, the daughter of our servants; he was crushed when she married. With us he sailed the world and mingled with a wealth of nationalities. Although he speaks Norwegian like a native, he's not really Norwegian at the core—he lacks the emotional restraint so characteristic of our national character and he has no fear of foreigners. If anything, his harrowing experience in Skagway made him more ready to seize happiness if he could find it.

I do not know if Lian loves him in the same way. I did not love Edvard at first. I simply married him to see the world and was shocked to find out all that marriage entailed. Edvard's experience, like most men's, came from prostitutes and one or two married women. He had never approached a virgin and his ways were rough. I was modest and self-protective. I made excuses and cried a little, and he stood at the porthole and smoked his pipe. On a ship you have nowhere to run.

Now all that has changed. As I lay in our bed last night holding Edvard in my arms, I thought how I had become his equal partner in desire. That graying reddish beard and chest hair, his burned arm, his continuing vigor—all, all were indescribably precious, and I had to stop myself from weeping and asking him not to leave me again. As a captain's wife I pride myself on accepting that my husband will always be at the helm if he can.

Kjell came into town yesterday, and he and Edvard had

a serious talk in the parlor. After which, we three went to the courthouse to be sworn in as American citizens. Edvard had filled out our paperwork beforehand, and I was surprised to see, when I glanced through it in the waiting room, that he had put down Kjell was born in Lima, Peru, and thus was a citizen of that country, not Norway.

"But surely that's wrong, Edvard?" I whispered. "Kjell was born in Stavanger."

"I have an idea," was all Edvard said. "And for it to work, it's best Kjell was born and grew up in Lima."

He must have explained it to Kjell, for our foster son answered yes when the judge asked if he gave up all allegiance to Peru in becoming an American citizen.

We all swore on the Bible, and it was done.

I thought of my family's small farm on the Sognefjord, and the hills and wharves of Bergen and tears came to my eyes. I did not give up allegiance to Norway in my heart.

June 12

I've not been able to think much more about Kjell and Lian's situation for worry about Edvard on the one hand and about Elle-Ristine and the Sámit living at Fort Townsend on the other.

This morning Edvard received another summons from a police sergeant to come to the office of the city magistrate. Apparently, Clarence Harrison has renewed his charges that Edvard stole money from his safe and then deliberately sank the *Fidelius* to cover the crime. No longer in Juneau, he has returned to Redwood City, California, now doubtlessly a much poorer man, and has filed a complaint with the authorities there. Carl Olafsson, the owner of the *Fidelius,* has added his name to the case, presumably so that he will not have to pay Edvard the salary still owing.

Edvard returned from the magistrate, furious that his presence is required in town for another two weeks before it's decided whether he should face charges. The lawyer Mr. Arnold Baxter must be re-engaged, and he is not inexpensive. Witnesses must be found and interviewed. Shall the trial take place here or in San Francisco? All this means that Mr. Talbot of the Puget Mill Company must hire another captain to take the schooner to Hong Kong. The company runs a tight schedule.

"I could sort this out myself up in Alaska, in St. Michael," Edvard said today. "No doubt that scoundrel Quayle is still there, waiting for the ice on the Yukon River to break up. The only place for him to go is Circle City or Dawson. I could track him down. And with all the men going north to the goldfields, it would be easy enough for me to find a ship to captain up to Alaska."

"You are a headstrong old man," I told him. "Stay here and fight it in court. You have witnesses to tell the story of how Harrison himself discovered the empty safe before you came into Juneau. As for the *Fidelius* breaking up on Ripple Rock, the crew can testify to that as well."

Grumbling, Edvard agreed and rehired Mr. Baxter. Tomorrow they will begin the process of trying to locate the scattered crew and passengers. They do not have to come to Port Townsend. It will be enough for someone to take their sworn testimony.

Meanwhile, the Sámit at Fort Townsend are now more or less in open revolt against Mr. Dahl, whom they accuse of arbitrary rules and depriving them of their rights. In particular, the preparations for getting the herders to Alaska have become quite bewildering.

Two days ago the famous Dr. Samuel Jackson arrived at the fort with plans for their evacuation, and I was asked to come and translate—from English to Norwegian, since the herders no longer trusted Dahl's word. Edvard came with me.

Dr. Jackson strikes me unfavorably, although he is a very shipshape sort of fellow, short, but iron-backed, with a sharply pointed beard. I cannot help but imagine the small scissors with which he must trim it. He wears a captain's hat, though he is no seaman, but a missionary and teacher. His words were calm and optimistic; he speaks to the Sámit as he doubtless speaks to the Eskimos up north, as though he is their wise father. Unlike the native people of Alaska, however the Sámit have had a centuries-long experience of missionaries and settlers. They keep talking about their contracts and other legal obligations of the U.S. government, that is, the War Department, which originally hired them. They are not easily reassured that Dr. Jackson has ever had their best interests at heart. Wasn't it he, after all, whose grand idea of importing reindeer led to the needless deaths of so many animals?

I do understand that Dr. Jackson has done a good deal to help the natives of the Alaska Territory. Before his posting up there, only a handful of missions ministered to the education of a people spread over a vast land and dependent on whaling and sealing. When foreign ships came into the Bering Sea and the sea mammals began to disappear, starvation and death seemed likely. It was Jackson who had the idea to import reindeer from Siberia and build up herds that the Eskimos could slaughter and sell for their hides and meat. The first Sámit came in 1894, just a dozen of them, to teach the natives how to herd, breed, milk and slaughter the animals. Now, with so many spare Sámit on his hands and contracts that run through January of next year, Jackson thinks naturally of employing them at different "reindeer stations" in the far north of Alaska. Sincere as Dr. Jackson appears to be, it's clear he blundered badly with the absurd rescue mission and is probably quite desperate to get the herders from Lapland away from any place there are journalists and newspapers. Unfortunately, the visits of some of Sáme men to Port Townsend's many saloons have been increasing, with predictable results.

What I translated, from English to Norwegian for Elle-Ristine, who then told the others, can be summarized this way: Jackson has hired a sailing ship to transport the Sámit to Alaska, a ship that is currently tied up in Seattle, but that will be ready to board everyone at Fort Townsend, from men to children, on June 19. Only a few will be left behind. Those who will not go to Alaska include Margrete Utsi's family, because their youngest child caught a case of whooping cough and is in quarantine. She says they will return to Norway once the boy is better. Others talk of wishing to return to Norway but are still bound by their contracts.

No sooner had I finished my interpretation than a herder who had already gone to Alaska in March asked why it must be a sailing ship, not a faster steamship? The men and reindeer, after all, had spent ten days on the *Seminole* just getting to Dyea and then only with the help of a tugboat. St. Michael, he understood, was three or four times as far. Were they to be towed all the way up there?

Dr. Jackson assured the man that the group would be far more comfortable on a sailing ship. He planned to join them up in Unalakleet, their final destination. Someone shouted out, "And will you be taking a fast steamship, sir?" in Norwegian.

Edvard went up to Dr. Jackson afterwards and introduced himself. I heard my husband offer to go to Seattle and inspect the sailing vessel, which they are hiring from the Seattle Hardware Company. Edvard told Jackson he was an experienced captain who had been to St. Michael last summer. He had a good idea of what was needed for a voyage that far up the Alaskan coast.

Given the clamor of questions and argument in the group standing before Dr. Jackson, Edward's steady demeanor and blue coat with its shining brass buttons must have impressed the fellow, and Jackson accepted Edvard's kind offer to inspect the ship, especially if he would take two of the herders with him so as to mollify the crowd.

It can be imagined the sinking feeling I had, to see the two of them talking about a ship to St. Michael. I knew Edvard would not be content to just inspect the ship. He would end by convincing Jackson to hire him as captain of the voyage. He could easily persuade Jackson that the Sámit were his countrymen, and he could communicate with those who spoke Norwegian. I knew my husband. He had found a way to combine service to the Sámit with an adventure at sea, while also pursuing the men who had taken the money from the safe. He would not rest until he had caught Lloyd Quayle and Jeff Harrison and seen justice done. When you have been the captain of a ship and have been judge and jury and meted out lashes to wrongdoers for many years, it is not easy to sit by and pay a lawyer and his clerks to track down a few witnesses and collect depositions.

Edvard sent me word from Seattle that he has been commissioned to sail the *Louise J. Kenney* to Unalakleet, an Eskimo village north of St. Michael where Dr. Jackson plans to establish a reindeer station. The only problem is that the ship's owners had already sold passage on the schooner to thirty-five prospectors. How could there also be room for all the herding families, their gear, their dogs—and what about Leksu?

When I was at Fort Townsend again today, I expressed my fears to Elle-Ristine. Already the white reindeer looks thinner to me; the grass around the fort's parade ground is not as lush as that of Chinese Gardens. How could Leksu survive a month at sea? Mikkel had had the foresight to back bring two bags of lichen collected near Haines Mission—this might not be enough for the voyage.

Elle-Ristine of course had had the same thoughts but was too strong to let them overwhelm her. She had decided that she must leave Leksu behind. A husband was a husband after all, and she must follow him. A reindeer was only a reindeer. Reindeer live and die by their ability to forage. Why subject the animal to another sea voyage of strong waves and eventual starvation?

So Elle-Ristine reasoned, with her usual good sense.

"If we do not stay long in Alaska, I will come back next summer for Leksu. Our contract is only through next January. Perhaps Mikkel will find gold nuggets in the rivers and make our fortune," she added with a slight smile. "And then perhaps we will settle in Port Townsend or nearabout."

I knew that she liked it here in the Pacific Northwest, in spite of the fact they could have no reindeer herd in Port Townsend. But Elle-Ristine understood that even in Lapland the days of reindeer herding might eventually come to an end. Already there were many conflicts over the herding districts. Sweden and Norway fought between themselves, but they also fought the Sáme herders. The governments wanted to build dams and railways; the farmers claimed more land for agriculture; and mining companies looked for ore and copper.

In America, Elle-Ristine could observe that she and Mikkel

were already treated much better than at home. In ordinary clothes, they could be seen as Norwegians if they chose. And their children would grow up without an accent, knowing only American ways. Why, only a few days ago, dozens of Sámit had been sent to the courthouse and sworn in as American citizens, en masse. Elle-Ristine and Mikkel had not chosen to do so, but they still could become citizens at some point. The U.S. government had treated them properly, many thought—much better than the provincial authorities in Norway.

"Then, I will be glad to take on the task of finding a home for Leksu until you return," I said. I suggested that we bring the reindeer to the farm at Chimacum, where green grass grew abundantly along the creek and Leksu would have a goat for company.

I will remember this day for a long time. Elle-Ristine and I walked together the four miles to the farm, leading the ever-placid Leksu, in her colorful harness, behind us. A warm, breezy, blue-skyed day it was, and easy to imagine ourselves back in Norway. Much of the dense forest along the bay has been logged off, and now red alders and vine maple grow amidst stands of second-growth hemlock, so that we had filtered shade along the dry dirt road.

We talked on and off about our hopes for the future. No matter if they stayed a long or short time in Alaska, she wanted to have children. I could not promise that I would have a child, but I told her that I would like to keep writing and publish more articles in Norway and the Norwegian press in America. Maybe someday I would write a book.

"What about you, Elle-Ristine?" I asked. "Do you still think of being a teacher?"

"If I have a daughter," said Elle-Ristine. "I would like her to be a schoolteacher. A proper one, like your cousin Katrine. But in Alaska, yes, we will need teachers, and I will teach what I know, so that the children know our language and our stories."

On our long walk we sang each other songs, being quite alone in the filtered light of the forest. My songs, rusty in my throat, were from the Sognefjord, while hers were a form of chanting that had few words and went from deep in her throat to high and eerie. It's called *joiking*, this singing that belongs to the tent and to the wilderness, and that suggests the wolf and the reindeer and the shape of mountains and valleys. Sometimes, Elle-Ristine said, there is drumming as well, and I was reminded of the Klallam people on the beach in the evening, once when Edvard and I came across a group of them unexpectedly and heard their drumming and chanting.

Yes, I will remember this day for as long as I live, how close I felt to Elle-Ristine, even though she is ten years younger. And yet how different our lives have been, and how different our futures may be.

When we arrived at the farm, we found Lian and Kjell out in the field behind the shack, clearing brush and hoeing. Lian, in her dress and bonnet, looked like any farmer. She dropped her hoe when she saw us and came running—lightly, as is her way, as if she were more leaf than girl—and on her face was pure joy, until she saw I didn't have Susan Berit with me.

I explained that I had left the baby in her cradle at Adele's establishment. Adele adored Susan as much as I did, and already had sewed exquisite clothes for her. Kjell had also come up to us by now, wiping the sweat off his sun-browned face. I explained that we had a favor to ask of them.

Elle-Ristine had meanwhile unhooked Leksu's lead from the harness, and the reindeer made straight for the creek and the sweet green grass growing beside it. The tethered goat, *Yang Yang* she is called, strained to see the strange new beast. *Yang Yang* apparently can mean sheep or goat, so perhaps it can mean reindeer too.

We sat outside, in the shade of a big-leafed maple, listening to the sound of the creek and drinking its clear water in jars provided by Kjell. Port Townsend, at the tip of the Quimper Peninsula, has wetlands, a lagoon, and a spring-fed pond or two, but no running streams or rivers. Drinking water is piped from some miles away to town. So it was pleasant to hear the gurgle of Chimacum Creek. Kjell had brought a chair for me and a packing case for himself. Elle-Ristine and Lian sat cross-legged on the grass.

Lian was more talkative than I had ever known her to be

in town. Her English vocabulary—in spite of the accent that Americans enjoy mocking, just as they mock Italians, Irish, and *Norwegians*, I might add—progresses quickly. She described to us the pleasure of being outdoors most of the day and tending to the new chickens and the goat. They planned to sell eggs, along with lettuces, and later in the summer, carrots and potatoes. Kjell said he was learning about chickens from Lian, who had given their hens Chinese names. They might get a pig as well. Lian knew a good deal about pigs, he said admiringly.

Three hours passed quickly, and we laughed often, though Elle-Ristine was quiet at times and looked at Leksu, and Lian seemed to have an empty space where a baby should have been on her lap. Only Kjell was unreservedly happy, glancing at Lian with a tenderness he didn't disguise. I was glad for them, though of course their situation is perilous. Edvard had not yet had the inclination or opportunity to explain every detail of his plan to me, only the barest outline, which depended on a lie: for both of us to assert that Kjell and Lian were *already* married. In Peru.

With Edvard departing in just a few days, this plan would need to wait until September when he returned. I should have been used to his absences by now, since over the course of the last two years he's been gone far more than he's been home, but the suddenness of this journey back to Alaska—so far away, so unimaginable to me—was a thorn in my heart.

Finally, the fresh breeze of midday turned into the familiar offshore afternoon wind. Kjell offered to drive us both back to the fort and then me to the house on Morgan Hill, for I had taken to walking to Fort Townsend this last week, finding it more convenient than hiring a horse and buggy. I did not walk alone in the evening, of course, and was glad for Kjell's suggestion.

Now came the parting with Leksu, combined with many instructions for the beast. The bags of lichen had been carried here by Leksu herself. It was explained to Kjell and Lian that the lichen was to be saved for an emergency. Elle-Ristine expected from all she had been told that there was plenty of reindeer lichen growing in this far away place, Unalakleet, and she would make sure that Captain Bergland brought back a large load with him when the *Louise J. Kenney* returned later this summer. She hoped to return next summer herself; she said this with both hope and sadness in her voice.

Elle-Ristine and I were quiet on the trip back to Fort Townsend, which took far less time than our meandering walk to Chimacum. Kjell wrapped us in blankets, against the wind, and we sat side by side in the back of the wagon, bouncing around. I knew that I would see her again before the ship sailed. I would be on the dock to wave them all good-bye. But still, there would never be another day quite like this.

Once home again, I write here to conjure it up again: the filtered sunlight and taste of summer in the air, Leksu eagerly eating green grass, the stories shared, the sound of the *joik*, mixed with birdsong. Yes, it has, in spite of every potential sadness and loss to come, been one of the happiest days I remember, and will remain so, I promise myself.

The Housekeeping Ledger
Alaska

July 1898 - July 1899

Letters to Dagny Bergland
from Elle-Ristine Persdatter Aikio

First Letter

July 5, 1898
Aboard the Louise J. Kenney

Dear Dagny,

You have asked me to record my impressions of the passage north to Alaska and although it may be a few weeks until I can post this, I have decided to write you today and continue the letter when able. Captain Bergland says we can leave letters at a place called Dutch Harbor to be sent south on another ship.

You will remember all the problems with deciding who should go on which ship because of the overcrowding and how half of our group was taken off this schooner and sent to Seattle to take another ship. Often, I wonder if we too, Mikkel and I, should not have taken that opportunity. Perhaps it was a larger, bigger ship those others are on now, perhaps sturdier and more comfortable.

Before this year I had never been on a ship before, but now I have taken two long sea voyages and, if I am ever to return to Norway, I will need to take two more. I cannot say at the moment that I like the idea. You, with your long experience at sea, will perhaps smile at my timidity, yet compared with traveling across Finnmark in a reindeer caravan in dark winter with a blizzard raging, I would choose that over sailing in an open sea on what seems a very small and unsteady craft. At least in a blizzard you can bury yourself in the snow and take a nap until the storm is over (you must make sure your ski pole sticks up though, in case you need to be dug out). At least under the snow it is silent.

Here it is never silent. The wind howls in the sails and the waves slap at the sides of the ship, and over the sides. And the men—the prospectors—speak and laugh with loud voices and the crewmen shout to each other about the sails and the cook shouts "Come and get it," and even your husband the captain must speak loudly, so that he is heard above the other shouting, so all obey him. We Sámit are like small birds in the underbrush, very quiet. We have no reindeer to call to and only a few dogs to tell what to do. If Margrete Utsi was here, she would speak up, but as you know she stayed behind because of her sick little boy. Perhaps they have gone back to Norway by now. Ravna is wretchedly seasick. Her mother-in-law Inga just smokes her pipe and looks on in disgust.

I am glad that your husband is the captain. He keeps good order and does not allow any drinking. The first day out the crew made a search of the ship and tossed some barrels of whiskey belonging to the prospectors overboard, and since then a few hidden bottles have gone over the side as well. I hear grumbling because of this, but Captain Bergland is so tall and so big in his blue jacket with the shiny brass buttons and captain's hat that he is respected. You get a feeling your husband would toss a troublesome man over the side just like a barrel of whiskey and think no more about it.

We Sámit, of course, are easily cowed. We are not a fist-fighting people. Most of the time when we have fought against the sheriffs, it has gone badly for us.

I wrote that we are in the open sea, but it is not that we do not see land still, as we are less than a week out from Port Townsend. Sometimes the land is far-off and sometimes much closer, when we enter a channel with big rocks and deep green forests on either side. When the sun is out it is very beautiful, but often it is misty or raining and then the huge, dripping trees seem to press in on our little ship. We have seen many animals. Big mother bears with a large hump on their shoulders and small playful cubs fish among the leaping salmon in rivers that pour into the sailing channels. My people have many traditions and tales related to bear hunts and ceremonies, but most of them are from long ago. Before this, I had never seen a bear so near.

There are other marvelous sights in this new land, the white-headed eagles that also hunt the salmon, and the woodpeckers whose thrumming can sometimes be heard across the water. We see seals lying on the rocks, and dolphins follow us sometimes. A curious kind of whale, black and white, moves in groups of four or more, jumping and spouting sometimes quite close. And sometimes when they leap from the water, they turn an eye upon us and peer with curiosity at our faces. Ducks and seabirds gather along the shore or on the rocks, or sometimes fly in a great hurry away from our noise and our sails. And there are houses along the shore too, cedar houses with carved posts and drying racks for fish and firepits, and sometimes these small villages look empty, but at other times we see Indians congregated on the stony beaches, gathering seaweed or digging clams and oysters. And we also see them in their canoes hollowed out from cedar trees, trees so huge that many men can fit in them. They row so fast they almost match the speed of our sails. Almost always they row away from us.

About the prospectors, what is there to say? Graybeards or youths, they are almost to a one bigger than we are, with loud voices and wide gestures. When they swing their arms, they seem already to be groveling for gold nuggets. Their eyes are dark with greed and sparkle with the gold dust they imagine will soon fill their leather pouches. They imagine how rich they will be and what they will do with all that money. They want only to take from the earth, take and take and take.

Some of them are very rough men indeed, with teeth stained from tobacco (or missing), and badly healed broken noses, but some few are more refined. These men are in the "first class" cabin—although, aside from a door that shuts, there isn't so much difference between our quarters. We are separated from the prospectors by wooden slats and canvas hangings that afford so little privacy we never change our clothes (though we do wash our faces, unlike some of the prospectors). Most of them make it plain that they see us as a species of Indian, with our "peculiar" leggings, tunics, and bonnets or hats. They—who are paying a good deal of money to live in shacks in the wilderness, eat nothing but beans and corncakes, if they can get them, and dig in the earth like moles—think of us as savages, we who have been hired by the United States government and brought at great expense to this country with a job to do. Our passages, at least, were paid, and we receive a monthly salary. Who are the foolish ones in this case?

Still, I must add, in fairness, that some of the men are kind to the children, giving them a coin or two to see a smile. These men, I think, must be fathers, and my heart pities them. They may not see their children grow up, I fear, if they see them at all again.

Mikkel and a few other men, who also cannot help but dream of the goldfields and easy money, would like to speak to these men, I suspect, and learn more about where the gold is and how to find it. But the language separates us. Not a single miner speaks Norwegian or Finnish, and the two or three Sámit who managed to learn English in the last four months are on the other ship. Mikkel knows some words, but the sentences come out wrong somehow and they only laugh at him. Thank God, I say again, for Captain Bergland, who is from our country and understands what we say if we can speak Norwegian. And thank God for the luck of knowing you, Dagny, for that means the captain watches out for us.

We sometimes talk a little about life in Port Townsend and how the captain hopes that when this voyage is over, he can settle down quietly with you in your beautiful house. I believe he has some particular reason for wishing to go to St. Michael, but I have not understood what it is, only that there are two men there who have done him some injustice and he wishes to make it right.

July 19, 1898

We hope to make port in Dutch Harbor in a day I hear, so now I will continue with my letter, so it can be sent south with the post. The voyage has been very difficult, more than I knew when I first wrote you two weeks ago, for we have encountered much bad weather including one terrible storm that lasted four days. But there have also been days of little wind and strange events. The strangest was some days ago when a river steamboat was spotted drifting in the sea, seemingly abandoned. The Captain sent a rowboat and several men to investigate. They found evidence of a hasty departure from the ship: valises and trunks open, clothing everywhere, bedding flung on the floors. There were twenty chickens, but not a single person. It is suspected the steamboat was under tow and perhaps during the storm cut loose. The tug picked up all the passengers—it is hoped. The seamen brought back the most valuable objects, including some guns, and the chickens for the cook. And then the steamboat was left to its fate, drifting on the great Gulf of Alaska.

The situation below decks is no better; the prospectors complain that we Sámit are filthy and yet across the wooden partition they continue to chew tobacco, spit, and to retch and curse. Everyone who can spends much of his time on deck. Though it is cold and foggy, at least the air is fresh. I have now seen several great whales, lazily swimming along and spouting water very high. One whale threw itself several times high in the air and hit the water with a slap, creating waves that nearly swamped the forecastle. Captain Bergland ordered all the children immediately below.

We have seen many albatrosses, or "goonies" as they are called in English, with wingspans of many meters. Some of the men had the idea to lasso the birds out of the air, and soon they had several to give to the cooks. The other passengers would not eat them and in truth they were not very delicious. Better is fresh cod. A few days ago we passed over great cod and halibut beds, fish without number. It was the rare sunny day that put everyone in a good mood. Some fish were over thirty pounds. We feasted that night.

Now, when the fog clears, we see islands and low hills partially covered with snow. We will only take on water at Dutch Harbor, they say. Time is precious now and everyone wants to get to St. Michael. I hope that soon we will be settled in our new home and that in time you will receive this letter, and also that I will hear from you. I think every day about my time in Port Townsend, and about Miss Lian and Mr. Kjell and Miss Pennybaker, and all the strange and interesting things that happened there, which now seem so far away.

With best greetings from
Elle-Ristine

Second Letter

August 15, 1898
Eaton Reindeer Station, near Unalakleet, Alaska

Dear Dagny,

The post came yesterday and with it a letter from you. Just think, how a letter could travel all the way from Port Townsend, Washington. I also received the short letter you enclosed from my uncle in Karasjok, who said the spring migration went very well and many calves are still living. His letter was sent in April, but it went slowly to Port Townsend and then came here with your letter, written in June. You tell me that Leksu is well in Chimacum and that makes me glad. The ships will be leaving in early September for the south, before the seas begin to freeze. This letter will come with six bags of reindeer lichen that I've been collecting. I can only write at night because there is so much work to do. Mr. Kjellman makes us labor long hours to build our houses and make ourselves ready for the winter. But he has given me paper and the envelope from the stores and says he will find a ship to take the letter to you with the sacks of reindeer lichen.

I thought we would stay in the village of Unalakleet, as that is where the Eskimos live. There is a Swedish mission there too, the Swedish Covenant Church, which is run by the Reverend Axel Karlson, and there is a schoolhouse where the Eskimo children learn English. Our group arrived on the *Kenney* on at the end of July. The steamship with the rest of our people, the *Navarro,* had arrived in St. Michael a few days earlier. Then we all took another steamer boat north to Unalakleet. Dr. Jackson and Mr. Kjellman are here too, having taken a better class of steamship to Alaska. I wish Dr. Jackson had been on the *Kenney.* Then he would have seen what we had to go through. But his mind is always on God and reindeer, so maybe he doesn't care.

Soon after all of us, Sámit and Norwegians alike, were gathered on the shore at Unalakleet with our bags and boxes and sleds and chests, there was a quarrel between Jafet Lindeberg, the young Swedish-Norwegian man, and Dr. Jackson. Jafet did not want to go on to Siberia to collect the reindeer the government had bought for us and to bring them back on a ship. There were angry words, and Jafet left on the *Kenney* for Golovin with your husband as captain. Captain Bergland agreed to deliver some supplies to the villages and missions around Norton Sound before returning to St. Michael. I think your husband had not expected that, but anyway, he said he would do it, because there are not many sea captains up here.

Dr. Jackson went away again on another steamship, and we were told by Mr. Kjellman we were not to stay in Unalakleet but would move upriver eight miles and build a village for ourselves. This will be called Eaton Reindeer Station. None of us know why it is to be located here except perhaps there are more trees to cut for building and much reindeer lichen. Yet so far, we have no reindeer, they are still on their way overland. We were given tents to live in and we are to live in them until all four houses and the main building are finished. This is so none of us moves in before the others and has it better. Only the doctor will be allowed to move into a log cabin. We herders are used to living in tents, but the young Norwegians and Finns do not like it so much.

So far, the weather has been good, even hot. It is beautiful here and reminds me of Finnmark. The river is broad and clear and along it grows willow and small birch, just like home. While the men cut trees and saw them and hammer them together, we women gather berries and hay to dry. In the winter we'll stuff the hay into our boots to keep our feet dry and warm. I cannot tell you how good it feels to me to be on land again and to be doing ordinary tasks, tasks I always did at home all my life. There is a kitchen tent and meals are made for us. We also make some of our own food from the reindeer that were finally brought to us. There are 150 of them, very poor reindeer from Siberia, with thin legs that easily break. Our own reindeer, from Norway, are still, we believe, on their long trek through Alaska and will not be here yet for some time.

I am again with child, perhaps three months along, but I work just as much as the others. Ravna will have a baby as well, it was not seasickness after all. She lies in bed, and she cries for her mother back in Karasjok. Inga Pulk smokes her pipe and tells her son not to worry about Ravna, but to work. It will turn darker and chillier in a month, so all the buildings must be done by then. Many people are discontented with Mr. Kjellman because he makes us labor so hard, and the rations are small and not what was promised when we left Port Townsend. Dr. Jackson said we would have monthly rations of food, but we have only about half that. There is fear about the winter, since no one knows whether it will be the same cold as Norway or a different cold.

August 25, 1898

I will add two pieces of news we heard a few days ago before I close this letter. Mikkel and I are in Unalakleet, where we had permission to come and visit the Reverend Axel Karlson and his school. As you know, Swedish is not so different from Norwegian, so we understand each other. I had a thought that perhaps I could help the school a little bit with teaching. It was a pleasure to sit in a room and drink some coffee without the sound of hammering and Mr. Kjellman's voice urging all to work harder. The pastor has been in Alaska for twelve years. He was sent here to turn the Eskimos into Christians, and in this I see he has succeeded and for this effort I congratulate him, even as I feel a familiar sadness. When Christianity comes, the old customs and memories begin to die out.

   I hope, my good friend, you won't worry about my soul or think less of me for still remembering the old traditions. What I mean to say is that when I look upon the Eskimos in their sealskins and hear them singing hymns in church, I am reminded of my own people in the past and all the old ways that are now forbidden and forgotten.

   But I have not told you the two pieces of news, both good. First is that your husband was saved from a shipwreck! The *Louise J. Kenney* went aground south of Point Hope. Although some of the supplies were lost, the crew and your husband are well. The ship was seen on the beach, on its side, by the *Bear,* the revenue cutter, and everyone was taken to St. Michael. The men had been out in the rain overnight but apparently are well. This was on August 20. So I can imagine that your husband will soon be on his way home to you if he is not already, as a captain or passenger on one of the many ships going south.

The other news is that our Jafet Lindeberg has found gold at Golovin, where he traveled after his quarrel with Dr. Jackson. He has staked a claim with two other Swedes, and they plan to explore some other places as well. When Mikkel heard this, he was quite wild to join Jafet, and many of the other men working here to build the reindeer station are keen as well. Even Mr. William Kjellman seems excited. Sometimes I can wonder why the United States government was persuaded to bring us all here. We build a reindeer station at top speed, but have few reindeer, and no Eskimos to instruct upriver. And all the men can talk about is gold digging and how, when the year-long contracts are finished at the end of January, they will all go the new goldfields around Norton Bay and become rich men.

But here I must end, dear Dagny, for the letter must go on the ship if it is to go at all. I send, as I said, six full sacks of lichen. And here are the instructions you must give to Lian and Kjell. They must allow Leksu to graze on the grass until it becomes tough and hard. She will eat mushrooms in the fall if she can find them. When the rains and snow come, begin to feed her a little lichen every day, until she gets used to it. The lichen must last the winter. But I think that she can begin to eat grass again in April, along with leaves on the bushes. I will send more lichen as soon as the ice breaks up and the ships can sail again next June.

Your friend always,
Elle-Ristine

Third Letter

October 20, 1898
Eaton Reindeer Station, Alaska

My dear Dagny,

I imagine by the time you receive this letter that you will know the sad news and I will not be the first to tell you of your husband's fate. The last ships of the year left Norton Sound sometime in late September. Over the winter they say that the post will be carried by dogsled, at least once a month, along the river from St. Michael to Dawson City and from there south to Skagway. They even talk about reindeer carrying the post soon, since the reindeer don't need to be fed meat along the way. But it is such an unimaginable distance that I do not know whether to believe it. In truth, I feel no great rush to write you with this news.

Today it is very cold and most of us continue to freeze in our tents. Because I am with child, I am allowed to move into one of the wooden houses that have been sitting empty for two months, along with several other women and their children. The main building is almost finished and will be very grand, with two stories. Almost everyone is sick, because of the cold and poor food, but still everyone who can work is made to do so.

In this cold weather, with some snow falling, a kind of calmness comes over me. I have not seen snow for many months, and I have missed it. Soon the reindeer will begin to pull the sleds, the *pulkas* we brought with us. The Eskimos are already using their dog sleds on the frozen rivers.

You must believe me very distressed to know that Captain Bergland has died. I only heard yesterday when news came from St. Michael, and I am still in a kind of shock. It was at the military hospital there that he died, three weeks ago. All this time I had imagined him on one of the last ships going back south, to you. I thought he would surely be in Port Townsend by now. When I first heard the news, there were two accounts. One was that he developed influenza after the shipwreck and after spending the night outdoors, all wet and cold on the shore, and that it became worse on the passage down to St. Michael. He was admitted to the military hospital and there, after a long struggle, he died.

The other account is more confusing. It has to do with some "unfinished business" with the two men who had blackened his name last year. In this account he heard that one of the two men had been to Dawson City but had returned to St. Michael again and was about to take a ship south. Your husband rose from his sickbed and went looking for the man and found him, but the Captain was too weak, and he collapsed. Captain Bergland was then brought back to the hospital and eventually was called to heaven. They have buried him in the cemetery there.

Whichever one of the accounts is true, the fact is that the captain is no more. And for that I am truly sorry, dear Dagny. I remember his blue coat and brass buttons, and his firm voice on the ship. His boots were heavy, and I always felt some relief to hear them coming down the ladder to our quarters, for I knew that any disputes would be settled quickly and that the prospectors would again behave themselves, for a time. He would take no nonsense, but never did any man ever have a kinder look in his eye.

One evening comes to mind, this was on board the ship to Alaska. One of the young children, a boy of only five or six, was irritable and crying because of a cold. His mother had held him as long as she could, and his father had spoken to him sternly, but nothing did any good. It is hard for young children to sit still, especially those who have always had an active life outdoors. Captain Bergland had come down to visit us and asked how everyone was. He could see for himself that all was not well with the boy. First, he gave him a peppermint from his pocket and then he set the boy on his back and shoulders and told him to hang on to the big bear. And then the captain walked around and around the steerage hold like that until the little chap simply fell asleep. I never saw a man do something like that. I could tell he liked children. He always had a friendly word for the girls and boys and liked to see them smile.

My sympathies, dear Dagny.

November 16, 1898

I continue this letter with further news. Most of the time there is no news to write. Everything is frozen now and, as in Finnmark, that makes it much faster to get around. We harness up these reindeer to our sleds and go back and forth to Unalakleet, mainly to get away from Eaton Station and to visit Reverend Karlson. The situation here is not so good. The rations are even fewer than in the fall and it is very cold, so that people suffer. The doctor is kept very busy with our illnesses. He is angry that we Sámit do not take the medicine he gives us for what he calls scurvy. I think if he were not always so angry, we might believe what he says, but many among us do not know this disease and wish for familiar remedies. I understand from the pastor that scurvy is caused by lack of vitamins in the diet. Reverend Karlson eats what the native people eat, seal and walrus meat, and cloudberries soaked in salmon roe and then buried in the ground for a time. But Mr. Kjellman does not give us such things, only flour for bread, cornmeal, rancid ship biscuits, and some tins of beans and pork.

I have not been well, like the others, but I do not have scurvy, only colds and coughs, because of the weather. At home I was almost never ill, and I thrived in the winter. I slept outside all night sometimes, watching the reindeer, so the wolves did not carry them off. Yes, many are ill, and every night, as we all try to sleep in the rooms of the big house, we hear each other sneezing and coughing and groaning.

That is probably why the news of just a week ago made so many of us, the men at least, so excited. Jafet Lindeberg left Golovin and went farther west, to a place called Anvil Creek, near Nome. There, he and two Swedish immigrants found a good deal of gold on the beach. He wants Kjellman and all the men here at Eaton Station to know about this strike, before the word gets to the prospectors in the Yukon goldfields and they all begin a new gold rush at Norton Sound in summer.

Night after night there has been discussion of this. All talk of reindeer herding has been suspended, even by William Kjellman, who helped bring everyone here. We have not many reindeer to speak of and no one is certain who is meant to own them—is it the United States government or Dr. Jackson or the Sámit or the Eskimos?

Some Sámit wish to return to Norway. Several plan to leave by dogsled in March for Seattle and then travel the long journey back home. Others are content with the possibilities of Alaska—if they could just get reindeer, they could have large herds, thousands of animals. For many traditional Sámit, this is the greatest wealth, and what they dream of at night. Here in Alaska, they argue, there are vast new lands to graze and as much reindeer lichen as anyone could need. The rivers are large and clear. Every condition is met here for good reindeer pasture. There is only one national boundary, with Canada, and it is far away. Compared to the laws and tax collectors in Norway, Finland, and Sweden, all of whom fight over the Sáme rights and how much money we must pay in fees and damages, there are few laws here (none that we understand anyway) and no taxes. The U.S. government wants to *give* us lands to graze the reindeer on, not take land away from us. Many families are convinced that if they can survive this winter and become free of Kjellman, Jackson, and the contracts, that it will be possible to live here very well.

Mikkel does not want to go back to Norway, at least not yet. I wish he were more like some Sáme men here, men and women who love the life of a reindeer herder and want to teach the skills to their young sons and daughters and make a life here. But Mikkel, even with a child on the way, is always the dreamer, and more like the young men from Norway who find inspiration in Jafet Lindeberg's gold strike. They all want to head over to Anvil Creek and stake claims, and Mikkel is among them. He says they will go in December, register their claims, and return in February when our baby is due. What then? I ask, fearing the answer. Will I raise our child alone here at Eaton Station while Mikkel looks for gold on the coast? I don't know what will be worse—if he finds gold or if he doesn't. For I see now I have a husband who will never be satisfied and who will not work for what he needs. He will always be dreaming of something else.

Excuse me, Dagny, for writing of my troubles. In our culture, we have strong women, but the man decides. If Mikkel decides to go to Anvil Creek, he will go.

In friendship and, if by some strange luck, the dogsled manages to bring this letter south in time for Christmas, a very happy holiday to you!

Elle-Ristine

Fourth Letter

January 6, 1899
Eaton Reindeer Station, Alaska

Dear Dagny!

I wish a good new year to you and to my other friends in Port Townsend, Miss Lian, Mr. Kjell, and Miss Pennybaker. In spite of your recent loss (which I now think you must certainly know of, though I have not received a letter from you), I hope to hear that your Christmas holiday was a cheerful one. I like to think of you with your friends in your beautiful house, with a tree, candles, and many good things to eat. Is Miss Pennybaker still sewing pretty clothes and does Miss Lian help her? I wonder if by this time Miss Lian is married to Mr. Kjell? I think of her and Susan Berit. And of course I think of my beloved Leksu, and I hope very much that the reindeer lichen is enough and that they are not feeding her too much, so that it can last the winter.

Mikkel left December 7 for the place they are calling Anvil City or Nome, with six or seven others, including William Kjellman himself, in his haste to make gold claims for himself. They went with reindeer sleds. The rest of us are left in the doctor's charge. Dr. Gambell spends his time caring for the sick, of whom we are many. I do not seem quit of the cough I have had for many weeks, but it is not worse, that I can tell you. Our own Christmas was rather quiet, for the doctor is very much against offering spirits to the Sáme people. A group of us made an excursion to Unalakleet to hear Reverend Karlson preach a sermon. It was a good sermon, though in English, and the Eskimos filled the schoolroom to hear him. Two days later he came to Unalakleet and preached the same sermon in Swedish, which gave me much to think about. In Unalakleet there was coffee and cake for all after the sermon, but here we had little to offer in the way of festivity, only barley flour pancakes with some dried berries soaked in reindeer milk. The doctor is as tight with the rations as ever Mr. Kjellman was.

On New Year's Day I went out by myself for a short while on the skis that Mikkel made for me for Christmas. The weather was clear and cold and over the snow lay violet shadows, while the sky in the middle of the day was light blue. I was reminded of my home and of my girlhood. People have often said our life in Finnmark sounds so difficult—to live in a tent on the snow and to live, winter and summer, with what the land gives you. I did not find that difficult—it was what I knew. I found it beautiful. And I find Alaska beautiful too on a day like today, fresh with beginning.

I skied some ways from Eaton Station, but very slowly, listening. For I wondered if the land here holds some of the same secrets as our land. Do you remember on our walk to Chimacum, that we spoke of the *uldas,* the underground beings, who live mirror lives under our feet? They have tents and fires, and forests and lakes. And they have herds of reindeer as well. They sleep when we are awake and are awake when we are sleeping. Sometimes they take our reindeer, but often they give us reindeer as well. The clear-eyed among us have sometimes seen their reindeer in the distance, a herd crossing a frozen river, or a few stray beasts in the forest. The sharp-eared among us have heard them humming and singing. Their *joiks* are like our *joiks,* but not everyone can hear them.

Sometimes when I was young and out by myself, I imagined that I heard the *uldas* singing far below. I felt a kind of yearning then, as if time had stopped, and if I held my breath, I might see one of them. Perhaps my double, another Elle-Ristine who had come up from the depths for a glimpse at our world.

Several times I imagined I saw my double in the distance, with her white reindeer, just like Leksu. Today I looked for this girl, to see if she would be a woman now, carrying a child. But mostly I looked for the white reindeer.

Again, greetings to you for the new year, and to our other friends. I do not know what the future brings, if I will come again to Port Townsend or stay here in Alaska. You will not receive this letter for many months. But still it gives me pleasure, and comfort, to write to you.

Your friend, Elle-Ristine

Letter from the Reverend Axel Karlson

March 15, 1899
Unalakleet, Alaska

Dear Mrs. Bergland,

This unmailed letter of January 6, 1898 was found among Mrs. Elle-Ristine Aikio's possessions after her death ten days ago. It was in an envelope addressed to you, so I take the liberty of sending it now. Mrs. Aikio perhaps was going to wait to send it by ship from Unalakleet, but I shall take the chance that the dogsled can deliver the post sooner to Dawson City and from there on southwards. I want to send it as soon as possible, with my condolences.

I can tell you that none of us was expecting Mrs. Aikio's sudden death. She had had a cough for some time, but many people at Eaton Reindeer Station have had some form of illness since the autumn. She gave birth to a healthy baby girl in mid-February, and I am glad to say that her husband Mikkel was present, having returned from Nome to formalize the end of his service with the U.S. War Department in the matter of the Yukon Relief Expedition.

There were many cold days in February and Mrs. Aikio's cough grew worse and she began to have trouble breathing. In spite of all the doctor could do, she expired the night of March 10. She will be sorely missed in our small community. I believe from what she told me that you had met during the time that the Laplanders stayed at Fort Townsend and that you were very kind to her. Her letter, which I apologize for having read, shows a degree of warmth that I expect is mutual. May God support you in this loss and only know that Mrs. Aikio is now in a happier place with God and his angels.

As to Mr. Mikkel Aikio, he has now departed Eaton Station for Nome, following other men, mostly Norwegians. They leave behind the Lappish families who are to manage the reindeer herd. The baby is one of four born since the first of the year and has been wet nursed since Mrs. Aikio's untimely death by a young Lappish lady, Mrs. Ravna Pulk, with a child born around the same time. The baby has been baptized and is called Anna Mikkelsdatter Aikio.

I pray that you receive this letter in good time and regret that my news is not of a happier nature.

Your humble servant in Christ,
Axel Karlson

***

St. Michael and Unalakleet, Alaska
July 15, 1899

Adele and I arrived in St. Michael a few days ago at about six o'clock in the evening. I didn't bring my last leather journal, since I was near the end of it, but instead grabbed the housekeeping ledger from the secretary drawer in the parlor, along with sufficient funds to pay for the voyage and a month away. We left in something of a hurry.

Of the voyage north there is little to say except that we came by steamship. We didn't travel up the coast, but instead struck out across the Gulf of Alaska for Dutch Harbor, and from there crossed the Bering Sea. I could not help but think of Edvard's opposition to steam, his steadfast loyalty to the world of sail that he grew up in. I have no longer any loyalty to sailing ships.

Our ship was crowded with would-be miners as well as those who had tried and failed to get to the Yukon last year. Nome was said to be even richer than the Yukon goldfields. We heard some say, especially those who had only recently managed to travel to Seattle from the East or even abroad, that they were glad they had waited to join the gold rush. Unlike the men who had braved the steep slope of the Chilkoot Pass or lost horses (and fingers) along White Pass in 1897, these tenderfoots believed all they had to do was walk along the beaches and rivers of Norton Sound and pocket their gold nuggets as they walked.

Adele found the whole journey a great adventure, and her good spirits were a comfort to me. She never complained about the close quarters and was not seasick but strode about on deck in her mackintosh like a born sailor. It was she who suggested coming with me on this voyage north as a companion in my grief.

We were among the few to debark in St. Michael—most of the rest of the passengers were going on to Nome. The steamship anchored offshore, beyond the mudflats. As St. Michael has no proper wharves close to the town, we were lifted onto a tender, along with many crates of foodstuffs and supplies. Machinery and other metal boat parts emerged from the hold; they were taken ashore by barge. These were sections of sternwheelers that had been built in Seattle and now only needed assembling in the boatyards of St. Michael. Here in the town almost a hundred boats were built over the last winter, to ply the Yukon River. The irony of course is that far fewer men are going upriver to Circle City and Dawson. The sternwheelers will be taking up supplies for the miners and merchants who remain. Their more important task is to transport people *out* of the Yukon fever dream and its freezing, muddy reality.

Americans, when inspired, are capable of unleashing stupendous amounts of energy. And nothing inspires them more than greed: Seattle and Port Townsend have been changed by the gold rush, and it appears that St. Michael has been transformed as well, for the town bears little resemblance to Edvard's description of it as a trading post with an onion-domed Russian church. Now there are mercantiles and warehouses, saloons, and boarding houses, in one of which, if it is respectable, we hope to find lodging for a night or two before going on to Unalakleet. The streets are mucky from rain and snowmelt and the steady tramp of boots.

The mood is reckless and a little desperate. The men who have just come down the Yukon are a dirty, grizzled lot, clothes stained and torn or badly patched, boots in need of new soles, or any sole at all, some of them. Some fellows boast about their claims and flourish pouches of gold dust when they pay for drinks or a meal; others slink ashamed and hard-faced around the town, bedroll on their back, trying to cadge a bite of food. They wait for the government to send them back to Seattle. There are women too, the painted kind for the most part, ready to move on to Nome and to new friends to wine and dine them.

Looking at their tattered flounces and stained bodices, Adele whispered mischievously to me, "Don't you think St. Michael is in need of a good dressmaker's shop? If I'd had the foresight to bring some bolts of silk and muslin and my scissors and needles with me, I could have made a fortune this summer and returned to Port Townsend a wealthy woman."

I smiled, but distractedly, as we pushed our way through the crowds along the main street of St. Michael holding our valises close. For I was staring at the hill overlooking the harbor, its neat buildings clustered inside a white picket fence and a large American flag flapping in the gray sunshine. This is the fort with its military hospital, I realized, where Edvard spent his last days. Here too will be the cemetery where he is buried.

"I think this boarding house would suit us nicely," said Adele the evening we arrived, pointing to one where the landlady had made an attempt at decoration—there were at least curtains in the windows upstairs. "It is just for a night or two." For our plan tomorrow was to go to the military hospital at Fort St. Michael, and afterwards to find a ship to take us to Unalakleet.

I thanked her for her presence of mind and her calmness, both of which seemed to have deserted me in this strange new town full of wild-eyed people coming and going. I needed to pay my respects to my husband's grave in the cemetery here in St. Michael and equally to Elle-Ristine's resting place in Unalakleet or Eaton Station.

The death-work of the living who survive is the hardest burden to bear.

By the time I received Elle-Ristine's letter telling me of Edvard's death, a letter sent by dogsled many thousands of miles to Skagway and then further south by ship, it was the middle of May, and I had known since late October that Edvard was gone.

The officer in charge at Fort St. Michael, Lieutenant Colonel Briggs, sent his letter of condolence directly to Port Townsend, on one of the military ships, with the news explaining that my husband had died that day, September 17.

Fearful and anxious I had been for some time, knowing that something might have happened to Edvard to delay his journey home. I suppose my mildest fear was that he had pursued Harrison and Quayle to Dawson City and would be trapped there over the winter. My midnight fears were worse: I imagined one of the thieves had shot and killed Edvard. Or that Edvard had shot them and had been hanged. So it was strange to read the letter from the commander of Fort St. Michael with its more prosaic explanation that Captain Bergland had developed a fever brought by exposure after the schooner grounded on Point Hope. "Although his was a strong constitution and he fought manfully," wrote the captain, "at his age the body is less able to fight off infections."

At his age. Edvard was fifty-two. He should have left the sea after the *Matilde* burned. We should have taken passage on the next ship to Norway. With the insurance we could have bought a house in Bergen and lived quietly the rest of our allotted time, close to Katrine and Aunt Inger. And perhaps there could have been more children. At the very least he should not have returned to Alaska, not after what happened a year ago. He *knew* the Arctic seas were dangerous and icy. Oh, I was angry!

And with my anger came the desire to flee homeward, to those I loved and who could comfort me. If Edvard was dead, there was no reason to stay in Port Townsend, a town where I had never really been accepted and where I had no ties. I could sell the house and everything in it. A train would quickly take me across the country. From New York I could easily find a steamship sailing to Liverpool and another to Bergen. The idea intoxicated as much as it comforted. To be in Norway in a mere month? To sit at a table eating dinner with my dearest Katrine and Aunt Inger, looking out at the familiar hills of Bergen and the harbor below? To see spring come to Western Norway in all its glory, to visit the Sognefjord and see my older sisters and their families? To speak Norwegian all day every day and read it and write it and live it?

But it was not true that I didn't have ties to Port Townsend. There was Adele. And there was little Susan Berit and her parents, Kjell and Lian, now married. Yes, married, though not after a great deal of effort. A year ago, last June, before he set off in the *Kenney*, Edvard confided a scheme to me and to Kjell, a plan he wished to put into effect as soon as he returned from Alaska. All summer and fall Kjell and I waited, uncertain if we could carry out the deception on our own and hoping that the captain would return. Neither of us felt able to act on the ruse without Edvard, for it would need Lian's participation as well as the captain's presence to swear to its truth.

Lieutenant Colonel Briggs put to rest the story that Edvard had risen from his sickbed to pursue the two men, Harrison and Quayle. Briggs was the officer in charge of Fort St. Michael. The doctor who had attended Edvard was busy when Adele and I arrived first thing in the morning; he was attending to new cases of men who had just arrived from Dawson City with fevers and ulcerated wounds. Thus it was the crisply uniformed lieutenant colonel himself who escorted us into his office and related the events of almost a year ago.

"Your husband was brought to us last August from Point Hope with a cough and fever. The *Kenney* had a heavy load of machinery and lumber and had anchored off Point Hope in the Chukchi Sea. A gale blew up and she dragged her anchor and was caught in the shoals. Most of the cargo was lost, but the crew were fine. By some miracle, the revenue cutter *Bear* saw the ship and men on the beach and picked them up. They were wet and exhausted, and on the voyage south to St. Michael, your husband developed a bad fever. He lay in bed at our hospital for several weeks and seemed to be getting better, before rapidly turning worse. I remember him well. He spoke of you often, Mrs. Bergland, though he did not wish me or the doctor to contact you, as he thought you would only worry. As you might know, we don't have the telegraph yet, but there are plans to lay cable next year. I was uncertain whether to write or what to write on my own.

By this time it was likely, given the weather, that he might have to overwinter with us in St. Michael. He seemed to carry a burden of guilt that he had stayed on in Alaska long past the time he should have turned back home. I wasn't ever sure why he had taken on the task of skippering the *Kenney* northward with a cargo. I only know that we were all sorry to see him suddenly decline. He began to talk wildly, he couldn't catch his breath, he spoke of waves taking him and his family."

Adele gave him a sharp look, and he added, "But rest assured, Mrs. Bergland, everything that could be done for him was done, and his end was as peaceful as one could wish."

I interrupted, "So there is no truth to the rumor that Captain Bergland left his hospital bed in order to search for two men, the two men who had wronged him the year before?"

"The captain would not have been able to leave his bed," said Briggs. "Unfortunately he had suffered a grievous wound to his leg during the shipwreck and by the time the captain was brought to the hospital, it was badly infected, and it needed to be ..." he did not continue, but, seeing my face, he hastily pulled out a chair.

But although I sat down and accepted a glass of water, I pulled myself together. Oh, I had seen it all aboard the *Matilde*. Our first mate, who had skills as a surgeon, had several times to amputate feet or hands that had been smashed in one way or another. That did not mean the thought of Edvard suffering such a fate was bearable. The words "He began to talk wildly, he couldn't catch his breath, he spoke of waves taking him and his family" pierced me like a fishhook.

"I believe," said Briggs, "that the captain had something on his mind when he first came here. The doctor told me that he shouted out that he would find these thieves, and bring them to justice, and talked about a safe. But most of it made no sense and he seemed to forget about it as he grew better."

I told the lieutenant colonel about the events of almost two years before on the *Fidelius,* and how Edvard had been summoned to the magistrate in Port Townsend on a charge of grand theft, and how the case had been dropped by the judge but was still not resolved. Edvard had been dismissed from the employ of Carl Olafsson in San Francisco and then the Puget

Mill Company in Port Gamble. And it was not over yet, when Edvard left Port Townsend on the *Kenney* in June. The accuser, Clarence Harrison, had returned to California and had vowed to press charges against Edvard again. And it was all because Mr. Harrison's younger brother had fallen in with the tinhorn gambler Mr. Quayle.

"Harrison, you say? Quayle?" said the lieutenant colonel. "Why, those are the very names of two men who murdered each other in St. Michael this last winter. Both pulled pistols at the same time and shot each other in the heart. Of all the murders in Alaska, it was the one that attracted the most notice at the time."

"Why did they kill each other?" said Adele faintly, for I only sat speechless in my chair.

"Miss Pennybaker, no one knows why men kill each other up here, except that they do it on a regular basis."

So Edvard need not have come up here after all, I thought. And again I was angry.

Briggs escorted us to the cemetery, which already had two dozen wooden crosses, Lloyd Quayle's and Jeff Harrison's among them. The morning weather was like yesterday's, a gray sky even though the sun was visible, the clouds very low, and the wind whipping at the flag in a most mournful way. From the hillside we could look out at the ships anchored beyond the mudflats. Our steamship from yesterday had already departed and another had taken its place. There was also a motley group of schooners and small steamers at anchor, and tenders and barges coming and going. Since I had first come to Bergen at fourteen, I had loved the sight of ships, but now I saw them as enemies, not as friends. Boats had caused me almost every grief in my life.

Adele and I stood at Edvard's grave, and she joined me in silent prayer and tears. And again I wished only to be back in Norway, sitting at my Aunt Inger's dining room table, safe and among friends, not here in St. Michael, always an outsider.

I remembered the first time Edvard came into that room in the Bergen house, with its beautiful bow window overlooking the harbor. How tall the man was, how broad-chested and straight-backed. He wore his best nautical jacket, and his boots were polished to a high shine. He had a tidy beard, dark red like his hair, the color of autumn leaves, and blue eyes, a sort of twinkling, friendly blue, as when the sun strikes the water's surface. He was not exactly handsome, his face was long and even then it was weathered, but his expression was one of hope and resolve. He seemed quite old—he was thirty-two then—but not old in a fatherly way. Edvard was seated across from me, his back to the bow window. In a deep, pleasant voice he answered all my questions about sailing and his ship with a smile, but a smile that took me seriously. He was weighing me as I weighed him. Later Edvard told me that he had longed to be married for quite some time and to begin a family.

"You must come and visit my ship the *Matilde* soon, Miss Dagny. And I will show you everything, from the hold to the captain's quarters. You are even allowed to stand by the wheel and turn it. Your uncle showed me the newspaper photograph with you at the wheel of a ship in harbor a few years ago. The *Matilde* has a fine wheel, if I do say so."

"And are you really sailing to Chile and Peru?"

"To lands of sunshine and warmth," he said, and he smiled.

"But it's sunny here," I countered, for it was ripe summer in Western Norway and the birds sang and all the fruit trees hung heavy with apples and plums.

"Oh, Miss Dagny, you will never see anything to match the beauty of the Chilean coast. It will be spring there when the *Matilde* arrives, at the time when Bergen is dark with rainclouds."

I saw myself then on the ship, standing at the wheel, sailing along the Chilean coast. Of course, one of the first things I learned aboard the *Matilde* is that a woman never steers the course.

July 18

After Adele and I left the cemetery, we found a restaurant in town and for an exorbitant price ate plates of salt cod and beans. Shortly afterwards, we heard that a small steamer was heading north to Unalakleet and so eager were we to leave St. Michael's muddy streets and chaos that we rushed to buy tickets, retrieve our valises, and go aboard.

By early evening we were walking into the quarters of the Swedish Covenant Mission, asking for the Reverend Axel Karlson. We found him having a meal in a kitchen smelling strongly of fish. When I spoke in Norwegian, the pastor switched from English to an old-fashioned, courteous Swedish and then back again to English to greet Adele.

"Mrs. Dagny Bergland, how very glad I am to make your acquaintance. You surprise me with your visit. And Miss Pennybaker, welcome. Two ladies appear from nowhere in Alaska. You ladies are an unusual sight this evening!"

"We came to St. Michael to learn more about my husband's death," I said, and could not help but think he was just as unusual a sight. His face was brown, and his blond-gray hair stuck up in cowlicks, like a small boy's. His face, cheerful and alert, had the radiance of the true man of God, not the fixed expression of the zealous missionary, the sort I had met with around the world, men who hold to a high standard in morals and cleanliness and wear out their wives, who must do the cleaning. Reverend Karlson, perhaps because he had no wife, was an entirely more disheveled being. His dog collar was stained with sweat, as were the armpits of his striped shirt. He wore patched skin trousers and sandals, which looked as if he had cobbled them himself.

"But good Mrs. Bergland and Miss Pennybaker, sit down, please. If you have come from St. Michael, then you will not have had dinner. Are you hungry? What I have is seal meat, fried in its own oil, and reindeer pemmican, and a pie of dried apples and berries."

I took some pemmican, but Adele tried the seal meat, which was as oily as it smelled. Afterwards we took our pie outdoors and the queasy look on Adele's face immediately vanished in the fresh bright sea air. The sun was still high, and the birds sang in the green coin leaves of the many birch trees by the river. For the first time since landing yesterday in Alaska I looked around and thought how beautiful this country was—especially away from the rumble and rubble of St. Michael. The quality of light was much the same as Norway in high summer, clear as ice, but warm. Even though I had come to Alaska on a mission of mourning, my heart lifted with the freshness of the ocean air, and with the sight of green trees fluttering with small birds that were not gulls.

Reverend Karlson asked about Edvard and said that he had never met him but had heard that he was a fine sea captain and a better man, who had done all he could to make the long voyage to Alaska more bearable for the Laplanders last summer. Wisely, the pastor did not speak immediately of Elle-Ristine's death but of his own enjoyment in getting to know all the Lappish people who had become part of his pastorate.

"Peaceful, humorous, good-natured," he said. "And willing to teach their knowledge of the reindeer. They get on well with the natives here. The Inuit, that is what the Eskimos here are called, are good Christians, but they also share some traditions. These beliefs, I have come to understand, have to do with believing that the natural world has a soul, that objects are alive, and that animals speak to us. The only problem so far with the reindeer project is that Mr. Kjellman has built Eaton Reindeer Station some eight miles from here. There is also the problem of language between the two people."

"Is the translator Mr. Dahl still here? He did not return home or go to the gold fields?"

"He did not go to Nome with the others. To have just one arm is a disadvantage for digging and panning for gold. But I do not suppose he will be here much longer. The remaining Laplanders do not care overmuch for his authority. I believe they have had too much of it, and from Mr. Kjellman as well."

"The remaining Laplanders?" I asked. "How many are left?"

"Just a handful, most with families. Some returned to Norway, some have gone to Nome, others continue to be employed by the government to transport troops and equipment to Golovin Bay from St. Michael in order to keep the peace in the mining districts. There is also a plan to transport forty or more of the reindeer from Eaton Station to St. Lawrence Island so that the Inuit people may be instructed in herding management. Two families will go there this month. And more plans! Dr. Jackson and Mr. Kjellman hope to set up postal delivery by reindeer in

Alaska, since the reindeer can go much faster and farther than the dog sleds. The dogs need food, but the reindeer will eat lichen along the route."

I inquired about Mikkel Aikio, as I was too afraid to ask about Elle-Ristine's infant daughter. With all the plans for the Sámit to be transported here and there, what was to happen to a five-month-old child with no mother? Or had the baby already died, and the pastor had not yet had the courage to mention it?

"Mikkel Aikio is still in Nome, I believe. From what I understand he has extracted a good deal of gold from his claim. He no longer wears his Lappish clothes and, in many ways, he has become like the rough miners all around him. He is a good man at heart, but given to drink, and the thirst has increased without the staying hand of his late wife. So Mr. Kjellman writes. It is easy to trade away your claim when you are drunk and gambling or be attacked by robbers. I hear Nome is filling up with claim jumpers and thieves as well as the hardened criminals from Skagway and Dawson who have by now a good deal of experience in separating men from their gold."

"Then, Mikkel has not been back here to see his child?"

"It is perhaps better he stays away, for now." The pastor sighed. "I do not know in fact whether we shall see him again, between the sad memories and the drink and the gold. The little girl does not know him enough to miss him."

"But surely," I said, my heart speeding up. "As the father ..."

"Fathers are little good without wives. In my view."

"Will the child then be brought up at Eaton Station in another herding family?"

"It is either that or in an orphanage in the Lower States," said the pastor. "The Mission here is not equipped to raise a baby. Mikkel has not even sent any money for her upbringing. And the family that has taken the baby in, the Pulk family, they are the ones who think to move with the herd to St. Lawrence Island. The Laplanders travel with their infants in cradles. I have no doubt of their good will. But it will not be an easy life. The island is closer to Russia than Alaska."

But surely there were relatives in Norway, in Karasjok? I remembered that Elle-Ristine's mother and father were both dead. Wasn't there an uncle? Uncle Aslak, yes, the one who had written her last year.

The pastor looked at me closely. "You ladies will of course stay here tonight and for as long as you like. I suggest that tomorrow morning we go to Eaton Station. So we will certainly see Elle-Ristine's child as well."

I nodded. "You said her name is Anna?"

"I christened her myself: Anna Mikkelsdatter Aikio. Her foster mother Ravna calls her Elle-Anna," he said. "Ravna recently had a little girl herself, so she had milk for Anna."

July 20

I know from Elle-Ristine's stories of growing up that the Sámit are an active people when it comes to herding, hunting, and doing all that is necessary to keep body and soul together in the wilderness. Elle-Ristine had a hundred skills, honed since childhood, which had kept her hands busy all day long. But here at Eaton Reindeer Station, as at Fort Townsend, the tasks were far fewer now the shelters were built, and it was summer. The large building where the remaining Sámit sleep had been William Kjellman's great project, and now he was in Nome, trying to make his own fortune. The families and herders who remained were waiting for his return and meanwhile continuing on with daily chores such as hauling water from the river for washing and cooking, sun-drying reindeer and caribou meat for pemmican, picking berries, and sewing or repairing shoes. The men, of course, were out with the reindeer, but the herd was rather small and did not move around much. All the men were still employees of the War Department and received a salary, however unclear their duties.

Reverend Karlson said there was still some confusion over how long the Sámit were to live in Alaska and just what their objectives should be. William Kjellman and Dr. Sheldon Jackson had many ideas for how to best utilize them and their skill with reindeer, but Kjellman was in Nome and Dr. Jackson was in constant movement, here and there in Alaska and back and forth to Washington D.C. The pastor himself did not quite understand whether the Sámit had been brought here to teach the Eskimos herding on a temporary basis or whether they were now American citizens with the right to buy great tracts of land and their own herds of reindeer. Were these particular reindeer, brought from Siberia, owned by the Inuit, or the Sámit, or merely the United States government? The native people were not allowed to own land in Alaska, nor were they allowed to stake mining claims.

"My Inuit parishioners think of the Laplanders as white people with a strange affinity for these caribou-like animals," the pastor told me. "They see the Laplanders having privileges they do not. Yet they also see a people in furs and boots, well used to cold and darkness, and with a simplicity about them that is not like white people. Simplicity is not the right word—I should rather say, a stillness."

For now, said Reverend Karlson, the Laplanders taught the Eskimos what they could. The women worked and waited, and the children explored their new world.

When we arrived at Eaton Station, we found Mr. Dahl gone on a hunting expedition with several of the men, and five women sitting on the porch of the main building sewing and doing other handiwork. I recognized Inga, the older widow, and her daughter-in-law Ravna. Inga wore a wool dress in spite of the warmth and had on a pair of cast-off men's boots, but otherwise looked just the same: wrinkled and no-nonsense. Ravna was healthy but thin and tired looking, with blue circles under her eyes, and a strand of hair falling out of her tight cap, its lace edging now torn in a few places. She wore a patched calico dress, open at the neck. There were two calfskin cradles by Ravna's feet, each with a sleeping baby. I recognized the cradle Elle-Ristine had shown me once for the miscarried child. A chain of metal with two silver balls was secured across the upper opening.

All exclaimed to see me, the Norwegian lady from Port Townsend. What was I doing here among them?

"I have come to see where Elle-Ristine lived," I said in Norwegian and then in English. "And to meet her daughter."

"Ah, Elle-Ristine," was the sad murmur. Ravna pointed to the cradle with the silver balls and said, "Elle-Anna."

Coffee was already on the boil. Adele and I were offered mugs, with a kind of dried berry cake, and then Inga and another woman pulled out clay pipes, filled them with tobacco, and smoked. Adele was taken aback but fascinated. She had never been to Fort Townsend and had only known Elle-Ristine briefly.

I could see Elle-Ristine's face among these women, the brown hair pulled back in a bun or braid under the fitted cloth cap, the careful efficient movements. All that was different now is that they had all picked up English over the past year. Only a few knew Norwegian; there was no reason to speak it in Alaska.

I told them that Adele and I had only just arrived, and that we had gone to see my husband's grave in St. Michael. Much sympathy was expressed. They all had something kind to say about Edvard: the peppermints he dispensed for seasickness; the way he kept order on the ship; how comforting it was to hear his strong voice in a storm. They had been very sorry to hear of his death.

I asked them how they liked Alaska. The Sámit in my experience are courteous and honest people. Yet the honesty, if I may say so, is not always expressed directly. One woman said something about Siberian reindeer with legs like soft waxy candles. Another mentioned a doctor who did not follow his own advice. There was some laughter about William Kjellman or "Gullman" and his lengthy stay in Nome, *gull* being gold in Norwegian. Or maybe they were referring to how he had gulled them to come to North America.

Underneath I sensed loss and longing. They missed their companions who had returned to Norway, and one of the women was openly sorry she and her family had not gone back as well when they had the chance. Still, they did not complain. If I hadn't read Elle-Ristine's letters, I would have been hard put to understand just how miserable and wearing the whole experience had been over the last year and a half since they embarked from Bossekop one blizzard-white day in February. But if they didn't grumble, neither did they express much hope. It was an attitude I only partly understood and seemed most similar to elderly farmers I had known as a child on the Sognefjord, deeply superstitious men and women, who feared to mention good weather lest it turn against them in spite.

We drank our black coffee, and I told them that Leksu still lived and even thrived on a combination of grass and lichen over the winter. I had been instructed to bring back at least six sacks of lichen to Chimacum, more if possible. The women told me that reindeer lichen was abundant in the area, and they would be glad to pick some of it for me. "Just think," marveled Ravna. "At least Elle-Ristine's Leksu is alive!"

This was the closest we came to mentioning Elle-Ristine until an hour later, when Inga and Ravna brought me to a small altar made of stones in a wooden area away from the buildings. Their friend had been buried in the cemetery in Unalakleet, but they had made this sacred place of remembrance for her. Along with the stones were some coins and a cross made of wood. In spite of all the illness up here at times, Elle-Ristine was the only one to die this winter. Ravna said that the end had come suddenly. "The little one was at her breast until her last breath. Then," she pointed at her own breast, "I fed her. I had just had my own baby two weeks before, so I had the milk."

Ravna had brought the one cradle with us, slung over her back. She now placed it on the ground and took Elle-Anna out and put her in my arms. The baby was quiet, a little small for her age perhaps, but inquisitive. Her eyes were dark blue like Elle-Ristine's, with a light brown curl on her forehead under the cap. The blue eyes stared at me unblinkingly, as a baby's eyes will do.

July 22

The last time I held an infant in my arms was almost a year ago, in September, when I finally gave Susan Berit back to her mother. At first, I told myself that I was only fostering Susan in order to protect Lian from discovery. Almost no one came to visit the secluded farm down by the Chimacum Creek and Lian kept close to the house, so that if anyone did arrive unannounced, she could quickly hide in the storage lean-to. A baby could not be so easily hidden or kept silent. All summer I brought Susan out to Chimacum once a week for a visit. The rest of the time I had her to myself. I bathed her and changed her, just as I had my little Agnete, and smiled at her until she laughed, and walked up and down with her at night. Edvard had told me that I must not get too attached to the baby. We had tried, before he left for St. Michael, to make a baby ourselves, but there was so much else to do, and Edvard was preoccupied. That too was postponed until his return, and now will never happen.

Edvard was right. I was already attached to Susan, hopelessly so. I was jealous when I handed her over to Lian on those visits and eager to take her back again in my arms for the ride back to town.

Even though I saw the tears in Lian's eyes each time.

It was Kjell who finally spoke the truth to me. "When I went to the orphanage in Lima after my parents died, there was an especially kind nun, who held my hand at night so that I could go to sleep and called me her little brave one. I grew to love her. But she was never my mother. You will never be Susan's mother, Mor Dagny. Susan already has one."

What I heard him saying was that I was not *his* mother. I was hurt. I never said I was, even though I undertook much for his sake, teaching him Norwegian properly so he read and wrote it, instructing him in the Protestant Bible, teaching him table manners, geography, history, and how to dance.

It was different with a baby. Holding Susan in my arms restored my own children to me. Through her I was able to remember Agnete and, farther back in time, my little boy Jan. Susan's baby scent, her simple but strong needs cast a spell on me. I did not see it as a kind of madness with greed at its heart.

I was angry with Kjell but knew he was right. Within a few days I made a special trip out to Chimacum. Adele came with me. Kjell was in the fields, and it was just as well, for I did not wish to see him that day.

Lian ran out to greet us, as she always did, her face in smiles, her arms yearning. The baby knew her but forgot her in between visits and always clung a little to me as I passed Susan over to her mother. In my weakness I told myself the baby loved me, not just that she was used to me because I had made her so.

"Lian," I said firmly. "Now that autumn is upon us and fewer people travel this way, I think it is time that your daughter stays with you for good. Adele and I have brought everything from the house. What she needs most is you, her mother."

"I have longed for this," said Lian. "And yet I thank you, Mrs. Bergland. I know you love her too. You will come often and see her."

I nodded, not trusting myself to speak, and Adele and I soon left. She drove the carriage, as I bit my lip and stifled my tears. For a time I visited Chimacum very little. I continued to stoke my fury at Kjell, though I should have been grateful. If I had been allowed to persist in my madness, I might have continued to justify keeping Susan forever.

It was only when I received the news about Edvard that I turned to Kjell for comfort. I went out to see him and Lian on a rainy day at the end of October and told them the news I had received from Lieutenant Colonel Briggs in St. Michael. We all cried, Kjell most of all.

It was some time before we could revive ourselves to talk about Edvard's plan to help him and Lian, and how we could carry it through without him.

Edvard's proposal for protecting Lian from being deported rested on a simple assumption: that many foreign people looked simply foreign to white Americans—not of any particular race. After all, most whites had never been to China, Japan, India, or Mexico. Foreigners were identified not so much by their skin or eyes or hair, but by their dress, their habits, their accents, or difficulties speaking English. The Celestials in Port Townsend, for instance, were quite recognizable as Chinese by their cotton trousers or shifts, their padded coats, their queues. Even when they put on "our" clothes and wore suits and hats, their way of walking, bowing, and speaking identified them as Chinese gentlemen in suits.

But Edvard was counting on the idea that though people in Uptown knew we'd had a houseboy named Henry, word was out that Henry had gone off to Butte to join his uncle. It would not occur to anyone that this very same Henry could turn up on a Chimacum farm as a woman with a child. Those few who knew about the baby might be persuaded I had placed her

in an orphanage in another city. Since Ah Song had left Port
Townsend for Seattle, he was unlikely to reveal what he knew. I
thought, too, that I could trust the Reverend and Mrs. Smith.
Edvard saw potential difficulty with Jeremiah Comstock, who
knew what he had seen that night—Lian in a dress—and must
be persuaded to forget it. It was our good fortune that Jeremiah
was eager to exchange the boredom of carpentering on land for a
life at sea, and that my husband had managed, in the two weeks
he was home, to find Jeremiah a place as the apprentice to a
ship's carpenter on a lumber schooner headed to Australia.

Yet there was a greater problem we faced, and that Edvard
attempted to solve. Lian was Chinese and Chinese immigration
was illegal. Only as the wife of a merchant in Port Townsend
could Lian have entered the United States lawfully, but all the
wives of our town's Chinese merchants were accounted for. Still,
for a few days last June Edvard had pondered seeking help from
the merchants in town. If Lian were to marry one of them, she
would be among her own people. He broached this idea to Lian
quietly. Her answer was a resounding no. She admitted she had
a strong affection for Kjell and wished to stay with him.

That left Edvard to devise another scheme, the one that relied
on making sure Kjell became an American citizen, one whose
birthplace was Peru. After all, Kjell spoke Spanish and no one in
Port Townsend could be certain whether he was born in Lima or
Stavanger. If Edvard and I said we had found him in a Peruvian
orphanage and taught him Norwegian, who was to know the
difference? The difficulty would be persuading the authorities in
Port Townsend that Lian was Peruvian as well, and that she had
married Kjell some time ago—and that Edvard, as the captain
of the *Matilde,* had married them at sea. When I protested that
performing a wedding was not actually a prerogative of the
captain, Kjell told me that most people believed it and therefore
it was true.

Edvard said we could pretend Lian was the daughter of a
Chinese laborer and a Peruvian girl, our servants in Lima, Chan
and Maria Rodrigues. That would explain Lian's Chinese look.
We would pretend they had married two years ago but, because
of her ailing parents, Lian had needed to stay behind in Lima.

Several things were necessary: First, Lian must be taught some Spanish, and must also practice a Spanish accent when speaking English. Her name must be changed to something more Spanish sounding: Liana. Then she must be smuggled away, perhaps to Seattle so that Kjell could go there to meet his wife and bring her back to Port Townsend. It was Edvard's intention to swear to their marriage two years ago when he returned from Alaska. It was a bold idea, which rested, as I've said, on the fact that no one in Port Townsend or Chimacum could be very sure what a Peruvian-Chinese girl would look like.

After the captain's death, the central idea, of Edvard attesting to having married the two of them onboard the *Matilde* was impossible. Would a judge simply accept our word for it without wishing to see some form of documentation? How far were we prepared to go to forge papers and possibly put ourselves in danger of committing fraud?

It was then I thought of another solution. A way of turning one of the most painful nights in my life into a boon for Kjell and Lian.

It was July 5, 1896. Edvard, Kjell, and I had been in San Francisco for Independence Day and were staying in a hotel, when a fire broke out in the *Matilde*'s hold in the harbor and rapidly spread throughout the ship. The cargo, more than a hundred bales of fine Peruvian cotton, had not yet been unloaded, due to a dispute over import duties. Most of the crew had gone ashore; only the second mate and a couple of seamen stayed aboard to guard the ship, and to drink themselves under the table.

Sometime around midnight there was a heavy pounding on our hotel room door.

The *Matilde* was burning, the first mate shouted. I rushed to the window overlooking the harbor. Edvard was already pulling on his trousers and boots. The ship was not yet in flames, though licks of yellow fire could be seen through the smoke. There might be still time to save the logbooks and ledgers, perhaps even the valuable cargo. The *Matilde* had two pumps, and the harbor fireboat could be seen approaching.

I would have never thought to beg Edvard not to go, nor

to dissuade Kjell from going with him. All that night I watched from the window as the flames lit the sky above San Francisco Bay. The masts burned like upside down candles, the flames creeping up from the bottom. The decks were ablaze and all the water spraying from the sea could not squelch them. The ship was dry as tinder from the heat of the equator and California's arid summer. The cotton bales were kindling.

Dawn illuminated a charred hull that would soon sink or be sunk to prevent collisions. A message came from one of the crew that the second mate, who in his drunkenness had knocked over a kerosene lantern in the hold, was dead, and that two others were badly burned. Kjell was fine, but Edvard was taken to the hospital for smoke inhalation and burns to his arm.

Of everything that the *Matilde* had contained, nothing was left to us except the clothes we wore and my sea chest, now in my bedroom of the house on Morgan Hill.

I went upstairs to the chest and took out some papers—clippings about the fire from the San Francisco newspaper—and then removed a flouncy skirt and jacket, wrapped in layers of tissue paper. I walked over to Adele's shop. With the autumn card parties and dances approaching she had more than enough to do, and she glanced at my large parcel a bit fearfully.

"Dearest friend, please don't let that package be something you're hoping to have sewn or repaired. I am already desperately behind. I miss another helper since Pearl's sister married."

"This is nothing for me," I said, glancing at her assistant, Pearl Cooper. I had bought a ready-to-wear black dress at Waterman & Katz and altered it myself—it was all I wore now. "But I require your help."

Adele said quietly, "Pearl, could you possibly walk over to Aldrich's market and buy a half pound of tea, some milk, and biscuits? Thank you so much." When her assistant was gone, "Now, Dagny, what is it?"

I unwrapped my tissue parcel to show a full cotton skirt with many gathers, blue in color, and much embroidered. With it came a wool jacket in red, also heavily embroidered, with animals and trees and flowers. There was also a shawl, woven in blue and red stripes. "From Peru," I said. "A gift I wish to give

Lian. And I would like your help fitting it to her shape. But it requires a trip to Chimacum."

Before she could say no, I added, "And since we're going to the farm, why don't you bring a few of the gowns that need lace or buttonholes and let her help you? You know how good her work is, and I'm sure she would be glad of the money."

"And you will explain everything to me on the way," said Adele, already taking boxes down from a shelf and beginning to fold up two gowns.

Adele and I arrived to the sound of wood chopping. I saw Leksu wandering in the fenced enclosure, chewing on grass and bushes. The bags of reindeer lichen that Elle-Ristine had managed to send back from Alaska were now beginning to be of use. I noticed the horse in the buggy I'd rented was wary of Leksu; now that her antlers had grown thick and strong, she looked twice as large and a proper reindeer.

When I had spoken a few days ago with Kjell, he had led me to believe Lian would accept his proposal of marriage; indeed, he blushed, she had long ago accepted him as her husband. Now I spoke frankly to them about my idea, that instead of my husband, I would be the one to say I witnessed the marriage at sea, performed by Captain Bergland off the coast of Peru. "I will say I saw him write it in his logbook."

"His logbook!" said Kjell confused. "But it burned ... Ah!"

Lian asked, "What is a logbook?"

"A record of all that happens on a ship during its passages. Weather readings and miles covered, ports, and other ships passed, and anything else of note. When our ship *Matilde* burned in San Francisco Bay, its logbooks were destroyed. Who can say what was written in them?"

"But how did I come to Port Townsend? Why only now, after our marriage was long time ago?" Lian demanded.

"We could say that you stayed in Lima with your parents until Kjell was settled here and could send for you and your child. That's why he went to Skagway, to earn money to buy the farm."

"Baby is still little." Lian looked at Susan doubtfully.

"Nobody knows how old a baby is when it's all wrapped up," said Adele. "We'll keep Susan out of sight for a bit and sort it out later."

Lian still looked unconvinced, so I moved on to the details, which I had discussed at length with Adele on the drive here. We could carry this plan out anytime, but perhaps the sooner, the better.

"Lian, you and Adele will go to Seattle, not from Port Townsend's wharf, but from some other small harbor on the peninsula. And Kjell will travel to Seattle a day later, openly. I will explain the situation to the immigration officials, that the logbook with the record of the marriage was burned with the *Matilde.* I have the clippings about the fire. I have the insurance papers. When that is sorted out, I'll send a telegram to Seattle and all of you can return to Port Townsend on the evening packet. Lian will wear the Peruvian skirt and jacket."

I pulled out the brightly colored clothing. "Adele has agreed to help alter it."

Lian looked at the skirt, touched it, and then burst out laughing. "No."

"No?"

"Fine to being Peruvian. Trying to speak Spanish. If that is the way to stay here. But I can not wear *this.* I cannot act this way. I am Chinese. Yes, please, Mrs. Bergland, do what is necessary with the story and the logbooks. I trust you. Say I come from Peru to join my husband with our baby. Say my name is Liana and I was born in Lima to the Rodrigues family. But do not make me land at Union Wharf in these funny clothes. To white people maybe all Chinese look alike. But to Chinese every face is different. They remember me as Henry, I think. So, no trip to Seattle, all that business. Let me just stay here, quiet, at the farm, and you may fix it another way."

Adele said, "She has a good point, Dagny. The clothes might only draw attention of the wrong kind to Lian. As long as they live in Chimacum, who is going to know when and how it all happened? The word will just quietly seep out ... *Remember that young Norwegian Kjell, feller with a lucky strike in Skagway, turns out he's got hisself a wife. From Peru way down in South America.*

Pretty little thing, works hard too."

I smiled at Adele's spot-on imitation of some of the locals and thought about it. What would Edvard do? I said slowly, "I think I will talk to that lawyer who represented Edvard last January. No reason really to go to the immigration officials directly if I don't have to."

The next day I made an appointment with the lawyer Mr. Arnold Baxter. After accepting his condolences for my recent loss, I got down to business. I showed him the clippings about *Matilde* burning and the explained that the logbooks had been destroyed. I explained the situation about my foster son's marriage to the Peruvian girl. He naturally had sympathy for the recently reunited pair and if he thought anything was strange in the story, like a good lawyer, he kept it to himself. I willingly signed an affidavit attesting to the marriage onboard the *Matilde* off the coast of Peru, in the spring of 1896. Mr. Baxter submitted it to a judge who declared it valid. The marriage between Kjell Fossen and Liana Rodrigues was then recorded at the Jefferson County Courthouse without them having to be there at all. Was all this irregular? I don't know. I paid Mr. Baxter well enough to grease all palms. Liana Fossen then took the oath of citizenship. Nothing could be done about Susan's birth certificate, for there was none, only a record of her christening at Trinity Methodist.

But one ever suggested Susan was not the Fossens' child.

Mrs. Smith once asked me how that young man Kjell was getting on. Now that he lived in Chimacum he went to a church out there and she never saw him at Trinity Methodist. She had heard he'd been married all this time, to a lady from Peru! "And a very pretty one," she smiled.

July 30

Adele and I are in Nome now, waiting for a boat back to Unalakleet. From there or rather St. Michael, we will travel by steamship back to Seattle. I hardly know how it happened. During the few days we were at Eaton Station, I asked permission to take Anna out of the cradle and hold her. She was unused to being held much, I noticed. Sáme parents tend to leave their babies longer in the cradle than we do, sometimes as much as a year. This has been, I understand, for safety's sake. You can't have a baby crawling near an indoor fire or outside the tent in icy weather, with dogs and reindeer running around. But I am of the school that thinks a child should be moving its limbs early on. Each time I picked Anna up out of the cradle, I moved the chain with the silver balls aside. I thought she seemed to recognize me and to smile when I held her.

Ravna was happy to let me do it. I could see that it was not easy to handle two infants as they grew. She told me one day that two families had been asked to move to the western tip of St. Lawrence Island, out in the Bering Sea somewhere. They will take around forty reindeer with them and instruct the natives there in herding. This is another project of Mr. Sheldon Jackson's, but he will pay them well. "My husband has agreed with Mr. Jackson to do this, and we will earn good money. I worry only about the two babies. We are to leave soon."

"But what about her father?" I had asked Ravna and Inga earlier about Mikkel Aikio, but they had only shaken their heads. The Reverend Karlson had written to him in Nome, to ask what they should do. "From Mikkel comes no word whether Anna Mikkelsdatter goes or not with us," Ravna said. "We wait to hear and then we either take her or leave her, I do not know."

I asked the pastor about this when he came to Eaton Station. "Can this be, that Elle-Ristine's daughter, hardly six months old, is going to an island in the middle of the Arctic seas? Surely Mikkel Aikio would object if he knew."

"I do not like the idea," he said. "But Oula Pulk wants to go, and his wife and mother are willing. There will be another family too, one with two sons. We could keep little Anna in Unalakleet for Mikkel, if we knew he would come and take care of her, but I doubt he will. He was drinking heavily after his wife died, and then he returned to Nome. We have not heard from him since." He paused and took my hand. "Mrs. Bergland, I can't help but feel you arrived here on a mission from Our Lord. I would feel so relieved if I knew the little girl had a better future. Not one here, all alone in the world, but back in someplace like Port Townsend, someone who knew Elle-Ristine, and would raise her daughter as her own."

I said nothing and he looked at me, in the searching way of clergymen everywhere, and said, "It would be the Christian thing to do, Mrs. Bergland."

I didn't say that I wasn't the Christian woman he took me for. If I adopted Anna Mikkelsdatter it would be for other reasons. For the dark blue eyes, the baby smile, the feeling of a child in my arms.

Adele, bless her, had not shied away from accompanying me to Nome.

"This shall be my life's great adventure," she said. "My Oregon Trail. And after this I shall probably be quite content to return to my quiet little shop in Port Townsend."

Reverend Karlson had been very anxious to think of us in Nome and had tried to prepare us for the squalor and chaos we might encounter. The town was said to be running over with the worst elements from Skagway and Dawson; drinking and violence were rife. He told us that we must immediately find William Kjellman and he would protect us. We were given a few letters and tokens from those at Eaton Station for their friends and relatives digging or panning for gold in Nome.

"I do not know what condition you will find Mikkel Aikio in, Mrs. Bergland. It would be better if you discussed little Anna when he is not drinking. I have prepared a document for him to sign in English. He does not read, so you will have to ask Mr. Kjellman to explain it in Lappish. Mikkel's Norwegian is not good, as you probably remember. Whether it is legal, I do not know, but Mr. Kjellman can advise you."

"Do you think it is right?" I asked. "To offer to take the baby away from her people? From her father?"

"I think it is right to wish to give the child a better life. It is an act of charity."

Mr. Kjellman, whom I had only met briefly in Port Townsend, was a forceful man of a certain stamp, combining the ambition of an American with the dogged sense of duty that seems to characterize people from Finnmark. He had been recruited by Dr. Jackson around six years ago to bring over the first group of Sáme herders from Norway, along with 170 reindeer, to Teller Reindeer Station, north of Norton Sound. The intention then was for the Sámit to instruct the Eskimos in the skills of reindeer husbandry. It had been Kjellman who Dr. Jackson turned to again and again with the whole failed Yukon Relief Expedition. Much of the fiasco had not been Kjellman's fault; in fact, one could say he had tried his utmost to correct the problems created by weather, circumstance, and the War Department. All the same his role seemed to have shifted once gold was discovered in Nome. He had wanted to be among the earliest to stake a claim, and now he apparently felt he had to stay in this horrid new mining town to protect that claim.

The pastor's cautions about Nome could hardly prepare us for what we found when we disembarked, though the ship we traveled on from Unalakleet to Golovin Bay to Nome gave us some forewarning. The steamer was filled with gimlet-eyed men whose humanity had already been coarsened by life in the Yukon over the past year. The two of us were a strange anomaly—neither wives nor school mistresses—but not prostitutes either, though we had to bunk with one of them, a gaily painted girl named Juliette.

The weather, which had been pleasantly warm with a fresh breeze in Unalakleet, was positively hot by the time we reached Nome, yet fires were burning on the beach, a hundred cook stoves, and a smell of fish grilling and coffee boiling made the place seem more congenial from out at sea than we found it. The scene debarking was chaotic—it was as if our ship simply tipped the whole lot of us into a frothing wasp nest. The hovels and saloons were cheek by jowl with mining operations and everywhere men, some of them shirtless, and all of them sweating, ran back and forth with hammers and shovels and pickaxes, shouting and swearing. A town was rapidly taking shape here, practically on the beach itself, buildings with no foundations, put up hastily and with signs announcing Whiskey, Cafe, and Bank.

Before we had gone a few feet—towards the "Bank" where

we hoped we might find someone to tell us the whereabouts of Mr. Kjellman, there were gunshots, and everyone dropped to the ground. A robbery had just taken place. Or perhaps it was just an altercation. No sheriff appeared, there was no chase. It seemed to be such a normal occurrence that, after a pause, the shouting and swearing and rushing about with boards and hammers continued.

Kjellman was as rough looking as the rest, with a beard and longish hair. He was in a bunkhouse a short way from the center of town, and immediately put on coffee and offered us some food. He offered to clear out the bunkhouse for our use and we accepted gratefully. The others were all at their claims—it was warm enough they would probably sleep there.

When I explained my mission—the wish I had to adopt Anna Mikkelsdatter Aikio and take her back to Port Townsend with me—the necessity of gaining Mikkel's permission—the pastor's insistence I talk with Mikkel when he was sober—Kjellman looked grim.

"You will not find Mikkel Aikio drunk. The poor fellow is very ill. He has been taken to a rough field hospital where they are treating typhoid fever cases. Conditions here are extremely bad. There was no town here before a few months ago, and with the arrival of hundreds and hundreds of miners, sanitary conditions are deteriorating. You must not expose yourself to typhoid, Mrs. Bergland. I suggest you and Miss Pennybaker think of leaving as soon as possible."

"But I have a paper he needs to sign! Reverend Karlson has prepared an agreement in English. It asks Mikkel Aikio to relinquish his daughter to me in adoption. I must wait until he recovers, so he can sign it."

"Let me see it," said Kjellman. He read it carefully. "To be honest, dear lady, I do not think there is much possibility Mikkel will survive this fever unless he can be transported away from here by ship to a hospital. They give him one or two days at most. And even if he was not half out of his mind, Mikkel neither reads nor writes."

I was silent and Adele asked me to translate our conversation.

"But we have come all this way!" she burst out. The great

adventure she'd dreamed of was more disturbing than she'd imagined, like something out of the Wild West stories her parents had told her, but not softened by memory or romance.

Kjellman looked at the paper again. "I am used to taking responsibility for the Laplanders," he said. "They rely on me, and they know I have their best interests at heart." He picked a pen and, where Mikkel's signature should be, he made an X. And next to it he signed his own name as witness and dated it. Sweat ran down his brow and a drop splashed on the paper.

Adele looked taken aback, much the way I felt, but neither of us protested. I told Kjellman, "If Mikkel *does* recover and someday comes looking for his daughter, I will explain that we only thought of little Anna. He will understand."

"If Mikkel recovers," said Kjellman, echoing my thoughts, "I'm sure he will be grateful to you. Without a wife, a man finds it hard to raise a child, much less a girl, much less here in frontier Alaska. If he does *not* recover, as they say he won't, you will be blessed in Heaven for taking in this little orphan girl and giving her an opportunity in life."

I accepted his words, because I wanted to. And because Nome was a foul place. And because if Adele and I hurried back to the ship we could depart this afternoon.

August 11

And so, with the paper safely folded up in the inner pocket of my skirt, I left Nome with Adele. Two days later we were in Unalakleet, which seemed a paradise. I did not lie to Reverend Karlson but explained the circumstances.

"This is not legal," he said. "But I believe it is right."

I did not go to Eaton Station again—there was no time, for a steamship was leaving the following day for Puget Sound and I wanted to be on it.

Instead, Inga and Ravna brought little Anna in her cradle to the parsonage. They asked about Mikkel, and I said he was very ill, would almost certainly die of typhoid. Then I said something about a paper giving me custody, that Mr. Kjellman signed as a witness. Ravna handed the big cradle over trustingly, but with tears in her eyes.

"It is a long way to Port Townsend," she said, letting go. "Keep her safe. Raise her as Elle-Ristine's child."

"I will," I said, trying not to remember Agnete and the moment when she slipped from my arms into the sea for burial. It was now up to me to keep Anna alive, and that I fiercely promised to do. I also promised Ravna and Inga that I would write them as soon as I arrived home, and that I would tell Anna who she was and where she came from.

It is only now, on the small steamer to St. Michael, that I notice someone, perhaps Inga, has removed the chain and two silver balls from Anna's cradle.

The Third Journal
Ballard, Washington

August 1905 - January 1907

My daughter's hand in mine. Sticky-warm like a peach cut open.

"Mor," Annie said, squeezing. "Let's not go today. Let's go tomorrow."

"Things don't get any easier if you put them off," I said, continuing to march us down the sloping street, in the direction of the red-brick business district where the Central School had been built, too close for my liking, among the hotels and saloons of Ballard Ave.

A hot dry wind blew the cedar and coal smoke from the sawmills up into the hazy morning sky. From the hillside I could see vast tracts of logged-off land to the west, where the bluffs meet Shilshole Bay. Around us the land had been cleared and platted, a few houses built, and gardens planted; still, you could glimpse massive stumps, wounded and fragrant, among the apple orchards and dahlia beds. Thirty years ago these hills would have been a wild dark forest of Douglas firs and western red cedars, home to bald eagles, cougars, even bears. The tall trees were boards and shingles now, the land almost empty except for the stumps and half-burned slash and fireweed. Still to be seen among the growing rows of bungalows were older farmhouses on large lots, like the one where we lodged with the Svansson family above Ship Street, tall, spindle-porched, white-painted, rose-trellised, many with a goat shed or chicken coop, perhaps a horse with a buggy or a cart in the side yard.

More damp and unconvinced tugging, but wordless. My other hand was strangely damp as well, from heat or nervousness. It held my leather case with articles I'd written for newspapers in Norway. Most of them were from some years ago, before motherhood and the boarding house took over my life. Still, I hoped that they were sufficient evidence of my abilities.

I had come to Seattle to get work on a newspaper.

I looked down at my little girl, at the stubby light brown braids with bows at the ends, at the small, anxious face with the upturned nose and the dark blue eyes so much like Elle-Ristine's. I said, "But Annie mine, today *all* the children will be new. If we came tomorrow, you would be the only new girl."

I remembered my own first day at school, not the little school in Kyrkebø, but the female seminary Katrine attended. Katrine held my hand that day as we went up the steps: me walking stiffly in my new button boots, uncomfortable in the new corset; she, self-confident and relaxed, greeting friends and introducing me firmly as her beloved cousin: Dagny Kvam Vesterman. On the way to school she had told me, "Remember, Dagny, there's nothing to be frightened of! You're a Vesterman now." Katrine was two years older, she knew everything, she would protect me. One of the ways she chose to protect me was to give me the Vesterman name. In short order Kvam disappeared from my registered name at the school, just as surely as the wooden shoes were burned and the bunad packed in a box in a closet.

Who would protect Annie, if not me? And yet in school she would need to learn to protect herself. I wanted to tell her that I'd often lacked courage and then regained it, that I knew she would find her own bravery: find it, lose it, find it again. She was my daughter after all, more and more every year that passed.

All the same, she seemed so tiny, taking her small steps next to me down the hill, through the dusty streets that would turn to mud when it rained. The blue and green plaid dress with the white collar was a little too long; we had bought it last week ready-made at a Ballard mercantile. Her polished black shoes were coated with pale brown dust. Would people wonder about Annie here in Ballard, as they'd wondered in Port Townsend? "The captain's love child that he left behind in Alaska," they gossiped. "Taken in by the betrayed wife, can you imagine?"

"Does Annie speak English?" The teacher for the combined class, grades one to three at Central School, was very young but I could sense resolve behind the pretty face. Probably because she was a little afraid too. Miss Smithson is her name.

"Yes!" said Annie suddenly, and loudly. "I know English. And Norwegian. I know *two* languages."

Miss Smithson couldn't help but laugh. "Clever mother for teaching you two languages. You'll be a great help then to some of the others, Annie. I'll put you next to Hilde. She and her family just arrived from Norway a month ago."

I stroked Annie's plaid arm, fussed a little with her lunch

sack, forced myself to allow her to be led to her seat by the teacher. "I'll be back for you in a few hours," I whispered.

And by that time, I told myself, trying to be brave, *I'm certain I'll have a job.*

Now it's evening, twilight and still warm. I've been sitting writing about the morning's adventures at my small oak secretary under the open windows. It's one of the few pieces of furniture I kept when I sold the house in Port Townsend with all its contents, all the heavy wardrobes and settees and lamps Edvard had purchased in San Francisco, all the imported carpets, and the many beds and chests of drawers I had purchased after his death, when I began to take in boarders. The walnut dining room table, and six upholstered chairs for the paying guests, the chandelier above, the huge sideboard with the marble top, even the paintings were part of the sale. A well-to-do judge and his large family moved in.

All I took was this secretary from my bedroom, our clothes, photographs, and books, and the painted sea chest that's been mine from the time I sailed off with Edvard on the *Matilde* when I was eighteen. Inside it I keep my two previous journals, a housekeeping ledger, letters and newspaper clippings, unpublished articles and stories, legal papers, and everything to do with Elle-Ristine and Annie. It's always locked, and I wear the key around my neck together with the locket that has my mother's face on one side and Edvard's on the other.

From outside come sleepy clucks from the hen house, the soft whinny of the horse in the barn, an owl in the near distance. This house isn't Chimacum, but it's as near as I could find to the farm at Chimacum where Kjell and Lian live with Susan and Susan's younger brother John. Annie likes animals as much or more than people and is happiest outdoors. I know she's wrenched by the loss of the familiar, and especially by the loss of the children we call her cousins. Annie never complains, but she feels a great deal.

She didn't argue with me when I said we would be moving to Seattle or Ballard, so that her Mor could get a real job, not just be a cook and hostess to fractious, demanding guests (oh, those long, tedious dinners, making conversation with people I cared nothing for). I had, in truth, thought of moving to the Upper Midwest, where most of the Norwegian-American newspapers are, but Seattle was closer and more known. Adele Pennybaker lives here in the city. And Chimacum is only a long day's journey away.

Downstairs, the comforting voices of Vera and Oscar Svansson float up, mostly in Swedish with English words thrown in. I picture them: Vera with her full, square face and crown of heavy, whitening-blond braids; Oscar short and muscular, balding at the crown, with a clipped toothbrush moustache. She'll be knitting or embroidering hand towels. He'll be reading a newspaper or the *Saturday Evening Post*. Oscar is a barber and needs to be well-informed. Their younger son, Bill, started his junior year of high school today. I can hear him too occasionally, laughing at something in his book. He's also a reader. He likes Jack London and detective stories. The older son, Nels, I've only met once or twice; he works out to sea as a fisherman in the Ballard fleet, and bunks in a hostel with some other Swedes down by Shilshole Bay.

One late-blooming, clove-scented rose bush is below my window and there's a kerosene lamp on the night table, a candle on the oak secretary, lighting this journal, my third journal, which I bought a few days ago, but haven't opened until today.

I've been unused to writing about myself. It is strange to begin again, yet begin I will. I even thought of trying, once again, to write in English, but the words don't come easily to my pen even now, after nine years of living in this country. My inner life is still inscribed only in Norwegian. Only Norwegian words convey my emotions. When I write the Norwegian word for courage, *mot,* I feel my head lift a little in the wind, my narrowed eyes search the horizon, my feet anchor me more firmly on deck.

For *mot* isn't only the noun *courage,* it's also an adverb in Norwegian and has the unusual double definition of both *toward* and *against.* Exactly like standing on a sailing ship as the sudden squall whips the sheets of the fore and main masts, and the captain and first mate reckon with how much sail to haul down, how to make headway into the wind.

*

This afternoon, while Annie picked beans in the garden with Vera Svansson and told her about her first school day, about sharing a seat with Hilde Torvaldsen ("I said to Hilde, this *pult* is a *desk*. And I told her other words for other things. And Hilde gave me a piece of *lefse* with butter at the lunchtime, like our *lefse,* but thicker, with *poteter.*"), I lounged in a wicker chair under a shady lilac bush and described our morning to myself in Norwegian. And now as Annie lies sleeping in the other room and I sit here by myself in candlelight by the open window, I continue, bravely, to write down the sad tale of my interview today with Mr. Geir Vik, the editor of the *Washington Posten,* and to find comfort and resolve if I can.

The office of the *Washington Posten* is in a brick building on Front Street near Blanchard, a part of downtown Seattle I don't know. Blanchard is a vigorous street carved out of a bluff above Elliott Bay, where all the ships come into harbor and embark again. Even more of the bluff to the north is in the process of being shaved away by water canons and huge, snaking hoses. The houses that remain on the steep hill above are perched on wooden foundations, some tilting precariously. I boarded the streetcar from Ballard to the downtown directly after leaving Annie at the Central School, but it took me some time to find the newspaper office and it was past ten when I arrived, with perspiration soaking my fresh shirtwaist under the long gabardine jacket. Adele had made me the jacket and skirt as well as a new hat—"not too large or feminine," I'd instructed— and I'd bought new boots, which I attempted to dust off before I went into the building.

I hoped, between the fashionable suit, the hat, and the boots, and with my leather case full of articles, to make a creditable impression.

"I'm sorry, Mrs. Bergland," Vik said in Norwegian, after perusing my clippings for an uncomfortably silent period. He had graying, curly hair and a bulbous nose pinched by spectacles. His blue suit jacket hung on a peg behind him; his white shirt had a detachable collar and sleeve protectors. I smelled ink, heard the sounds of a steam press in another room, an old press by the sound of it, clanking as platen met plate. There were piles of old issues on one of the chairs, a bedraggled aspidistra on a battered wooden file cabinet, a framed oil painting of Norwegian mountains in the National Romantic style of thirty years ago. Behind the editor, bird-spattered tall windows with shades half-drawn looked out on Elliott Bay, late morning sun glancing off the water's flat, shiny surface, darkening the shapes of clippers and steamships.

"You write Norwegian well. But. A female reporter. At—pardon me—your age? Traveling around the city gathering information requires stamina, long hours, arriving and leaving the office at all hours. In the dark. In winter. This neighborhood can be rough at night. And you say you don't type?"

"I could learn quickly," I said. "And I have traveled and lived in other countries. My husband and I sailed around the Horn several times. I'm tall and used to port cities. No one will bother me. I carry a knife."

Editor Vik inclined his head in a half nod—acknowledging my captain husband? My height? My pluck? My knife? I heard the press come to a screeching stop; one man shouting and another answering, both in Norwegian. I'd passed a woman in the large front office. Plump, sweet-faced, but suspicious after she discovered I was not an advertiser but a prospective journalist. At my age? Vik was my age, or older. But apparently a man's forty is different than a woman's forty. An immigrant who came from Telemark as a child, he had been raised in Decorah, Iowa. I understood that he'd purchased this paper last year after owning a series of smaller Norwegian-language papers in the Midwest.

"We could possibly use your work," he allowed. "If you wrote a short article from time to time, something about women, like those in *Woman and Home*. We are progressive here at the *Washington Posten*. We don't pay much, but, Mrs. Bergland, please think of us in future. Ladies' stories, yes." He put the clippings in a neat pile and made to hand them back to me.

"But I've also written about shipping on the Olympic Peninsula and the Yukon Gold Rush. I took the clippings and pulled one out. "Here, published in a Kristiania paper. I know

I could contribute from Ballard on a regular basis. I understand boats. Not just from a woman's perspective. Shipbuilding. Trade. Maritime news."

"Ah, Port Townsend," he said, declining to look at the clipping. "I've yet to visit the town. The City of Dreams, didn't they once call it? Do you have children, Mrs. Bergland?"

"Yes, a little girl. Six. It's her first day of school today in Ballard."

"Wouldn't it be a far better thing, now that you've moved to Seattle, to find a husband? Ballard is full of Norwegian men looking for wives. A young child needs its mother. When a mother is away from home, doing men's work, everyone suffers."

"But I had heard ... doesn't your wife also work here at the paper? Isn't that her in the front office?"

Editor Vik looked annoyed for a moment, then his face resumed its genial expression. "Yes, you've heard correctly, Mrs. Bergland. Mrs. Vik is a helpmeet to me here as well as at home. She types my correspondence and deals with the classified ads. Our three sons are almost grown. One is at the university, one in high school, a third son works here at the press in the composition room. My wife types," he repeated. "What I would advise, if you feel you must work somewhere, is to learn to type. Typing offers opportunities for women," he added, rising to escort me from his office. "But also, if you like, send us a small article from time to time. On women's issues. Send it to me, personally, and I promise to look at it."

September 6

"Advertising!" said Oscar Svansson yesterday over Sunday dinner: roast chicken, green beans, corn on the cob, and a large number of potatoes with white sauce. A real Swedish-American farm meal of the kind that Vera had learned to make when they lived in Illinois, and that Bill was shoveling up "as if there was no tomorrow." An American phrase if there ever was one. Annie looked with shy fascination at this strange new being, a hulking tall *boy* with thick blond eyebrows and rosy cheeks, while she picked at some white meat and mushed the floury sauce into half a small potato.

"Advertising," Oscar repeated. "Don't bother with reporting news. Most of the papers around here get their news from the East and from gossip around town, and then they write their columns and editorials. What fuels the papers is advertising. They need people to not only go out and rustle up the ads but to *write* the ads. The copy, they call it. They never have enough good writers for that."

"I've only written articles," I protested. "It must be very different, writing advertising copy. How could I learn?"

"On the job," he said. "Like all of us. You think I knew how to barber anyone but myself before I picked up a razor? I practiced on myself and my friends for two weeks before I opened my shop." Oscar grinned. "You go see the fellow at the *Ballard News,* his name is Voss. Show him your stuff, mention me, and he'll hire you. I shave him twice a week."

"You just eat your meal, now," said Vera comfortingly, seeing that I looked perplexed. "You will find something. There are so many people here, so many jobs that need doing." She knew I'd already been to the *Ballard News,* the main English weekly here in the city. I'd gone to the office a few days after my unsuccessful encounter in Seattle with Mr. Geir Vik. But I hadn't even been able to get in to see the editor, Anders Voss. The mere fact that I was a woman purporting to be a journalist was enough to freeze the face of the clerk at the front desk.

Advertising? I'd never imagined such a thing. That wasn't writing.

These are a few things I know about my kind hosts: They are about five or six years older than me and were both born somewhere in central Sweden, on neighboring farms. He was the fourth of eight children, and she was the sixth of twelve. As children they shared beds with their siblings and helped with the milking and haying, planting, and harvesting. They knew about hunger, but they also knew about throwing snowballs and sledding, swimming in the lakes and fishing. Their families were musical and fond of dancing. They left school at fourteen. Vera mastered baking and sewing and knitting and stayed home with the family, Oscar picked up some basic carpentry and went to work at a more prosperous farm as a laborer. This family decided to emigrate to Illinois when Oscar was around twenty. They asked Oscar to go with them and offered to pay his passage from Malmö to New York and on to Chicago. Before he left, he and Vera betrothed themselves and he promised to send for her. Remarkably, he did just that, within two years of arriving in Princeton, Illinois.

For some years they worked on his employer's large dairy farm before deciding to move on to Puget Sound for more opportunity. By that time, their first son Nels was four. A baby girl had died. They arrived in Ballard around 1898 with some savings and many hopes. Oscar got a job in one of the first shingle mills, but the work didn't really suit him and after a shocking accident in which a man working by his side lost his arm, Oscar turned to barbering. He set up a shop in a very small space on Ballard Ave, but his cheerful ways and talent with a razor and warm towel soon allowed him to take larger premises and hire an assistant.

He cuts the hair of Swedes, Finns, and Norwegians, and keeps the peace between them. He shaves the chins of businessmen and sawmill workers. His discreet ear and congenial smile makes him the center of easy-going social knowledge. He knows who's hiring, who is on the edge of financial losses, who you need to talk to at Ballard City Hall to get your permit approved or resolve a dispute with your neighbor.

Oscar told me that they bought their two acres early, when Ballard's hills were still littered with stumps and logging debris. The two sons and Oscar, along with several of Oscar's customers, built the farmhouse, a small barn, and a chicken coop. Vera added that they only began to take in boarders when Nels went off to sea. They'd never had a widow or a widow and child before.

When I know her better, I'll ask about her little girl who died and tell her about my own lost children. I won't ever tell her or anyone in Ballard about Elle-Ristine and Mikkel. On one of the walls of the adjoined rooms we have upstairs, the sitting room, I've hung photographs of my family, the Norwegian family: Edvard and my wedding picture in Bergen, Edvard and I in Lima with young Kjell, Edvard on the deck of the *Matilde* in San Francisco, me and Katrine. Aunt Inger and Uncle Theodore, a stiff studio portrait. Aunt Inger died three years ago. Katrine lives by herself in the large house in Bergen. "Your room is always waiting for you," she writes, but less frequently. It hurt her that I did not try to return to see Aunt Inger one last time before she died.

These photographs all hung in the parlor of our old house in Port Townsend as well, and I used them to tell Annie about her relatives in Norway, in Bergen and Kyrkebø. When she asked about her grandparents, I told her about my parents, and how my papa had died in a boat accident when I was eleven, and how my mama was long dead too. I didn't put the photograph of Elle-Ristine and Mikkel Aikio on the wall, of course, nor did I have pictures of Jan and Agnete.

Once, unexpectedly, Annie asked me why her father and I didn't have more children. Caught off-guard, my tears came swiftly. I said that we had had two children, a little boy Jan, and a little girl, Agnete. But both had died. "Agnete was very little when she died, of illness." I could not bear to say how Jan died, how I had seen his eyes before the wave took him.

Annie's eyes flooded. "So I had a brother," she said. "And a sister." She repeated the names. "Jan," she said. "Agnete." *Stakkars mor,* she said. "Poor mother."

"But I have *you,*" I hugged her tight. "And I will never let you go."

September 8

A warm late Saturday afternoon. Oscar is taking a nap while Vera is teaching Annie to knit. She has a natural aptitude for it, just as she does for baking. I've just returned from an excursion with Adele: to the new tearoom at the Frederick and Nelson store downtown. Adele was beautifully turned out as always, in an enormous hat and a striped poplin dress. I wore the gabardine suit she'd made me for my job interview and felt too warm. Now it's hanging in the closet again and I sit at the secretary in my loosened corset and dressing gown wondering why I feel more sad than satisfied to have seen my dearest friend.

Unsurprisingly, Adele has thrived here in Seattle as a dressmaker, cultivating ladies of taste and money. At first, she lived with her brother and his family, now she has rooms above her shop on Capitol Hill and has purchased property in an upcoming area called Ravenna, north of the University. Her brother Knox's skills as a carpenter are much in demand; he has a company now. He plans to build his own house soon and will build Adele's as well. Everything about Adele today— from the magnificent hat to the neat, buttoned boots to the elegant earrings, to the way the waitress took our order— suggested prosperity and independence. It's hard not to envy her sometimes, much as I'm grateful for her constant kindness to me and Annie. When we first met, I was a well-off woman employing her to make my dresses; now I penny-pinch and feel my future is uncertain.

"You're not without resources," Adele reminded me today. "First of all, you have savings from the house sale. You have the ability to work hard at whatever you do." She paused, "And then you have your pen—your greatest asset!"

It was kind of her to mention my writing. All she's ever read of it are my letters to her over the past few years, in an English far from perfect. She takes it on trust that my Norwegian is much better. "My pen is a friend," I admitted. "But I'm not sure I'd call it an asset." I have since looked that word up in the dictionary and see how many meanings it has: it can be a skill or a benefit, an advantage or a blessing. Most often I've heard it used to mean money or physical property. The only such material asset I've ever really owned was the house on Morgan Hill, which Edvard had bought outright. For the first year after Edvard's death, I had assets in the bank, but the savings dwindled faster than expected. The only good thing was that Clarence Harrison had dropped his lawsuit against Edvard after it became clear that his brother Jeff had colluded with Lloyd Quayle to steal all the money from his safe.

On Adele's suggestion, I began to take in boarders, first a

seamstress friend of Adele's, then a widow, later a young woman teacher. Women were rarely in a position to pay as much for their lodging as captains in port and traveling salesmen. Men eventually became my primary guests. But men also required substantial meals and laundry services, not to mention the use of the parlor as a smoking room. I hired a cook and a housemaid, yet found I was expected to preside over the evening meal and be at the boarders' beck and call. Some wanted me to entertain their clients or provide introductions to eligible ladies or to attend the theater with them.

More than one man proposed marriage and was offended or embarrassed when I declined. Why would I consider making a home for male lodgers when I could so easily put myself and my daughter under his protection and make a home for *him*? In vain I explained I was fine on my own with Annie, and that I also had a career as a writer for newspapers in Norway. They smiled or scoffed in amusement at my scribbling, and gradually I stopped speaking of my literary efforts altogether. But for a time, writing still sustained me, if not financially, then emotionally. When I wrote, I was not Mrs. Bergland, a widow with a young child who ran a boarding house, I was a thinking woman with stories to tell. Within two years after I went up to Alaska and brought Annie home, those dreams of writing hid under the demands of men's voices every night in the parlor and piles of laundry and surly cooks and incompetent housemaids.

"How is Annie?" Adele asked me today. "So hard to believe she's in school now. And does she like living with the Swedes?"

I told her that she had settled in well, and already had a good friend, little Hilde, and that Vera and Oscar petted her so dreadfully I feared she could be soon spoiled. "Vera is teaching her to knit. She's already very good at it. Unlike me, Annie is clever with her hands."

"You must bring her to my shop and let her help me a little," Adele laughed. "I'll have her sewing buttons in no time."

Adele is the only one really who knows the story—most of the story—of how Annie came to me. Neither of us were sure Annie would survive a sea voyage from Alaska back to Port Townsend, and Adele, never having been a mother, was particularly worried.

Ravna had started the process of weaning her and her own child, but the two babies were still used to the breast. I'd first imagined that if I were to take Annie's welfare on, I might have to stay the winter in Alaska until I could return to Port Townsend the following summer. But as it turned out, Reverend Karlson had heard of a steamship captain from Seattle whose wife had given birth in St. Michael. They agreed to carry me and Adele and Annie to Puget Sound. Mrs. Abbott had enough milk for two and took pity on baby Annie.

I didn't call myself her mother, not at first. In fact, I considered, briefly, the possibility of allowing Annie to be raised by Lian and Kjell, on the farm where Annie's origin might be less remarked. She might grow up resembling Susan and John a little. In Chimacum she would have a brother and sister, a mother and father. I could still remain an aunt or great-aunt and contribute to her welfare.

Yet even by the time Adele and I reached Port Townsend from Alaska, I knew that giving Annie up would be impossible, and Adele saw it too. The empty space in the center of my arms was filled when I held her, the pain in my heart was eased when I looked into her face. I saw my Agnete in her, I saw the baby I had miscarried that first year in Port Townsend. Then I saw Annie herself. Annie was at first a replacement for my lost children. She came to be a beloved daughter in her own right.

Perhaps I believed that this was God's way of consoling me for the loss of my entire family, Jan, Agnete, the unnamed little girl, and Edvard, especially Edvard. Perhaps I saw myself as a do-gooder, Annie's savior, who took on the duty of raising a child in better circumstances than a reindeer station in Alaska. Perhaps I was responding to the Reverend Karlson's belief that Elle-Ristine wanted me to have her child and bring her up. That Elle-Ristine trusted me more than her friends and certainly her wayward husband.

I eventually wrote to Katrine and my sisters that I'd adopted a little orphan girl, of Norwegian parenthood. I did not say that Annie was Lappish, a word that all of them would recognize. Indeed even to myself I never used that word, only Elle-Ristine's word, Sáme. While I could not raise Elle as a Sáme, I did not erase every trace. Reverend Karlson had given me the birth certificate of Anna Mikkelsdatter Aikio, with the names of her parents: Mikkel Aikio and Elle-Ristine Persdatter, and with it a photograph of the pair, taken in Port Townsend before they sailed. I hid these things but did not destroy them.

I must dress and go downstairs shortly, find Annie and play with her in the garden, have her show me her knitting. "Your pen is your greatest asset," Adele told me. No, Annie is my greatest asset. My blessing. For her, I'll find a way to make a living for us both.

September 10

I have a newspaper job.

Not at the *Ballard News,* even though I geared up my courage and reappeared there this morning in a new guise as an applicant seeking work in their advertising department. I did manage to talk to someone, an interview that lasted approximately three minutes with editor and publisher Anders Voss, a man who, unlike Mr. Vik, didn't bother to hide his disdain for the female sex and told me frankly, "Many of our advertising customers are men. The big mills, the shipyards, the manufacturing companies. They will expect to deal with a man who understands their business."

I bit my tongue and held my head high as I left the office and walked the few blocks to Oscar's barber shop. He was alone, after the morning rush, sweeping up threads of hair from the floor and replenishing some of his stinging face tonics and scented hair creams. It smelled like men in the tidy shop, but I didn't mind that. If you live on a ship you live with men and get to know their ways. You smell their working sweat and see their wounds and pustules as you nurse them. Sometimes you'll see them shaving and washing as port approaches and they anticipate visiting the ladies of Rio or San Francisco. It struck me suddenly that I had never seen Edvard clean-shaven, and now I never would. A wave of grief passed like a shudder through me. Oscar thought I was upset about being dismissed out of hand by the editor at the *Ballard News.*

He comforted me: "I have another customer, Kurt Schiller, who just started a paper for working men: the *Shingle*. He bought the equipment of another paper that went out of business. He told me yesterday he was looking for some help selling classified ads. He may not last long either, but it's a start. Go see him, right now before he hires someone else, and tell him I sent you."

I promised him I would and slipped out again, just as a portly fellow with a few strands of black hair plastered across his skull appeared in the doorway. "Oscar! A shave and make it quick! I've got a meeting in fifteen minutes."

"Certainly, Mr. Smith. Shall I leave the haircut for another time?"

"I need all the hair up there I can hold on to," I heard him say. And the two of them laughed, men in their element: the barbershop.

October 15

Now that I'm working at the *Shingle*, I find myself with almost no time to myself. I've always been a fair-weather journal keeper at the best of times. Not for me the ship's log that Edvard kept daily for years aboard the *Matilde* and his other ships. I write when something happens, or when I have hours to fill. Today is a Saturday, and Adele came by to collect Annie for an excursion to some sort of Autumn Fair being held at the Broadway High School where her nephew is junior class president.

I have been for a brisk walk and have helped Vera put up some applesauce from the last of her orchard's crop, and now I have three blessed hours alone at my desk to describe my new life.

Kurt Schiller, editor of the Ballard newspaper the *Shingle,* is of German stock, born in Wisconsin, drawn to the Pacific Northwest by reports of booming growth and the prospect of workers and their families avid for news. His weekly four-page broadsheet is the latest of various papers he's owned in Wisconsin and North Dakota, most of which, I've come to realize, had failed. Not, Schiller assured me, because he didn't publish an excellent newspaper, but because either the population of the small town where he'd set up shop didn't grow as predicted, or because there had been Competition. As a democrat and idealist Schiller firmly believes in Competition, but as a business owner he resents it. It does seem, from the stories he eventually told me, that Competition has not been kind to him, whether it was in the form of an established newspaper that didn't take kindly to an upstart espousing "radical" political views. Or whether Competition came in the form of a new upstart, which had moved into Schiller's territory.

Schiller is about fifty, rotund of belly and skinny of leg, with a big intellectual forehead, a head made larger by a crackling brown beard. His forebears were Forty-Eighters fleeing Munich, educated men persecuted for loving freedom and promoting revolution. In America they had established a printing firm in Milwaukee, where his father and uncles are still issuing pamphlets and books in German. Expressing himself with capitalized nouns is in Schiller's blood, and so is Socialism and earnest fellow feeling for the Working Man. Schiller was attracted to Ballard because the town is full of Working Men, and he'd initially taken a job in town as editor of the *Millman* before, as he likes to put it, "hanging out my Shingle." The *Millman* went out of business, not because of Competition from the *Ballard News,* but possibly because many Working Men are more inclined to spend their money on Suds than Subs. Even though the *Millman,* like the *Shingle,* had its fervent readers, who followed local and national news eagerly and enjoyed writing letters to the editor demanding various investigations, better pay for Working Men, and even, occasionally, Rights for Women.

Schiller purchased the *Millman's* printing equipment and type cabinets, two desks, a few chairs, and a typewriter, and installed everything in an unheated former barn behind the rented house he shares with his wife, a pale, red-haired woman with a persistent cough who adamantly refuses to have anything to do with newspapers. There are two workers, Jimmy Jay, formerly of the *Millman,* at the composing table, and Robert Vincent, known simply as Vince, on the press. Jimmy organizes the classified ads on the page and designs the display ads, while Vince and his youngest son see that the papers are delivered. Much of the paper is cribbed from "Eastern papers," or even, very much rewritten, from the *Seattle Star* or the *Union Call.* Schiller writes all the headlines and some of the more local news, what he calls Fresh Reporting, and weekly Opinions. Often there are more Opinions than Reporting of the fresh or even stale sort.

When I went to work for him in September, the paper had been in existence only about six weeks and most of the advertising was the briefest sort of classifieds—rooms for rent—horses for sale—jobs opening up at new sawmills north of Seattle. There were only one or two larger display ads per issue and Schiller told me that he had offered them gratis, to help drum up business. Competition, mainly the *Ballard News,* had the advantage of the *Shingle.*

I told Schiller I was certain I could get him more advertising. Maybe not from the owners of the shipyards and mills, but if the *Shingle* wanted to appeal to the families of the millworkers and shipwrights, it needed a woman's touch. The men might want to read reports of unsafe conditions in the shingle factories or fiery editorials about workers who banded together to demand higher wages, but the women would be more likely to read the paper if it also carried ads for children's clothes at reasonable prices and lists of sale items at the grocers. The *Ballard News* should not have a monopoly on every shop and service in the booming city.

I would make it my personal mission, I told Schiller confidently, to get to know the Ballard business owners and to convince them to take out ads in the *Shingle.* I would work on commission, I added. "If you don't get paid, I don't get paid."

He liked the sound of that. Advertising is the meat and potatoes of newspapering, as he well knows. He had only one concern, and that wasn't my sex. It was that I wasn't a native speaker. "I can't afford mistakes in grammar slipping through, or unfortunate word choices. The only newspapers you have written for, I understand, are published in Norwegian. *Can you write English?*" he asked when I appeared to ask for a job. His beard crackled and his near-sighted eyes bored into mine.

I've found in dealing with men that it's best to act as if every disadvantage is in reality an advantage. "The fact I was born in Norway is a plus," I said. "Norwegians will trust me, and others, who hope to hoodwink me because of my accent and the reputation of the Norwegians as blockheads, will be taken by surprise. And then pleased, I hope."

Schiller grinned suddenly and rather frighteningly (his teeth are large and wolfish) and said yes, he would give me a trial run. He handed me a list of businesses and a deadline for the following week. The issue could accommodate four small ads and two large ones. If I got more, he'd cut one of his articles.

In less than three days, I had ten ads, mostly small ones, but two quarter-page display ads, with illustrations of fall suits and dresses. Schiller said later it was my choice of the words *hoodwink* and *blockheads* that sold him on me during the job interview.

I studied the ads in the *Seattle Star* and the *Ballard News,* and I went to the stationer's shop on Ballard Ave and looked for lexicons to help me in my new job. What I'd had on my shelf for a long time was a Norwegian-English dictionary I'd bought in Liverpool twenty years ago when I first sailed with Edvard. Along with that I had an Oxford dictionary, which had once caused no end of confusion in Port Townsend shops when I asked for food stuffs using their British names. Over the past nine years I'd picked up thousands of American words and phrases from sailors, merchants, boarding house guests, servants, and friends like Adele, and I used them when I spoke, but my writing in English was admittedly basic and perhaps old-fashioned. On the advice of the clerk at the stationer's shop, I purchased the 1900 edition of *Webster's International Dictionary,* and also a volume called *Roget's Thesaurus,* a novel way to me of thinking about the English language, not in terms of exact definitions, but as collections of words related to other words by family, friendship, and passing acquaintance.

"What do you ask for in a new suit?" I wrote, next to an illustration of an elegant man in a nicely fitted jacket and trousers, with a bowler hat and dapper boots. "We are particular here at Hansen's Clothing for Men. We are critical and exacting. If the jacket doesn't fit at the *collar,* if the jacket pulls at the *shoulders,* if the *lapels* don't lie flat, we won't sell you the jacket, simple as that. We will find you another jacket from *our large selection.* Our reward for this time and effort is your *respect* and continued *business.*"

The owners of Hansen's were delighted with the response and became regular advertisers and boosters, and after a few weeks I could carry around a sheaf of extra issues of the *Shingle* and point to the attractive display ads,

For Solstad's Bakery, run by the two Solstad sisters, I praised their many varieties of bread, "baked daily in sanitary ovens," their "flakey pastries and airy doughnuts," and their "Scandinavian cream cakes just like home." Jimmy Jay pointed out that Ballard *was* home, but I knew my reader. For most of them, Sweden and Norway were home, Finland and Iceland and Denmark were home, and a powerful yearning for familiar tastes and smells would bring them into Solstad's Bakery and keep them coming back. From *Roget's,* which I now read before sleep and carried in my leather case to peruse whenever I had the chance, I often pulled words that would be understandable yet enticingly new to immigrants, like "mouth-watering" and "lip-smacking," though occasionally I threw in adjectives like "scrumptious" for pure pleasure. Just to make sure, I always looked up the word definition (*scrumptious: delightful, excellent, esp. delicious*) in Webster's before allowing the word to be set in type. Jimmy was an excellent type compositor and a decent proofreader, but his own vocabulary was unimaginative and from time to time he protested. "If it means delicious, why not say delicious?"

In spite of a few disagreements, Jimmy and I worked well together. He often added italics and bold lettering for a stronger effect or inserted boxed "Guarantees" or "Reasons Why You Should Shop Here." Schiller was happy with me, paid me on time, and even hinted that I might be allowed, in a month or two, to write some articles—not Opinions or Reports, but short news pieces. In the meantime he appreciated how I rapidly came to know the community and how much care I took to cultivate our advertisers.

In Ballard I am simply the respectable widow of a Norwegian

sea captain who died after a shipwreck in Alaska. I am Mrs. Dagny Bergland, born on a farm on the Sognefjord, educated in Bergen, the mother of a little girl, well-traveled, well-spoken, in Norwegian and English. An American citizen, a modern woman with my shirtwaist and smart jacket and hat, my leather case, but with touches of the old country—a small silver *sølje* brooch at my neck; hand-knit mittens in a snowflake pattern in cold weather—that could be reassuring to newcomers. Shopkeepers smile when they see me coming. The many Scandinavian women business owners in Ballard always offer me *lefse* and *krumkake* or cardamom rolls with boiled dark coffee and cream and sugar, but I also enjoy *rugalach* and *piroshkis* from the Lowensteins and Radnowskies.

Sometimes our advertisers put the *Shingle* ads in their windows and often they become subscribers to the paper and carry copies in their shops, in spite of the fact that the socialist views espoused by my employer Mr. Schiller conflict with their own capitalist dreams. One thing that everyone can agree on in these times of development: Ballard is a place to be proud of. A vote for annexation to Seattle is coming up in December, and Schiller, like many of his readers, is against it. That view has gained more subscribers than lost them.

Since I started at the paper, we've been able to increase the weekly print runs and expand the number of pages to eight. My ads and Ballard pride have done it.

November 26

Annie and I went to Chimacum for Thanksgiving for five days. We've only returned late today, and now my tired Annie sleeps dead to the world in her little bed while I write here. I'm exhausted by all the travel too, but so many thoughts course through my mind that I must put them down.

We hadn't seen Kjell and Lian since last summer. This wasn't down to disaffection on my part, but the difficulties of finding a good time to go, now that Annie is in school, and I'm working every day. The *Shingle* has continued to grow, though the finances still seem unsteady. It may be that it's growing too fast. Schiller has been distracted as well by his wife's chronic cough, which has worsened with the arrival of the rain and winds of early November.

Susan is almost eight now, and John is five. Susan is lithe and energetic like her mother, with the same eagerness to read and learn, the same shiny black hair, while John is sturdy and even-tempered and lightly freckled. English, in all its variations, is the language of the house, English and music, for Kjell fiddles almost every evening, and John has followed him in that talent and has a small violin himself. The young ones look half-Chinese, but the story still holds that they're both Kjell's children and there's a Peruvian connection. No one seems to mind in Chimacum, where there are several mixed marriages, mostly between the local Chimacum Indians and the dairy farmers.

Lian, or Liana as she's known in Chimacum, prefers simply to call herself American. She doesn't associate with the few remaining Chinese people in Port Townsend; her accent is not strong, and she never speaks Chinese, only a bit of Spanish now and then, which Kjell taught her (*Buenos dias* and the like). No one but me, Kjell, and Adele know her full story. She's one of many immigrants in this country who has muddied her traces. Even with me, she can act as if she's been in the country for many years, and she identifies with America in a way I never have. I still think of myself as Norwegian and probably always will.

The little family is happy and more prosperous year by year. They have two cows, several goats and many chickens, and a vegetable and fruit garden tended by Lian, whose green thumb is legendary. They sell vegetables and fruit, as well as milk and eggs, and Lian also uses her skills as a fine seamstress to bring in more income. Kjell often works in the winter in one or another sawmill, but from spring through summer he farms. He is still my boy and the only person who remembers Edvard as I do. Strange that Kjell is a husband and father himself now. He is twenty-eight and has a full blond beard and a broad chest. His shirts are striped or plaid. He wears suspenders and boots. Annie calls him Uncle, though I suppose they are really sister and brother if I am foster mother to them both. We have never gone fully into the exact relationship.

I see he worries about me sometimes. This new life I have, in Ballard, is strange to him. The writing I used to do, years ago, was my hobby. That I now work on a newspaper and walk around Ballard soliciting advertising seems almost incomprehensible to him. He has always known me in my maternal role. He can't help but want me near, to be a granny to his children.

The day after Thanksgiving, Kjell and I went to Port Townsend by wagon. He had some supplies to pick up and I decided to go with him, leaving Annie to play with the other children and help Lian with her wooden jigsaw puzzle. Lian loves these things, especially the geographic maps of the world, and Annie has an unmatched eye for shape and color. I'd brought this one from Ballard, having purchased it from one of my advertising shopkeepers. It showed all of South America, including Lian's supposed home country of Peru. She'd smiled at that.

As we drove along the familiar dirt road to Port Townsend, Kjell talked about the farm and his family before telling me that he had picked up a bit of news a month or two ago that might interest me. We spoke Norwegian of course. We always speak together in our own language when alone. "There are rumors of Lappish folk living in Poulsbo. Immigrants from Norway and a few who've come down from Alaska to buy farmland. Cows this time, not reindeer." He scratched his beard, and his eyes sought mine. "Have you heard that?"

My breath had stopped for a moment, but I said, "No. I haven't heard that."

I'd heard of Poulsbo of course. The small town on the Kitsap Peninsula, somewhere in between Port Townsend and Seattle, was the center of scattered dairy and fruit farms all around Dogfish Bay. It was one of many thriving little settlements and mill towns around Puget Sound that could be visited by steamship. The Mosquito Fleet is the popular term for the hundreds of small vessels that ferry cargo and passengers back and forth.

"A fellow down at the sawmill told me this back in September. We were trading stories about our goldmining adventures.

He was up in Nome. He made a little money, like me, but he gambled most of it away. He knew about the Laplanders at Eaton Station, but he didn't realize they'd come through Port Townsend years ago. I told him all about it and that's when he said he'd heard some Lappish families had turned up in Poulsbo. He has an aunt there."

My heart was now racing, but I said nothing beyond, "*Jaså.* Well, well."

"I thought you'd be pleased to hear about them in Poulsbo, Mor Dagny." He seemed slightly crestfallen, and I realized he'd been storing up this news for weeks, waiting for the time to share it. The story reminded him of Edvard, and his own adventures in Yukon. Kjell probably wasn't thinking so much of what it might mean for me and Annie.

"I don't suppose your friend mentioned Mikkel Aikio?" I finally said. "He was in Nome, years ago. Another gold miner."

"No, but then, I didn't ask. I'd forgotten Mikkel was in Nome. He died there, I recall. Of typhoid, you said."

I nodded, "Yes, he was very ill." I had told Kjell the bare minimum when I returned with Annie to Port Townsend that summer of 1899. That Elle-Ristine was dead when we arrived in Unalakleet. That Mikkel had left her and the baby to go gold panning in Nome and was seriously ill and not expected to live. That he had signed a paper witnessed by Mr. Kjellman, on the advice of Reverend Karlson, which had entrusted Annie to me because he wanted to give the little girl a better chance in life. I had told Kjell at the time that I planned to raise Annie on my own.

What I never told Kjell directly, but what he'd gradually understood, was that I didn't plan to tell Annie that I was not the woman who had given birth to her.

We dropped the subject then, but it haunted me during the several hours I spent in Port Townsend alone that day. While Kjell attended to his affairs, I wandered around the familiar streets. It was November now, chill but sunny with a light breeze out of the south. Ships crowded the bay, some still carrying sail, though most were steamers now. On the towering bluff above Water Street the Customs House still stood watch over the bay, and the wharves below were packed with men loading and offloading the ships: water barrels on and boxes of salt cod and provisions off. Some passengers milled about the wharves and streets as well, stretching their legs after a long journey from San Francisco or Hawaii into the Puget Sound. Most of them would reboard for the last leg into Seattle or Tacoma. Others were heading to smaller towns around Puget Sound.

In the near distance around Point Hudson, I saw the canneries onshore, where the Klallam had once camped in summer. And beyond, on another bluff, rose the buildings of Fort Worden.

I couldn't help it—my eyes scanned the bay for one of Edvard's ships.

In spite of the noise and bustle on the wharves, the boardwalks, and on busy Water Street, where the wagons and carriages and even one or two automobiles made crossing a hazard, I could see that some of the storefronts were as empty as they had been when I left in August. That included all the Chinese shops except the Zee Tai Company, once the most profitable business in all of Port Townsend. I went inside to buy tea and rice for Lian and was met by the familiar scents of sandalwood and polished teak, of oolong and jasmine. The other scent I recalled from the past, sticky sweet opium smoke wafting from a back room, was gone, and so was the clicking of the mahjongg tiles and the crack of fan-tan cards. Sacks of rice still were piled high in one corner; tin canisters holding many varieties of tea lined the shelves behind the counter. Yet the pickled vegetables and tins of fish, along with the household goods and garden tools that had once crowded the shop—woks for frying noodles, bamboo sieves and baskets, pointed straw hats and hoes and rakes—were mostly absent. Instead, the shelves were stocked with bolts of beautiful silks, with porcelain teapots and bowls, with small figures carved of jade and ivory, and small teak boxes. Portable souvenirs, chopsticks and fans were always popular with tourists, and it seemed today that all the other customers in the shop were tourists. A well-dressed Anglo-American bargained loudly with a clerk in a tasseled Mandarin cap, while his children rummaged untidily in baskets of rings and bracelets. A young couple debated over a tea set, delicately painted with dragons, and a woman on her own, with a soft, dreamy face under a large, fashionable hat, let her fingers brush the silks.

I wondered if the merchant I'd known best, Charlie Tse Hong, was upstairs or in back. He used to ask me about Lian occasionally, though he never asked me why she didn't come into town, alone or with her children. Most of the established Chinese families in town belonged to one of the merchant clans. The men established the shops, and then went back to China for a wife. Lian was outside all that and always had been. No woman from the clan would befriend her, few men respected her. She was commonly considered a prostitute who had married a white man. The fact that there were fewer Chinese in Port Townsend every year meant that Lian's secret grew safer. The Chinese who tilled and harvested the lands of Station Prairie and Chinese Gardens had largely departed, leaving just a few truck farmers to continue selling vegetables door to door from their wagons or baskets. A handful of laundries and noodle shops were left; most had vanished in the fire of 1900.

I left the shop after paying for a twenty-pound bag of rice and packages of tea, along with a length of silk I would give Lian as a gift. Kjell and I would pick them up later. With two hours at my disposal, I walked in the direction of Washington and Adams Streets, to where a tangle of blackberries and poison hemlock had taken hold in the weedy expanse, a full city block, over the site of the burn.

I remembered that night in September 1900. How I'd smelled smoke and rushed outside, closely followed by our cook, Polly. In the direction of town we could see flames and smoke, and then a neighbor ran by, a volunteer fireman, shouting that Chinatown was burning. I told Polly to take care of Annie, grabbed my coat and hat and ran down the hill after him. There were always fires in Port Townsend—the one in Uptown this past June had burned down Adele's seamstress shop—but most of them were centered on a single building, a house, a barn. I thought at first it was a laundry or noodle shop, but as I came down Monroe Street, I could see that a whole block, from

Madison to Adams along Washington Street, was blazing. Every rickety wooden workers' dormitory building and brothel, every grocery and mercantile and cafe, all three laundries, including the one that had employed Ah Song, was aflame, with people running crazily both away from the fire and toward it, some carrying bedrolls and baskets, others hauling buckets of water and trying to set up hoses from the two fire wagons.

For once, unfortunately, it wasn't raining in Port Townsend.

No one was much hurt, but little was saved from the conflagration. Afterward, there were stories of how it started. A whore threw an oil lamp at a rival whore, some said. No, it began at the stove of a noodle shop. No, it was a cigar left burning in a room. Others shook their heads and whispered that it might have been more intentional, a cleansing of the "vermin and filth" of an undesirable part of town. People said the firefighters were only told to rescue any white people who were there and not to bother about the Chinese or their businesses. Others who were there disputed that account, saying that the Chinese and whites worked together all night with hoses and bucket lines to save anything they could.

At the time I found it hard to believe it was calculated. I saw men working together that night, and I saw women working with them, women in light clothing hauling buckets of water, women bringing wet cloths for the firefighters to briefly bathe their faces and eyes with. No, I couldn't believe at first that it was a conspiracy to destroy Chinatown. And yet, five years later, not a stick of the Chinese quarter has been reconstructed. After that night, many Chinese left, out of necessity or fear, for Seattle, Victoria, Vancouver, even China. And without the Chinese merchants to rebuild, the city's ambitions began instead to turn to making the burned lot into a ballpark or leaving it an open field for traveling circuses and fairs.

Whatever one believes about the origins or reason for the fire, the fact is that restrictions on Chinese immigration into Port Townsend have only grown stiffer. Two years after the fire, the Chinese Exclusion Act, subject to renewal every decade, became permanent law. In 1904 Canada banned most Chinese from landing on its shores. The route that Lian and so many others had followed, of embarking in Victoria and paying to be smuggled across the Strait of Juan de Fuca to North Beach, was almost impossible now. The Customs House in Port Townsend turned away most Chinese; the few merchants who managed to land here needed sworn affidavits that proved they'd lived here previously and were only returning from a visit to China. No women were allowed to come unless they were the merchants' wives.

What could be more different than this country's policies toward Scandinavians? Oh yes, we Norwegians complained that we were mocked for our accents and a kind of oafishness and naïve stupidity, and that the "Yankees" held most of the power, including naming rights over all the streets and buildings and parks. But no one stopped us from pouring into America in our hundreds of thousands. No one stopped us from moving from Brooklyn to Chicago, from Minneapolis to Fargo, from Port Townsend to Ballard. No one checked our registration on the streets. No one threatened us with deportation or burned our homes and businesses because we were Norwegians.

I walked all the way around the burned and weedy area and was halfway up Monroe Street, out of habit returning to my old house, when I stopped and retraced my steps back to the seafront and walked out on one of the wharves to gaze at a steamer leaving for some of the small towns around the Sound. My mind turned to what Kjell had told me on the way here: Sáme families were in Poulsbo.

Who were they, and why did they come to Poulsbo? Had they been here for a long time, or had they recently arrived from Alaska? Did I know them? Would they have any connection to Mikkel and know where he was? For if they had been in Alaska, they would surely know that he had not died of typhoid fever.

I knew this, because one day, in early 1902, I received a letter from Norway.

It had no return address but was postmarked Karasjok, and was much delayed, in part because the envelope read only: "Fru Kaptein Edvard Bergland, Port Thownsen, Seattle." It's a surprise it even reached me, and I have been sorry many times that it did.

It was from Mikkel Aikio, written in painstaking English

and a smattering of Norwegian. He addressed me as Fru Kaptein and thanked me first for coming to visit him in Nome when he lay so very ill. Then he explained:

In the end I did not die, but before the ice came, me and another found a whaling ship. They had lost sailors to the gold fields, so we signed on and sailed to Japan and then took another ship and another and finally we came home to Karasjok after eighteen months at sea. Now I have my reindeer back and a wife and a boy child.

Fru Kaptein, I am writing to find out about my Anna. Mr. Kjellman told me that when I was feverish, I told him you could adopt my daughter. I don't remember this. But I know she is safe with you unless she has died, and you will be very kind to her as you were kind to Elle-Ristine. But Fru Kaptein I wish I could know how my little girl is and if there is a chance you can bring her to Norway someday so we can meet her, and she can meet us.

Fru Kaptein, Norway is a long way away from America, this I very well know, so if you cannot do this I understand. But one day soon I hope I will hear from you. I thank you and praise you very much.

Inside the envelope was a photograph that showed Mikkel in a Four Winds cap and a woman wearing a very beautiful shawl and a silver bridal crown on her head. My heart contracted so swiftly that I thought I might collapse for lack of air on the spot.

Mikkel lived and he wanted to see my Annie. The little girl who was by this time three years old and my darling. I had reasoned that there was no harm in my taking Annie as my own, with her parents dead so young. I thought at first that yes, I would of course, someday, tell her part of the circumstances that made her my daughter. But she was so small, how could she understand this complicated story? I would have to explain how her mother and father were born to reindeer-herding families in Finnmark, but traveled far across the globe to Port Townsend, where I met them. I would have to explain Sheldon Jackson's misguided grand plan to ship reindeer to Alaska to feed the miners, and how that changed to another grand plan, to employ the herders to teach the Inuit people how to tend to the reindeer's habits in order to build a slaughtering business. I would have to explain the crazed years of the gold rush in Yukon and Nome. I would have to explain that I had at times blamed Elle-Ristine's death squarely on Mikkel for taking her to Alaska.

I would have to explain that she had family in Karasjok. An Uncle Aslak if he still lived, for one. And a father and a stepmother, and a half brother. People who remembered her mother Elle-Ristine, people who would want her to grow up in Lapland.

It was too much for me and far too much for a toddler. I said nothing. She thought I was her mother. I acted like her mother. I became her mother. Her Mor. And the years passed.

I admit that, for a few weeks after receiving Mikkel's letter, I considered writing back. To say that that Annie was well and that I had taken good care of her. Once or twice, to my shame, it crossed my mind to tell him Annie had died. And then I simply put his letter and photograph back in the envelope and locked it away in my sea chest.

On the wagon ride with Kjell back to the farm, I was quiet. I thought of walking with Elle-Ristine and Leksu through the forests from Fort Townsend to Chimacum to visit Lian and Kjell and to leave the reindeer with them. Leksu died some time ago. Susan vaguely remembers her but not her one-time owner. Lian and Kjell remember Elle-Ristine, of course, but they don't speak of her, because of my wish. They say only that Leksu was left behind by some Laplanders who passed through town once. Annie herself has no memory of the white reindeer and thinks Susan is telling her a fairytale set in Chimacum.

That day we walked in the forest, Elle-Ristine and I told each other stories from our childhoods, of the beautiful *huldras* with their cow tails and the *uldas*, the underground people who stole babies and raised them as their own. These are not tales I have ever told Annie. I have been a baby stealer and raised a changeling whom I have loved beyond all regret. I may tell her someday. Likely I will not. And yet I feel a constant fear that someone will find me out, someone will suspect. These Sáme people in Poulsbo, who are they?

*

When Kjell and I returned to the farm, Annie and John were running about the yard with the dog, while Lian and Susan were on the shaded porch, reading. Susan was deep into *Anne of Green Gables,* and Lian had a newspaper that she put down when she saw us pull up before the house. Over the years I'd asked Lian twice if she ever planned to tell Susan that Kjell is not related to her, but that another man, a Scottish doctor, was her real father.

"I will never do that," she answered the first time. "She loves her dad, it would only hurt her. She wouldn't understand."

The second time I mentioned it was soon after I'd heard from Mikkel Aikio. I went out to Chimacum and sat on the porch with Lian. It was summer. She was wearing a gingham skirt and blouse with a long apron on her slight frame. Her lustrous dark hair in its long braid hung over one shoulder catching the sunlight. She still looked hardly more than a girl, though she was twenty-two now. She had some sewing in her lap. I told Lian that Mikkel was not dead as I had thought, but back in Norway. I said I was tempted to write him, to tell him that I had Annie still, but I was afraid he would come and take her away from me.

Lian said promptly, "Don't write him. She is yours now. You are her mother."

"But that means I'll be keeping a secret from Annie about who she is, where she comes from, *who* she comes from. I will be lying to her if I tell her I am her mother, and Edvard was her father."

"Life is like that," said Lian. "You must think only of the children's happiness. What purpose would be served if I told Susan that Kjell was not her father? Nothing! It would make her feel separate from her brother, from her father, from me. I don't know where that man is now, that doctor, and I will never know. He was nothing to me, and he can be nothing to Susan either."

Her voice had risen on a fierce, protective note, and Susan, hearing her name from the porch, looked over, asking, "Mama? Did you call me?"

I think of that summer scene from time to time when I've wondered about telling Annie that her father isn't the bearded man in the photographs, the sea captain in his nautical jacket and cap, but instead a reindeer herder halfway around the world. The difference between Kjell and Edvard is that Kjell has helped raise Susan and loves his daughter as his own. Susan has two parents, a blood mother and a responsible father, while Annie has only me and Mikkel, a father thousands of miles away who must never be allowed to take her away.

December 21

Christmas is almost here and for me and Annie it will be the first time we've celebrated it in Ballard. During the last years in Port Townsend, we always went to the Chimacum farm for the day and brought presents to Susan and John and a few store-bought delicacies to contribute to the dinner. I worried a little that Annie would miss them but if she did, she was quiet about it. When we first left Port Townsend, she mentioned Susan and John all the time, and Vera had asked me who they were. "I have a foster son who is married, and those are his children." Out of habit I did not mention that his wife was Chinese. Or Peruvian. "They live outside Port Townsend on a farm."

If I were more confident in the Svanssons, I would have asked Kjell and his family to come to Ballard for Christmas. Yet, in addition to the problem of where we would fit everyone in the house, I worried about introducing the people I love to the Swedes. What if, like others in Port Townsend, they saw a superficial likeness in the three children's faces? What if Oscar and Vera began to doubt that Annie was my daughter? What if they were disapproving or worse? Then Annie and I would have to leave, and I didn't want to risk that.

Early last summer in Port Townsend, I'd welcomed a guest to my boarding house. Mrs. Holt, from Tacoma. Her business in town had to do with her late husband, a traveling salesman who'd died unexpectedly while making a call in Uptown at the hardware shop. A heart attack. I was sympathetic to her, naturally, and told her she could stay as long as she needed to, I would find room for her.

During the second day of Mrs. Holt's stay, I came into the parlor with a tray of biscuits and sherry, knowing Mrs. Holt had had a trying morning.

Susan and John were staying with me overnight for reasons I don't recall, something to do with an errand of Kjell's or possibly as a treat.

As I entered the parlor, I heard my guest say in displeasure, "What are you Chinese children doing in the house?"

Five-year-old John simply stood there, puzzled. Susan, always confidant, explained, "We are Americans." And then added, because she found it fascinating, "A little bit Peruvian. That's in South America."

I almost laughed at Mrs. Holt's astonishment, but then I saw her take in Annie standing next to Susan and John, Annie so small and neat, blue-eyed, brown-haired, with an uptilted nose and a ready smile. My guest had probably seen Annie around the house, and knew she was my daughter, but, in her agitated worry about paying her late husband's bills and collecting on his sales, had paid little attention to her. But now Mrs. Holt stared rudely at Annie, appearing to see a resemblance. "Are you related? To these Chinese children?"

"They're my cousins," Annie said, aware that something was odd abut this conversation. She added helpfully, "We're Norwegians."

"That's enough," I said, coming into the room, and then to Annie in Norwegian, "Take your cousins up to your room, and I'll bring up your dinner soon. Polly is making fruit pudding too, for dessert."

I gave Mrs. Holt her biscuits and pointed to the bottle of sherry and glasses on the shelf. "Help yourself, please. The whole bottle if you like." But I needed to do more. I continued, "I think you said you wanted to stay a week. But I'm sorry I made a mistake. An old, valued guest sent a telegram. He's coming to town this evening and I'm afraid I must accommodate him, in your room. I can suggest another boarding house that's within walking distance. Polly will help you carry your things there."

She was so shocked she couldn't speak, and then she marched upstairs without availing herself of the sherry. I knew she'd gossip about me at the next boarding house, and that the gossip would be added to the rumors already in circulation.

But I didn't care. She had no right. She could sleep under a bush in the rain for all I cared.

Only later, after Mrs. Holt had huffed off in anger with her suitcase, and Polly and I had brought up the children's dinner and read to them and tucked them into bed, Susan with Annie, and John in blankets on the floor, did I go to my room and slap a pillow in the face.

The next day I called a lawyer and said I wanted to sell my house.

Kjell knew some of why I was unhappy in Port Townsend—"too many memories," he said once—but it still surprised him that I'd sold the house so quickly and moved to the big city. *Jeg long til deg, Mor Dagny,* "I long for you," he wrote in a letter soon after I left, unaffectedly and incorrectly, for he had never really learned to write Norwegian well and now it was mixed with English. "You are the nearest to a mother I ever had." In every letter he wrote that he missed me and signed himself "your son, Kjell." He was shocked and saddened that we weren't planning to come to Chimacum for Christmas as usual. I had excused myself by saying the weather was bound to be bad, and that the lead-up to the holidays was very busy at the *Shingle.*

This was no lie: I had been "pounding the pavement" as the American expression has it, in search of new advertisers and urging our current clients to put in larger display ads. The *Shingle*'s circulation was modest compared to the *Ballard News,* so every dollar we earned from advertising was necessary. In addition I'd been writing more articles, short ones for the *Shingle* in English and several longer pieces about Seattle and Ballard for the Midwestern Norwegian-language newspapers. The editor at the *St. Paul Gazette* was particularly keen on my descriptions of immigrant Scandinavians in Ballard. I wondered occasionally what he'd think if he found out that D.B. Bergland was a woman.

I mailed a few presents for the family in Chimacum, including some candy and *Little Women* for Susan and a wool cap for John. And then I turned my attention away from those

I'd left behind and back toward Annie and our new Swedish family.

The Svanssons revel in Christmas and preparations for the holidays seem to have gone on since Thanksgiving. Cakes and cookies baked and packed in tins, the entire house decorated with wreaths and ribbons and candles, a pig butchered for ham and sausages. They hosted a party for Bill and his high school friends and another for clients of Oscar's at the barber shop. All kinds of people began to drop in for a glass of hot clove and cinnamon spiced glögg or coffee and cookies. Vera played the piano when she wasn't cooking, and Oscar was the most genial host imaginable. Their joy when Nels came back from his fishing trip was magnificent to behold. Into all this jubilation they wrapped Annie tight: they taught her Swedish songs and dances; Vera made her a beautiful white dress for St. Lucia Day, and Bill, her hero, took her out sledding one afternoon, well-wrapped up in old sweaters and scarves.

Annie came with me on my advertising rounds one day, into shops decorated with bows and small elves and toys. She was treated with candy so often I had to hide it in my pockets. People said, "Your daughter!" and a few were even kind enough to say, "She looks like you." And stories came to my lips of Bergen at Christmas, and the windows of the storefronts there, which had so delighted and amazed me during my own first Christmas with Uncle and Aunt and Katrine.

I had left my mother and sisters behind and found a new world in Bergen, and so will Annie in Ballard.

March 10, 1906

Only two months after the new year began, unfortunate news struck in the form of a notice plastered to the office door of the *Shingle* that the landlord of the building was planning to evict Schiller and the bank to auction off the press and other equipment. I didn't understand how things got so bad, when I had been working so hard to bring in advertising and expand our circulation.

Schiller had gone into debt last summer to buy the machinery of the defunct *Millman* and although he had some success, he never had the wherewithal to pay off the balance. Medical bills from various doctors had added up as well. His wife's health worsened in January. She was admitted to the hospital with lung disease, and it was then he stopped paying rent and his other bills.

When I lost my job at the *Shingle,* I panicked, though of course I had my savings, and I knew that the Svanssons would never throw me and Annie out on the street even if I couldn't pay the rent for several months. But after the initial scare subsided, I had to think what to do. It was then that I remembered the Danish entrepreneur, Ida Krantz. She had advertised with the *Shingle* and I'd interviewed her in January for a short piece the editor of the *St. Paul Gazette* had agreed to, about Scandinavian businesses in Ballard. Together with her husband, she runs a large real estate company. She's one of many people engaged in some form of what they call "boosterism," a word once new to me, but one I now see everywhere.

The first time I encountered Ida Krantz, I was expecting a much more substantial woman in furs and a feathered hat, with a hat pin like a weapon, a greedy mouth, and hard eyes. Not just a businesswoman, but the "Ballard Land Queen" as she was sometimes called in the papers. She owns one hundred and twenty acres of prime, cleared land on the hills above the waterway, and is selling lots. I was surprised that January day to find a nondescript door on the third floor of a brick building on Ballard Ave, with the simple sign: KRANTZ LANDHOLDINGS. The clerk in the front space ushered me into a side office, with a single large desk, and I found myself face to face with a small, tidy woman of around forty-five. Her pale blond hair was puffed into a rather elaborate pompadour, but otherwise she looked like a schoolteacher in a shirtwaist with white cuffs and collar.

"Ah, Mrs. Bergland," she said affably. "I received your note about an interview and am glad to oblige. I have been hearing good things about you from the Ballard Business Council in Ballard. The *Shingle* is a little radical for my taste, but you say this is for a newspaper in St. Paul with a more pro-business view?"

She pulled out a bottle of schnapps and two small glasses and offered me a drink. Her eyes were not the typical blue that went with pale Danish hair, but Irish green, and they regarded me with mischief. "I hope you're not a temperance follower."

I assured her I wasn't.

Ida Krantz, like her husband, the lawyer H.C. Krantz, was born in Chicago. His parents were older German and Danish stock, and hers were Danish immigrants. She'd grown up speaking Danish, but now mainly remembered only some of the stronger expressions. The couple had come out to the Pacific Northwest ten years ago in search of milder winters and new opportunities and had parlayed some initial land purchases into greater wealth. They had not been blessed with children, Ida told me, adding that she knew it must be unnatural in her, but she had never felt the lack. She was her husband's partner in all things, she told me, but I suspected that she might be the driving force.

That day I felt the intoxicating power of Ida Krantz's strong will. It was a kind of American optimism that I'd often had cause to distrust in Port Townsend. So many dreams came to nothing, not through lack of hard work and spirit, but because of unforeseen complications and hindrances. A railway was not built, steamships replaced sail, another city was suddenly the winner in the race, and a thriving town was reduced to empty Victorian houses and bankrupt businesses.

But Ballard-Seattle, as Ida often called it, was not Port Townsend. The main hindrance to growth had been the lack of sufficient water, but now water flowed freely to the lands above Salmon Bay, and the city government of Seattle had been forced to contribute to the paving of streets and to better law enforcement here. Meanwhile, the land available for building stretched far to the north, to the city limits at Northwest 85th Street and west to the bluffs over the Sound. Thousands of people were pouring into Ballard for work. True, some of them were young men who only planned to make a lot of money and then return to home to Scandinavia. But many were looking to set down roots in Ballard-Seattle, to buy, to build, to send their children to school, to put their money into local banks.

Ida was no idle Ballard Booster. She sat on the Ballard Business Council, the only woman to be invited, and had her finger in any number of Scandinavian pies, from Norwegian choirs to Danish charities to Swedish hospitals. And if, because she was so well connected, she was able to sell newly platted lots, to buy up houses and resell them, to lease buildings to businesses in the downtown, to buy land along Market Street in anticipation of a shift from Ballard Avenue northwards, she was also a supporter of the library, the schools, and community organizations.

Today when I went to her office, Ida wasted no time on pity for Schiller and the radical *Shingle,* whose demise she had confidently predicted. Instead, she held up a thin pamphlet from her desk. I recognized it as something Schiller had printed for a railway agent with information about Ballard. It was in Norwegian and English, with one or two photographs and various statistics. Its aim was to lure the newcomer to Ballard, and I had written it.

"I understand you're the author of this. What a very good idea. Would you be able to write one of these for Krantz Landholdings? I need it very quickly."

"Of course," I said, and then paused. I'd learned a little about negotiation since I came to the city. "Though an immediate deadline means I'll have to put aside other work. It will cost extra."

The glint in her clever eyes showed me that she knew how to bargain with the best, but that she'd liked my considering pause as well as my initial yes.

April 15

My busy working life has left me little time to write here. First, Ida commissioned an eighteen-page booklet in English, with a photograph on every page, the photographs illustrating Ballard businesses and schools, along with a map of the Krantz Addition with lots for sale. It was printed in an edition of five hundred copies by the printing arm of the *Ballard News.* The booklet was an immediate success and went into a second printing, although I was only paid once for my work on it and the words "Krantz Landholdings" are three times as large as "by D. B. Bergland" on the title page. The important thing is that Ida Krantz began to employ me for other work, and to recommend me as a writer to many of her fellows on the Ballard Business Council, who also wanted to get their business before the public eye. Now this has led to a new commission, one offered by the Ballard City Council, to be titled *Ballard for Everyone*. It is to be a full forty-eight pages long and filled with photographs to be taken by a professional photographer and with a map or two. I am to be the sole writer, and to find advertising to accompany the minimal text. It is a booster project for Ballard and should be written in the advertising language I perfected while at the *Shingle*.

My deadline is June 15, two months from now, and I have been given half the fee in advance. I bought shoes for my growing girl with part of the money, and new boots for myself. I asked Adele to make us each a new summer dress and sent small presents to Chimacum. The spirit of entrepreneurship has infected me, and I suddenly see how I can support myself and Annie. Ida encourages me in every way. She is one of the boldest women I have ever met.

Like the other booklet about the Krantz Addition, *Ballard for Everyone* is to be printed by the *Ballard News*. On my first humiliating visits to this establishment in search of reporting and advertising work, I saw nothing of the pressrooms at the back of the one-story brick building. They connect with the newspaper's front office, but have a separate entrance on the side, and this is where I now come when I am delivering copy, discussing photographs, and reading proofs. There's a small office with a counter where customers place their orders and pick them up, and this leads directly into a larger space with marble composing tables and wooden typecases. A second room holds a massive iron printing press, for the daily newspaper and for outside jobs like the booklet; a proof press; and two smaller platen presses with large wheels for business cards, stationery, and circulars. All except the proof press are powered by electricity. The door between the two workspaces is usually closed, but even when it's closed you can hear the whirring and clanking of the ungainly metal machines at work and smell the ink and kerosene when the door opens. The typesetting is all done by hand and requires two men and an apprentice working steadily and at speed. The compositors work standing at job cases, the compartmentalized boxes where the moveable type is stored, under a row of small-paned windows that face an alley. The men rapidly fill their composing sticks with lead type, words separated by em and en quads, sentences by leads and slugs. On a high marble table is the metal frame or chase with the lines of type, along with ornaments and the engraved plates of illustrations mounted on wood blocks. The space around the type is filled with furniture, small blocks of wood or metal that are tightened with a key, called a quoin.

I often have reason to talk with the compositors, as I did with Jimmy Jay in the *Shingle* days. They might have a question about one of my proof marks or how the type should be set around a photographic engraving, or I might need to explain that I got a fact wrong and a paragraph needs resetting. We discuss what the display ads should look like: how to satisfy the client but also keep the design in harmony with the booklet. One of the compositors is older and well-experienced, but gruff. He prefers to be addressed as Mr. Sampson and for me to speak in soft and supplicatory tones. The other, younger man is a Norwegian immigrant, Tom Nilsen, and far more patient, so it is usually him I approach if I have the choice. Tom Nilsen works hypnotically fast. I could watch him make sentences of single letters all day. He holds whole paragraphs in his left hand and attaches them to other paragraphs, and apparently never misspells a single English word, though sometimes he has to use a dictionary to understand how the word breaks.

If I didn't know Tom Nilsen was Norwegian, I could have imagined he was Russian, perhaps a revolutionary who'd had to escape from Moscow or St. Petersburg because of illegal meetings to overthrow the Tsar. He is my height, not tall for a man, slender and active, clean-shaven with high cheekbones, straight dark hair falling on his forehead from a side part. He wears wire-rim spectacles. His eyes are dark too, observant but gentle. His fingers are smudged with black ink, and he often wears a striped blue and gray collarless shirt under his heavy blue canvas apron. I suppose he is Kjell's age, around thirty. He is from the north of Norway. I can hear that in his accent.

May 12

It's been explained to me that one of the aims of *Ballard for Everyone* is to make sure Ballard doesn't become a mere neighborhood of greedy Seattle. The members of the business council, unlike most of the workers in Ballard, are not all Scandinavians. They want me to stress that our city within a city isn't only a destination for Swedes, Norwegians, Finns, and so on. Everyone is *velkommen,* but I've been instructed to emphasize that there are *abundant* real estate and business opportunities for people moving to Ballard from elsewhere in the United States. I am, of course, to include Solstad's Bakery—"a beloved spot where those-who-know-what's-delicious gather for fresh-from-the-oven *boller* and *wienerbrød*"—but I've also been charged with explaining that many of the larger sawmills and cargo shipping concerns are owned by Yankees from New England and the Midwest, with names like Taylor and Greene, and that merchants and hoteliers aren't only called Johansson and Seierstad, but Weissman and Radkowski.

Because of my work on the pamphlet for the railways and the Krantz Addition booklet, I'd already expanded my circle beyond the shopkeepers on Ballard and Shilshole Avenues to the offices of the shipping businesses along the waterway and the shingle mills. I've taken down facts and figures about sales and employees, tons of shingles produced monthly, and so on. I've now spent over a month gathering fresh information on real estate and local geography, schools, churches, benevolent societies, social groups, parks, and amusements. I'd written before about all the Nordic community groups—the Lutheran churches and male choirs, the Sons of Norway's Leif Erikson Lodge, founded in 1903, followed by the ladies' Valkyrien Lodge—but now I also tracked down other benevolent societies, Elks and Redmen and Shriners, and other places of ritual and community. I've also gathered information and statistics about real estate companies, banks, land surveyors, and lawyers.

This morning I accompanied Annie to school as usual, then had a cup of coffee at Solstad's Bakery, and went to the stationer. As I came out of the shop with a box of pins and a bottle of ink, I was surprised to run into Tom Nilsen. I would have thought he would be at the pressrooms already, but he said he'd had to work very late last night on a special job, so his boss had given him two hours off this morning. He had thought to stop by the stationer and look at their display of new books. I noticed a copy of a book jammed in his jacket pocket. This morning was warm, and he wore no hat. A lock of his dark hair fell forward, and he blinked behind his wire spectacles at the sun. He gave off a faint smell of ink and sweat. He said with a smile, "I almost feel like we're in back in Norway, with the return of the light."

I noted that he didn't say "back home" as so many people did around here. I asked him if he was from the north. We'd been speaking English, but I switched to Norwegian now, so he could hear my dialect, as I could hear his.

"Yes, near Alta," he answered. "And you must be from Western Norway. Bergen?"

"Sognefjord originally, and then Bergen."

"The fjord country, I knew it! Are you on your way to the print shop?" he asked. "Because we could walk together."

I hadn't been planning to go there, but for some reason I said yes. We fell into step quite naturally. I liked the way he swung along beside me, not offering to take my parcel or help me over a clump or two of horse dung in the street, but assuming that I was strong enough to walk half a dozen blocks to the office.

"Have you been in America long?" I asked. In the morning light I could see that he had hardly any beard, surprising for a man with such dark hair.

"Yes and no," he said. "I first came to Minnesota when I was seventeen to join my older brother. He lives in Minneapolis with his wife and children. I learned English and went to high school, and then studied two years at Augsburg Seminary before I went back to Norway. And you? How did a girl from the fjord country come to be in Ballard working as a writer and editor? That's uncommon."

I felt a little embarrassed to be called a *jente,* a girl, but perhaps better that than a *dame,* a lady, as if I were his grandmother. "I came by sea," I told him. "My late husband owned a ship, and we ended up in Port Townsend. He died seven years ago, after an accident in Alaska, and last summer I moved here with my little daughter. I've always been interested in writing and newspapers. For years I've sent out my work to be published in the Norwegian press. I worked until recently at the *Shingle.*"

"I am sorry about your husband," he said. "I think you must be very brave to start again, on your own." He spoke sincerely, and again I felt embarrassed.

"It's not bravery," I said a little brusquely, "but simple financial need. I must support my daughter." We crossed a street, avoiding a horse and buggy, and I continued, "What about you? How did you become interested in printing?"

"I worked on the student newspaper at Augsburg," he said. "We produced it ourselves on a tabletop press. After my second year, I found a summer job at a newspaper in North Dakota. I learned to typeset and print there and ended up staying a year to learn the trade. Then my parents wrote from Norway, asking me and my brother to come and see them. My brother didn't want to go, so I did. I ended up staying six years, fishing with my father until he died. Then I worked on a newspaper farther south. My mother died, and I decided to return to America. I was curious about the Northwest, so took the train to Seattle. Work is not hard to come by here."

I calculated the years: He must near Kjell's age, without Kjell's fatherly gravitas. "I thought at first you must be Russian," I said. "I had a whole story about you in my head. You have an anarchist's look about you, you know."

"No, I didn't know that." He smiled and then hesitated a long moment, "I am from a Lappish family. But there is probably some Russian in there as well. Up in the north people traded every year with the Russians. The Russians carried grain from the White Sea, and we sold them dried fish and furs. Perhaps there was a Russian sailor who took a wife and settled in my village of Kokelv."

I stared at him without speaking, then managed, "Lappish, you say?" just as we reached the entrance to the pressrooms at the back of the *Ballard News.* Anders Voss, the editor of the newspaper, along with his assistant, was standing outside the door. Both were smoking pipes and seemed surprised to see me with Tom Nilsen.

"Mrs. Bergland?" said Voss. "Can we help you?" In spite of the fact that he knew very well I'd been commissioned to write *Ballard for Everyone* and that the *Ballard News* was printing it, he managed to make it sound like I was inconsequential and possibly even lost.

"No," I said, without further explanation, and turned to leave. "Good-bye, Mr. Nilsen," I said.

"Good-bye, Mrs. Bergland."

I heard Voss say, "Good morning, Tom. Rested up?"

"Yes, thank you, Mr. Voss," said Tom. I felt him looking after me as I walked quickly away.

May 18

Today, to give me a break from proofing the pages of *Ballard for Everyone,* Ida and I went out together, what Ida calls an *udflugt.* A jaunt or outing, though oddly, the word in Danish, similar to the Norwegian, also means *excuse, prevarication.* I almost always go with her when she summons me. Sometimes I've been at her office, asking her some questions for the booklet, when she suddenly says, "I must see Pastor Svendsen," or "I simply have to take a look at some properties." She makes a call on her telephone to the nearby livery stable and by the time we get there the two-person carriage is ready. She always takes the reins, and she is a very good driver, even when she's had a glass or two of her "herbal medicine," as she sometimes calls it with a wink.

Today our expedition took us up to a far section of her property, where there were still forests last spring. The clearcutting has all been finished, but there are piles of slash everywhere and the men who agreed to burn it or cart it away aren't working fast enough.

"You'll see," said Ida, "in mid-October the rains begin, and this is all mud and broken branches. I don't care about the stumps, but I can't have these piles everywhere." She cracked her whip playfully in the air. "You'll help me, Dagny, with your stern Norwegian face. The men are all Norwegian. You'll remind them of their wives."

"I'm not stern-faced," I laughed.

"Well not with me, naturally. I see your cheerful humor often. But you must admit, you have a serious face. You have lived a lot, lost a lot, you know what's what."

"Oh, I don't know about that," I said, but I was pleased.

"Tell me," she said, "Why did you marry so young?"

"Circumstance," I said. "I wanted to see the world. I had no money of my own and didn't want to study to be a teacher like my cousin Katrine. My uncle had an acquaintance, Edvard, a sea captain of substance, much older. I liked him," I paused. "And then I grew to love him."

"The opposite of me," she laughed. "I can't stand my husband now, though I adored him once. I think."

"That can't be true," I said. "He seems an agreeable man."

"Others think so," she said lightly. "It's a useful trait to be agreeable, especially if you're a lawyer." But, as so often, Ida moved on quickly to the subject at hand: Would I help her organize a charity evening to raise money for a worthy cause: building an old age home? "I want to introduce you to more people, as my friend and colleague. And I think it makes a difference that even though you must work for a living—as I do—that you are not only the widow of a sea captain, but a relative of the Vesterman family in Bergen. Do you mind if that's how I introduce you?"

"No," I said, though a little hesitantly. I had only mentioned my connection with Bryggen Kaffe og Kakao in passing, but clearly she recognized the company (their coffee was sold even here in Ballard), and my standing went up in her eyes. It occasionally strikes me as odd that for all her apparent confidence and her notable business skills and wealth, Ida seems to rely on her family's social status. I have heard her drop her husband's name during negotiations, and she always introduces herself as Mrs. Helmut Krantz. His name is on her business letterhead and although I have rarely seen him at the office of Krantz Landholdings, the receptionist takes messages for him there on business matters. Of course, women have fewer rights than men, especially when it comes to voting, education, and wages. I assumed that like Adele and me, Ida would be for equality, but in fact she doesn't seem to care very much about suffrage. "Real power is money," she said. "The vote means very little if you don't have a sizable bank account."

I believe Ida has a great deal of money, but in fact, I don't know if it's her own or her husband's or whether it's all an illusion based on real estate and investments. I've never been invited to her house on Queen Anne Hill. All our dealings take place in her office, where I occasionally work on my ad copy, or in the horse and buggy. She doesn't come to my house either, except to whisk me away occasionally on her jaunts and outings. She seems busy in the evenings—she tells me that she and her husband often attend social gatherings at the homes of his wealthy clients. But she doesn't mention dinner parties at their own home. He is often out of town. Apparently, he likes to fish and sometimes goes for a weekend or as long as a week "into the mountains." But whenever she says "fishing trips" her lips curl slightly, as if she wants me to understand something else.

I spend my evenings with Annie of course, and usually with the Svanssons. Adele and I sometimes meet for a musical event, in Seattle or Ballard and we try to have coffee or take a walk at least every two weeks. Recently, Adele came over with another friend, Irene, and the three of us attended an evening of Magic and Vaudeville. Afterwards, I walked them to the streetcar stop on Ballard Ave and passed by Krantz Landholdings. I looked up and there was a light on in the brick building. I had the strange feeling then that Ida might be up there working, with her bottle of schnapps and a glass.

June 1

I've not spoken much with Tom Nilsen since he told me he was Sáme. I suppose he thinks me prejudiced, like most Norwegians.

Nothing could be further from the truth! I was only taken aback. The fact is, I thought that all Sáme people had reindeer and lived in tents. Elle-Ristine never mentioned any other kind of life but the nomadic one. And yet here is Tom, who also comes from Finnmark, where his parents had a farm and fished. Here is Tom, who went to high school and began college in Minneapolis. Who speaks perfect English and Norwegian and who seems comfortable in this country. Can he really *be* Sáme, does he know other Sáme people here, *are* there others in America besides those in Poulsbo and Alaska?

This Saturday afternoon I was on my way down Market Street after a meeting with Ida. I had taken an after-lunch tipple with her, only enough to feel slightly elevated. As I made my way down the street, leisurely enjoying looking in the shop windows, I noticed Tom Nilsen purposefully walking toward me.

"Mrs. Bergland!" he said, lifting his hat. "I saw you from the streetcar and jumped off. I've wondered how you are."

"Thank you, Mr. Nilsen. I'm well. Are you shopping today?" He had a heavy, square parcel in his hand.

"Yes, books. I like sometimes on Saturdays to go down to a bookshop in Seattle." His dark eyes held mine with a certain firm bashfulness. "I haven't seen you in some days."

"No, I've been proofing the last round of the booklet," I said calmly, though I felt my heart pounding with the need to explain myself. Perhaps it was pounding for some other reason; I did find the way he looked at me both unsettling and agreeable. It was the cheekbones and the sensitive, soft-looking lips. "I should be stopping by the pressroom soon with the last of the corrections."

We had begun to walk together and again I was struck by the easiness of his stride, matching mine. "I had a business meeting, and I'm going home for a special treat. Our landlady is teaching my daughter how to bake and today they're making cinnamon rolls."

"*Kanelboller!*" His nostrils flared as if he could smell the cardamom and cinnamon.

I made a quick decision. "Are you in a hurry? Why not come back with me to the Svanssons? There will just be the four of us. Vera is always welcoming, the coffee is always on the stove, and Annie, well, I would love for you to meet her."

*

It was only when Annie had left us in the parlor that Tom Nilsen said in a low voice, "Were you married to a Lappish man?"

A flowered plate of gingersnaps, along with a dark blue coffee pot, was on the table before us, along with the remainder of the cinnamon rolls, delicious if a bit unshapely.

"Then she looks like a Sáme girl to you?"

"I can recognize my own people. But how is possible? I thought perhaps,when we talked last time, that you might have felt that my being Lappish was unfortunate. But I now hear you saying Sáme, not Lappish?" He had taken off his jacket, and again I caught the smell of ink and something like the sea, as if he had washed in salt water.

From the kitchen came Annie's voice, chattering freely to Vera as they washed up.

"My husband, Edvard, was not Sáme. But there were circumstances that led to me adopting Annie. It began during the Klondike Gold Rush, when a group of reindeer herders came through Port Townsend on their way to Alaska. One of them, Elle-Ristine, became my friend."

I was also talking in a low voice, feeling the strongest desire to unburden myself of the whole story, to someone who was Sáme himself. I had kept my secret from everyone, for so long. But today, I told Tom Nilsen about Elle-Ristine and Mikkel Aikio and the reindeer, about the abortive trip to Haines, and the second trip to Eaton Station, about Edvard's death and Elle-Ristine's, about Mikkel going to Nome and falling ill, about Reverend Karlson in Unalakleet suggesting I take the baby back home with me so that she would have a better life and a good education.

He asked no questions while I spoke, and simply looked at me with those dark, gentle eyes, magnified a bit by the spectacles. Only when I ran out of words, did he say something. "You have been through a great deal, Mrs. Bergland."

"Call me Dagny, please. It has been a long time now, but yes, I still feel the losses. My husband of course, but also Elle-Ristine. I was so fond of her."

"And then there are Annie's losses," he added.

"Yes, though ... she doesn't know. She thinks I'm her birth mother."

"She doesn't know she lost her mother and her father in Alaska?" He was clearly shocked.

I fumbled with my cup, so it clattered on the saucer. "It wasn't my original intention to keep that fact from her. But she wouldn't have understood. And by the time she was old enough to understand, I thought it would only create confusion in her mind."

I did not correct his assumption that Mikkel was dead too. I rushed on, "I had already lost two children at sea. I didn't want to lose a third."

"Dagny—two children—I don't know what to say," he began, but then Annie came in, sent by Vera to ask if we wanted more fresh coffee. I guessed this might be Vera's way of nudging Tom Nilsen out the door. "Mor," she said, coming to my side, "Can you help me with something? She ran her eyes curiously over him, at the two of us. "Upstairs, Mor!"

"Yes, yes," I said, rising. "I have kept Mr. Nilsen here too long."

Tom rose with alacrity, and I walked him to the coat rack next to the door, as Annie ran up the stairs. He put on his coat but not his hat and thanked us for the coffee and cakes.

"Please say nothing about this," I asked him under my breath. "I mean, Annie."

"That will be easy," he said, with a smile. "For one thing, I'm not inclined to chat with my coworkers much. And for another I'll be leaving the *Ballard News* in early September. I've enrolled again at Augsburg Seminary as a junior and will be moving back in with my brother and his family to save money."

"But that's wonderful," I told him, though I felt oddly flustered at the news he was returning to Minneapolis. "I know you've wished to continue your education. I imagine that everyone will miss you here though."

"Perhaps." He looked at me searchingly. "Will you call me Tom, Dagny?"

"Mor!" called Annie from the top of the stairs. "*Kom!*"

I watched Tom go down the walk, hat in hand, sun glinting on his dark hair. He is the first person in Ballard to know some of Annie's true story, and it seems like a great relief.

June 20

Ballard for Everyone is being printed and bound at the moment and the first copies should be available this week. Ida and I celebrated yesterday evening with dinner in a restaurant. This afternoon, Sunday, Tom accompanied us to Woodland Park, one of the Seattle parks designed by the Olmsted brothers. Ballard, strangely, has no parks at all. It was Tom who suggested taking Annie there. We went by streetcar part of the way and then walked. Before the Olmsteds turned their hand to it, this was a wilder place owned by a man who kept a private menagerie. There were no signs of wild animals now, however; we strolled on paths through firs and maples, huckleberry, and Oregon grape to open hillsides above Green Lake.

I remembered from the newspaper articles back in March, 1898 that the reindeer that came with the Sáme had grazed here in this very park, but I said nothing to Tom about that. Instead, whenever Annie was preoccupied with chasing squirrels and picking up twigs, I asked Tom questions about himself and how he grew up.

I admitted to him that much of what I'd known about the Sáme people was what Elle-Ristine told me about reindeer herding, hunting, trapping, and gathering berries.

"They had the reindeer, those Sáme in the interior. We on the coast had fish," said Tom good-naturedly. "Not as romantic, I know."

"Did you own a boat?" I asked.

"Several. My father built the larger one, a Nordland boat, with his brother, my uncle. They were accustomed to sail down to Lofoten Islands for the winter cod fishing when they were young, but later we fished mainly for coalfish and halibut in the inner fjords and out to sea. My mother tended the garden and milked the goats. We had a cow as well."

It wasn't so different than my own family's farm on the Sognefjord, I thought, and I thought of my father in the fjord trolling for salmon in spring, the pretty little goats we had, and our one cow. But then the conversation turned, and I realized how very different we really were. For Tom had grown up in a sod house, called a *gamme*. He had grown up speaking Sáme at home, Norwegian at school. And there had not always been harmony with the neighbors and the authorities.

"The Norwegian state, especially in the north, long ago set in motion regulations to destroy our culture," said Tom. "Against our will, they took our grazing lands and they tried hard to erase our language. They made it difficult or even illegal to own property if you don't speak Norwegian and have a Norwegian name. That's why my father became Nilsen. He was born *Nilsa-Bierra*. Peder, the son of Nils."

He told me this when we'd come to a playground with a kiosk selling ice cream. Tom bought us three cones, and Annie left us to play with some other children in the sandbox nearby. I allowed her to take off her stockings and shoes.

"But is there nothing you can do?" I asked. I had not heard this story when I lived in Norway or afterwards. The Sáme or the Laplanders were a distant folk, and we learned little about them in school. They were not part of our glorious history of Vikings, kings, and Constitutionalists. I had counted myself among the few, because of Elle-Ristine, to know about the daily lives of the reindeer herders, but she had never spoken of such persecution.

"We are few; they are many. In the distant past we often just abandoned a place and moved inland or farther north. But we can't so easily do that now. Some go to cities in the south and forget their heritage, find jobs, and marry. Some emigrate, like me and my brother. In America you can simply be American."

I have never found being American simple, I wanted to tell him. Instead I just watched him with a sense of warmth, of pleasure in his company. He was licking his mound of pale vanilla tidily, unlike me, who had managed to get some of the melting strawberry ice cream on my sleeve. Having come to meet us from church, he wore a jacket and a tie; his shoes were polished. Only his face, if you knew how to read it, showed he was from Northern Norway, that he was Sáme. For the world passing by on this Sunday afternoon we must look like Americans ourselves, not two people who had grown up in the same country, but worlds apart.

"You said your brother was the first to come. He must be well settled here by now?"

"Yes, he's been here for fifteen years now," Tom said, turning to me so his jacket rubbed against my arm in its summer dress. "When he was in Hammerfest working, Jouna was set upon by men who called him a dirty Lapp. He fought back and went to jail for a week. He was not the same afterwards, he said he was leaving. Our parents thought he meant to go only to Tromsø, but he found work on a cargo ship to Boston. In America he worked on the docks for six months and managed to get to Minneapolis by jumping a train. Once he was there, he studied bookkeeping at night and became a clerk in a shipping company. Now he calls himself John and stays away from Norwegians. When I first came to join him years ago, we spoke our familiar language, *davvisámegiella,* when we were alone. But he refused to use it when I came back last summer to Minneapolis. He has a wife, Trudy, who doesn't want their children to know we are Sáme."

He looked at Annie, pouring warm sand over her arms and legs in delight. "It makes me sad to see my nephews growing up not knowing who their people are or anything about our culture."

July 5

Adele has now met Tom. I brought him and Annie to a picnic at the home of her brother and sister-in-law. They live in Ravenna, down the street from where Adele's property is, and where Knox will build her a house. At one point we all walked down the street and looked at the lot, which is still wooded, and overlooks a deep ravine. I could see that Adele liked Tom, but afterwards she took me aside and said, "He is nice-looking all right and well-spoken, but— Dagny?—isn't he a bit young?"

"Yes, I know," I said with some asperity. "It's fine that Edvard was eighteen years older than I was when we married. But things are different when the woman is older. People would be shocked at such a marriage."

"Marriage? Surely not, Dagny."

"Don't be silly," I said, flushing. "Tom is a friend, to both me and Annie. Can't a woman have a friend? Besides," I added, "He comes from Northern Norway!" A Norwegian might have understood that meant Tom could be a Sáme, but Adele looked at me uncomprehendingly. After all these years, Norway and everything Norwegian that is not related to food is still a mystery to her. She knows little of my country's geography and history. Of course she would recall the reindeer herders, but what could this dark-haired young man speaking perfect English have to do with them?

That was the nearest I came to blurting out that Tom was the first person since Elle-Ristine I'd been able to talk with about Lapland, the first person I'd been able to tell anything important to about Annie and her family. The first person who *saw* my daughter for all she was. I pressed my lips together and said, "What I mean is that he was a type compositor and printer when he lived in Northern Norway. That's of course very interesting to me."

It *is* interesting. And it's one of the reasons that Tom can seem so much older than his years. His experiences are more varied than most men his age and his understanding greater. He has lived in three different cultures, not just two countries.

The other day he told me more about his newspaper work. A few years ago, a Sáme named Anders Larsen, who'd once taught primary school in Kokelv, where Tom's family lived, decided to start a newspaper in Norway for Sáme people. It wouldn't be the first Sáme publication, but the first in the North Sáme language.

"That was where I came in," said Tom. "In 1903, while my mother was still living, I moved down to the village Sigerfjord to work for a pastor named Lund who was publishing a Christian paper in the Sáme language. Not only did I know how to set type and run a printing press from my time in North Dakota, but I knew the North Sáme language. I also had studied theology at Augsburg Seminary and was a member of the Free Church already. In 1904 Pastor Lund agreed to begin printing Anders Larsen's newspaper, *Sagai Muittalaegje*. I was able to work on it for over a year. Larsen was sorry when I left; he wanted me to be part of this Sáme political movement, along with his friend Isak Saba. Saba is hoping to be elected to the Norwegian parliament this autumn, and Larsen and the paper support him. 'Samiland for the Sáme people!' is their slogan."

"But you didn't want stay in Norway and become part of the movement?" I said, a little taken aback by the fervor in his voice.

"No," he said. "I believe in the cause but knew it wouldn't satisfy me to live in a village and work as a printer. Not after having been to America and seen how many doors could open to someone with education. Before my mother's death last year, she made me promise to finish my schooling. What she most wanted was for me to become a pastor who would preach in Sáme and Norwegian and lift our people up."

"Is that why you're returning to Augsburg Seminary then? Are you really intending to be a pastor?"

"And if I were, Mrs. Bergland?" His eyes glinted, teasing but serious behind the wire spectacles.

"I would admire that," I told him. But, somehow, I didn't feel enthusiastic. Tom as a pastor? Wouldn't he be happier working on newspapers?

July 9

Ida Krantz has complained that I'm never free any longer for our jaunts. "I hear that you have a young compositor as your escort now," she teased when we met by chance outside her office one day. Her pompadour was high but she was still tiny next to me, and she held a riding whip in her hand. She was off to the stables.

I turned bright red, or at least I felt as though I did. "Tom Nilsen is just a friend."

"Dagny, a woman can't have a male friend without people talking. Especially not a younger man." She winked at me and added half-seriously, "If you're looking for a husband, look for a man of substance. There are plenty of solid, ambitious men in Ballard, God knows. Someone with an established home to offer you. And if you're looking for a lover, keep it quiet. Don't go parading around the streets with him."

I've wondered about her from time to time, she and her mysterious evenings in the office. Does she have a lover? I suppose it might make sense, given her unhappy marriage.

How could I tell Ida about my Sáme daughter and the guilt I carried, how Tom understood my situation in a way I'd needed for years. Even if Annie didn't know Tom was Sáme, I did. It made me happy to see Tom with Annie, apart from the happiness his presence gave me.

"Oh nonsense, Ida," I said firmly. "I am far too old to think of such things. And we are not parading around the streets. I have work to do, and if sometimes I meet Tom in the street on the way to the *Ballard News*, that's no one's business."

But, alone in my room at night, I sometime touch my breast or my thigh gently, and think how long it's been since I lay with Edvard, and I wonder if those memories of what it means to love a man will ever be revived.

July 16

A few days ago, the Svanssons invited Tom for Sunday dinner. They asked him about his work and his plans, but in their usual friendly way they didn't probe too deeply. Before the meal Tom and I played croquet with Bill and Annie, and afterwards Tom good-naturedly pitched softballs at Bill. Of course Tom played softball when he was in high school in Minneapolis years ago, but I was still surprised at his skill. In many ways, he is more American than most of us, and Bill has quite taken to him. He was excited to discover that Tom had done a lot of fishing in Norway. "Nels has a boat now and wants to teach me to sail. We should go out into Shilshole Bay next weekend," he said. "You too, Mrs. Bergland. You like the sea."

"Yes, I love the sea," I said. "But I don't like small boats.

They capsize too easily."

"But not with Nels as our captain," insisted Bill, with all the faith a sixteen-year-old has in an older brother. "And Tom is experienced too."

Tom modestly said he would be glad to be the first mate and looked at me questioningly. I thought about Edvard. My husband had never been modest, nor was it a question of small sailboats, but a barque called *Matilde,* with its huge sails and cargo hold and captain's cabin. All the same, I realized I wanted to be out on the water with him, to see how he handled a boat.

Later, while Annie was taking a nap upstairs, I showed Tom the studio photograph of Elle-Ristine and Mikkel. It seemed a century since it had been taken, not just nine years ago.

"Ah," he said, studying it carefully. "Annie has her mother's eyes but her father's smile, doesn't she? You can tell her parents come from Karasjok by the style of the clothing. Our dress is similar, but my father wore oilcloth overalls over his *gákti.* In my family, it was my mother who made our clothes and many of the other things we used each day, bowls from tree roots, small leather pouches, woven shoe bands. My father made me a knife with a sheath of bone. He etched patterns on it, and patterns on our bone spoons and my mother's needle case. He taught Jouna and me to make fishhooks and fish racks. He taught us to build a dingy and whittle some oars. I still have the knife. The rest I gave away to relatives or sold with the farm."

I knew now that the farm was located near the *Ruoššajohka* or Russian River, where it emptied into the Revnsbotnfjord. The village of Kokelv was close by.

"Do you feel you've left your heritage behind?" I asked, thinking of myself. "I sometimes wish I still had some of the little, well-loved toys I owned as a child, things I left behind when I went to Bergen."

"My heritage is inside, Dagny," he said. He was still warm from playing ball and I smelled the sweat in his shirt. We were sitting together on the sofa. His dark hair fell onto his forehead as he bent over the photograph again. "Like yours. You don't wear the dress of a Sognefjord peasant girl, and I wager you didn't bring your milking bucket with you when you set off for parts unknown with your captain." He raised his dark eyes to look at me and they had a new expression, almost tender. "But you'll always be a girl from the western fjords, won't you? I hear it in your accent, I see it in how you walk, as if you are well used to hiking outdoors in the mountains."

"Yes," I said, pleased but self-conscious. "I suppose I am and have always been a country girl from Sognefjord. I still have my sea chest. There's a bunad inside, folded carefully in silk cloth, that I wore when I was eight. My mother made it for me. I thought that Agnete ... or Annie ... might wear it someday."

"Annie will love to wear it," he said. "You have nothing else of Elle-Ristine's for her to wear with it? No jewelry or a belt?"

"Silver balls on a chain," I said. "But they are lost. They were to be hung on the cradle to protect her against the *uldas*."

"You know about the *uldas*?" He was startled.

"And many other stories," I said, "Elle-Ristine knew many legends and folk tales, from her mother and grandparents in Karasjok. Her father was Norwegian, and Elle-Ristine grew up partly in Alta and partly in Karasjok."

"Then there are still relatives in Karasjok, I suppose? And in Alta?"

"An uncle in Karasjok perhaps," I looked away. "Though I believe Elle-Ristine's father came from farther south."

I could not bear to bring up the fact that Mikkel and his new family were in Karasjok. Bill came in then and flung himself into a chair. It was easy to change the subject and to tease Tom about his pitching prowess. I can well imagine Tom knows that I am keeping some part of the story from him.

July 25

I've just returned from seeing Kjell and Annie off on the steamer to Port Ludlow. Foster siblings but also uncle and niece. Related to each other and to me through bonds of love, a love that was in the way Annie held his hand as she skipped up the gang plank, braids bouncing under her straw hat, in the way he carried her small suitcase on his strong farmer's shoulders. It was in my wave and in the tears that I hid by turning away before the steamer loosed its hawsers, as if I had something important to do and must get back to work.

It will be my longest separation so far from Annie, a whole month almost.

Kjell and I had a fine time with Annie before they set off to Chimacum. We rode the streetcar, visited the zoo, and had taffy apples. I told Kjell that I was considering buying two lots from Ida Krantz. On one lot I would eventually build a house for me and Annie. The other lot I'd hold on to as an investment.

"Are you doing well enough with this booster writing that you can afford to spend your savings?"

Having just been paid the final installment for my work on *Ballard for Everyone* and already busy with more such work for different businesses and rail agents, I thought I was doing well indeed. My mind is full of English words and phrases from my booklets: *Opportunity. Prospects. Chance of a lifetime. Splendid views. Invest in land. You won't regret it. Booming. Soaring. Roaring. Going fast. Get in while you can.*

"It's spending to earn," I said. One of Ida's phrases. "Adele thinks it's a good investment." Adele gets on very well with Ida. There is something in Adele, lady-like as she can be, that is bold and decisive, that understands risk and is willing to take it.

"Yes," he countered, "but after you've bought the property, you'll still have to pay for a house to be built, you have to furnish it."

"That's true," I said. For I'm not as bold as Adele, in spite of having seen far more of the world. I've had more losses than she has and have seen more dreams fade and crash into reality.

"Well, just be cautious," said Kjell. "Don't be in a hurry. After all, you might not stay in Ballard. You might want to return to be nearer us sometime. The children miss you and Annie." I thought about the young man who jumped on a ship to the Yukon without a care for the consequences. That Kjell was gone forever, replaced by a sensible, nine-fingered farmer with a family. Still young, but more conservative, a man who now thinks of me as his elderly relative who has to be protected and scolded. We didn't only disagree about my possible land purchase, but about my friendship with Tom Nilsen.

It was a chance remark or two that Annie made about walks with "Onkel Tom" that made Kjell glance at me in alarm.

"He's a nice man who gives us presents and takes us for walks. Once we had ice cream," said Annie.

"Who is this man?" Kjell demanded.

"He's compositor in the pressroom at the *Ballard News*," I said. "I got to know him because I often have to talk with the typesetters and printers about my work. He's Norwegian, so we have that in common. That's all," I added, hoping to discourage any further questions. I was certainly not going to say in front of Annie that Tom was Sáme. She still did not know what that meant.

"But he gives you presents?"

"Annie just means he gave her a bentwood box he made."

"Yes," said Annie jumping up and down. "And he knows how to fix things too. He fixed my little doll house, where the roof came off. And he can sew too. He says that where he comes from, boys learn to repair their clothes."

"But Mor Dagny, what does this mean? What is his situation?" Kjell's deep voice rose irritatingly.

"He has no situation!" I said crisply. "He's a young immigrant, still a student, taking some time off from his studies at Augsburg College by coming west for a year to work. He's returning to Minneapolis in a month. We have tried to be kind to him, as a young Norwegian, that's all."

"Oh, that is kind," said Kjell, mollified. "It is hard to be alone in a foreign country."

I felt like a liar. Something very frequent these days.

August 10

We set out on our sailing adventure today with Nels and Bill and a picnic basket packed by Vera Svansson with meat pies and cold potato salad. The sailboat, the *Marianne,* is a trim little vessel of around twenty-four feet. Nels calls it a cutter because while it has just one mast, it has two foresails, a jib, and a mainsail. Tom didn't know words in English for these types of boats—cutters, sloops and so on—but he quickly picked up the vocabulary. He had grown up sailing the lapstrake-hulled Nordland boat with its single big square sail and its ballast of stones.

The day was clear, with a sharp wind from the north, tossing puffs of white clouds around. We were all on deck, and Nels took the helm as we set out into Shilshole Bay. We steered across the Sound toward Bainbridge Island, tacking back and forth as Bill worked the sails with Tom's help. The boom swung back and forth, but Nels kept the boat steady. Nels was a larger version of Bill. Although he had been born in Illinois, there was something still Swedish about him, the broad face, the sun-bleached hair, the emphasis on certain words, and most of all his way of nodding his head like Vera, in approval and occasional doubt as he says, "Joh!" And "Jooh ... ?" He'd been out fishing on large ships off the coast of Washington for much of the year and would be returning to open ocean again in the fall. Tom asked him questions about the fishing grounds, the nets they used, the size of the catches.

I could have felt ignored—I don't care much about fish—but instead I was happy, trailing my hand in the water and bringing it up to my nose to sniff. All salt water connected me to the world's seas and to Norway. I never learned to sail properly. My father only taught us to row the *faering* and raise a single sail in the fjord. I learned as soon as I married that I would never stand at the wheel of the *Matilde* except to have my photograph taken. Still, I remembered the names of all our sails on the barque; the vocabulary of wind and weathers, the regular shouts of the men as they raised and lowered the vast canvas sheets. On some voyages there were twenty-five or more crewmen, seasoned sailors and apprentices, crawling around the masts and riggings, calling out *Whale, land, iceberg* from the crow's nest.

For once I found myself thinking less of Edvard and more of Tom. With Bill and Nels he seemed more boyish, even wild, though also careful and fast with the sails, making sure we didn't capsize as we tacked. As we swung away from the shores of the forested island of Bainbridge, back out into the lace-edged blue

waves of the Sound, he gestured to snow-capped mountains of
the Olympics to the west. He was standing next to me in the
stern where I perched on the one padded seat. He said, "Don't
you get the sense in a boat that you could go anywhere? Be
anyone you wanted to be? There's nothing like it, this freedom!
Can I give you the tiller, Dagny?"

I understood that sense of freedom, of course I did, but at
the same time, as a woman, as a mother, I couldn't go where I
liked, not freely, not without responsibility. And I knew the sea
could kill as well as rescue. I thought, *don't lean over like that.
Can you swim?* My father couldn't swim. Tom wore a heavy blue
sweater and no hat, so his hair blew forward and back. When it
flew away from his face, his cheekbones were sharp and his eyes
very narrow, his glasses speckled with spray. He was pale from
his work indoors, compared to Bill and especially Nels who is
brown and muscular. I wanted to put my face into Tom's salty
neck or feel his arm around me. I wanted to go down to the
berth below. Let others pilot us while we slept and were carried
away to someplace new and strange.

I took the tiller and felt the power of the sea. The wooden
boat was almost too much for me to handle, in this wind, with
this current, yet I managed to keep us heading in the right
direction, back toward Ballard, the sails filled, for a good ten
minutes.

I passed the tiller back to Tom. "Thank you," I said. Not
many men so willingly give the helm to a woman.

In just two or three weeks, Tom is leaving on the train to
Minneapolis, and I still don't really know how he feels. The
tenderness in his eyes is shy and he never yet has touched me
more than to take my arm occasionally as we walk. How different
from Edvard, who seized me by the waist on our wedding day
and never let me go.

August 18

Today, everything is different.

First of all, this morning I told Tom that Mikkel is alive. I hadn't meant to, but I had a dream last night that frightened me. The dream took place in Finnmark, where I have never been. I was standing on one side of a huge river and on the other side stood Mikkel, holding Annie by the hand. She was crying. They were both in skin clothing with fur gloves and boots, while I was in a dark green skirt and embroidered bodice, the bunad I keep in my sea chest. The river was so loud that my voice couldn't be heard, but I know I was shouting in the dream, shouting in Norwegian: "Don't let me leave. I don't want to go. Don't forget me."

And yet, I could see that it was Annie leaving me.

In sad and fearful confusion I woke and stumbled around my room, putting on shoes before my stockings and forgetting to tighten my corset. I grabbed a shawl and dashed out of the Swanssons' house. It was already a warm day, but I clutched the shawl to me. Was it my mother I was leaving behind, or was Annie leaving me for Mikkel? It all felt real and terrible. I was almost ready to set off for Chimacum and to fetch Annie back early, but instead I went to Tom's boarding house, not far from the *Ballard News* building. I had never been inside before, of course. It wouldn't have been proper. But what did I care about that now? He'd mentioned that he had a room on the second floor. I went up the stairs and called out his name. "Tom? Tom!" The boarding house seemed quite empty and smelled of vinegar and soap. I knew he wouldn't be at work; he had given up his job. He was leaving tomorrow for Minneapolis.

He opened one of the doors, and motioned me in. "What has happened, Dagny?"

The room was spare, just a metal bedstead and washstand, a worn armchair and table piled with books. Faded wallpaper in a fleur-de-lis pattern, a rag rug, multicolored. I could see a black leather Bible, but also Knut Hamsun's *Pan,* opened and flattened. He had obviously been reading. His shirt was half unbuttoned, with the suspenders down. His feet were bare. They were slender, like his hands.

"I needed to see you," I said, my teeth chattering in spite of the morning heat. "I have to tell you something. You see, I had a dream last night. It frightened me so. Annie was on the other side of a big river. I couldn't get to her. She was not alone, she was … she was with her father, Mikkel. In Finnmark."

"Sit down," he said, gesturing to the armchair and pouring me a glass of water. I caught a glimpse of myself in a speckled mirror hanging over the washstand. In my mind I was still a young girl standing on a ship waving good-bye to my mother at Kyrkebø, but the woman in the mirror was forty-one, with heavy dark brown hair in a bun, strands trailing over my temple. My shirtwaist was one button off and the collar had a stain. The ribs of the loose corset were visible through the fabric. I had dressed so carelessly this morning. I began to weep, at my slatternly look, at his going away tomorrow, at the dream, which still had a hold on me.

I sat and gulped some water. "She was with her father," I repeated. "I'm sorry. You were reading and here I am, making a scene, shouting for you in the hall, crying, everything."

"I'm happy you came," he said. He had buttoned his shirt and had put on his socks. "Though you see me at my worse." He gestured to a trunk in a corner of the room. "I just finished packing and was relaxing a little before I pick up my last wages from the *Ballard News*. Some of the fellows and I were going to have lunch."

"I should go," I said, and half-rose.

"No," he put out his hand to stop me. He touched my shoulder, left his hand there, and in my confusion all I could think was that no man had desired me since Edvard, at least no man that I'd desired back. I sank back down in the chair and gulped more water, wrapped the shawl closer. Tom moved away and sat on the bed to put his shoes on. They were polished but old-fashioned and worn at the toe. Why did that move me so? I wanted to go to him and be with him and it wasn't from a maternal urge to take care of him.

"Don't leave, Dagny." His voice was soft and urgent. "I want you to tell me more about the dream. It almost sounds like an omen. If she is with her dead father, perhaps that means she is in danger. Is Annie well? That would be my first thought. Yes, I am a Christian, but I come from a place and a people that takes dreams seriously. Have you heard anything from Chimacum?"

"No, it's not that, Tom. I'm sure Annie is fine. But I haven't told you something." I hesitated and then plowed ahead, meeting his eyes. My tears had abruptly stopped. Why lie any longer? Tom deserved better. "Mikkel is alive, as far as I know."

"Annie has a living father?" He stared at me, sitting on the edge of the bed, one foot still unshod. I knew this was all unseemly, but I didn't care. My own desire mixed with my shame. I must put an end to lying.

"Yes. I'm sorry I let you think otherwise, Tom. It was so wrong of me."

I rose from the chair and went over to the open window and looked out onto the empty, dusty street. The morning heat made it seem more like a town in South America; all that was lacking was a mule or two. The sun burned the windows in a brick building opposite. It was silent in the boarding house, not even a housemaid seemed to be stirring. I suppose everyone was at work. I turned and approached the bed (five steps) and sat beside him.

"It's true that I thought for a long time that Mikkel was dead. Adele and I had gone to Nome to find him. I didn't see him, he was so ill with typhoid they said he would be dead soon. I had an agreement Reverend Karlson had written up, giving me custody of Annie. In Nome, someone who knew him from the Relief Expedition signed Mikkel's name with an X and witnessed it. But then, years later, when Annie was three, a letter came from her father, from Karasjok. The letter had taken a long while to arrive in Port Townsend. Mikkel said he had recovered from the typhoid fever and had spent a year or more on whaling ships before managing to get back to Norway. He told me was married again and had a child. He asked about his daughter, as he had heard I was given charge over her."

"But what did he say when you told him about Annie?"

"I didn't."

"You didn't answer Mikkel's letter, Dagny?"

I couldn't speak, but shook my head, like a small child in trouble. He put his arm around my shoulders. "Ahh," he said, in that considering way he has. "But you are going to?"

I sighed and leaned against him. The warmth of his body

lulled me, and I wanted to agree to everything. "Yes, of course. I don't know what his address is, but I will try to find it. Perhaps someone in Alaska knows where he is now. If he is still in Karasjok."

He leaned me back on the bed, gently, and looked at me lovingly before he bent over me and kissed me, such a light kiss. His dark hair fell on my face, his lips were warm, soft. He was not experienced, but he was eager, affectionate. It did not occur to me, though I see it clearly now, he was a virgin. A virgin at twenty-eight or thirty, whatever he is. A man of the Church, or studying to be one.

"No, Tom, not this. When you're leaving," I murmured, not convincingly. It was my last sensible thought.

I put my arms around his back and pulled him closer for another kiss, a fiercer one. That salt smell he had was intoxicating to me. His lips so firm, his unbearded skin so soft. Heat enveloped us and I lost my head, opened my mouth, groaned with pleasure, and felt his hands on my breasts, again that light touch, exploring. The nipples stood up, exquisitely swollen and tender. I only knew one way to make love and that was rough, playful, and strong: Edvard's style. He would tilt me this way and that on the bed, suck my nipples, lean me up against the wall of our cabin, take me silently from the back, so the men wouldn't hear. Or I would get on top of him and ride him back and forth, which he loved, especially in his later years. All of that was coming back to me, all the pent-up waiting to make love again: the desire to be shaken down to my bones and to moan and direct, to push and spread and rock and finally let go with all my being. It wasn't enough to be gently caressed, to have Tom tenderly kissing my lips and touching my breasts as if they were precious porcelain bowls. Impatient, I unbuttoned his shirt, stroked his chest, marveling at the lack of hair, I unbuttoned his trousers, wanting to feel his hardness and unleash it. To make him as excited as I was. I pulled up my skirt, pulled down my drawers, displayed myself. I wasn't looking at his face, my eyes were closed, remembering Edvard and yet wanting it to be Tom. If I had been looking, I might have seen shock on his face. Felt Tom's resistance, his modesty.

"Dagny, I don't know," he tried to say, "This may not ... Can we ... ?" But I thought he was only shy and that he would learn quickly, that he was a man and being a man meant strength and even violence as the need took hold. I tried to guide him into me, wanton and wet, I recall now with horror. I felt him pull back, though he was hard. "No," I whispered, "I need you inside me, *please*."

And so he entered me and came almost immediately with a gasp, and did not know what to do afterwards, but withdraw in embarrassed softness, dripping.

"I am sorry," he said finally. "That wasn't right, was it?" He was already buttoning up again, and he pulled my skirt down in the same haste. I wanted to cry, discomfited and unsatisfied. "I have wanted you," he said uneasily. "Don't think that. But it's more the kisses I thought about."

He didn't try to kiss me though. He retreated to the window, discreetly tucking his shirt back in, staring out at the dusty street. He was probably thinking about being late for his lunch with his mates. Would he tell them what he'd been up to with an older widow woman, would it become a joke to him to disguise what he must surely see as failure?

I stood up, pulling up my damp drawers, buttoning and tugging at my clothes, wrapping the shawl tightly around my shoulders, only wanting to leave now and get back to the Svanssons and to slip upstairs before Vera saw me in this state.

"You don't have to leave," he said. "Can't we talk?"

"You were about to go and meet your friends," I said coldly. "You must see them, since you're leaving tomorrow." As if to punish both him and myself, I added, "It's too bad that Oscar and Vera and Bill won't get a chance to say good-bye to you."

"But I'd thought to spend the evening with you at the Svanssons or go for a walk." He made as if to come closer, his hands were out to touch my hands or hug me.

"If you like," I said, indifferently, already half out the door. "If we're there."

It's late now, and the birds are singing their last small songs. He hasn't come. I don't know why. But do know: He's embarrassed.

Or else he thinks I'm no better than a brazen old hussy. Or else he heard the coldness in my voice and is afraid of me. Bill was the most upset not to see Tom again. He went off to bed an hour ago, still muttering, "Where is that fellow anyway? Wake me if he comes." Vera simply wrapped up her cake for tomorrow and said softly to me, "Never mind, dear. Annie will be back in just a few days."

August 30

First thing this morning, after taking Annie to school, I signed papers at Ida Krantz's office to purchase a corner lot on the currently stump-ridden hillside overlooking Shilshole Bay. My compromise with reality is to buy the one lot and keep more of my savings against the day when I can afford to build a house without going into debt. Ida says she understands, and I believe she does. "I've lived in debt for so long that it seems natural," she confided, as she took a glass of schnapps with her coffee and offered me the same. "But you know best."

We toasted. "What made you decide to do this now?" she asked. "Are you ready to settle down? Maybe get married again?"

"I want to make a commitment to Ballard," I said lightly. "It will make me more credible as a copywriter if I buy land and build a house myself. It will be good for Annie as well, to have her own room as she gets older. We can't live with the Svanssons forever."

"And what happened to that fellow, Tom?" she asked.

"Tom—oh he's long gone. Back to Minnesota, to study *theology*," I said and drank another glass. I thought I'd seen love in his eyes when he bent over me, but it was only a passing desire. I shuddered now to think what he might have bragged to his friends about me, and for some days now I've avoided stopping by the pressrooms of the *Ballard News*. How they must have sniggered to see me pursuing Tom, chatting with him, *parading* with him. Too many times I remembered my face in the mirror at his boarding house, the face of a woman over forty. With shame I remembered my hitched-up skirt, my hard nipples, my moaning. That part of my life was over. It had been over for a long time.

It was a sunny morning when I left Krantz Landholdings, and I didn't want to go back to the Svanssons just now, I wanted an adventure. An *udflugt* as Ida would say. The streetcar took me to the Seattle docks where the steamers of the Mosquito Fleet set off for dozens of stops around the Sound. I saw that one of them was about to depart for Poulsbo, and I stepped aboard the *Hattie Hansen* without much thought, just pleased to be on the water again. The little, white-painted boat had a cargo deck forward and a railing around the main deck only a few feet above the waterline. We bobbed around at first between the other vessels before gaining speed and tooting off towards Dogfish Bay.

It took about two hours, given that we put into a half a dozen named places around the bay—Scandia, Pearson, Lemolo—as well as a couple of unnamed docks jutting out from an unprepossessing cluster of cabins with a sawmill. Logging was everywhere, logging and fishing boats. The waters hereabouts are full of small craft as well as larger steamers filled with coal, lumber, and other cargo. Sometimes you still see an Indian canoe carved from a long cedar log. The passengers on the *Hattie Hansen* were mainly men and a few families. I heard some Norwegian. No one spoke to me, but I pretended to myself that I was going to write an article about communities around Puget Sound, especially those with Scandinavian immigrants and when I took out my ever-present notebook, this made me feel less lonely.

As the *Hattie Hansen* approached Poulsbo, I could see wooden buildings on the shore and rising up on the hill behind. Where once there would have been a dark Northwest forest, there were only a few evergreens, maples, and fruit trees. Other steamers from the Mosquito Fleet were tied up around the dock and several cargo boats. High on the hill was a white-painted church.

I set off to explore the town in my role as journalist, stopping in at several establishments and soliciting brief interviews with the shopkeepers and customers. Where in Norway did they come from, I asked, and why had they come to Poulsbo? The stories were not much different than those in Ballard. They came from villages in the south of Norway in the main, but also from Telemark, Hardanger, and the Lofoten Islands. They came because relatives were here before them, or because they'd heard of towns where Norwegian or Swedish were the main languages. They came because they were one of eight children on a parcel of stony land that couldn't be divided any longer; they came because they were hungry, young, and adventurous. Because here in Dogfish Bay they had opportunities not available at home, yet they had also managed to recreate Norway somehow, down to the houses they built and the church on the hill.

My notebook grew full and instead of the short hour I expected to spend in Poulsbo, I was there until three o'clock, drinking coffee, eating *smorbrød* and cookies, and speaking Norwegian. When I began walking back down the dock in search of a steamer that would be leaving for Seattle, I was certain that I had the makings of not just one article about the immigrants just outside Seattle, but possibly a series of two or three. I strode happily back to the wharf, imagining how I could write these articles but also find a way to use my booster skills to create a pamphlet for Poulsbo as I'd done for Ballard. The words were already in my mind: *views, farmland, community, prospects,* and *invest in the future.*

A steamer was just letting off its passengers. I made for it quickly, hoping it was the Seattle vessel. In my hurry I did not see the woman before she was practically upon me, when it was impossible to look away. She was dressed in a plain, calico dress, with a red silk scarf at the neck. She carried two large, empty egg baskets; they were the same kind Lian used to collect eggs and carry them to her customers in the Chimacum Valley. I imagined the woman in the calico dress had been delivering eggs to some of the shops in the local communities served by the steamer.

Her dark hair, parted and pulled back tightly, was just visible under a flat straw hat string-tied under her chin. Something about her face was familiar but not so familiar that I could place her, and I was about to pass by when I glimpsed a long, white scar above one dark brow. At the same time her eyes lit up to see me, and she opened her mouth to speak. Up close I saw not only the scar, but the woman's triangular silk scarf, held at the throat by a clip of antler etched with a reindeer figure.

I was past her before she could say anything, and I hoped that she hadn't glimpsed recognition in my eyes. If she followed me, I would deny knowing her. I fumbled with my purse, found some coins, and gave them to the deckhand as I stepped into the little vessel. I resisted looking back and in a few minutes the steam whistle shrieked. It was not the boat to Seattle that I wanted—it only went to the next stop—but I had to get away. The sky, sunny most of the day, had darkened with gray clouds. Memories washed over me: Elle-Ristine at Fort Townsend, sitting and sewing on the porch of the barracks with her women friends, the way the spring light fell on their red, lace-trimmed bonnets and smiling faces. Elle-Ristine at my house on Morgan Hill, tucked into bed after the miscarriage, wearing one of my flannel nightgowns, her soft brown hair in two braids, as if she were a younger girl. Sáme women crowding into the room, talking in their own language: Ravna and her mother Inga. A young girl named Sunna, who stared at everything and said she'd never seen a bed for just one person before. And Margrete Utsi, Elle-Ristine's outspoken friend, who had told off Kjell for displaying Leksu in a corral by the house.

Margrete, that's who it was. My heart was pounding but I dared a peek out the steamed-up window. No, she wasn't on the dock staring after me. She probably just assumed that I wouldn't remember her, especially after all this time, especially when she was wearing calico and a straw hat and looked like nothing more than an egg-woman. I recalled that at the last minute, back in June 1898, when the Sámit were leaving on the *Louise B. Kenney* for Alaska, Margrete Utsi and her husband had stayed behind at Fort Townsend because their little boy had whooping cough. I was under the impression they were going to return to Norway when the boy recovered. Instead, they must have come to Poulsbo and settled here.

I admit that I had been curious as well as afraid when Kjell mentioned there were Sámit in Poulsbo, but I had not expected to run into someone I knew, someone who would have known Mikkel Aikio and Elle-Ristine Persdatter. As the boat set off, I wondered, was Margrete in contact with people in Alaska or back in Finnmark? Perhaps Margrete had heard from Ravna

Pulk or someone else that I had stolen Annie from her still-living father. What if Margrete were to mention the unexpected encounter with me to others in Poulsbo or in letters back home? If so, might Mikkel try to contact me again or even come to find me? I have a witnessed statement that he gave me the child to raise, but no formally filed papers of adoption. He could contest the X on the page. He has every right to say he didn't sign it, to expose me as a baby thief, even if I did have the encouragement of William Kjellman and Reverend Karlson. Mikkel is the father. He could take her. How could I have been so foolish as to travel to Poulsbo?

I have burned the notes I took today. I will erase this memory as I have erased others. All I told everyone at dinner was that I had signed papers today with Ida Krantz. We now own property again, I told Annie. We will build a house someday soon.

September 6

A letter came today from Tom. He confessed that the reason he had not come to see us that evening was that he had been drunk. Drunk! Of all people I would not have expected that of Tom. In fact, I thought of him as unusually strict. He often mentioned that his parents, like others in the Free Church, had taken vows of abstinence. He refused a glass of beer even when Oscar Svansson offered it.

It is not that I have never had a drink, but that I never drink to excess. Yet that is precisely what I did with my companions that day in the saloon. I am not used to it, you see, and yet within an hour I had downed several beers and some whiskey, and after that I don't recall much. We went to another saloon, and then those who were still able to walk went home to their families, and I staggered back to my room and slept for some hours, waking up in the middle of the night with a terrible thirst and an angry headache. My train left early the following day. I was ashamed, Dagny, and remain ashamed. I wanted very much to see you and I let you down. It was too much to think that you might come to see me off, as I had once hoped. The worst is that I never had a chance to say good-bye to you and the Svanssons. No, that is not the worst. It's that I didn't have the chance to talk to you about the news you gave me. When we were together, I couldn't think straight, but now I must speak out.

You let me assume—you wished me to assume—that Annie was an orphan that you had taken in from charity, because of your friendship with Elle-Ristine. I accepted that, and in fact I thought how kind you were, to have befriended a Sáme woman, to be close enough with her to raise her child. I put away the thought as best I could that you might not want to tell Annie she was Sáme because of prejudice in favor of the thought that, for now, you wanted to protect her from prejudice. But when you told me that her father still lived, that Mikkel had written to you, and that you had ignored him, I saw that your fear went deep. You do not think of us Sáme people as equal to you. You share the Norwegian view, I can see that now. But even that wasn't as painful as my realization that you didn't trust me with the truth. Oh, Dagny, why not? I would not have judged you, I would have tried to help you.

Then, abruptly, as if he had resumed the letter on a different day, he went on to tell me more about his first two weeks in Minneapolis, his classes, and his difficulties with his brother and his wife, his sense that theology might not be his path after all.

I barely read that part. I was consumed by anger, shame, and humiliation. Anger at myself for telling Tom about Mikkel just before he left, shame that I had misled him for so long. But most of all, humiliation. For the last several weeks I've felt the mortification of our failed lovemaking. Without wishing to I've relived those moments when he buttoned his clothes and went over to the window. I've imagined him bragging to his friends about me, or even joking about what a tigress I was. At first I blamed him, for being so puritanical, then myself for being so aggressive and insensitive; then I had simply tried to put it behind me. I had striven to forget about it, but now—to get this letter chastising me for not telling him about Mikkel, to realize that Tom wasn't even going to mention what happened between us—that was insupportable.

Humiliation turned into anger, anger that he was taking

me to task. It was the first time someone had ever seen my choice to raise Annie as my own and hide her heritage from her as something ignoble. Those who knew—Kjell and Lian and Adele—had understood my need for silence. Especially Lian. But Tom was the first one to know that Mikkel lived and to accuse me of prejudice. Yes, all right, perhaps, yes, I was prejudiced. But didn't he see that the real reason was that after receiving Mikkel's letter I was terrified that I would lose Annie? I was still terrified, especially after encountering Margrete on the dock in Poulsbo.

Tom says he wouldn't have judged me? Of course he judges me! He is a Christian, after all, and dishonesty, even through omission, is a sin.

I put the letter aside. Of course I know that he is right about some things. He would have tried to help me or at least listen to me and support me. Nevertheless, I'm glad he's in Minnesota and that I'll likely not see him again. I am a widow with a child, a dozen years older, and he is a college student preparing to become a pastor. Oh hell.

October 14

I've had another letter from Tom, and I have written back. His second letter was milder in tone, though still without any mention of a warm day in August, a room with a bed, and two people wrapped around each other on that bed, one of them inside the other. All that is over, but at least we can still, I hope, be friends. I've accepted his apology for being drunk. And he, to his credit, has tried to understand my excuses for why I didn't tell him the whole truth, excuses that largely rest on the fact that I didn't know him well enough. I've explained that Mikkel's letter came as a shock, as if a dead person had come to life again. I said that I had not meant to be prejudiced, that I was trying to protect Annie, but that in fact until I met Tom I had very little sense of the Sáme people other than as reindeer herders. He had educated me, and I hoped he would continue to do so. I did not want to be one of "those Norwegians." All I wanted was the best for Annie and I realized that I must contact Mikkel and let him know about his daughter. Even though that could mean that I might lose her.

Tom, in his return letter, forgave me for my untruthfulness, and said that perhaps some of his anger had to do with his difficulties living once again with his brother and sister-in-law. He sees so painfully how Jouna hides his identity from his coworkers and his sons. He hates how Trudy demands that Tom never say anything about their family heritage to his nephews. "I've realized I can't stay here much longer," he writes. "I have taken a job as a compositor in a job printing shop three evenings a week. When I've saved up some money, I'll consider finding another place to live. In the meanwhile I am studying all the time. I spend hours in the library, and those are my happiest time." And he ended by saying, "I wish I could have seen you again before I left, Dagny. I don't believe you meant to be prejudiced against me and my people. Things did not go as I had hoped. I can't put this in a letter."

No, such things can't be written about, not between a man and a woman at a distance. But couldn't he write that he still cares about me? Or ask if I care about him?

November 4

I haven't heard from Tom in several weeks and if he's moved, he hasn't given me his new address. At first, I only thought he must be very busy with classes and his new job as a compositor, but now I have written two more letters, neither of them returned, and have had no reply. Perhaps I was too forward in my response. I did write that Annie missed him, as did I.

I've been busy myself with new booklets and articles for Ballard businesses. There is excitement and worry since the vote ten days ago on the subject of annexation. Although the vote was close, it was decisive. After sixteen years as a city, Ballard citizens have chosen to become part of Seattle. Next May is set for the handover. Meanwhile none of this affects my work; indeed, as Ida Krantz points out, properties in Ballard have become even more desirable now that the water supply is secured. She wants to loan me money to start building on my lot early in the new year. I have resisted. Although every day I write optimistic lines about growth and success, in my inner heart I am anxious. In that I'm not unlike other immigrants here, heady with dreams one day, panicked by nightmares of debt and disgrace the next.

I often think about what I owe my daughter: not just a new house in Ballard, an education, a mother who loves her. I owe Annie her history, her parentage, her living father. It would have been so much easier had Tom stayed in Ballard. He could have helped me tell her. He could have explained, so much better than I can, what it means to be Sáme. Perhaps we could have all, in time, traveled to Finnmark to visit Mikkel. I am conscious that if I had waited, had not thrown myself on Tom that day, we might have courted in a circumspect way. Or at least remained friends. Now, without Tom, I am on my own, and once again, hesitant and fearful. For to tell Annie even the slightest thing means that she will know I have been withholding the truth all her life.

November 18

Today, a rainy day thick with low dark clouds, I boarded a boat once again for Poulsbo, this time with the intention of finding Margrete Utsi and asking if she is in contact with Mikkel or any other Sáme people in Karasjok. Mikkel's envelope had a return address in Karasjok, but after several years I didn't trust it. And it was important that if I did write him that he get the letter.

A secretary at the small city hall in Poulsbo told me that the Utsi family's property lay about two miles from the ferry dock, along a main road. There was no form of transportation other than foot, so I was thoroughly soaked and mud-splashed when I came to an unpainted wooden house and knocked on the door. It was a tidy if wet farmstead, with cows in the barn and some damp chickens outside a large coop. There was nothing to distinguish the buildings and outhouses from those of any other immigrant farmer from Norway.

I'd remembered Margrete as talkative. She stood up to

William Kjellman. She told Kjell off for exhibiting Leksu and wearing a Sáme hat. She had never spoken Norwegian well, as Elle-Ristine did, but among the Sáme women at Fort Townsend, she'd been confidently at home. She wore silver buttons for everyday, I recalled, earrings and a ring or two; she had two bonnets, one of them with extra lace. On the Poulsbo dock in August she'd had looked more American, with her straw hat and leather shoes. Here at home, alone, she was wearing the familiar tight red bonnet with a bit of limp lace, but her past finery was not in evidence. Her house dress was faded under a full white apron, stained with something brown. She had on thick socks and an ordinary shawl against the chill. Her face was careworn and the white scar above her eye more visible than ever with no hair showing under the bonnet. Her expression was wary when she saw me standing on the doorstep. Almost frightened. She knew me, of course. I had interrupted her cooking the midday meal of what smelled like beans.

I asked if I could come in for a moment, and silently, she stepped aside.

"It has been some years," I said quietly in Norwegian, to try to put her at ease. "I am sorry I didn't recognize you right away on the Poulsbo wharf last summer. I had no idea your family had settled here. I thought you had gone back to Karasjok."

She shook her head, and said, "English? All my Norwegian, I don't remember more."

I nodded, and so for the next while we spoke together in English. She didn't berate me for ignoring her in August, perhaps she thought it was natural I didn't recognize her. She obviously remembered me as a lady of consequence from Port Townsend. *Madame* she called me. "Would Madame like some coffee?" She put on the kettle. The liveliness I remembered from years ago had gone out of her.

The room, which was both kitchen and living room, was clean but dimly lit on this gray day, just a kerosene lamp between us at the table. There were several armchairs, a fire in the wood-burning stove with its pot of brown bean soup, but nothing in the grate of the fireplace but ashes. Nothing to suggest that a Sáme family lived here except a carved and painted reindeer and sled on mantel above the fireplace, along with a few of the wooden cups hollowed out from tree boles that must have been part of their traveling gear when they came from Lapland. There was evidence of children around, a few toys and small mittens.

Margrete told me they had gone from Fort Townsend to Seattle, then here to Poulsbo where there were a few other Sáme families. It was her husband's wish to stay in America, not hers. They'd bought an acre of land outside of town with their wages from Sheldon Jackson. All they'd known at home in Lapland was reindeer husbandry. Here they'd relied on help from their neighbors; now they had chickens and three cows. Her husband, Niilas, worked at a local sawmill. I gathered, from her gestures, that he fed logs into a sawblade. The children were in school. One boy was twelve; the other, the one whose whooping cough had prevented the family from going to Alaska with the other reindeer herders, was ten. I asked if they still spoke the Sáme language.

"Not much," she said, touching her heart, "only me, with the two other Sáme women in Poulsbo. We are Americans since Port Townsend when we got citizen papers. Life better here, it will be better for our children." She did not look optimistic. I wondered how they fit in with the neighbors here in Poulsbo, whether the Norwegians carried old biases to the new country. She confirmed this when she said, "We only know other Sáme people. My husband, the Norwegian men don't always like him at the sawmill."

She didn't ask me much about myself, or why I'd come from Seattle to Poulsbo to see her, though I could see she wanted to. I told her that my husband, Captain Bergland, had died and afterwards I had run a boarding house. Now I had moved to Seattle and worked for newspapers. "With my little girl." I observed Margrete as I said this—had she heard about Annie?

She didn't seem to, and at first, swallowing a sigh of relief, I was inclined to say nothing more. The fear I'd had, that Margrete would expose me as a baby-snatcher, was groundless. And yet, in spite of myself, I told her the story:

That I had gone to Alaska to see where my husband was buried and found Elle-Ristine's baby at Eaton Station, being cared for by Ravna who was shortly to set off for a remote island with her other baby and family. The pastor had suggested it would help Annie if I took her back to Port Townsend. Mikkel had been deathly ill. "I do not know if I did the right thing," I said to Margrete, hoping she would say, "Of course you did."

Instead she simply stared at me. "Elle-Ristine's baby lives with you?"

"Yes," I said. "She is seven years old now."

"But where is her father, Mikkel Aikio? Is he dead?"

"I thought he died," I said. "I honestly did. But it turns out, he recovered from his illness. He returned to Karasjok." I pulled out the photograph Mikkel had sent me four years ago, of him in his Four Winds cap with his new wife holding a baby.

Margrete held the photograph in two hands. "I know that girl he married," she said. "Her name is Káren. She is a distant relative of mine." Tears wet her dark eyes and her lips pressed together. Her face suggested a fount of grief for home and family that was daily suppressed and that not even a wooden house, chickens, cows, and American citizenship could assuage. "We hear a little about the people in Alaska. But nobody said anything about Mikkel Aikio."

"Do you know where I could write Mikkel?" I asked. "When he wrote me, the only address he gave was Karasjok."

"I don't know how to write," she said. "And my family in Kautokeino don't write me neither." She considered. "I think you must write to the pastor in Karasjok. Mikkel will get the letter. Everyone goes to church at least at the holidays."

I left soon after that. We shook hands tentatively, though I wanted to embrace her. She had known Elle-Ristine, she had been to my home in Port Townsend. That I had managed to tell the truth about Annie was a miracle. And yet, I must also be honest here, as the glow and relief fade, that other familiar thoughts come to the fore. Margrete has had no easy time of it in America. The Norwegians in Poulsbo brand her and her husband as Lappish and inferior. For everyone like Tom, who manages to keep hold of his past identity while embracing a new one, there are probably dozens like Margrete and her husband, who live in the shadow of old prejudices. What does that mean

for Annie, who was born Sáme but has been raised to believe
she's Norwegian and American? I could wish I had Tom to talk
to.

I could wish it so very much.

December 20

The streets of Seattle around Third and Pike were arrayed with
wreaths and garlands and electric lights earlier today when
Annie and I went downtown to see Santa at the Bon Marché.
In the show windows of the department store were mannequins
in fur coats and capes. Sleighs piled high with packages. Sleds
carrying dolls and stuffed bears. Annie wore her red wool coat
and buttoned boots, with patterned red and white mittens and a
matching beret knitted by Vera. Her straight hair was in a single
braid with a red bow, and her small cheeks were flushed as we got
off the streetcar into a mass of shoppers with wrapped parcels.
The cold, expectant feel of snowfall was in the air. "Mor, so many
people, hold my hand!" I clutched it firmly as we made our way
through the crowds into the Bon Marché.

I've been to many cities around the world, to vast markets
and bazaars, but these new American department stores take
my breath away. Marble and thick carpets, elevators with metal
grilles, woodwork of mahogany and brass, glass cases, mirrors,
and crystal chandeliers. Not just for the rich, but for anyone
who might walk inside. In some of them you can have your hair
cut or your shoe soles repaired, you can have a meal or put your
baby in a nursery for an hour. You can send telegrams and mail
packages; you can buy everything from confectionary to corsets
to fabrics. You can buy whole suites of furniture and carpets
and lamps. There are tables full of crockery and china, shelves
of linens. There is a bookstore. The millinery department is full
of the latest styles, whether they're sailor hats or turbans, and
the selection of leather footwear in the shoe department is deep,
suiting every taste (see how my booster language begins to infect
even my journal writing!)

But we didn't linger in the luxury aisles of the sales floor, even though we both gasped a little at the electric chandeliers. I'd bought all the Christmas presents I required two weeks ago. I had promised Annie a visit with Santa and afterwards a cafeteria lunch. I inquired from a floorwalker in tails and stiff cravat where we might find Santa's Workshop, and he pointed at one of the elevators, which had just opened. A uniformed operator with white gloves stood inside. "Fifth floor, Madame? Young Miss? For Lapland?"

I smiled but was startled. Other children and their parents crowded in, and we rose together, Annie keeping close by my side.

"Where is Lapland?" she whispered.

"Where Santa lives," I said. "And other people."

We got out and followed a few signs to "North Pole, Lapland," and "Santa's Toy Workshop." The scenery was everything one could have expected. A full toy workshop with some mannequins dressed as elves, and out the window a painted snowy landscape with the northern lights glimmering in the sky. A Christmas tree with ornaments and tinsel and near it, a white-bearded Santa in red settled into a big armchair. Toys of all sorts peeked out of boxes and bags around the chair. A half-sized sleigh pulled by two tan-colored, plaster reindeer was on display. The animals had stubby antlers and strangely painted brown eyes with long lashes.

"What are they?" Annie wanted to know.

"Reindeer," I said, but she rejected that. Reindeer, she knew from stories about Leksu, were always white and their eyes were shiny like black mirrors.

Santa Claus was foreign to us, as Norwegians. In Port Townsend we'd followed the traditional Norwegian customs, of opening presents on Christmas Eve. In Ballard last year we'd had happily gone along with the Svanssons' Swedish festivities, like our own, yet even more beautiful with St. Lucia Day, and many, many candles. This year would be our first attempt at an American Christmas. Annie had been singing Christmas carols and making cards in school. Now it was time for her to be introduced, like other immigrant children, to American customs like Santa's Workshop and a sleigh pulled by plaster reindeer.

I gently pushed her into line. When Santa finally asked her what she wanted for Christmas—a doll, perhaps, she appeared indignant. "I have a doll, she's Helen."

"Maybe Helen would like a friend?"

"I want a sled," Annie said. "A red sled."

"Then I will try to bring you one," said Santa, and glanced at me. I nodded, already thinking of an explanation for why Santa wouldn't be able to deliver. I had purchased books for Annie and a new dress.

I could not keep my eyes off the reindeer. I could not stop thinking of Leksu, with her white coat and shiny dark eyes, her heavy hooves, and her calm air. How she grazed, how she moved. And when I thought of Leksu, I thought of Elle-Ristine.

Annie joined me without another glance at the sleigh. "Santa said he would bring me a sled."

"I hope he can," I said, and added, "But aren't you hungry? Shall we have a sandwich and hot chocolate?"

We found the cafeteria and seats at the counter. It was splendidly crowded, and the waitress was "jolly" (a new and favorite word of Annie's) with a Christmas tree brooch on her white uniform and a spring of holly in her topknot.

This Christmas is less jolly than last year's, though not because the Svanssons haven't done their best to make it wonderful. Their holiday party was larger than last year, and with Nels back from fishing and now courting a girl from Ballard, they had even more reason to celebrate. Annie was their St. Lucia, she wore a white dress and a ring of lit candles placed carefully in her hair (a bucket of water in Bill's hands just in case). Vera played Swedish carols on the piano. Adele came with her brother and his family, and so did the Solstad sisters, bringing Norwegian pastries. Even Ida Krantz stopped by and had a glass or two of *glögg* before going on to another party. She toasted me and my good sense in buying property: "This coming year we'll build you a house!"

I have not heard from Tom in over two months. I thought he would at least make time to respond to my letter about meeting Margrete. Two weeks ago I wrote him again to tell him that Mikkel had responded to my letter in November. Still nothing.

I can no longer pretend that he is just busy with his studies and work.

Mikkel Aikio's letter was short and free of blame. Once again, he thanked me for taking care of Annie, and asked that I tell her she was often in his thoughts. He prayed for her every Sunday. This was not the Mikkel I had known, so briefly, in Port Townsend, the man with the bold white smile, nor the man possessed by gold fever and drink described by Reverend Karlson and William Kjellman. He was now a convert to the Læstadian faith, he told me, and he wanted to send Annie a prayer book. He said he had another son now. We would be very welcome to visit. He did not wish us a God Jul or Merry Christmas. I had the feeling that Læstadians might disapprove of such things.

I kept the letter hidden, of course, and hoped he wouldn't send a prayer book. At least he knew that Annie lived and was sound and healthy, that she was in school, and well-cared for. I did not exactly say that I considered her my daughter now and that she knew nothing of her heritage. I will wait until January to write back.

Katrine's Christmas letter left me much sadder than usual. She is not unhappy, no, she would never want me to think that, but she is feeling her age. The burdens of being the headmistress weigh on her, she wonders if she should consider stepping down. Three or four older friends, her mother's friends, have died. Soon that generation will be gone. She writes as if she is sixty-three not forty-three. Her health is not as robust as it once was, she suffers from mysterious aches and pains, but the doctor finds nothing. She asks, but only in passing, about Annie and Kjell, and once again I am reminded how little I have told her about my life in America, my real life. She knows that Kjell married a girl in Port Townsend, but not a Chinese girl. She knows that Annie had parents born in Norway, but not that they were Sáme. Of Tom she of course knows nothing. I have never mentioned him, all these months. I never will mention him now, there is nothing to mention.

All the same, I can't help feeling wretched for Katrine, alone in the big house without Aunt Inger, and no other family. My own sisters had never met Katrine, even though for years I had mentioned our cousin and her aunt in my letters. Truth be told, they connected the "fine folk" in Bergen only with the sacks of coffee beans delivered to their two farms at Christmas. I'm reminded in Katrine's closing paragraph that I don't write to her as much as I once did, and that I haven't been to Bergen since Edvard and I sailed off on the *Matilde* over ten years ago for Lima. "I remember when I came down to see you on the dock before the ship sailed," Katrine writes dejectedly, "You held me close and said you'd be back in two years or less. I have been waiting ever since."

Recently, in the office of the Ballard Chamber of Commerce, I picked up a brochure from a desk that advertised the White Star steamship line. It leaves Boston every week for Liverpool and, among other enticing illustrations, there's one of a woman standing by herself at a ship railing, the streamers of her hat blowing in the breeze. Seattle to Boston by train. Boston to Liverpool by ship. Train to Newcastle and another ship to Bergen. Annie and I could be in Bergen in less than two weeks. The copy is written in my kind of language: excellent accommodations for both first and second-class passengers: a promenade deck, a drawing room for ladies, "richly upholstered in moquette," a dining saloon with two sittings, "finished in hard woods and upholstered in frieze plush." Staterooms with two berths, detailed in polished mahogany. Photos show the staterooms and wash basins, a library, and retreats for ladies from the presence of cigars and men.

I can see myself standing at the railing. I can feel the strong sea breeze in my hair.

January 14, 1907

I've been sitting on the floor with my sea chest open, sorting. Annie is at school, and I should be working on my next project. This is to be another booklet for a land development company, a competitor to Krantz Landholdings, but Ida doesn't mind. They are developing housing lots in Wallingford, so I've been over to that district several times. The trees have not yet all been logged off and I hope they spare some.

Around me are spread packets of letters, mostly from Katrine, some from Aunt Inger, my sisters, and my mother, along with a box of family photographs. Others are in frames. Most are studio portraits taken in Norway twenty or more years ago: My mother in her bunad with my two sisters, taken by a traveling photographer, the only photograph I have of all of them together. Uncle Theodore and Aunt Inger, prosperous and a little haughty. Me at fifteen at the wheel of the ship in Bergen's harbor: flat-chested, dreamy. Katrine alone and Katrine with me in the parlor of the Bergen house. Edvard and I on our wedding day in Bergen, in that same parlor. Everyone is so formal looking, so Old Country with their stiff postures and stern faces. No one smiles and I don't either. I look very young in that wedding photograph, a girl with a rather boyish body, wide shoulders and big hands. A peasant girl who became a female seminary student, a wife at eighteen, and a world traveler. Who could and did pass as a young sailor occasionally.

In one photograph, I am a mother and hold a little boy on my lap, while Edvard, in his captain's uniform, stands behind me, the proud father. We were in Liverpool, in port before setting off for South America. All I recall now is the light weight of the boy, his wiggly legs, the scent of his neck in the starched little collar. Edvard and I were also photographed with Kjell at different ages, mostly in Lima, several in San Francisco on the *Matilde*. The first mate took them with a camera he'd bought in Buenos Aires. In these pictures I look happy, so do we all. In one of them I am pregnant with Agnete.

There is another photograph of Edvard and me together, taken in a photography studio during the first year we lived in Port Townsend. Our age difference is marked. His hair and beard appear completely gray, and his long face is serious, with its wrinkles and furrows clear in the sharp picture. A man of fifty who has spent his life at sea looks much older than one who has worked in an office. When we were first married, when his hair was still red-brown and thick, his muscles strong, and his teeth all there, I could imagine him a younger man, still with boyish energy. He grew up with two brothers in a village near Ålesund. There was a tradition of boys who went to sea, and so they all went, one after the next. His brothers never came home. One died young, falling out of the rigging into the Atlantic during a storm; the other perished of fever off the African coast. His parents were still alive when we married in haste; I met them later. There was no love between them and little love for Edvard either. He'd gone to sea at fifteen.

After Edvard died, I missed him deeply, for all that he had often left me alone in Port Townsend for months on end. I saw only my misfortune as a widow. But today, looking at his dear, weathered face in the photograph, I wonder what it really would have been like had he given up sailing and settled in Port Townsend. There would have been no Annie in our lives, but there might have been other children, for I was still young enough then. Yet Edvard himself would have declined and I might still have been left alone with a family to raise. Or I might have spent years caring for him.

I tell myself I *would* have cared for him, willingly and gladly. But there would have been no *Shingle,* no Ida Krantz and building lot in Ballard, no booster writing, no Tom Nilsen.

I put Edvard's photograph aside and continued looking for something else: the photograph of Elle-Ristine and Mikkel from the Port Townsend studio, which I'd taken out a few months ago to show Tom. I found it in a large envelope along with a few other things: correspondence from Elle-Ristine and the birth certificate for Anna Mikkelsdatter Aikio. There's also a small notebook from 1898 where I jotted down notes for the story I eventually wrote of Elle-Ristine's travel from Bossekop to Port Townsend, all the details she recalled from the Yukon Relief Expedition.

In this notebook I wrote down other things Elle told me as well, various customs around marriage and childbirth, some superstitions and beliefs. Why you should always hang or attach silver balls or other ornaments to the cradle to make sure the *uldas* don't take your baby or exchange it for one of yours. About Madderakka, the earth goddess, the goddess of childbirth, and her three daughters: Sarakka, Uksakka, Juksakka. All of them watched over the child as she grew, and they all had different functions. Sarakka placed the child in the womb and Uksakka aided in the birth. Juksakka helped raise the child. Elle told me all this as she lay in my guest bedroom after her miscarriage. Although she was a Christian, she made offerings to Madderakka and her daughters.

I'd once thought that I might make use of such information in an article about the Sámit. Gradually I'd realized that these were not my stories to share with the curious outside world. This was knowledge that Elle-Ristine's mother and grandmother had passed down to her, and that should rightly have been passed down to Annie. It should have been my job or someone like Ravna's to pass this knowledge along, to tell her stories of how her parents met and married, how they decided to leave Karasjok and to take part in a big adventure across the ocean. I never told Annie any of her family's stories. Instead I told Annie my own stories, the ones I should rightfully have told Jan and Agnete had they lived, about our farm at Kvamnes and the little village of Kyrkebø on the Sognefjord, about my father who drowned after a sudden storm upset his boat, about our one cow and three goats, about the mountain trolls and the best wild blueberry patches, about the day when Uncle Theodore came to invite me to live in Bergen and go to school.

I still remember my arrival at that house on the hill behind the warehouses and wharves of Bryggen. Uncle Theodore and I had had to walk up from the harbor, along cobbled streets and narrow stone stairways. The wooden house was light yellow with gray trim. Inside it was stuffed with padded horsehair settees and chairs, Turkey carpets on the floors, heavy velvet drapes at the windows. But most of all I remember Katrine leading me up the stairs to my bedroom, the first bedroom I'd ever had. I had always slept in a room with my sisters, and then my mother. Katrine showed me the wash basin and towels. A maid would bring me hot water and take the chamber pot, Katrine said. The maid would also light the fire in the morning and bring coffee, though the family breakfasted together.

Then the door closed, and I was in my own room. My own room for the first time in my life. I went to the window and opened it to the summer's day. The breeze was salt and sweet; the lace-trimmed, white cotton curtains fluttered. I looked down at the ships filling the harbor, tied up to the wharves, or departing on the tide, with a local pilot boat. Offshore, the sails would rise, one after the next, billowing their way onward to foreign seas. How grand they were, how enormous, those barques and barkentines, those square-riggers and schooners of years gone by.

My old room! What a longing I had suddenly to be there again, to be in that house with Katrine, with all my future before me. I'd a wooden desk, and I knew with sudden certainty that the desk must still be there, that no one else had stayed in that room since I left home and that it was waiting for me still, just as Katrine was waiting for me.

Wouldn't it be possible to walk into that room again after all these years, to open the window and smell the sea and the harbor again? Once again, someone would make my bed and our meals, once again I would not have to support myself. But this time I could write—not booklets about Ballard, but real writing. Articles and stories that I could place in the Norwegian newspapers and journals. Perhaps I could begin the novel I'd dreamed of writing about my seafaring adventures around the world. Annie could be raised to learn Norwegian in a respected family, she could go to school with other girls. And in the summer we could visit Karasjok. My enthusiasm faded slightly at the thought—*How would I explain all this to Katrine, to Mikkel, to Annie herself?*—and then revived.

We needed to go to Karasjok, and we would.

I looked down at the photographs of myself and my relatives and realized how few images I had from Port Townsend. I had never wanted to live in America! It had been Edvard's idea, and all it had brought was trouble and his death. Ten years I'd been here, and I was hardly closer to feeling American than I had been when we arrived. In spite of the citizenship, in spite of my efforts to speak English, to write English, to raise Annie as American, to buy land and talk about building a house and settling in Ballard, in spite of all that I still wanted to be back in Bergen, in my old room, looking at the ships out the window.

We would go. If only for a long visit.

I wrote Katrine first, telling her that she was right, it was time for me to return home to Bergen and to introduce her to my daughter. We would sail in March. For the first time in years I spoke of Norway with affection not guilt.

And then I wrote Mikkel. "We will come to you this summer and you will see your Annie once again."

The whole chimera of America seemed to shiver and disappear, and it was hard for me later to go downstairs and help Vera peel potatoes.

The Fourth Journal
Karasjok and Bergen, Norway

June 1907 - November 1907

The Sáme summer camp is much as Elle-Ristine had described it: juniper and bilberry bushes, dwarf birch and pine trees. A high blue sky. The wide Karasjok River flowing past low banks of sand and scrub. Eight or so pole tents covered with cloth, *lávvus* they're called, in a cluster, each with a curl of smoke.

But it's also different. The dogs bark more loudly, the campfires crackle more vividly, and the voices speak in the North Sáme language: *davvisámegiella.*

Two days ago, Annie, lifted down from my horse by the guide, looked around in some bewilderment. Biettar, a Norwegian-speaking Sáme man who had brought us from Porsangerfjord across the Finnmark Plateau, busied himself with tying up our horses as people began to gather around us, It was only fifty miles we had traveled, but this time of year the land was wet and marshy in many places. It had taken us two long days of riding, and we were hot, mud-splattered, and mosquito-bitten.

Mikkel came forward to greet me and Annie. I saw her hesitate, as if she wanted to hide behind my skirt. He was ten years older now, no longer the handsome, reckless fellow with the dare-devil white smile and shock of dark hair. His skin was weathered, and his eyes were warier. He knew we were coming. I had sent a message from Bergen.

Mikkel said to Annie in English, "I am your father."

Of course he must remember some English—he had been in Alaska for a year after all—but it was still startling to hear English in these surroundings. He said something else, "*áhčči,*" and pointed to himself. His eyes were damp. Was he seeing Elle-Ristine again in the face of his daughter, or recalling the hard times in Alaska? His drinking and his near death in Nome? His long voyage alone back to Karasjok? Next to him was a skinny, vigorous woman, eyes shiny as black currants, a few months pregnant, with a toddler in her arms and a four-year-old boy clinging to her skirt, staring wide-eyed at the horses nearby.

Mikkel said, "Your new family, Anna. This is Káren, my wife, and Mátias and Ánde, our sons. Your brothers."

"Hello, father," Annie said in English and smiled shyly at Káren and the boys. She took a step forward and held out her arms.

Mikkel pulled her to him then, and others crowded around, pointing to themselves, using words we didn't know. I gathered that some of them were related to Annie on her mother's side; they looked more like Elle-Ristine than Mikkel, the same upturned nose and high cheekbones. But if Uncle Aslak was here, he didn't announce himself. Everyone wore *gákti,* mostly tanned leather or woolen tunics with decorative woven belts. The women's red cloth caps sat back on their heads, with long ear flaps; the men were mostly bare headed in the summer warmth. Many curious children crowded around Annie too.

I stood aside, awkward and disregarded, merely the custodian, until Annie pulled away from the hands touching her face and tugging at her arms, looking for the lost Elle-Ristine in her dark blue eyes. She ran back to me, sheltering under my arm. "It's too much all at once, Mor," she whispered.

I had not considered fully—how could I?—what it would be like to return with her and to explain everything that had happened since Elle-Ristine died to a crowd of her relatives.

I said to Mikkel in English, "Perhaps? Just you? Can we, and Annie, go off a short distance perhaps?" He nodded and we walked down to the flowing river and sat together on the bank, saying little at first. The image of Elle-Ristine was so strong it hurt. Then the words came, from me, from him, halting at times, but warm with memories of his wife and my friend.

It was a moment of remembrance, even for Annie who could not recall Elle-Ristine but had lived nine months inside her mother and had for a short time been held in her arms.

June 27

There was a journal, paper-bound, that I kept between late January and early June this year. I started it soon after I made the decision to leave Ballard for Norway, and it recorded the story of my resolve as well as of my struggles and waverings. It told the tale, week by week through February and March, of how I often changed my mind, especially when praise for my booster pamphlets brought in more work, and when Ida showed me designs for houses that exactly suited my wishes and needs. The journal, its entries penned often late at night, complained about how difficult it was to explain to everyone in Ballard and Chimacum why we were going to Norway and how long we'd be gone. In the end, from weakness perhaps, but also as a safeguard, I left my sea chest and many of our possessions in the Svanssons' attic. I did not sell the property I'd purchased from Ida Krantz. And I promised Kjell and Lian that I would return in the autumn, that this was just a journey to see my family. Surely, they could understand that? It had been *years* since I'd been to Norway. I mentioned nothing about Karasjok to anyone. Nothing about Mikkel and Káren, nothing about my plan to visit Elle-Ristine's homeland and take her daughter with me. Thus, my lies and evasions of the past eight years continued.

That journal was burned, by mistake, two weeks ago, when I told Katrine's old maid servant, Josefine, that a pile of newspapers and drafts of some short stories written on foolscap could be fed into the fire. As it turned out, my journal, which was not part of the pile, but was also on the desk, went into the flames as well. Josefine has been with Katrine for decades and is half blind. I did not blame her, but bought this new journal bound in tan linen. I wouldn't have minded if the first half of that journal had burned—it was so full of ambivalence and worry—but I regret I don't have more of record of the last three months. I will try to summarize a little of our journey from Seattle to Norway and the weeks we were in Bergen before coming to Karasjok.

We left Seattle's Union Station on the Great Northern train on the afternoon of March 21. The steady downpour turned to sleet and snow as we approached the mountains. The train shook over trestles and on switchbacks, until we blasted out a long whistle and rumbled through a long black tunnel stinking of coal. Annie clung to me in panic, even after we came out into a wonderland of heavy snow and evergreens. I recalled such snows and mountains from Norway, but everything was new to

Annie. New and terrifying. She'd cried when we parted from the Svanssons, who had sheltered us for the last year and a half in Ballard. Not for a minute had she let go of her doll Helen. As for me, I was imaging the Sáme herders making the same journey, but eastwards, in March of 1898, accompanied by cattle cars filled with five hundred reindeer.

I thought of Elle-Ristine and Mikkel much of the journey. What it must have been like to see this great country with its mountains, plains, and rivers, everything covered in snow and frost. There were large towns, but many small settlements, each with their wooden railway station, general store, and saloon, each with one or more church steeples. Some were lively with buggies and farmers' wagons in the streets and well-dressed people on the platform, getting on, getting off. Many stops had a lost and lonely feeling. I saw farmhouses with picket fences and windmills, hay barns and outhouses. More often there was little sign of habitation for hundreds of miles, only a few sod houses and shacks with tin chimney pipes. After Spokane there were no real cities until Fargo and Moorhead, built on either side of the Red River that divides North Dakota and Minnesota. These cities had grain silos and mills and tall brick and stone buildings pushing up out of the landscape, almost piling on top of each other in their haste to make an impression of power and wealth, laughable in the midst of this huge and almost empty country. I'd expected to glimpse Indian life, but from the train there were no buffalo, no tipis, no men and women on horseback. There were only white people. Pioneers they called themselves. Homesteaders. You might just as well call them invaders. Had they really managed to take the whole country for themselves?

I also often thought of the Chinese workers who built this railroad, or at least the western half of it. I thought of them with sorrow and awe, hammering spike after spike into the railway ties through mountains and valleys in all kinds of weather, blizzards and heat waves. When the train left Seattle and began its climb into the Cascades, over wooden trestles and iron bridges across deep valleys and through tunnels blasted out of hard basalt and granite, I looked out the window and saw the ghosts of young men from China blinded and broken by explosions, falling rocks, and accidental falls from high places. They came to America with dreams of a new life and were cruelly used and discarded.

Leaving Seattle, Annie asked, "Will Uncle Kjell and Aunt Lian visit us where we are going? Will we ever see them again? It's so far away." I choked a little as I reassured her. "I'm sure we will see them again, Annie mine. I know we will." But the journey, in fact, felt like a farewell. I was resolved at that point to see if we could make a fresh start in Norway.

The train stopped for half an hour in St. Paul before going on to Chicago. If I'd been traveling on my own, I might possibly have changed my ticket, dashed from the carriage, and found my way to Augsburg Seminary or to the house of Tom's brother and sister-in-law. I had John and Trudy's address in my purse; that was where I'd sent all my letters. But I wasn't alone, Annie was with me. And besides, what further humiliation could I bear if I were to actually encounter Tom? After the initial surprise and shock he would doubtless look at me with embarrassment, standing there in front of his family or his fellow students. I would not be able to say anything coherent, only, *Why did you write to apologize only to stop writing again?*

I knew why: Tom needed to explain himself, and having explained himself, he felt it wise to let our connection go.

And so the Great Northern train roared out of the Twin Cities, with their granaries and flour mills along the Mississippi River, and onward to Chicago, where we changed for Boston and boarded the White Star line for Liverpool. I was not exactly the girl I'd seen illustrated on the steamship brochure, with the ribbons of her straw hat fluttering in the breeze, nor was I the captain's wife, who never knew a day of seasickness and in her younger years climbed all around the ship with a spyglass or tucked herself up reading in some cranny or other as the *Matilde* swayed through the rollers of the South Atlantic. But I was still glad to be at sea and was only sorry Annie didn't share my strong stomach.

I had not meant to tell her the story of her parents until we had been in Norway for a week or two at least. But somehow, once we left American shores, I couldn't refrain. There were long conversations in our small cabin as the waves threw the vessel up and down, back and forth, and Annie sat in her berth as I held her close and kept a basin nearby. It was more painful than I could have imagined seeing her wide eyes and tears, feeling her shaking shoulders, listening to her questions as she tried, with all the effort of a child's mind, to grasp that important things she thought she knew about herself and her life were not true. To grasp that I, her trusted Mor, had misled her. She didn't believe me until I showed her the photograph of two strangers in their Sáme clothes: her parents. Then she could see that she resembled them.

She wasn't angry, she was afraid.

"Are you still my mother?" she asked me over and over, and I said, "Yes." And then, "I will always love you as my daughter." And then, "I'm a mother to you like I am a mother to Uncle Kjell. You know how he calls me Mor Dagny? That's what I am to him, a foster mother. I am the same to you."

I saw the pain in her eyes at that. As a piece of whole cloth tears, or a sturdy cup falls and smashes on a marble floor. As yet, there was nothing to replace this loss, and I could only hope that in Karasjok we would find something to bolster us. A real father must be better than a false mother, I reasoned then.

Now here at the Sáme camp we will see if that is so.

July 9

Today marks our second week here on the Karasjok River, or the Kárášjohka as they say here. The language is pleasant to listen to, softer than Norwegian. We now know enough to say hello and thank you (*bures boahti* and *giitu*) as well as increasing numbers of words for domestic objects and reindeer. *Boazu* is the main word for reindeer, but there are at least a dozen other specific names: males and females, castrated, pregnant, one-horned, no horns, draft reindeer and wild reindeer among them (an all-white reindeer is a *gabba,* but there are none here at the moment). Annie plays with the other children, and they are generous with gifts. She now owns a wooden doll wearing *gákti,* as well as a hand-carved toy reindeer pulling a sled. She has been given a shawl and soft moccasins that fit her perfectly. These were made for her by a cousin of Elle-Ristine's, a childless widow named Gunvor.

The camp is situated on the river, about two miles from the town, if town it can be called, with its handful of wooden trading shops and houses, and a small white church and parsonage. I walked there two days ago with Gunvor to send a letter to Katrine to say we had arrived. I met Pastor Kielland, originally from Trondheim, but long resident here. He speaks *davvisámegiella* so he could translate between me and Gunvor. He welcomed me somewhat wonderingly, even more so when he heard we planned to stay the summer. It's rare that Norwegian travelers visit Karasjok, unheard of that they stay in the Sáme camp.

During the day, the camp is largely quiet. The men and older adolescents, boys and girls, are usually out with the reindeer. Often, they're out at night as well, to guard against the wolves. The herds are large, though it seems everyone complains they are not as large as they could or should be. New regulations from the state have come into effect since Norway became independent two years ago. There will be a culling in August and a migration in late August to another area farther away from Karasjok. When the men and adolescents come home from the herds in the evening or late at night there is always a storm of barking and renewed activity, no matter what time it is. Every family here has at least one dog. I don't know how many reindeer different families own; it is apparently impolite to ask. But no family seems much better or much worse off than another.

While Annie plays, I spend my time walking by the river alone, sometimes sitting with my journal, or with the women who are often sewing in small groups inside and outside the tents. Uncle Aslak, as I suspected, is dead (two years ago) and so is his wife (long ago), but they had children, two sons and a daughter Gunvor, who takes her responsibilities towards us seriously. Mikkel's wife Káren seems to see us as part of her family now; we often sit near her in the circle of women. I'm more comfortable with Káren than with Gunvor. I also like two of the younger wives, Birit and Siri. Both speak Norwegian and can explain what they're doing, though mostly I just watch and learn what I can. The women use thread made from reindeer sinews to sew tanned leather purses and clothing. They make shoes and hats. They are dexterous and help each other; they teach the older children, both boys and girls, the art of the needle. Everyone needs to know how to repair their possessions. I am most interested in the weaving that they do with a bone or wooden heddle. They tie strands of woolen yarn to a pole in the tent and then run the strands through the heddle. Their fingers move like water rushing through a weir.

Several of the women have babies of various ages in the calfskin cradles. Many of them have one or two silver balls or other silver tokens hanging over the opening. Some are more elaborate, more like charms in different shapes. If I didn't know better, I would think these baubles were for the babies to play with, not to protect them from child-stealers and *uldas*.

I can help with some things, like picking berries and preparing food. The men of the household often make the main meal of reindeer meat in a large iron kettle over the fire, but the women seem to prepare the rest of the food, whether porridge or flat bread. They have a few reindeer cows here at the camp for milking, and from that milk they make cheese in a mold woven of thin birch roots. They drink a large amount of coffee, sometimes with thick reindeer milk in it, but no sugar. I find the food agreeable but unvarying and bland, while Annie, initially cautious, seems to love it.

She loves sleeping in the tent as well. We have our own small tent, constructed of poles and cloths, with a smoke hole at the top and a wooden door. Inside the tent is another mosquito tent, a *raggas*. We sleep on sheep skins, wearing our clothes, often with a puppy that Mikkel gave Annie. Most of the day we are outside with the others or inside their much larger tents. Gunvor began to call Annie "Elle-Anna" the second day to distinguish her perhaps from another little girl called Anna-Káren or perhaps to claim her for the family. Now everyone calls Annie that.

I watch her all the time, trying to see if she is enjoying herself, if she is learning, if this would be a place for her to grow up. I see little evidence of punishment in this society; sometimes a mother's voice is raised, or a father grouses, and the child listens. The children have a good deal of freedom, though they help when asked around the tents. They play all day, ranging far afield, and organize themselves with games of lassoing each other and constructing little tents and fire circles from sticks and stones. They wade in the river, but none seem to know how to swim.

I don't see any books or know what or even if the children study. I asked Káren if there is a school nearby, using the Norwegian word *skole.* She shook her head, no *skuvla,* which must be the Sáme word. The young mother Birit explained that for many years here in Finnmark a traveling teacher had come in summer months to the camp site for a few weeks, and that in winter some of the children of reindeer herders had also studied in small schools run by the church. More recently, boarding schools were being built by the government with a large one in Kautokeino finished just this year. Sáme children over seven in the surrounding area were supposed to live there in dormitories and study for months at a time. Birit had heard these schools were places where *davvisámegiella* was not allowed, only Norwegian. She hoped her own little children did not have to go there, for it was many miles away.

Mikkel, I've hardly had a chance to speak to, and when we do catch a few minutes, he asks me questions not about Annie but about America. He gives me to understand that he liked Alaska and wishes it had turned out differently. He said, "Now I do not drink anything. I am 'awake' like the rest. Sometimes I still wish I had the money from the gold I mined, but I have something better now. My strong faith." By *awake* he means that he belongs to the Læstadian sect now. I gather he must have gambled his money away or else it was stolen from him when he had typhoid. He doesn't remember any of that. But he recalls his great adventure crossing the Atlantic Ocean to New Jersey and the rail trip across the continent. He remembers the voyage to Alaska, with Edvard at the helm, the harshness of the winter up north, certain people like Kjellman and his companions. He rarely mentions Elle-Ristine or the baby they lost or Annie, for that matter. He's made no special effort to get to know her, nor has Káren, though Káren accepts that Annie and I are in her charge. Mikkel has said nothing about taking Annie on as one of his children.

Annie doesn't seem to know what to make of Mikkel. "Does he like me?" she asked me last night in our tent. I hear the uncertainty in her voice. Most people in her short life have been kind to her. Shouldn't the man who is her real father want to spend more time with her?

I explained that he has a job to do with the reindeer herd. I thought I might experience an end to guilt by bringing her here, but I sometimes feel more sadness than expected. The older women might wish to talk about Elle-Ristine, but we lack a common language. The younger women who speak some Norwegian have few memories of Mikkel's first wife, who went off to Alaska ten years ago and died there.

July 12

I must add more about Gunvor, who has taken to Annie far more than Káren has. She's Elle-Ristine's cousin. Her father, Aslak, was a respected man in these parts, meaning he had many reindeer, and Gunvor, the elder of the two cousins, played with Elle-Ristine when she and her parents visited from Alta. Aslak's sons inherited the herds, and Gunvor married out of this *siida,* as they call the collection of families here, and went to live with her husband near Utsjoki in Finland. The Finnish border is only about seven miles to the east and there are good relations and intermarriage with the *siidas* there. Gunvor's husband perished in a snowstorm when they had only been married two years, before they had had a chance to have children. Afterwards Gunvor came back to Karasjok, to live with one of her brothers and his family in their tent.

She is in her mid-forties, so ten years older than Elle-Ristine would be had she lived. That surprises me. In my memory Elle-Ristine is always twenty-three, with smooth skin and an abundance of brown hair in a long braid, Gunvor's darker skin is rough and webbed with lines, especially around her eyes. She has a cough that makes me think her unwell; she says it's from the campfire smoke, but she's also a pipe smoker. She is a fast walker, much faster than me, but her back is a bit stiff when she sits and stands. Her teeth are stained brown from her pipe.

The day I walked with her to send the letter to Katrine, Gunnvor asked Pastor Kielland a series of urgent questions, which he relayed to me in Norwegian. They were, in order: *Did Elle-Ristine die in childbirth? Was I with her when she died? Why did Mikkel leave the baby? Why have I come to Karasjok?*

I gave my answers, as best I could, and the pastor he translated them for Gunvor. I could not answer the last question and said only that Annie wanted to meet her father.

The pastor had only a few questions for me: *Was I a member of the Læstadian sect? Or was I raising little Anna in the Lutheran church?* I said she had been baptized and that we had attended church in America, and that we were not Læstadians. This satisfied him and he said he hoped to see us on Sundays. Læstadians are not generally part of his congregation most Sundays. They prefer to worship in the tents at the camp, something I have since witnessed myself. He had heard of the Sáme herders who went to Alaska almost ten years ago. The majority had been from Kautokeino, a village to the south, and he'd heard that some of them had returned from America. Only Mikkel Aikio seemed to have come back to Karasjok, however. "He is a good man, but he has another family now," said Pastor Kielland, translating for Gunvor. She had spoken at greater length, pointing at herself and Annie. Had she said something to him in *davvisámegiella* that the pastor hadn't translated?

I saw an expression in Gunvor's eyes that I recognized and feared, a hungry look that came of empty arms. It was one thing to hand Annie back to her true father, assuming that he and Káren wanted to raise Annie and Annie agreed, but quite another to offer up my daughter to satisfy the longing for a child in another women's eyes. What did the pastor think? That I was abandoning this child? That I was returning this child to her people?

I'm her mother! I wanted to say. If only that were true.

Gunvor and I were silent on the return trip to the camp. I

was glad I didn't speak *davvisámegiella,* so she couldn't question me further.

July 18

At least I can see that Annie is much happier here than in Bergen. She, like me, prefers the outdoor life with its minor discomforts (mosquitos being the greatest of our trials), to sitting in a parlor sewing and reading or to being polite to old ladies who come to call. Every day she gets browner and stronger and more confident. Yesterday I saw her climbing a tree with bare feet and hanging off a limb with her knickers showing. Katrine would gasp in horror. For myself I am greatly relieved to be away from Bergen. My hope that Annie and I could find a permanent home with Katrine is over, though I can still flush with anger and sorrow at how the visit ended.

The familiar old house of the Vesterman family above the harbor, the house I'd longed to see again, soon seemed stuffy and old-fashioned: heavy velvet drapes, horsehair sofas and chairs with antimacassars and footstools, no electricity yet, only gas lamps and coal-burning stoves. Several rooms on the second floor were closed off; the whole upstairs had a musty smell. There were the same two servants, Josefine and Hanne. Now old and shuffling, they treated Katrine like a queen and were suspicious of me and Annie. Katrine herself was older, naturally. Her blond hair was turning white, her jaw was sharper, and her light blue eyes more critical behind her spectacles. She dressed behind the times, with long, sweeping skirts and a high lace collar. She moved a bit stiffly, perhaps with a sense of her own importance as the owner of the house, the head of a prestigious female seminary. Her mouth was pinched; she laughed less and lectured more. Of course she'd always had a tendency, with all her affection for me, to lecture and prescribe. Yet I was no longer fourteen, but forty-two.

I had prepared Katrine, in a letter I sent before we left Ballard, by telling her that Annie's parents had been reindeer herders but that I had raised her as Norwegian. Whatever

Katrine had been expecting, it seemed to sink in, at the moment she saw Annie for the first time, that the little orphan girl I'd taken in really was the daughter of Lappish nomads, an exotic species hitherto only glimpsed in Christmas illustrations or in encyclopedia entries about a primitive, non-Norwegian race that was vanishing from the north. "She's very small," Katrine said later. "But her manners are good. I can tell you've raised her well. Is she clever?"

To her credit, Kathrine never cared if girls were pretty or not. It was their minds she was interested in. "It's too late to enroll her for the school year," she went on. "We'll find her a private tutor, I know just the young lady, and we'll soon get her up to scratch. Then she can begin fresh in the new fall term. You've been taking her to church, I assume?"

"Yes," I said, half-amused and half-irritated. I caught Katrine's meaning. Was my little girl a heathen or a Christian? In Port Townsend, we had not often gone to church, but in Ballard we attended the Lutheran Church regularly. I could not override my own parents' insistence that we three girls should all know our Bible.

For her part, Annie was subdued around my cousin and did not call her Aunt, but Miss. *Frøken Katrine.* The curious little curtsey she'd had as a younger child returned; she bobbed when she addressed Katrine or her lady friends. My little girl had been raised to think of Katrine as part of my family, like my two sisters. But over the course of the voyage on the ship across the North Atlantic, Annie had come to understand that none of the Norwegian people I'd talked about—not Edvard, not Katrine, not Marit or Solveig and their children, belonged to her. She had others who were her family, people who lived in the far north, in "Lapland," including a father she had never met.

The tutor came every morning to give Annie lessons in Norwegian, in history, geography, reading, and arithmetic. She was another Miss, a former student at the seminary. With Annie occupied and Katrine at her office all day, I had the run of the house, but I usually stayed in my room or else wandered the wharves and narrow cobbled streets. It often rained. That did not deter me.

In Ballard, even more than in Port Townsend, I was used to walking everywhere around town, taking Annie to school and back, visiting business clients, having a cup of coffee with the Solstad sisters, popping into see Ida Krantz, or simply taking a stroll with Adele. Here in Bergen I had nowhere to go, no one to meet, and I didn't enjoy sitting and writing in the *konditoris* with a pile of newspapers and a slice of apple cake, being treated as something between a pathetic widow and an eccentric scribbler. So I walked and walked and gradually I passed from the city I'd remembered, both staid (the National Theater) and lively (the fish market), to another world that I didn't recall well from my years here as a student and member of the Vesterman household: factories where children work, hovels where families squeeze together, and alleys near the harbor where the whores live and ply their trade. Eventually I took to climbing up the steep hills on to muddy paths that gave me a good view of the city. From here I could see the Bergenhus Fortress and Vågen, the narrow bay at the center of the city, its wharves and wooden buildings dating back to the times when Bergen was part of the Hansa trade. I stood in the rain, the umbrella never fully protecting me, watching the ferries and fishing boats and passenger ships coming into port and making for sea again, and from time to time glimpsed a schooner among the steamships or even an old three-masted barque. I thought of Edvard and my youth, and sometimes my tears mixed with the rain.

Back at the house, sitting at the small desk in my old room, looking out at the harbor, I first tried my hand at fiction, as I once dreamed of doing. On foolscap, for I had not brought a typewriter, I wrote two long stories, based on memories from my years of sailing with Edvard, and sent them off to literary journals. Both stories were rejected, several times, with notes that said the same thing: "Sorry, this is not for us, not what our readers want today. Passenger and cargo travel are mostly steam-powered now; no one wants to read about the romance of sail to exotic ports around the world or tales set in San Francisco twenty years ago." My Norwegian has become out of date during the years I've been away. I didn't realize that until I returned. Or is it that the vocabulary of my mother tongue now seems more limited to me? Norwegian seems to have fewer words, at least far fewer energetic adjectives and verbs than English. Perhaps it's the result of my months writing advertising copy and booster pamphlets, but I miss the cornucopia of expressions that I daily found in my English dictionary and thesaurus.

After a few weeks of struggle, I gave up on fiction. I scribbled down some of my impressions of Bergen and embellished them with anecdotes and a few facts and sent a long article about the city to the *Minneapolis Tidende*. They were glad to have it and asked for more. Could I, for instance, write something about contemporary women in Norway: "What are the women of Norway doing and thinking?" the editor wrote to me.

I did make an attempt to find out. After all, Katrine has a wide circle of women friends, and we saw them often. Several were teachers in the seminary; others were well-born ladies, some married, some spinsters by choice. Some I had known long ago in school, most were strangers. They were friendly enough or at least polite, but my life in America was a mystery, not to be too closely inquired into. I'd had a husband, of course, but the little girl wasn't mine, and there was something a bit unsettling about us both. America could do that to a person, it seemed.

I chose the most congenial of the ladies, Mrs. Else Loen, to talk to at one of the larger gatherings, a rather large lady who dresses badly but expensively, as if to demonstrate she can afford everything but good taste. I knew her husband was a politician of some note and that together they agitated for rights for women. After we had discussed suffrage for some time, I confided that in America I'd been a writer and editor and that I thought of taking that work up again in Bergen. Could she think of anything I might do here in that line? She was at first enthusiastic and said that there were several national and local suffrage organizations that had publications I could write for. She could put in a word for me. At some point in the conversation, however, Mrs. Loen understood that I was talking about paid work with a newspaper.

"But my dear," she admonished me with a smile, "You have no need for money, I would imagine, not living with Katrine. Besides, you have your daughter. Writing about suffrage, an article now and again, I understand, but surely not an office job."

The fact was, none of these women, not even those who teach, work for the wage itself, but to elevate education for their sex and to advocate for better social conditions. They have family money inherited or earned by the men in the family. I wanted to tell Mrs. Loen that I *liked* to work, that it had given me independence and purpose, but simply nodded and said I would contact the suffrage organizations, while vowing to myself I'd try the newspapers here in Bergen as well.

It's hard not to compare these bourgeois Bergen ladies with my friends in America, the hard-working independent dressmaker Adele; Ida Krantz, the "Ballard Land Queen;" and Lian who keeps the family accounts and has figured out how to make the farm prosper.

In Bergen, for over two months, I tried to get used to being Norwegian again, only Norwegian, but the American I've become kept breaking through. I've become more forthright, more independent, pushier. I remember I thought of some of the editors in Seattle and Ballard as paternalistic or downright rude, but other men, business men at the Chamber of Commerce, for instance, regarded me as a good enough writer and editor to commission work from me. Here, the editors are far more conservative, and my American ways disconcert them. It simply isn't done apparently to just walk into a newspaper office and ask for work. One or two of the editors in Bergen sat me down and told me the brutal truth—no one would hire me—the others simply laughed me out the door.

Even Katrine, who had given me so much support in the past for my writing, did not know what to suggest when it came to journalism. Instead, she suggested that I might want to consider writing children's stories or even a novelette for young girls. About a Norwegian girl who went to America, for instance. Such fiction would surely find readers. She came home one afternoon with several such novels for young girls; they were of the improving sort, where girls lie a little about having eaten some sugared almonds in the pantry, have a falling out with their best friends, or struggle with their stern but loving mothers. The real world of many girls in Bergen and Kristiania is otherwise, I suspect: poverty, factory-work, prostitution, and too-early motherhood.

Nevertheless, I made an attempt at a short novel about an immigrant family in Ballard. Because my own experience of arriving in America was different than the normal trajectory of Ellis Island to the Midwest, I had to draw on stories I recalled from conversations in Ballard with the Solstad sisters, who had come as teenagers from Telemark to North Dakota to homestead land with their parents, or the tales that Oscar and Vera Svansson had told me about their early days in Illinois. I showed some pages to Katrine, and she encouraged me to dwell less on the hardships and sorrows the immigrants faced and more on school days, church parties, and amusing stories about learning English. "It's a book for young girls," she reminded me. But I had never been a girl in America, only a wife and widow.

I wrote a letter to Vera Svansson instead, telling her that we were well and enjoying our time in Bergen. In truth, I wanted nothing more than to sit beside her on the sofa as she knitted or pull up a chair at the kitchen table and peel potatoes or shell peas in her company.

Several weeks ago, in early June, things came to an unexpected head with Katrine. I had been vague about our plans for the summer. To Katrine's proposal that we make a family visit to Kyrkebø in July, after the school term was finished, I'd said little. I had written my sisters to say I was back in Norway, but my thought was to see them later in the summer, after the trip to Finnmark. One day at a shipping office, I'd investigated how best to get up the coast and inland to Karasjok. I kept wishing to explain to Katrine about Annie's father, but didn't find the time and place, or more likely the nerve. After all these years I was, in fact, still subservient to her, and uncertain of how to say what I wanted rather than simply accept what she wanted for me.

Then Annie, forgetting her secret, asked me over our bread and cheese in the breakfast room when we'd be going to Karasjok and the whole story came out. In the midst of it, Annie's tutor arrived and bore her away to an upstairs room while Katrine and I faced each other over a tableful of egg cups and lace doilies, cream pitchers, and blue-flowered china. She couldn't believe I hadn't told her that Annie's father was alive.

"Was *this* your plan all along, Dagny? To come to Norway

to return her to him?" Her nose was white, the way I'd seen it sometimes as a girl, and the words hissed furiously from her pinched mouth. "I thought you were planning to live in Bergen, with me, to make sure she had a solid education. For us to be together again."

"I'm not returning her," I said placatingly. "At least, not unless he insists. It's a visit. I want to see how they live. It's something I should have done long ago. Introduced her to her family. And anyway, I didn't know until a few years ago that Mikkel Aikio was alive. I thought he'd died in Alaska."

"You told me that you had adopted the girl, that her parents had died. You never said anything, anything about them being Lappish nomads."

"And if they were? The Sáme people I know aren't any different than you or me inside." I buttered a piece of bread, to show I wasn't rattled, but my hands were shaking. There had been times, and this was one of them, when I could see the strong resemblance between my cousin and her mother. Aunt Inger's wrath was something I'd avoided for the most part, but I had seen her lash out at Katrine sometimes, perfect as Katrine was.

"Dagny, I've been patient with you all these years," she said in a voice between cold and angry. "I've been sympathetic to your tales of woe, your losses with the ship, the court case, and Edvard's death. I've tried to help you get published, sent you what you wanted from Norway, offered to support you. I've done it because you're my family. But you've betrayed my trust, you've been less than truthful. And you've been pretending ever since you arrived."

"Is that what you think of me?" I jumped up from the table suddenly, unable to listen to this (and not caring that I had been calling myself a liar for months). The resentment poured out: "Yes, you probably do, you've never acted as if I was capable of doing anything on my own. But I'll tell you, Katrine, I've had a life, I've *made* a life in the great world. While you've moldered here in the house you were born in, I've seen the world, I've been married, I've had children that I loved and that died. My tales of woe, as you call them, are real events that happened to me and Edvard. I never asked you for much," and here I choked up a little with the unfairness of it all. "I had to support myself and I managed. I adopted Annie because I cared for her mother, and I'm taking her to Karasjok because Annie deserves to know her family. And by family, I mean her father, I don't mean you, however kind you think you are."

She was speechless, and then, with severe dignity, she also rose and said, "Do what you like, Dagny. I'll not stop you going to Finnmark. But please don't let that little girl grow up among savages. I may not be her family, in your opinion, but you are her family now, not those people."

She must have thought she'd made a good speech and a cutting exit, but I was angrier than ever. I heard the front door close; Katrine was off to her school office with her umbrella and her briefcase. Hanne came in to clear the table and gave me a look of undisguised horror that I had spoken up to her beloved Katrine.

She was not my beloved Katrine, I realized. Not anymore.

That same day I booked a voyage north for myself and Annie. Katrine apologized before we left, and I apologized too. But things had been said that could not be unsaid, and I still don't forgive her for the word *savages*.

July 24

Today, Sunday, a Finnish lay preacher came to hold a sermon in one of the larger tents. Almost all the adults in camp packed themselves inside, about twenty people. Standing and holding each other by the hand, they all began to sway as one, from side to side, while murmuring words of praise or other religious phrases. After his preaching ended, the murmurs got louder and a few people began to cry out and many more just to weep quietly. The swaying increased and then people broke away. Some fell to the twig-covered floor and writhed; others raised their hands and almost shrieked, calling out the name *Jubmel.* I don't know if that is a pagan god or another word for the Christian God, or both. The lay pastor went around and picked people up off the ground or embraced them. The cacophony continued until it seemed the tent wall was also moving in a circular pattern.

By that time I was outside with Annie, down by the river, where we sat on a large stone.

"Mor," she said. "Did my mother act like that on Sundays?" She had seen lay preaching on Sundays in the *siida*, and some of the same moaning and swaying in the tents, but the Finnish preacher seemed to have awakened a far greater zeal in the congregation. Mikkel and Káren had both joined in vigorously, and Gunvor was one of those who threw herself on the floor of the tent and sobbed inconsolably. It was certainly far from what went on at Zion Lutheran church in Ballard.

I tried to explain the little I knew about the Lutheran sect founded by Lars Levi Læstadius in the nineteenth century and how it had become especially popular in Finnmark. It had helped the Sámit find more meaning in their lives, as far as I understood it. "Your mother was from a Læstadian family on her mother's side," I said. "I suppose on the other side it was the State Church of Norway. You know, I've told you, that your grandfather, her father, was Norwegian, from farther south?"

Annie nodded. She was by now wearing a plaid shawl she had been given in colors of red and green, over her not-so-clean printed cotton dress from a Ballard shop, and the *kommager* or moccasins given to her by Gunvor. Her two light brown braids had become a single braid in back. She did not wear a cap, however; she still clung to her straw sailor hat with a blue ribbon. She was a blend of Sáme and Norwegian, but she was also American, and on this trip, she sometimes struck me as more American than I'd realized. She was learning *davvisámegiella*—Gunvor was making sure of that—but to me she had stopped speaking Norwegian and only used English. It was a way, I supposed, of holding on to the life she'd known in Ballard. She used English too with her *áhčči* Mikkel, though he now sometimes addressed her in the Sáme language as well. "Elle-Anna," he called her too, but a bit sadly, I always thought.

Looking at the river, Annie said, "I miss our Sundays with Tante Vera and Onkel Oscar. I didn't mind going to church because I knew however boring it was, soon we would begin baking and cooking *middag,* and I would help her, and you would go into the living room and read your books and newspapers. And then Tante would play the piano and we'd sing those Swedish songs she likes. And Bill and I would play croquet or go sledding."

"Yes," I said. "That was so nice, wasn't it?" I could see Vera's soft face bent over the piano keys, her crown of fading blond braids. I could see the living room so well: Oscar in his comfy chair, reading aloud occasionally from the *Ballard News* and adding his own commentary, the "real story" he got from his customers at the barber shop. Bill would be on the rug in front of the fire reading one of his detective stories.

"And then Tom would come, sometimes, do you remember? And we had such nice walks."

"I remember," I said, including him in my picture of the living room, black-haired, spectacled, he too with a book, a novel probably.

"I like it here better than Bergen," she said as we dunked our feet in the river and felt it flowing through our toes. "I didn't like Sundays there. The service was so long, and I got itchy and there was nothing to do except be quiet and eat a lot of pork roast and red cabbage."

"Well, at least you know now what Sundays are like in the well-off homes of Norway," I said, and I experienced a quick flash of freedom: that we would never have to sit through one of those formal meals with Katrine again. And at the same time, I felt like crying, as if something that had been part of my life for so many years, Sunday *middag,* had been wrenched away, leaving only the prospect of some reindeer stew in a wooden bowl to look forward to.

August 2

I have not heard from Katrine since I came to Karasjok, nor have I written her, though she or Josefine has forwarded on letters from Kjell and Adele and even a postcard of Ballard's town hall from

Ida Krantz with the message, "Your home is here, Dagny!! Come back and start building!!!" Today another letter from America via Bergen was brought to me in the camp. It's postmarked Seattle, June 20, and addressed to me in Tom Nilsen's neat script.

Dear Dagny,

It has been some time since you've heard from me. I don't know why you stopped writing last fall. At first, I imagined you were busy with all your work in Ballard, but then I supposed you were content to let our friendship fade. Perhaps you imagined that I was still disappointed with you for not telling Annie about her father. Or perhaps you were angry or embarrassed about our morning the day before I left. Perhaps you thought that I would simply forget you. I haven't been able to do that.

I am now back in Ballard, for good. It was a difficult year in Minneapolis. I left Jouna and Trudy's house in November for a room near Augsburg Seminary, on Cedar Street—Snusgatan, they call it, for all the Swedish men who use snoose or snuff and work in the mills by the river. A lot of Norwegians live there too, and there are many taverns. I am ashamed to admit I drank more than I wanted at times this past year. Loneliness mostly and loss of purpose. I saw Jouna occasionally, but I couldn't bear to be around Trudy. Somehow the silence I'd once kept on their account about our Sáme heritage was no longer possible. Trudy is firm that her two boys never hear a word about our family in Kokelv, our whole way of life, our every memory of our dear parents. Jouna goes along with it and expects me to do the same, "to keep the peace." That's a peace I don't want.

My studies didn't attract me like they did once and as time passed, I became ever more convinced that I did not want to be a pastor. As much as my mother wished it, it is not my calling. I don't know if I even believe half of what I've been taught. It's a result of reading all that Knut Hamsun, I suppose. I spent a lot of time in the library, so much so that the librarian started asking me to help him catalog our books and even to select some for purchase. As a result I have decided to become a professional librarian. I'm working part-time as a compositor again for the Ballard News *and following a course at the University of Washington in librarianship this summer. I will try to finish my last year of college here.*

*

The second day I was back in Ballard I went to the Svanssons' house, longing to see you and Annie. Imagine my surprise when they told me you had gone to Bergen back in March and were not expected home again until September. Vera and Oscar were as kind as always. Oscar cut my hair and Vera made an almond cake. I am now renting your old room in their house. I hope that doesn't seem strange to you. For me it is more comfortable than the boarding house. You will have it back, of course, when you return.

I think of you all the time, Dagny, and wonder how you are and what you're doing there. Vera (who gave me your cousin's address) said she thought you hoped to write more there, not just the booster pamphlets, but for a newspaper. If you have anything published, I would love to see it.

I wish we had been able to talk about what happened last summer. I know I disappointed you with my lack of experience. I had a religious upbringing, you know, and it seemed pitiful in me that at the age of thirty I didn't know the least thing about women, much less a woman like you. Dagny, when I think of you, I always think of your courage and your grandeur. That is the only word that comes to mind. You're like a ship in full sail, always opinionated, asking questions, taking on hard things, not waiting, but doing. When I remember all you've lived through, I feel almost overwhelmed. And yet, when I'm in your presence I don't usually feel quelled (except for that one day). I feel at ease. I can laugh with you, like a friend. No one I've ever met is like you, no one I've ever met is as interesting.

I can hardly believe that I haven't seen you in almost a year. In the Svanssons' house it seems like you might walk in any minute. I wish you would. I long for your presence.

Please tell Annie hello and I hope to see you in a few months time.

With affection, your friend,
Tom

Over and over I read this letter today until I finally believed that it was true, that his feelings were real, that he had not forgotten me. Of course it was all make-believe—I was hardly a ship in full sail. I was a forlorn little daughter, a poor relation, a much younger wife to a vigorous sea captain, a grieving widow, a failed writer, a bad cousin, and a false mother who had lied for years to her foster child. But in Tom's eyes—and suddenly I saw myself again through his eyes—I was more than all my weaknesses and faults, and I was more to him than a harlot who had forced herself on him.

And with that thought came a rush of long-suppressed desire. I'd turned our intimacy in his room that August day a year ago into a shameful episode, but now, blessedly, I could conjure up his dear, remembered face without the spectacles, the warmth of his soft lips, his fine-fingered hands on my body. His smooth chest, his muscular legs, the feel of him inside me. I heard his voice in the letter urgently calling me *Dagny*, as if from nearby, and I wanted to go to him, to walk into the Svanssons' house, into my old bed, which was now his bed, and be with him.

Only gradually did I shake myself out of this trance of rereading and wonder why he hadn't gotten my letters last fall. It must have been due to the falling out with Jouna and Trudy, perhaps Trudy was cruel enough not to forward my letters. So he would be a librarian now, not a pastor. That suited me. And he was thirty, he must be thirty-one now, so only eleven years younger. But he signed himself "your friend." What did that mean? Was that all he wanted?

"Annie mine," I said, catching my daughter up to me. "I have had a letter from Tom. Only imagine, he is back in Ballard and living with the Svanssons. He says he wants to stay in Ballard and become a librarian. He sends you greetings."

"Tom! Will he be there when we get back?" She wiggled out of my grasp and ran around me in circles. Since we came to Karasjok I've noticed that she clings far less. It isn't the way of Sáme children to hang on their parents; they are encouraged to be obedient but independent, yet they stay close.

I nodded, not trusting myself to speak. For the first time I no longer wonder if Annie, so obviously happy here and at home, wants to go back to Ballard. The only question is, will Mikkel try to keep her?

August 5

For the last two days the reindeer have been driven into a large corral made of wooden posts and branches some distance from the camp. They run counterclockwise, about a hundred of them at a time, and their leg joints click like a bone rattle. The dogs that have driven them into the corral stand outside, barking wildly. Added to the noise is the frog-like croaking many of the reindeer make, in fear perhaps. Some of them will lose their lives here, and the smell of blood is in the air. The men and some of the young women wade into the fray. They identify their own animals with the help of ear markings that were cut into the ears when the reindeer were calves, but also by the shape of their antlers or the color of their coats. Once they've found their animal, usually an ox-reindeer, they lasso the antlers and pull the bucking, kicking reindeer from the mass of animals and out of the corral. It can take three strong men to subdue a reindeer and bring it to its knees. They expertly slit their throats and then skin them.

I find it gruesome but fascinating. It is clear that this is no wasteful cull. Every part of the reindeer will be used: the blood will be boiled for nourishing soup, along with the bones. The stomachs are used as vessels for milk, and the bladders as bags. Children will play games with the knuckle bones; the antlers will be carved into spoons and knife sheaths. The skin of the forelegs is used for leg warmers and the soft pelts are bedding. The meat will be eaten fresh and then dried for the winter.

It is warm today and from time to time people go down to the river, to wash off their sweat and the blood on their hands. I followed Mikkel down to the bank when I saw him leave on his own. In my pocket I had the paper Reverend Karlson had written up in Unalakleet and that I took to Nome. It gave me guardianship over Annie and was signed with an X that was witnessed by William Kjellman.

I wasn't sure what I planned to say to Mikkel. Whether I planned to add to my dishonesty by claiming that he did sign the paper, when he was feverish and thought he would die. William Kjellman had been there and could attest to it. I could claim that I thought I was completely within my rights to raise Annie as my daughter. I could explain that I had seen it to be my duty to bring Annie to visit him and his family, and now, thank you very much, we were returning south, and back to America.

But I said none of those things. He was sitting on the grassy bank with his bare feet in the water, a quiet man with rough dark hair and tanned skin, well-muscled under his *gákti*. He had been the young man Elle-Ristine loved, and the father of two babies with her, one of whom still lived.

"May I join you?" I asked, and we looked silently at the water a while. Finally I pulled the paper out of my pocket and gave it to him.

"You may destroy this," I said. "William Kjellman signed it for you, because he told me you would not last more than a day or two in Nome, you were so ill with typhoid. I've never told you the whole story. How I came to Nome to find you and I didn't wait to see if you recovered. I felt I needed to get back to Unalakleet. Ravna had been feeding Annie, but she was leaving for St. Lawrence Island with her family, and they had to get there before the weather changed. The Reverend Karlson was afraid Annie might not survive such a trip to the island. But there was more. He wanted Annie to have a better life, for her to be cared for and educated in America. We had to leave too, my friend Adele and I, before the snow came. What I'm saying is that I took your daughter before I knew you would live. I took her because I wanted to have a child. That's the truth. I am sorry, and if you want to have Annie, Elle-Anna, with you and your family now, I accept that."

He looked at the letter and at me, then handed it back. "Mrs. Bergland. I understand. Elle-Ristine told me your children died. You have no children. I have two other children and maybe more to come. Elle-Anna needs you. You need Elle-Anna. You took her and you raised her, and you saved her life. I wouldn't have been able to raise her, not then."

I made as if to protest but he held up his hand. "I was not a bad husband to Elle-Ristine. But I understand now I was not a good one either. I went gold digging and I would have stayed gold digging, you understand? I would not have come back to

Unalakleet for Elle-Anna. I had the fever, not just typhoid, but the gold fever. I now see that I worshipped the false god of greed."

"But you wrote me a letter, and I didn't write you back. I hid Annie from you."

He said nothing for a while, and then he turned back to the river. "I have asked God's forgiveness, and He has given it. Now I forgive you, as God forgives you," he said. "Do you forgive me?"

I said, "Yes."

We still hadn't discussed whether Annie would stay on after the summer, but he got up briskly and said, "I must kill another reindeer today. My job!"

And I was left by the flowing river, not knowing whether to be relieved or still afraid. I put the letter back in my pocket. And although I don't know if I believe in God, I prayed for forgiveness today.

August 8

I can't help thinking that something more happened in my conversation with Mikkel than I was aware of. Perhaps he spoke to Gunvor, or Káren did. For shortly after that, Gunvor came to me with a tanned leather dress she had made for Annie and a woven belt for me. I had seen Gunvor making these garments, for all the women work together in company. I had seen her teaching Annie the words for what she was doing, and often touching her hand or her arm. But I had also seen Annie's polite indifference to Gunvor. Perhaps Annie saw the unmasked yearning in Gunvor's eyes. Whatever it was, it made her uncomfortable. She referred to Gunvor only as "the lady who coughs" and while she would never avoid her, she never sought her out either, she did one or two of the other younger mothers, who gave her treats and stroked her hair. The sharp worry I'd felt at the beginning of the visit, that Gunvor wanted my little girl, that she had some family connection that entitled her to keep Elle-Ristine's child, left me at last.

Annie was not a gift to be given or taken, I saw all at once. She could make her own decision. I knew she already had.

I said to Gunvor, *"Ollu giitu, ollu giitu."* Thank you. I wish I could have said more, told her that I understood what she felt. That I too had lost a son and a daughter, and another unborn child as well. That I'd long believed I would never have more children, but that after Elle-Ristine's death, by some sad miracle, I'd been given Annie to care for. My eyes filled with tears, and so did hers. She spoke a few choked words that I didn't understand and then went back to her brother's tent and remained there for the rest of the day. I will send her something from Bergen, there is nothing else I can do.

August 15

This is the last day of our visit to Karasjok. We left the summer camp yesterday to spend tonight at the parsonage in the village. The *siida* has been packing everything up and loading their possessions into bags and chests attached to the reindeer saddles. They are moving with the reindeer over the river to new grazing lands in Finland. Autumn comes early here, and already the willows and junipers are yellow and gold. Night comes earlier and earlier with a cool bite.

Tomorrow Annie and I set off in a different direction from how we arrived. The Karasjok River flows into a larger river flowing north, the Deatnu, and we can follow it up to the village of Tana and from there go overland to the Varangerfjord, where we can meet the coastal steamer and take passage for Bergen. As soon as I can arrange it, we'll be on a ship to Liverpool and then Boston. Pastor Kielland's son, Leif, who is studying civil engineering in Trondheim, is also returning south after a summer holiday with his parents at the parsonage in Karasjok village. The pastor and his wife feel strongly we should be escorted on our travels, and I agree. I had not thought it all out before coming here, nor realized the long distances.

I wrote to Tom this evening about our final days with the *siida* and will post the letter when we arrive in Bergen. We may get to Ballard before the letter does, but I want to put down my thoughts now, while the experience on the river is still so vivid.

Among other things, I told Tom about my last exchange with Káren. She touched the corners of her bright, dark eyes as if to suggest tears and gestured to Annie, playing with friends in the nearby forest, and she pointed to me. She said the word *eadni* several times, each time with meaning. *Mother.*

I knew the word for "mother" in *davvisámegiella* by now, but I had to come to Lapland to learn it. "*Eadni,*" I repeated "*Ollu giitu.*" I had thought Káren a cool character, but now I saw she understood what I must feel. She couldn't be Elle-Ristine to Annie, and she couldn't be me, the woman who had raised Annie from babyhood.

Mikkel told me the same thing yesterday when he brought me and Annie to the parsonage. A reindeer followed along with us, carrying our baggage as well as all the things we had been given. There was no dramatic good-bye. Mikkel took me aside and said, "She is my daughter, and she will always be so. My daughter. And she can come and stay again. She can decide herself what she wants from me. Now, she is too young, she does not understand our life. Now she needs you. You know her and love her. She belongs to your care."

Annie hugged him when she said good-bye, but he remained reserved and dignified. "You must obey this mother, Elle-Anna, and believe in God. And never forget you are Sáme and where you come from. We are here."

"*Mun ipmirdan, áhčči.*"

Her solemnity matched his own. *I understand, Father.*

Later, she cried, though she said it was because of the puppy he had given her, which we were forced to leave behind.

I described all this to Tom this evening but feel that even in my best Norwegian I can't get at the truth of the last six weeks. Lapland has been warmer than I expected. It has been far more beautiful here than I expected. It has changed me more than I expected.

I wanted Tom to know all this. He's the only person in the world who would understand, being Sáme and coming from this landscape, but also living in America. Knowing me, knowing Annie. Perhaps I will write him again from Bergen to tell him

that in spite of my struggles not to love him, I do love him, and
having been in Lapland, I love him even more.

September 25

I've left a large gap since writing last. The initial reason was the
weather. Floating and rowing down a broad river is wet at the
best of times. Only a day into the journey, rain set in, and the last
week of our travels was sodden and dismal. We arrived in Tana in
late August. Annie caught a cold first and then I did. We stayed
in Tana Bru at another parsonage an extra day to warm up. Leif
the pastor's son was good with us the whole way, but impatient
at the end to reach the fishing station of Vadsø, where the coastal
steamer docks. In Vadsø I wired Katrine to say we would be
arriving in Bergen within a week. Aside from the brief letter our
second day in Karasjok, I had not written her once since we left
Bergen for Finnmark. I held a grudge for those words of hers
about returning Annie to *savages*. My telegram strikes me now as
so business-like as to be brutal: "Arriving coastal steamer Bergen
September 4, soon departing for America. Greetings, Dagny."

Josefine must have received the telegram and realized I was
coming from the north. She sent a reply to our ship that reached
me somewhere around Hammerfest: "Your cousin very ill. Come
soon. Be prepared. Josefine."

I once loved this house above the wharves of Bergen, and I have
come to appreciate it again, in spite of my strong reaction a
few months ago. The furniture may be old-fashioned, but it is
comfortable and familiar. There can no better place for Katrine
to begin to recover from her illness or, if she can't recover, then to
peacefully pass away. I don't know yet what will happen.

I didn't realize it, but Katrine had not been feeling well for
some time before I arrived in Bergen in June. She did speak of
aches and pains, but I thought of them as minor, brought on by
inactivity and loneliness perhaps. I assumed that her pinched
expression of tiredness had to do with me and Annie, the strain
of having us there and making room for us in her ordered

life, however much duty told her to. After we left Bergen, she began to see doctors. One doctor thought it was to do with her monthlies; another gave her liver pills; a third said it was the gall bladder; a fourth wanted to investigate a mass in her uterus. His diagnosis of possible cancer was the one that frightened her most; but she listened to it, she told me, because he was the only one who treated her seriously. It turned out that there was a tumor growing in her womb. After he removed her womb, she developed an infection. For several weeks, her life was in danger. All this while I was in Karasjok. She hadn't wanted to contact me because there was nothing I could do.

"I could have been with you at the hospital. I could have made sure you got the best care," I scolded her once, but mostly I just said, "I'm here now, and I'm not leaving you until you are perfectly well again, however long that takes."

Now we were friends and family again, not the only child of the grand Vesterman family and the country cousin from Sognefjord, not teacher and student, not awkward relatives with nothing in common. I sat long hours with her in her bedroom, knitting something useless and reading aloud. Annie made a friend of the girl and boy next door. Why did I worry about Annie? She was speaking Norwegian now all the time, with a Bergen accent. She chatted freely to these children about her time in Finnmark, without hiding the fact that she was born to Sáme parents. She felt no shame showing off her shawl and soft moccasins, of telling stories of campfires and reindeer separations. She made our week on the northern rivers sound like an incredible adventure. I even overheard her telling a long tale about hunting wolves, and what you must do if you were ever caught in a blizzard.

The two children thought Annie was the most interesting child they'd ever met, said their mother. "Is it true that she was born to Lappish parents in Alaska?"

"Yes," I said proudly, leaving no room for misunderstanding. "That is her heritage. And they are called Sáme, by the way. That is their name for themselves."

*

At some point on the river journey to Utsjoki, I'd told Annie that Tom was Sáme, just like her.

"Oh," she said, as if something now made more sense.

"He didn't tell you, did he?"

"No, but he always seemed to know how the right way to do a lot of things. And everything had a story. Like our family in Karasjok. They would show me *exactly* how I should set the trap for the ptarmigans, and how I should chop the wood. Tom never let me use an ax. I'll show him when I see him that I know the right way to set snares and chop firewood."

I had to smile; she was so different from the little girl who had left Seattle on the train last spring. Tom would like this change, I knew. He would want to help her learn more about practical things. He could speak *davvisámegiella* with her. But did the Pacific Northwest even have ptarmigans?

I've written to Tom that we are not coming back as planned. I haven't said that it might be months. Katrine is still not at all well. Her temperature often goes up at night and she has little appetite. I sit beside her with a tray and make sure she has nourishing broth and oat porridge with milk. The doctor comes every day and commends me for my nursing. Privately he says that Josefine and Hanne are too old now to nurse, but it is still good they are in the house, it comforts Katrine.

October 13

As time passes and Katrine improves a small amount every day, sleeping longer and taking more solid food, some of her friends have come to call, in ones and twos, so as not to tire her. Mrs. Else Loen is one of the most frequent callers. To my surprise, Mrs. Loen has been intrigued by my time in Karasjok. She freely admitted that she, like many Norwegians here in the south of the country, knows little of her countrymen beyond the Arctic Circle. Her husband, the politician, has told her there is a Sáme politician in parliament, Isak Saba. He was elected last year to represent Finnmark for the Norwegian Labor Party. "My husband says Saba is intelligent, but obstructive. He is fighting for the right of the Lapps to allow their children to be taught in the Lapp language." She paused and added, "My dear Dagny, you must know something about this. For my part, I didn't even realize the Lapps had a language apart from Norwegian."

I thought of the loveliness of *davvisámegiella,* its long soft vowels, its many words for reindeer, for weather, and for terrains. I thought how as a journalist, if only I were *allowed* to be a journalist, I would like to take the train to Kristiania, find this Isak Saba, and interview him. Something is stirring in me. Like Annie, I am no longer afraid to speak up about our Sáme connection. But there is more—in talking to Mrs. Loen, I thought more about the kind of writer I really was, the kind of writer I *could* be. Someone who speaks the truth, someone who helps others speak the truth, someone who *educates.*

"Why," I asked Tom in my last letter, "did I turn my back on Katrine when she showed her ignorance of the Sáme people last June? Why didn't I tell her all that I had already learned from Elle-Ristine, that I had seen with my own eyes at Fort Townsend and Alaska, that I had heard from you, dear Tom? Why did I imagine that Katrine already knew everything I knew? I shut her out of my heart instead of taking the opportunity to change her mind."

I practiced on Mrs. Loen today. Instead of sneering, "Why wouldn't you think that the Sáme people have a language?" I said, "They have a beautiful and precise vocabulary. Let me tell you about their words for reindeer, and their words for rivers and fjords."

Never mind that after ten minutes Mrs. Loen cut her visit short. It is a beginning, and Katrine was in the parlor to hear the conversation. I can imagine she now regrets her words about *savages,* flung at me in June, but I want more than an apology. I want to see the side of her that can listen and learn. I want to be the person who shares what I know.

October 20

After I'd written Tom at length today about my revelation that journalism, the persuasive and educational kind, was my true calling, I went to Katrine and told her about him. "I thought of him as a friend, and then he wasn't a just friend any longer. We were separated for a long while. But it's all so different than Edvard, Katrine. He is younger than I am, much younger."

She was no longer in bed, but in the parlor, tucked into a chair by the fire. She reminded me even more than ever of Aunt Inger, now that illness has turned her hair white, yet unlike my aunt, who rarely stopped talking and jumping up to receive visitors or order the servants about, Katrine simply sat peacefully with a book in her lap. I was glad to see more color in her cheeks these days and hear the firmness in her voice.

She said, "I remember when Edvard came to dinner the first time. I liked him immediately, but I said to papa, 'He's far too old for Dagny.' Still, I could see you were very taken by him. You said right away that you wanted to see his ship. In one week it was all decided. You wanted to be married, you wanted to explore the world with him. You did not think him old at all."

"It was like that then," I said, smiling. "A wife could be much, much younger. It was expected. Even eighteen years was nothing between a husband and a wife."

"We both know that your different ages made for a gulf sometimes, Dagny. But it was not truly important. You and Edvard loved each other. That's the question you must ask yourself. Could you love this man Tom as a wife and friend, even he's younger by a few years?"

"Eleven years younger, perhaps even twelve," I admitted. "But yes, I could. Love him."

I had not yet told her about his background, but now I did. "He comes from Northern Norway. He first traveled to America at seventeen, studied, learned English and the printing trade, went back to Norway to help his parents, worked on a newspaper, returned to Minneapolis to study. He now wants to become a librarian." And at the end I finally managed, "He's Sáme. Like Annie. He's good to her."

Katrine had been listening with interest and then, for a moment, I thought I saw disappointment in her eyes. That was too much.

"It's different in America!" I said. "It's not like Bergen, everything so conventional and hidebound. On the West Coast, people come from everywhere. From China. From Russia. From Peru and Ireland and Italy and Lapland. It doesn't matter where people come from in America." I paused. Of course it does matter in America where you came from. Whether you are from China or England matters a great deal. "I know I have changed from the girl you once knew," I went on. "You've been here and I've been around the world."

"I know I haven't traveled," Katrine said. "I now see that as a lack in my life, not to have been more places, met more people. You mother let you go when you were young and that gave you the freedom to be yourself, to explore the world. But my mama—how could I have left her? She already felt that I shouldn't have taken the headmistress position. She was always disappointed that I never married, that she never had grandchildren." She smiled ruefully, "There was a time when a friend of mine, another teacher, suggested we travel to Italy one summer, rent a house in Florence for instance, and immerse ourselves in Italian culture. Mama had a fit to think of me being gone three months even though I was thirty-two by then. I could have gone anyway, but I probably was afraid. I used my mother as an excuse. I don't like change, Dagny. I'm not like you. But I love you." This was said so simply that tears came into my eyes.

Just as when we were younger, she took me into her lap and let me cry. Back then I was crying for my mother, big girl that I was at fourteen. Perhaps I was still crying for her, somewhere in my innermost being. Mor let me go, and I never found my way back to her.

"*Kjaere lille venn*," Katrine said over and over again now. "Dear little friend. It will be all right."

November 10

I haven't heard from Tom since I wrote him to say that Katrine's health was slow to mend and that it might be a long time before Annie and I are able to return, probably not until after the new year. At times I fear I've tested his devotion too far, and the longer I'm gone the more likely it is that he will find someone else, a girl his age, maybe someone also studying at the university.

The Miss has returned to teach Annie. If we continue here, Annie will be enrolled in school in January. For my part I'm writing again, though I have not found a newspaper editor in Bergen or Kristiania who wants to publish my opinion pieces. Only one of the feminist journals in Norway has shown an interest. They took my article on Sáme women's lives, intrigued by the notion that Sáme women often do the same work as men and have a more equal status in the tent.

Last week a parcel arrived from Karasjok containing a small wooden ptarmigan carved and polished by Mikkel, and a woven belt from Káren. Annie immediately wrapped the belt around her waist. In return, Annie and I chose presents for many of the family, including a silver charm for Gunvor. We went to a photography studio and had our portraits taken and sent them as well.

She asked me if she could sign her name Elle-Anna when she wrote to them. "Of course," I said. Then she asked if I could call her that sometimes as well. "Only when you want to," she said. "But it makes me feel more like who I am inside."

So Elle-Anna it is now.

November 14

Last night, it was late. We had all gone to bed, though I was awake and reading. Downstairs, a knock at the door, not loud, but repeated, as if by someone we knew. Josefine either didn't hear it or didn't want to answer it. I went downstairs in my nightgown and robe. Through the narrow glass window high on the door I saw a man in a dark slouch hat and a heavy coat. "What do you want?" I said as loudly and firmly as I dared.

"Just one thing," the man said in English. "I want just one thing."

"Tom?"

"Dagny, it's *you*. It's you I want."

He had received my letter, he told me when I flung open the door and threw my arms around him, but that wasn't why he was here. What made him come was a telegram from Katrine that said he must depart immediately for Norway. I needed him urgently, she said, and would explain when he got to Bergen. She also wired money for the train and steamship.

How and when Katrine had managed this, I had no idea. Her lawyer had been by the house two weeks ago; perhaps he'd helped.

"Are you all right? Is Annie? I answered your letter, but maybe you didn't receive it?" Tom said.

"I didn't. And you've come all this way. But truly, there is no emergency. Not now anyway. Katrine was ill for a long time but is much better. I'm so sorry, Tom," I said, but I wasn't sorry at all. And I felt a warm sense of thanks toward my cousin. "I can't imagine what Katrine was thinking to send a telegram. Nothing is wrong."

We had been standing in the doorway, our arms around each other, his cold cheeks against mine. His black hair, his gentle eyes, his freezing hands. Why did this man hate to wear gloves? He kissed me and said, "Then let's go in."

Five minutes after, I had Tom settled in the parlor. Josefine appeared, fully dressed, angry at being awakened and shocked to find a man unknown to her sitting, boots off, in a chair, with me on the footstool massaging his hands.

"Mrs. Bergland," she whispered loudly, scandalized. "Whatever does this mean? Who is this man?"

"Oh, it's all right, Josefine. This is Tom Nilsen from America. My friend. My fiancé, rather. Can you bring us some coffee? Katrine invited him. Thank you so much and apologies for disturbing you."

And only when she stomped out the door to the kitchen did we begin laughing quietly. We laughed so much we could hardly kiss.

"Your friend or your fiancé?" asked Tom.

"Both?"

"Both."

I led him to my bed that night, not caring what anyone in

the house might think. We took it slowly, we talked as much as we caressed, and finally we slept, wrapped close together as if in a promise that we would never allow ourselves to be parted again. I only woke up once, to see the snow falling soft as feathers outside the half-curtained window of this old and beloved room.

The only thing better than this reunion was the next day, when Katrine welcomed him with a handshake and kiss, and when Annie threw herself into his arms in delight. "I knew you hadn't forgotten us," she said. "I have so much to tell you. You and me, we are related, we are Sáme. My name is Elle-Anna now. I lassoed a calf this summer. I can use an ax. I can say, *Bures boahtin!* You know that means *Velkommen til oss.* Welcome to us."

"*Bures bures,*" Tom said, smiling widely, taking me by one hand and Elle-Anna by the other.

Everything was decided right then.

Welcome to us.

Last Entries in the Ledger

1932

I remember when Edvard and I moved into the house on Morgan Hill in Port Townsend thirty-five years ago we had hardly any furniture for ourselves and Kjell. For the first week we slept on blankets on the floor and picnicked on a battered table we found in the horse stable. The failed banker and his wife had sold everything except that. Kjell and Edvard scavenged dishes and kitchen pots and pans from a general store on Water Street, and I scrubbed and swept until some beds and chairs arrived. The weather was fresh and windy up on the bluff and we had a sweeping view of the entry to Puget Sound. I thought at most we'd be in Port Townsend a year and then Edvard would want to be at sea again or return to Norway to raise our many children.

I should have had Kjell with me here today. He wanted to come but I said no, I thought to revisit the past alone. I told him last night when I arrived at the farm in Chimacum that I'd been rereading all my journals from the years before I returned to America and married Tom. Kjell, the boy we found and cherished, was the only one who recalled that first year on Morgan Hill well as I did. Lian, once Henry, was the other person who had lived in that house, but she didn't want to go inside again. As she always said about those days, they were long ago and nothing to do with life now.

Susan had lived in the house too, as a baby, with Lian and then with just me for a few months. But Susan has been in China for two years as a journalist, covering the conflict between Japan and China from Shanghai. I thought about her often today, I must write her.

Whoever lived in the house now had painted it a different color I noticed as I parked in front—blue with white trim— and planted an extensive vegetable garden. Big yellow and red squashes tangled with each other in a fenced-in plot, and orange and maroon, and purple-edged white dahlias lined the path going up to the house. A youngish housewife answered the door, wearing an apron, and from the house came the smell of boiling tomatoes. These days everyone raises food and cans the harvest.

I was especially well-dressed, in a suit and polished shoes, and with the Ford parked on the street, I must have looked like a government official. She appeared a little frightened until I told her I was Dagny Nilsen and I had lived in this house many years ago. I happened to be in the area—I resided near Tacoma now, my husband and I had a summer place on the Hood Canal, my son and daughter-in-law lived in Chimacum—and thought I'd drive over for the day and visit Port Townsend, see the old place.

"Oh of course," she said, wiping a hand over her damp forehead, and invited me into the kitchen. Her name is Molly Adams. Her husband George is a supervisor down at the new paper mill, built about five years ago. They had no previous connection with the town but had come from Portland. The house, I gathered, had been empty for a year or two before they bought it. Times had been hard for Port Townsend over the years. The paper mill was the first industry to hire a substantial number of workers in decades, she said, pulling out heavy ceramic mugs and a milk pitcher. "I don't mind telling you that it was a lot of effort to get the house back in shape," she said. "But of course it has such lovely views of the bay. When did you live here, and, if you don't mind my asking, are you some kind of Scandinavian?"

I didn't want to sit in the steamy kitchen with a cup of percolator coffee and pans of skinned tomatoes ready to go into the canner. I wanted to see the old rooms, where Edvard and I had slept, where I had written my articles about America and sent them optimistically off to Katrine, where Adele and I had sewed and knit for the church bazaar, where Kjell had glimpsed Lian in a dress and fallen in love, where I had raised Elle-Anna, where the boarders had trod up and down the staircase calling, "Mrs. Bergland, more hot water please, can you send the girl up?"

"Norwegian," I said. "My first husband and I came here by ship in 1896. He died up in Alaska about two years later. He was a sea captain. I lived here several more years with my daughter before moving to Seattle. I remarried and now live in Parkland, near Tacoma. My husband is the head librarian at a private college there. I'm retired myself. I used to write for newspapers."

How blandly you could summarize a life when you wanted to. But in fact, life after Tom and Elle-Anna and I returned to

America has been absent of high drama, though not without adventure and uncertainty at times. Tom and I married in the Svanssons' living room just after returning from Norway in early 1908. Vera played the piano and made the cake. We lived for a few months with them while we sorted out our future. Elle-Anna went back to the Central School in Ballard, ahead in geography, but behind in arithmetic. She soon caught up, as did Tom. He graduated in the spring and found a job soon after. Eventually he would work at the Carnegie library on Roosevelt Avenue.

Ida Krantz rented us a house and found me a job in public relations for the upcoming Alaska-Yukon-Pacific Exposition in 1909 to be held in Seattle. I hadn't lost my old knack for booster writing and plenty of adjectives were required to tell the world about the glories of the Pacific Northwest. We couldn't have come back to Seattle at a better moment with all the excitement around the A-Y-P Exposition. Elle-Anna accompanied me often to the grounds of the fair, where I had a small office. Kjell and Lian brought Susan and John over several times to see the Pay Streak midway and all the educational exhibits.

Eventually we sold my lot in Ballard for a profit, and we bought a house in Ravenna near Adele's and near the university. I could have remained in public relations but that wasn't what I wanted. With times changing, I managed to get a foot in the door at the *Seattle Union Record*. I wrote scores of articles up to and through the Seattle General Strike of February, 1919. It was our finest moment when the whole city came to a stop. But the mayor closed us down and several editors and writers were arrested.

Tom asked me if I would consider stepping away from the newspaper. He had been offered a new job as head librarian at a private Lutheran college south of Tacoma in Parkland. It had suspended classes for a few years during the war and reopened in 1920 with a Sáme president born near Tromsø. Johan Ulrik Xavier is a remarkable man, related to some of those who went to Alaska. He had come as a young child with his family to the Midwest and he shared some interests with Tom (Professor Xavier had once been the librarian at the college). It seemed too much a coincidence and too great an opportunity to pass up, though it brought my journalism career to an end, at least the most thrilling part of it. I took a job with a small local paper in Parkland as a writer and de facto editor. We broke little news, but once you have ink in your blood it can be hard to give up newspapering. I still had a lot of opinions and a desire to educate the public, and I was no slouch at rustling up advertising. In fact, it reminded me of my days at the *Shingle* when I prowled around Parkland hunting for display ads from the shop owners and drinking coffee at the local diners.

I shook my head and returned to where I was when Molly Adams said, "Why don't you just take a look around the house? I've got my hands full here. I want to get these tomatoes canned before the children get home from school. Take your time."

I was grateful and immediately stood up. "I know my way."

A half hour later I came into the kitchen, thanked Molly Adams, and left. She wanted to give me a jar of canned tomatoes, but I said that my daughter-in-law was a champion canner. "Save them for the winter," I said and left.

I had spent most of my time outside my old bedroom, on the small balcony, looking at the sea and feeling the breeze in my hair. In the end it was all I wanted, other than to catch a glimpse of one of Edvard's ships heading around Point Wilson and making for home port.

I'm writing this now, with a few tears in my eyes, in a back bedroom at the enlarged farmhouse in Chimacum. It's late at night. Lian and Kjell have electricity now, but I prefer the old kerosene lamp. The window is open, and I smell the barnyard, hear a soft cluck or two from the chickens as they settle on their roosts. Lian manages a thriving business in eggs and along with vegetables and their dairy herd, they do well. John was here earlier, but he is married now too. He works as a logger, lives nearby with his wife, and has two young children. He's close to his mother and father. And then there is Susan.

This is her room, though it bears few signs of her now except a bookcase with old children's titles and a few college textbooks. When Tom and Elle-Anna and I returned to Seattle in early 1908, Susan was around ten. We made no great secret of the fact that Elle-Anna was Sáme and so was Tom. Among the Norwegians in Ballard we realized that there were others from Scandinavia who had the same heritage. Tom did not seek them out immediately; they found each other, one person telling another but still keeping it rather quiet. It was simply easier to fit in, especially during the times leading up to the Great War when we foreigners were often lumped together as outsiders, un-American, with allegiances to other countries. I had hoped to set an example to Lian and Kjell, given my relief that Elle-Anna now knew her parentage. Couldn't they offer the children, especially Susan, more of their history?

It was Lian's wish to say nothing, said Kjell when I asked him for his opinion. "And anyway, Susan never asks."

But that didn't mean Susan was not always thinking about this. Already in 1909 during the A-Y-P Exposition, she was intensely curious about the exhibits from Asia—the Orient they called it then—and about all the Asian people she saw at the Exposition. Six years later, when she was accepted into the University of Washington, Susan came to stay with us during the school year, a skinny, smart girl with glasses, not yet the beautiful woman she would become in her twenties. She had always been interested in reading and writing and enrolled as an English major. Lian expected her to become a teacher, even a professor, not a journalist. And certainly not a journalist who was interested in politics and China.

Earlier this evening, after John had gone home and Kjell had announced he was going to bed, Lian and I had sat up drinking tea. Her hair is now graying and bobbed softly around her face. She often wears a shirt and belted trousers and, inside the house, only socks. The years have filled her out, but she is still lithe and active. Long after her husband went to sleep, she would be reading or sewing. She asked me about my visit to the old house on Morgan Hill, and I told her how many memories it had brought back, of Edvard and Kjell and her own time there, but also of Elle-Ristine and the reindeer herders before they set off to Alaska, and of Elle-Anna.

"How is Annie?" she asked. She was one of the few who still called her that.

"Very well," I told her. "She has her own studio with a kiln in a shed in the backyard." Elle-Anna had discovered ceramics in high school and although she had decided not to attend university, she had taken many art classes and had built up a clientele who liked her work and bought it steadily. She still lives in Seattle and is married with three children, so it suits her to stay at home now. Not like Susan.

"I worry so much about her in Shanghai. What if the Japanese and Chinese go to war? How did it happen that my girl ended up there? Why couldn't she be like Annie? Husband. Three children. Work at home?"

I had made the mistake once of telling Lian that it would have been better if she'd acknowledged that Susan had a right to know her own history. That it was precisely because of the silence and mystery that Susan had sought out other Asian students at the university and had begun to visit Chinatown as soon as she got to Seattle. In the end she'd taken classes in Chinese and horrified her mother one day by addressing her in Mandarin. Not even knowing that her mother's language was Cantonese. Lian had never pretended she wasn't Chinese herself, but the result of all those years of hiding where exactly she came from and how she had arrived in America had made it impossible for her to ever tell Susan the truth about the nightmarish trip from Hong Kong to Victoria, and about the doctor who saved her, for a price.

Lian had raised her voice to me, and afterwards we never talked about it. I knew she blamed me for encouraging Susan to go into journalism. Those were the years when I was most engaged in politics and writing for the *Union Record*. "How could I not be a role model?" I'd asked Adele, who simply shook her head. There were a couple of years, I admit, when I couldn't have a conversation with anyone without lecturing them on labor politics. Ida Krantz had given up on me long ago.

Susan had been disappointed when I moved to Parkland with Tom and took the job at a newspaper where we wrote more about community events than union organizing. "But Aunt Dagny," she lectured me. "The world is at a boiling point; it needs journalists more than ever." She was only twenty-three when she went to China for the first time. She spent two years there, teaching English at a missionary school and learning Mandarin. She returned to Seattle but didn't stay long. Now a foreign correspondent for Reuters, she travels to London, and to India, to San Francisco and now back to China. The few times she's come back to the Pacific Northwest we've talked about her travels and her parents. By now she's a self-confident woman with a long black pageboy and exquisite taste in clothes.

"Daddy is all right with my life," she told me. "He doesn't talk about it much, but I think he envies me. He traveled so much when he was young and lived among other kinds of people. He's had so much more of an adventurous life than mama. So have you, and Uncle Tom and even Elle-Anna. The whole story of her family in Lapland is completely fascinating. You should write about it someday, Auntie. You told me you kept journals; can I see them sometime? Maybe there's a book there?"

She had never been able to figure out, journalist that she was, where her mother was born. I would not be surprised if she'd tried to find evidence of her mother's supposed upbringing in Lima, the daughter of Dolores and Chan Rodrigues. I could have told her straight-out that Lian was the daughter of poor farmers in the Pearl River Delta, parents who had agreed to give her to an unscrupulous "uncle" to be sold in marriage, and that her mother's life had held more adventure than most people's by a long shot. But what purpose would that have served, except to create more tension and distance between Lian and Susan?

Perhaps, if Susan reads my journals one day, she'll find out what really happened. Is that why I wrote them perhaps, to stand as a record of the truth? In the journals I didn't omit, I didn't smooth over, I didn't lie.

Who does the past belong to and how do you mend the errors you've made? I am ashamed of the long years that I kept Elle-Anna's truth away from her, but never sorry that I eventually told her about Elle-Ristine and Mikkel, never sorry I brought her to Norway and Lapland. I could not have done this work of repair without my dear friend and husband Tom, who showed me the path through his own pride in who he is and where he comes from.

Over the years we talked a good deal about another trip to Norway, perhaps with his brother Jouna, if he could be persuaded. We talked about going up to coastal Finnmark so that Elle-Anna and I could see where Tom had grown up. We even discussed hiring someone to take us from Alta to Karasjok by reindeer sled in winter. But it was only after the Great War, the Seattle Strike, and the move to Parkland that we returned to Norway as a family, to Bergen first, and then the Sognefjord, before boarding the coastal steamer for the north. In the end Jouna didn't accompany us. Too much had changed for him, he told Tom. It would only make him feel sad to see the old places and meet the relatives again. As for Trudy, I had never liked her since it came out that she had thrown out my letters to Tom that fall of 1907.

My sisters and their husbands were still on their farms near Kyrkebø, one family well-off and the other still struggling. There were children and grandchildren who called me the American Auntie and Elle-Anna a cousin. They were all shy of her until she showed them how well she could knit and embroider. It was a wonder to everyone that I came back again with a new husband and a grown child. No one had ever thought they'd see me again.

One day Tom and I went alone to Kvamnes where I'd grown up. We hiked there through the mountains, and I showed him places I'd loved as a child: a big gray stone shaped like a troll, a crooked tree, a brook that still sang the same song. We borrowed a *faering* from the family who now lived in the farm house, and we rowed out into the still green fjord, not far, just enough to take in the view of the rocky little headland and the wooden buildings with the steeply raked meadows of green above them. I was glad that the people who bought the farm hadn't changed anything, though they had more goats and cows than we'd owned. In the local dialect I said, "I'm the youngest daughter of Signe and Jakob Kvam. Dagny Kvam." My old name, my birth name, could now be woven back into the history of the place, could become one more story to be told, this one about the girl from Kvamnes who sailed around the world and ended up in America.

We spent two weeks with Katrine in Bergen. The coffee

company had fallen on hard times and her income was diminished after she retired from teaching. She lived alone in a flat that was still filled with old furniture from the great house, but she had added more of herself to the place, and it was far brighter, with large windows looking out on Bergen's harbor. She told Elle-Anna how glad she'd been the day her father brought me home with him from Kyrkebø. For Katrine, Bergen had always been my true home, even though, when I thought about it, I'd spent less time in this city than almost anyplace. I did not disagree with her though, for I too remembered my first days in Bergen: the shock and joy of my own room, the feel of my nervous fingers holding Katrine's firm, gloved hand on our way to school. "Remember, Dagny, there's nothing to be frightened of! You're a Vesterman now." Three years after our visit in 1920, one of her friends, Else Loen, wrote to me that Katrine had died suddenly, in her sleep.

In Karasjok we found much of the family still thriving, including Káren and Mikkel Aikio, with a daughter of thirteen, Ristine. The older two boys had taken on a good deal of the herding. I had been in touch with them every Christmas at least and sent them photographs of Elle-Anna and Tom, but I don't think they quite believed that Tom was Sáme until he arrived and spoke to them in *davvisámegiella* as old friends. Mikkel cried a little to see his daughter, and again I wondered if I had done the right thing in taking her back to America. But Elle-Anna, now with a boyfriend in Seattle, stopped me from brooding. "Mor, don't talk about it anymore. I forgive you. Mikkel forgives you. And it wouldn't have been easy, you know that, to grow up here instead of in America. I might have had to go to one of those boarding schools. I would have missed you. Every single day."

It was early summer when we arrived in Norway, and late August when we boarded the ship in Bergen for the return journey back to America. I had met some of Tom's relatives in Kokelv and we had spent several weeks at the summer camp on the Karasjok River. Tom took photographs and notes; he wanted to make an exhibit at the college library in Parkland. The reindeer herders here found it hard to believe that Tom was a college librarian, and that the president of Pacific Lutheran College had been born in Lapland. In Norway, in those times, things were especially difficult for the Sámit. The government regulations had grown more stringent, and the children were increasingly sent to state-run boarding schools. Mátias and Ánde, Mikkel and Káren's two sons, spoke of having been four years at a boarding school, where the teachers tried to stamp out their language. It was worse than I had imagined. Tom's relatives in Kokelv discussed it too, the erasure of language, the slights and cruelties. They talked about how difficult it was to keep to the older ways of life and yet be part of the larger Norwegian society, when they treated you as a primitive people who would fade away. They asked what it was like in America. We could have told them hard tales of racial prejudice and injustice. Instead we chose to speak of opportunities and possibilities and better times coming for all of us.

And so we helped prepare food, held the babies, and played with the children; we fetched water in pails from the river and chopped logs; we slept in a tent of our own. I learned to milk a reindeer cow and Tom fished. He also grew decently skilled with the lasso, even after his bookish life in libraries for so many years. Elle-Anna spent hours with the young people, more of whom now spoke Norwegian because of their time in the boarding schools. She learned to gather roots, soak, and bind them for basketry; she helped skin a reindeer and tanned its skin with alder bark. She did everything as she always did, with a sure hand and great curiosity for materials and methods.

She looked like some of relatives, how could she not? She was the daughter of Mikkel and Elle-Ristine. She was Elle-Anna Mikkelsdatter, and they called her that sometimes, placing her in their world. They teased her about her boyfriend and her lack of a ring yet, and they gave her little bits of jewelry and small leather pouches and taught her words for everything she'd forgotten. Gunvor, too, was there, now remarried and even more wrinkled. She said something to me, and Tom translated, "She says Elle-Anna is very much like her cousin Elle-Ristine. That makes her glad."

I was outside all this, but happy, and was sorry to leave. I thought at first I would write about that summer, but in fact I didn't even keep a journal on the trip. I'd already gotten out of the habit of journaling by the time Tom and Elle-Anna and I returned to Ballard. Perhaps my old journals were a form of conversation with myself, long ago, after I found myself in Port Townsend, a sea bird washed up on an unfamiliar shore. Perhaps I didn't need my journals when I married Tom, because I now had a friend to talk with, someone who never sailed off to Hawaii and Alaska, but looked at me mildly over breakfast and said with a smile, "*Ja*, Dagny, what battles shall you fight today, my love?"

September 18

I'm back in the little cedar-shake cabin on the Hood Canal. Tomorrow morning I'll leave for Parkland and its view of Mount Rainier. I must ask Tom if there's still a chance that we might travel to Norway next year, perhaps alone, perhaps with Elle-Anna again and her family. So they too can know their heritage. Elle-Anna's husband, a longshoreman, will probably say no, let's wait, the children are too young, and she herself might hesitate. Yet I feel the weight of my age. Since I made up my mind to marry Tom, I haven't wasted my time worrying what others think about the eleven years between us. I think instead about how long it will be until he retires—another ten years! And how I will soon be too old to go "gallivanting," as Elle-Anna calls it. For my daughter, I remain a restless spirit, while Susan only urges me onward: "Come to Shanghai!" she wrote in her last letter. For she knows that Edvard and I were in port there once, and that I had visited half the globe by the time I was her age.

Who was that girl I once was? I feel her still inside me, eager and impatient, longing for the wide world outside the windows of the Bergen house. When my chance came, I took it. I stepped on to the *Matilde* and sailed away.

The evening is pleasantly warm out here on the deck of the cabin with a little bite of autumn in the air. All the living children I've loved, none of whom are my birth children—Kjell, Susan, John, and Elle-Anna—have asked me what's in these journals and what I plan to do with them. As I write these lines in the last pages of the old housekeeping ledger, I think about buying a new journal. I think about typing up these old memories. Could I make something new of them or is it enough just to sit with the old stories and sift through them, not so much looking for meaning as trying to animate them, to inhabit them again?

When the three of us returned to the familiarity of the Swanssons' house to begin our family life together, Elle-Anna and I would sometimes talk about the two months we'd spent with Mikkel Aikio and the other Sáme people at the summer camp on the Karasjok River. For me, those memories had some sense of grief attached. I saw Elle-Ristine everywhere in the faces of her relatives and heard her voice in their voices. All that Elle-Ristine had told me about her life in Karasjok surrounded us for the first time, but the long summer days were shadowed by her absence and by my own fears that Mikkel would take Elle-Anna from me. He had the right.

For Elle-Anna, those summer days by the river in Finnmark were perfect, and she recalled the time often and in great detail. The names of the children, the games they played, the marvelous thunder of a reindeer herd circling inside the corral, the campfires at night, the moon and stars. She recalled Sundays and the trance-like singing and weeping. She could tell me the names of animals and plants and the things people carved and wove and the materials they were made of.

"Everything was so wonderful," she often ended, month after month as she told the stories until she began to forget them a little, "everything was so wonderful until the wet boat!"

By this she meant the long week we spent on the Karasjok and Deatnu rivers, especially the rain-soaked last days. "I was seasick," she told me. "And then we got head colds and we still had to sit there hour after hour in the rain, and Leif was nice, but he was always telling the boatmen to hurry, because we had to catch the coastal steamer. And my father had given me a puppy and you wouldn't let me take it with us. I can't forgive you that, Mor!"

"*Ja, ja,*" I said. "I'm sorry but that was how it had to be. The puppy would have hated the rain worse than we did." I sympathized with her seasickness, something I've never known.

The fact is, the days we spent on the wide Deatnu River were some of the happiest days of my life, days that went unrecorded in my journal because it was too wet most of the time to write. Even in the evenings in a tent by the river, we didn't fully dry out. Elle-Anna was soggy and sneezing, my own feet were constantly damp. Little happened outwardly for me to record anyway. All we did was row and float along the shallow, gravel-bottomed river and pull ourselves off a sandbank from time to time. Leif and the boatman fished for our dinners until Elle-Anna refused to eat any more salmon and begged for dried reindeer meat instead. We encountered few people for days on end. Only a few Sáme fishers in other boats, gillnetting in the waters, or solitary men with a pole standing on the shore—Norwegians or foreigners in tall boots and rainproof jackets. We sometimes passed turf huts of the Sámit and once or twice a larger encampment of tents on the Norwegian or Finnish side. One morning before we reached Utsjoki and could finally haul out and get thoroughly dry, we passed a whole herd of reindeer, some drinking from the river, others grazing onshore. There was one who stood out. It was white, like Leksu had been, and I could briefly imagine it *was* Leksu, Elle-Ristine's beloved reindeer, for it raised its head and seemed to look at me deeply, in that way that Leksu had.

"Why are you crying, Mor?" Elle-Anna asked me after we'd passed slowly by the herd. "Don't you feel well?"

"Something flew in my eye," I said. In truth, I didn't know. Was I crying for Leksu or for the loss of Elle-Ristine in her youth, or because Mikkel, in forgiving me, had released me from the fear I'd carried for so many years that I would lose Elle-Anna too? Was I crying because water had borne me away from my mother and sisters so long ago, or because Edvard had sailed off with me from Bergen, leaving Katrine behind? Was I crying for Jan, for Agnete, for Edvard, or my father? Water had taken so many of my loved ones from me, and still I wept for their absence.

But I also wondered if I was crying because, here on the Deatnu River, I no longer felt that the water had become an enemy to me, but that it had become a friend again. Shallow as it was, we could never drown; wide as it was, the land was always in sight.

For the first time, I knew that Elle-Anna and I would not be parted, and I knew too that we were on a return voyage home, however long it might take. No wonder I cried that day on the river, blessed with everything, wanting nothing, except to be a little drier, and perhaps not even that.

Sámi women standing in front of the Glendale Creamery Building,
Water Street, Port Townsend, WA, circa 1898.
University of Washington Libraries, Special Collections, UW5089

Sometime after my book, *The Palace of the Snow Queen,* was published in 2007, a kind stranger sent me a Xerox copy of a photograph from Special Collections at the University of Washington's Suzzallo library. The photograph depicted four Sámi women standing in front of a restaurant in Port Townsend, Washington, probably in 1898. The sender had read my travel memoir about several winters I'd spent in Lapland and Sápmi; he thought the photo might be of interest to me. He was right.

At the time I'd only recently moved to Port Townsend from Seattle, a city where I'd lived since my early twenties. In 2006 I reviewed a book for the *Seattle Times* by John Taliaferro, *In a Far Country,* which devoted a few pages to the "Reindeer Rescue" of 1898 when a large group of Sámi herders were employed to travel by ship and train from Northern Norway to America and up to Alaska. Their mission was to supply the Yukon gold miners with food and other supplies and to teach the Indigenous people there to herd reindeer. Thus, I knew that the Sámi, or "Lapps," as Taliaferro called them, and the five hundred reindeer that accompanied them, had stopped for a week in Seattle and had resided in Woodland Park before continuing on to Alaska. However, before I received the photograph and did some research, I didn't realize that the women and children accompanying the expedition had ended up staying behind in Washington for several months in the barracks at a decommissioned fort a few miles outside Port Townsend.

Over the years that I worked on this novel, I also discovered a good deal more about Port Townsend's history as a port city and home to a once-flourishing Chinese population, some of whom arrived clandestinely, by way of Vancouver Island, due to the restrictions of the Chinese Exclusion Act. The historical city has remained mostly intact except for the Chinese quarter downtown, which burned in 1900 and was never rebuilt. The lagoon and fields near North Beach and Fort Worden where the immigrant truck farms thrived remain only in name: Chinese Gardens.

Along with continuing to live in Port Townsend, while traveling often to Scandinavia as a writer and translator, I've relied on many sources for this novel, among them *City of Dreams: A Guide to Port Townsend,* edited by Peter Simpson; *Port Townsend: The City that Whiskey Built,* by Thomas W. Camfield; *Seattle, Past to Present,* by Roger Sale; and *Passport to Ballard* by Kay Rainartz. I also found the books published by Arcadia Publishing in their "Images of America" series of great visual assistance. They include: *Port Townsend* (Jefferson County Historical Society); *Early Ballard* (Julie D. Pheasant-Albright); *Norwegian Seattle* (Kristine Leander); *Poulsbo* (Judy Driscoll and Sherry White); and *Mosquito Fleet of South Puget Sound* (Jean Cammon Findlay and Robin Paterson).

For background on the history of Chinese immigrants and settlers on the West Coast I turned to *From Canton to California* by Corinne K. Hoexter and *Driven Out: The Forgotten War Against Chinese Americans,* by Jean Pfaelzer. Especially valuable were *The Chinese in Washington State,* by Art and Doug Chin and *Coming Home in Gold Brocade: Chinese in Early Northwest America,* by Bennet Bronson and Chuimei Ho.

General books about the Yukon Gold Rush that helped me with background and details were *The Klondike Fever,* by Pierre Berton, and the pictorial histories, *Queen City of the North: Dawson City, Yukon,* and *The Streets Were Paved with Gold,* both by Stan Cohen. The visitor's center at the Klondike Gold Rush National Historical Park in Seattle is a wonderful place to look at old photographs and objects from an era that transformed the city.

For stories of the extraordinary journey of the Sámi reindeer herders from Northern Norway, I relied on *Saami, Reindeer, and Gold in Alaska,* by Ørnulf Vorren, and the *Yukon Relief Expedition and the Journal of Carl Johan Sakarisassen,* edited by V.R. Rausch and D.L. Baldwin. In recent years the descendants of some of the members of the Yukon Relief Expedition who remained in Alaska have participated in research and exhibits on the contributions of the Sámi herders to the economy and communities of Native Alaskans. Faith Fjeld and Nathan Muus devoted space in the print journal *Baiki* to the subject and later released a publication, *The Sami Reindeer People of Alaska,* based on research by Ruthann Cecil. I'd particularly like to thank Marlene Wisuri, of the Sami Cultural Center of North America, for reading the manuscript. While I've included the names of a few real historical figures in the novel, including Isak Saba and Anders Larsen, early political pioneers in Sápmi, and Dr. Sheldon Jackson, William Kjellman, and Regnor Dahl of the Yukon Relief Expedition, the individual Sámi characters in America and Norway are entirely fictionalized. Their journeys follow the historical record, but otherwise I've invented characters and plot details.

In the archives of the Jefferson County Historical Society I was able to read original articles in the *Leader* and other local Port Townsend newspapers about the Sámi people's sojourn in the barracks at Fort Townsend and their visits to the town. Old issues of the *Leader* also contain stories about the Chinese businesses and inhabitants in nineteenth- century Port Townsend and about the years when the city filled with prospective miners on their way to Alaska.

The Carnegie library in Port Townsend, one of American's Victorian seaports, has an impressive collection of maritime books, through which I happily browsed for information about the age of sailing ships and steamships in the Pacific Northwest and about Port Townsend's significant role as an entry port. I also visited the museum in nearby Port Gamble for a better understanding of the lumber trade between the Northwest and Hawaii and San Francisco. Alert readers will note that Dagny describes a ship as *it* not *she,* as in English. This is because she is ostensibly writing her journal in Norwegian and Norwegian has gendered nouns; *et skip* (a ship) is a neuter noun.

Suzzallo Library at the University of Washington is where I read through old editions of the *Seattle Post-Intelligencer* about the Sámi arrival in Seattle in 1898 and their stay at Woodland Park. I also looked at copies of the *Ballard Tribune* and other newspapers published in Ballard in the early twentieth century. For a fascinating look at the immigrant Scandinavian press in the U.S. I consulted the substantial study *Norwegian Newspapers in America,* by Odd S. Lovoll. I was able to look through a number of issues of women's Norwegian-language newspapers at the Minnesota Historical Society in Minneapolis. The book *Adjusting to America: a Study in Kvinden og Hjemmet: A Monthly Journal for the Scandinavian Women in America, 1888-1947*, by Åse Elin Langeland, gave me valuable insights into how immigrant women from Norway and Sweden found community and advice in newspapers.

The Reindeer of Chinese Gardens is at its heart a novel about immigrants and immigration. While my own family (Irish grandfather, Swedish great-grandparents) followed the more common European journey to the United States via Ellis Island to Boston and Illinois, in my novel I chose to focus on travelers and emigrants who came directly to the West Coast. My main character Dagny Bergland was a seafarer before she became an unwilling settler and citizen; through her character in particular I hoped to show the ambivalence and difficulties of those generations who arrived in turn-of-the-century America, uncertain if this country could really be a home for them yet determined to land on their feet and make new lives for themselves.

Barbara Sjoholm
Port Townsend, Washington

About the Author

Barbara Sjoholm's many books include *The Palace of the Snow Queen; Winter Travels in Lapland and Sápmi* (2007; reissued with a new afterword in 2023) and *From Lapland to Sápmi: Collecting and Returning Sámi Craft and Culture* (2023). She is also the author of *The Pirate Queen: In Search of Grace O'Malley and Other Legendary Women of the Sea.* She is the translator of *With the Lapps in the High Mountains: A Woman Among the Sámi* 1907-1908, and *By the Fire: Sámi Folktales and Legends,* by Danish artist and ethnographer Emilie Demant Hatt. Sjoholm's novel *Fossil Island* won Best Indie Novel from the Historical Novel Society; she has also been awarded an NEA fellowship in translation and grants and awards from the American-Scandinavian Foundation. A longtime resident of the Pacific Northwest, she lives in Port Townsend, Washington.

[www.barbarasjoholm.com]